# HOUSE
## OF
# STRAW

# HOUSE
## OF
# STRAW

*Nobody Can Break A Girl Who Is Already Broken*

## MARC SCOTT

Matador
9 Priory Business Park,
Wistow Road, Kibworth Beauchamp,
Leicestershire. LE8 0RX
Tel: 0116 279 2299
Email: books@troubador.co.uk
Web: www.troubador.co.uk/matador
Twitter: @matadorbooks

ISBN 978 1789015 713

British Library Cataloguing in Publication Data.
A catalogue record for this book is available from the British Library.

Printed and bound in Great Britain by 4edge Limited
Typeset in 11pt Adobe Garamond Pro by Troubador Publishing Ltd, Leicester, UK

Matador is an imprint of Troubador Publishing Ltd

*For Marissa, Amie and George, for making this world a better place. I am so proud of you.*

*And in memory of Ian. One beautiful soul who I was truly privileged to call my friend in this journey of uncertainty. You are never far from my thoughts buddy.*

# CHAPTER ONE

The dark clouds opened over Oxley village on that treacherous November night, the heaven-sent rains cleansing the sins of most, but not all, of its residents.

Locals of the Rising Sun public house were becoming concerned that the car park at the rear of the main bar was in danger of flooding. The newly laid tarmac was certainly being tested to the full. Awash with a deluge of rain it had begun to resemble something out of a disaster movie. As the passing storm gathered pace, the constant thumping noises of the heavy rainfall sounded out like wild stallions racing across the rooftop of the bar. This was the worst weather that regulars of the establishment had seen for years.

Bree sat opposite Jamie in the middle of the main bar, the sour expression on her face a clear indication that she did not want to be here on this damp and dismal night. She didn't care too much for the rowdy crowd that frequented this pub and had planned to spend the evening at home finishing a work project. Her preferred choice of company that night would have been a photomontage and a chilled bottle of Prosecco. But Jamie had called her, in a drunken stupor, not for the first time that week, begging her to collect him from his favourite pub. She had been sitting here for nearly two hours now and her patience was wearing thin. 'That is definitely your last drink,' she said to him, trying hard to keep her composure.

Jamie simply smiled and raised his hands to acknowledge a song that had started to blare out from the pub's sound system. 'I bloody love this one!' he yelled, waving his arms and singing along to the tune, much to Bree's embarrassment. His drunken behaviour had attracted the attention of the bar manager, who had warned him earlier about his loud shouting and dancing in the middle of the seating area. The publican, like many of the patrons of the Rising Sun, knew Jamie, not on a personal level, but simply because he had become a constantly irritating source of amusement for them over the past couple of months. But in truth, that's all he was. Despite his six-foot frame and well-toned body, he was a harmless soul who avoided confrontation at all costs. He seemed to live in his own little world most of the time, oblivious to his surroundings, his headspace clouded by the excessive amounts of alcohol he consumed each day. Some of the regulars of the public house may have been hoping that he might be so drunk that he would fall into one of those large puddles forming in the car park when he left the bar that night. They would certainly find that entertaining.

'Finish your drink and let's go, Jay!' Bree snapped. 'People are looking at you!'

Jamie unleashed his inimitable childlike grin. 'When did you become so boring?' he asked. 'Give that resting bitch face of yours a holiday for once and smile. God, sis, you are turning into a right sour-faced cow!'

Bree did her best to contain her anger and tried to reason with him. 'Come on, Jay, the weather is getting worse, the roads will be flooded.'

Jamie simply smiled and put his hands together as if to beg. 'One more drink and I promise we can go.'

2

Bree swiftly rose to her feet and made her way to the bar, cursing him as she walked away. 'This is your last one, then I will just leave you here, Jay, do you understand? You can make your own way home.'

Bree was pleased to leave the table. Jamie's selfishness and drunken antics had really been getting to her and she did not want this night to end with an argument. As she approached the busy bar area, Bree spotted her best friend, Kayleigh, tucked away in a corner seat. She was with a strange-looking man. She waved and caught her attention, beckoning her friend to join her at the bar. Kayleigh acknowledged her wave and quickly rose to her feet. She had been around Bree long enough to know that her call was not a request, more of an order. She gave the man sitting beside her a friendly peck on the cheek and made her way to join her friend.

'Where the hell did you dig him up from?' Bree asked, as Kayleigh reached the busy bar area. 'Have you been robbing graves or something?'

Her friend looked over at her date for that evening, offering him a smile and a small wave. 'He is only thirty-six,' she said. 'He is thirty-six, he just looks a bit older.'

Bree laughed out loudly. 'Thirty-six! Fuck off, Kayleigh, his waist size may be thirty-six, but he won't be seeing his forties again anytime soon.'

Her friend felt slightly awkward. 'He is a neighbour of my boss, it's only a drink, don't start getting judgmental, babe.'

Bree shook her head. 'No, Kayleigh, we all know that it is never only a drink with you.'

'He is not that bad,' Kayleigh said, shrugging her shoulders.

'Twice your age, he looks at least twice your age. Are you really that desperate?'

The barman took Bree's order. 'A pint of lager, a fresh orange juice with ice, and you better give me a large white wine and some new contact lenses for my friend here.' This amused him, having caught part of their previous conversation, and he scurried off to fetch their drinks with a large grin on his face.

'Jamie looks like he is having fun,' Kayleigh said. 'They will miss him in here, he livens the place up.'

Bree was less complimentary of his behaviour. 'He has been here since four o'clock this afternoon. He acts like a complete idiot when he drinks like that.'

'He leaves this Sunday, doesn't he?' Kayleigh asked. 'Are you taking him to the airport?'

'No, 'the bitch' is taking him. She wants to make sure he gets on the plane. God, I fucking hate that woman!'

'It is only six months, the time will fly, babe. He will be back before you know it.'

'He can fucking well stay out there for all I care. He obviously doesn't give a shit about me now, does he?'

Kayleigh knew when to keep quiet and this was one of those moments. Her friend, however, had not finished her rant. 'Do you know what really pisses me off?' she said. 'He never even asked if I wanted to go with him. I could have sorted something out with my job, but he never even asked. It is as if he can't wait to get away from me.'

Taking a large mouthful of her drink, Kayleigh looked over at her companion for the evening. She wasn't put off by his rapidly receding hairline or the dark circles under his eyes at all. Maybe the amount of wine she had drunk that night had clouded her senses, but she felt strangely attracted to him. 'Tom and I are going to the Shallows club when we leave here,' Kayleigh said. 'They have a couple of bands playing down there tonight. I was told that one of them is quite decent.'

Bree shook her head and laughed. 'You and him down the Shallows? Fuck me, Kayleigh! I can see him in a museum or a steam train convention, but the Shallows! You really can be embarrassing at times.'

'Why don't you and Jamie join us? Tom is driving, he can drop you home afterwards.'

Bree looked over at Jamie, still slumped over the back of his chair, waving his arms around to the music and making faces at some girls at the side door. 'No, I really need to get him home and I have got some work which needs to be finished by tomorrow.'

'Come on, babe,' her friend insisted. 'He will be gone in a couple of days, might be good to spend some time together.'

Bree shook her head and repeated herself firmly. 'I said no, Kayleigh!' That was her best friend's cue to keep quiet. When Bree said no she usually meant it.

As the girls left the bar area, Bree felt slightly uneasy. She could sense that someone was watching her. She turned her head from side to side but did not recognise anybody. An uncomfortable feeling stayed with her as she returned to her seat.

Suddenly, the side door of the public house was flung open and a small crowd of students rushed in to escape the torrential downpour. They made their way through the bar dressed in nothing more than T-shirts and jeans. They were either very thick-skinned or completely stupid. As Bree sat back down and gave Jamie his drink, she noticed that he had been distracted by one of the new arrivals. 'God, doesn't she look like Jess?!' he said. Bree glanced over at the soaking wet students but kept her thoughts to herself.

The heavy rain could now be heard thrashing against the windows as the wind began to take hold of the stormy weather outside. 'Hurry up with that drink, Jay, I really want to get home before the roads get any worse.'

Jamie gulped down a third of his lager. 'There is that grumpy old woman back again. Liven up, girl, you are only young once, you know.'

Bree shook her head and frowned. The resting bitch face had returned to its usual place. 'Fuck off, Jay!' she said. 'You can be such a moron sometimes.'

As the cluster of drenched students walked back past their table with their drinks, complaining about the cost of the taxi fare and the rudeness of the barman, Jamie was once again drawn to the pretty girl with long dark hair. He couldn't take his eyes off her. 'She really does remind me of Jess, you know,' he said, the happy expression on his face replaced with one of sorrow. Bree's tongue rolled around inside her cheek and she bit the corner of her lip. She wanted to say something to him but instead chose to ignore his remark.

As he guzzled a little more of his drink, Jamie made a comment which he knew would not go down well with his companion, but it was something that he felt he needed to get off his chest. 'He came to the gym again yesterday, he came there when I wasn't on shift. He left a business card this time with his mobile number written on the back of it.'

Bree knew exactly who he was talking about. She did her best to change the subject. 'Kayleigh is here with her new boyfriend, well, I say boyfriend, I thought he was her grandad.'

Her comment passed him by. Jamie was anxious to continue with his conversation. 'Do you never think that it all could be true? You know, that he really could be...'

Bree let out a fake howl of laughter as she interrupted him again. 'She says he is thirty-six. They are going down the Shallows club later. She really needs to get her brains tested, that one.'

Jamie sat up in his chair. He was determined to make Bree listen to him. 'I may call him tomorrow, I may meet up with him. You might not care, but I need to know, I don't want to leave without knowing the truth.'

The tone of Bree's voice suddenly rose a few notches and she stared sternly in his direction. 'Stop it, Jay! Stop it now! We only have a couple of days left together, don't spoil it for me, please, don't spoil it for me.'

Jamie sat back in his chair. He knew that look of hers only too well. She was not going to listen to him. 'I am not going to the moon,' he argued. 'We can still keep in touch – Skype and FaceTime.'

Bree screwed up her face and folded her arms like a petulant child. 'No, not the moon!' she snapped. 'Just the other side of the

6

bloody world! It is not the same for me, Jay, you know that, it is not the same for me. When you go, I have nothing, nothing here at all.'

Jamie shook his head and put his hand on her knee. 'You are twenty-two years old, Bree, you really need to get on with your life without me now. I can't do this anymore, I need to get away from things, you have to understand that. You really need to sort yourself out now.'

Jamie had hit a nerve. She didn't want to pursue this conversation anymore. She couldn't bear to look at him at that moment and moved her head to see how her friend's date was developing with her older love interest. Bree knew deep down, however, that Jamie was right, that she was in the prime of her life, but that she had no life. She rarely ventured out these days, preferring solitude to the company of others. The world seemed to be passing her by and she had become a sorry spectator. She had few friends, but, despite her sullen demeanour, had no shortage of admirers, having inherited her mother's stunning Scandinavian looks and silky blonde hair. But Bree never seemed interested in the attention of men and made it clear to those around her that she was not looking for a relationship. She used the passion she had for her developing career as a fashion photographer as an excuse for her choice to be alone, but those around her thought that there was more to it than that.

Thunder broke across the roof of the public house as the storm began to show its anger. Heavy rain could be heard, pounding harder than ever on the skylight window above the bar. Suddenly, a flash of lightning lit up the sky, causing a stir amongst several patrons near the side door. Kayleigh had now left the dark corner seat and headed towards Bree's table with her new man in tow.

'And here comes the lovely Kayleigh,' observed Jamie, waving his arms around again, his words more slurred and slightly less coherent.

'This is Tom,' she said, introducing her new companion, who seemed to be ageing by the minute in the brighter lights.

Jamie shook his hand. 'Good to meet you, fella. I am Jamie and the stone-faced cow over here is my sister Brianna. But you had better call her 'Bree' or she will get the hump.'

Bree said nothing, simply aiming a small sneer in Tom's direction and a nod of acknowledgement. 'They are twins,' Kayleigh declared. 'Bree is twelve minutes older than Jamie.' Her comment met with a blank stare from her best friend.

Tom seemed a little nervous as he addressed the seated couple. 'We are heading down the Shallows club. Kayleigh thought you might want to join us.' Bree gave her friend one of her 'looks', an obvious indication that she was not happy with this intrusion. 'If you want to come with us,' Tom continued, 'I could drop you home later. It will be a nightmare getting a taxi in this weather.'

Jamie was up for it. 'Yes!' he shouted at the top of his voice. 'Come on, old girl, let your hair down tonight, let's go and have some fun.'

Tom had obviously been briefed by Kayleigh to persuade them to join the couple on their late-night excursion. She mimed a few words at him to keep him working on her friend. 'It's half-price entry before eleven o'clock,' he pointed out. 'And the first hour is two drinks for the price of one.'

Bree suddenly came to life. 'Oh!' she remarked aiming her comment firmly at Kayleigh. 'What a catch! Your new friend has one foot in the grave and he is a fucking skinflint! What a great combination!' Kayleigh screwed up her face in an attempt not to laugh. She knew her best friend never held back with her thoughts. She could be a master of put-downs when she wanted to be. Jamie started to put on his 'sad face' again, but his plea did not get him very far this time. 'No, Jay! You have had enough!' Bree barked.

Feeling slightly awkward, Tom nudged Kayleigh and the two of them said their goodbyes before heading out to brave the dreadful weather outside. Bree couldn't resist one further jibe at the man departing. 'I hope you didn't leave your zimmer frame out in the rain, Tom, it will be rusty by now!'

This clearly amused Kayleigh, who struggled to hide her laughter from her new man. 'I will call you tomorrow, babe,' Kayleigh shouted, as Tom opened the side door to face the deepening puddles outside. Jamie simply slumped back into his chair with a look of resignation on his face. He had accepted now that his evening was almost over.

There was a small silence before Jamie once again threw his arms into the air as another of his favourite songs played out from the speakers. 'What a tune!' he shouted. 'I really bloody love this one!' Fearing that their journey home may now take longer than usual, Bree made a trip to the toilet, leaving Jamie singing away merrily at the table. His words were probably not the right lyrics for the song playing, but so what! He was happy, he didn't care.

As she returned, Bree could see that the alcohol had finally worn her brother down and his head was resting on the side of his chair. Sitting down to finish her drink, something suddenly caught her attention. It gave her the strangest of feelings. There in the large mirror next to the bar, someone appeared to be looking at her, staring at both her and Jamie. Bree felt a small chill in her backbone, it was very unsettling. Her line of vision was obscured by patrons of the bar, but she could make out that the reflection was that of a girl, a small girl. She was not standing with anybody else, she was alone, just staring directly over at their table. Bree moved her head to get a better look, but the rain-drenched students were blocking her view. Then, in the mirror she could see her reflection again, she could make out the image of this strange-looking girl. She was dressed in a bright yellow coat, like a fisherman's coat. It was far too big for her, it made her look very small. Bree moved her chair slightly, trying to get a clearer view through the crowd. She could see her again, still standing there, completely still, like a mannequin, just staring at them, fixated on her and Jamie. Bree could just about make out a small face resting on the top of that bright coat. She had tangled dark hair. It was jet-black, like black coal. Her hair was messy and strewn across her face. It was ringing wet, so was her coat. She looked like she had been swimming in that coat. Her eyes were large, like giant marbles. They were dark and black, just like her hair. 'What does she want?' Bree murmured under her breath.

Jamie was oblivious to what was happening. His eyes were shut tight and his head was resting comfortably on the side of his chair. He was still clutching his empty glass, which Bree prised from his grip before nudging him to wake him up. As his senses began to return to him, he could see his sister's attention was elsewhere. The girl was still there, still watching them. She seemed to be completely captivated by her and Jamie. Sensing something was not right, Jamie piped up, 'Who has upset you now?' His words came out in the right order, but his slurring was much worse.

Bree nodded towards the bar area. 'That girl, over by the large mirror,' she said, clearly still agitated by the presence of the stranger looking over at them.

Jamie swung his head round to look but could barely see as far as the palm of his hand. 'Don't go and start anything in here,' Jamie said. 'If they bar you from here there is only that Green Dragony thingy place left. Or is that closed now?'

Bree did not hear Jamie's drunken rambling, the constant attention of the girl in the raincoat was making her angry now. Suddenly, her brother, sensing that his sister was about to react, got to his feet, swaying for a few seconds before grabbing her arm. 'Come on, sis, let's get you out of here, I know what you are like.' Bree did not need a second invitation. She grabbed her colourful scarf from her bag and wrapped it around her neck before tightening her coat, hardly taking her eyes off the girl's reflection in the mirror for a second.

As the two of them made for the side door of the pub, Bree could not resist a parting shot at the strange-looking stalker in the shiny coat. 'You are a weirdo!' she snapped and then repeated herself much louder and much clearer. 'You are a fucking weirdo!'

The pair left through the side door of the pub and waded through the mass of grey puddles that had engulfed the car park. The torrential rain was still thrashing down around them as they clambered into Bree's Audi convertible. Bree was not happy when she saw the mud stains on her footwear. 'I only bought these boots two weeks ago, they are Moncler, they cost nearly £500,' she moaned. 'Thanks, Jay, they will be fucking ruined now!' Jamie said nothing to his sister. He fell into the car through the passenger door and rested his head on the back of the passenger seat. He closed his eyes tightly and let out a small sigh. He had, by now, had enough of his sister's constant whinging.

'Put your seat belt on, Jay,' Bree insisted. 'These roads are going to be a nightmare tonight.' Her brother ignored her order, he just wanted her to be quiet now. His brain told him it was time to sleep. Bree was not prepared to let that happen, she wanted to voice her opinion and he would have to listen. 'What are you going to do without me in Australia, Jay?' she asked in a smug manner. 'You will be lost without me, you know that, don't you?'

Jamie's eyes remained closed, but a cheeky smile beamed across his face. 'I will have to find another chauffeur, I suppose!' he replied sarcastically, immediately evoking the wrath of his sibling.

'I hate you sometimes, Jay, do you know that? I really hate your selfish fucking ways sometimes.'

Jamie opened his eyes and turned to his sister. He had hoped to drift off to sleep but now chose to revisit that sensitive conversation again. 'I will call him tomorrow, sis. I need to know, we both need to know. Come with me, if I arrange to meet up with him, come with me.'

Bree had finally had enough of his taunting. 'Well I don't want to know!' she barked. 'I really don't give a fuck, Jay! So just shut up about him now!'

As the heavy raindrops fell on the Audi, making drumbeat-like sounds on the canvas roof of her car, Bree started her engine and adjusted her windscreen wipers to maximum. 'Put your seat belt on, Jay,' she said again, this time in a much firmer tone. 'The Chadbrooke road will be flooded. I am going to have to go the long way round and through the bloody Maple crossing.' Once more her advice fell on deaf ears.

Bree shook her head, she was furious with him now. She had wanted their last few days together to be special ones and he had spoiled things. As her Audi rolled through the deepening grey puddles and on to the main road her mind began to race. A thousand mixed thoughts jumbled through her head. Gathering speed, she set off through the slippery streets, turning left at the end of Oxley High Road and on to the dimly lit side road which led down to the Maple crossing. Looking over at her brother she could see he was fast asleep now, his head pressing up against the side of the window, his mouth slightly open, tiny noises escaping through his nostrils, like a small piglet with a cold.

Trying hard to concentrate on the rain-soaked lanes ahead of her, she found dark thoughts screaming out inside her head. Why does he have to meet him? Why was he so bothered? Why was he so desperate to change things? Her concentration wavered as she tried to work out why her brother seemed hell-bent on tormenting her that night. Why did he want to go all the way to Australia and leave her on her own again? She was sure that this had been her mother's idea. She was positive that it was her mother that had given him the money to travel thousands of miles away, to finally get her own way and split the two of them up once and for all. 'Bitch!' she said under her breath. 'Fucking bitch!'

As the car approached the Maple crossing, the windscreen wipers seemed to be losing their fight with the monstrous weather conditions. Bree could hardly see the faintly lit street ahead of her and was becoming increasingly frustrated. All she could think about now was the last two miles of this horrendous journey and that cold bottle of Prosecco waiting for her at home. As the Audi neared the crossing she could just about make out a green light ahead. A good sign, she thought, she would not be delayed any further. But as she pulled up towards the pathway across the railway tracks there were other lights blocking her way, brake lights from another vehicle. It had stopped, halfway between the barriers.

'What the fuck!' Bree said as she brought the Audi to a halt, several feet behind the obstacle. Her vision was still blurred by the constant rain, but it was obvious that the vehicle in front of her was stationary. She pushed hard on her car horn. 'Come on! Come on!' she shouted, but the vehicle made no movement. She looked across at Jamie. He was in a deep slumber.

Bree started to become more agitated and pushed harder and longer on the car horn. 'Come on, what the fuck is the matter with you? Come on! Come on!' Jamie was still oblivious to all the commotion. He fidgeted in his chair slightly, but nothing more. Bree felt a rage stirring inside her and once again pushed hard on the car horn, flashing her headlights at the same time in a bid to get some sort of reaction from the driver of the stranded vehicle. But there was nothing, those dimmed brake lights ahead of her were going nowhere.

'Fucking great!' she said as she wrapped her scarf tightly around her neck and buttoned up her coat. 'This is all I bloody well need tonight.' Exiting her car, she trudged through the murky puddles towards the stranded vehicle. Following the beams of her headlights she looked down to see the dark and dirty shades that had formed on her new suede boots. 'God, these are definitely fucking ruined now!' she moaned, as she drew nearer the obstacle ahead of her.

The object blocking her route was a Shogun, a large four-by-four. It seemed to be stuck, right in the middle of the railway tracks. The car's windows had misted over. She could not see anyone inside, but heard noises. Bree clenched her fist tightly and banged firmly on the driver's window of the vehicle. 'You are on the tracks!' she yelled. 'Can you hear me? You are on the tracks.'

Just then a whirring noise was heard from the front of the stranded vehicle, as if the engine was about to start. It lasted barely three seconds before it cut out. Seeing some movement in the front seat, Bree banged again on the window, this time much harder. 'You are on the tracks, you need to move the car.'

The swirling wind began to howl through the crossing and the punishing rain thrashed all around them as Bree tried one more time to get a response. But she suddenly became alarmed. She could hear a child, it sounded like a small child, sobbing inside the car. She froze for a second. She knew now that the situation was urgent, she knew that she would need Jamie's help. Trudging back through the growing puddles she began calling out to him, but her shouts were lost in the echoes of the constant downpour. When Bree reached the Audi and opened the passenger door, she could see that he was still slumped back in the car seat. The tiny pig-like noises had been replaced with a loud snoring sound. How could he be sleeping with all this going on around him? Bree thought. She shook his arm to try to bring him round. 'Jay, you need to help!' she screamed. 'There are kids stuck in that car, it is on the tracks, it can't move.' Jamie pushed her hand away and turned his head to one side, determined to return to his slumber. Despite her shouts and shoves, she couldn't wake him. The excessive alcohol seemed as if it had rendered him useless.

Stepping back, Bree looked down at her brother. An injection of unbridled rage ran through her veins at that moment, something sinister stirred within her. She felt as if she wanted to hit him, to hurt him, to punish him for all this stress and torment he was putting her through. She let out another shout, this time much louder than before. 'Jay, for fuck's sake wake up!' No sooner had those words left her mouth than a new and very real hazard reared its head. The barrier above them had begun to shake and the green traffic light had been replaced with a flashing amber. The danger had just become real, there was a train approaching. Bree began to shake her brother's body. She lowered her head and screamed loudly into his ear, 'You need to wake up, Jay! You need to help me!' Strange emotions began to take over Bree's body at that moment. A dark cloud appeared inside her head, she felt totally helpless and alone.

Suddenly Jamie's eyes opened. He took a few seconds to focus his vision before his mouth started working. 'What's all the fuss?' he said. 'I was soundo there.'

Bree started to panic, pointing at the dim lights of the four-by-four. She knew she had little time to explain, so kept it brief. 'There are kids in the car, Jay, they are stuck on the tracks, the train is coming! Jay, the train is coming!'

Looking through the misted windscreen Jamie's senses swiftly returned as it began to dawn on him what was happening. But by now the danger was almost on their doorstep, the shaking barrier was slowly starting to come down behind their car. Jamie didn't hesitate. 'Close the door!' he yelled. 'Close the bloody door!' Bree began to panic, she didn't know what to do, she froze. Jamie quickly reached out and pulled the car door closed. In an instant he had moved into the driver's seat and started the engine. The barrier was almost down, he needed to act quickly. Suddenly, the wheels of the vehicle began to spin as the car jolted forward, sending a spray of slimy water into the distance. The Audi hurtled towards the rear of the Shogun, the sound of the impact thundering through the night air, the loud clashing noise of bumper meeting bumper followed by an eerie silence. All that could be heard now was the heavy rainfall as it met the widening puddles that surrounded them.

Bree stood at the side of the barrier. The falling rain had clouded her visibility, but she could see enough to know that the stranded vehicle had not moved, it was still stuck on the railway line. Her heart began to pound harder and harder as the sound of thunder cracked in the dark skies above. And then, in the corner of her eye, she could see them, the lights of the train. They were faint, but they were growing by the second, larger and larger. She took a deep breath and screamed out as loudly as she could, 'The train, Jay! The train is coming!'

Jamie could see the same lights from his side window. In an instant, the Audi's engine roared back into action. The vehicle reversed, eight, maybe ten feet. The barrier was now firmly closed, so there was no room to move any further. A small silence followed at the poorly illuminated crossing. All that could be heard during these desperate seconds was the falling rain and the purring of the engine beneath the bonnet. Suddenly, the screech of the tyres broke that silence as Bree's car lunged forward at a searing pace. An almighty smash followed as it found its target again. This time it worked, the force of the Audi sending the larger vehicle careering across the puddles towards the barrier on the other side of the crossing. There followed a few seconds of nervy silence, almost as if someone had paused a scene in a movie.

Bree lifted her head and looked to her left. She suddenly became trapped in that moment. Those distant lights were no longer distant, they were there. They tore through the dark night like a spotlight falling from a stanchion. In an instant more than three hundred tons of speeding steel smashed full on into the side of her convertible, the screeching sound of metal meeting metal echoing through the railway sidings. The full force of the passenger train sent Bree's car hurtling through the air like a juggler's club in a circus ring, but in this tragic performance, there would be no one there to catch its fall. Time seemed to stand still as the car turned twice in mid-air and landed upside down further down the track. Bree stood rooted to the spot as she heard the screeching of the locomotive's brakes. They ripped through her body. They were louder than the rain, louder than the wind, screaming out as they desperately tried to bring the train to a halt. But their efforts were in vain. The engine struck the wounded carcass of the convertible for the second time, rolling it over and crushing the remains beneath its wheels of steel. Scattered bits of the battered car frame flew up into the soggy countryside, showering the idyllic backdrop with tangled pieces of metal.

Bree finally caught her breath. Filling her lungs, she let out an ear-piercing scream that ricocheted around the Maple crossing. 'Jaaayymmeeee!'

Her legs gave way beneath her and she fell to her knees. She squeezed her head tightly, bowing it down, lower and lower until her rain-soaked hair was lying in the sodden earth. She tried to scream again, but nothing came out of her mouth, like a small injured child that could not catch their breath to release a cry of despair. The first of a million tears left her eyes as the gushing rain lashed down around her body. That was the second that she knew, she knew she had lost him, she knew he was gone. In her heart she knew that her brother was dead.

The level crossing suddenly came to life. Car doors were slamming, people from both sides of the barrier were scurrying backwards and forwards. Some people braved the elements to venture further down the track, to where the remains of the car might be. Bree could not hear anything, her mind had completely shut off. People were talking to her, but there were just no sounds, it was as if she had suddenly been struck deaf. In the middle of all this pandemonium, a grey-haired man without a coat on reached down and wrapped his arms around her shaking torso, clutching her tightly to his chest in a bid to offer her some comfort. She looked around to see more people arriving. Some were on their phones calling for emergency services, others were trying to make sense of the catastrophe that had taken place. As her senses slowly returned Bree could hear the frantic screams of a woman and could make out the sobbing cries of a small child. She would, however, have taken no solace from knowing that the passengers of the stranded vehicle were safe and well. Jamie was gone, that was all that mattered to her.

Bree raised her head slightly as the old man, now soaked through, attempted to help her to her feet. The merciless downpour continued to fall around her aching body and the howling wind carried the remnants of her final scream into the distance. But just then, beyond the darkness, she heard a small voice call out to her, a voice she recognised. Suddenly, through the punishing rainfall, amidst the growing number of do-gooders arriving to offer their assistance, she could see her, she was as clear as anything now, the girl from the bar. She was there, on a small hill overlooking the level crossing, her bright yellow coat standing out like a beacon for lost sailors. The tiny figure was motionless. She was watching, just staring, as she had done in the pub. She was looking down from the hill, studying the aftermath of the tragedy. What unsettled Bree more than anything was that she realised now that she knew who that girl was.

# CHAPTER TWO

I t is often said, yet never proven, that when a man is drowning, his whole life flashes before him – images of the path he chose to follow and the world he is about to leave behind.

Dean Jarvis was drowning, he was sinking fast in a turbulent sea of his own self-pity. He would not have liked most of the scenes that were playing out before his eyes, but whether he would have changed any of them or not would be highly debatable. He had spent the best part of his sixty-four years on this earth caring for no one other than himself. And now, as he approached an age where most men would be looking forward to a happy retirement, he had become a bitter and twisted old man.

He looked down at the sodden streets from the window of the warm hospital room, watching intently as the torrential downpour caused havoc below. The heavy rains and strong winds had been ceaseless that night, bringing chaos to the streets of South London. The weather forecasters had, not for the first time, underestimated the severity of the oncoming storm, leaving many people stranded in their homes. The screaming sirens of ambulances had been coming and going for at least four hours.

The paramedics would certainly be earning their crust on this awful night.

Through the quagmire below Dean could make out the figures of two nurses braving the appalling conditions to visit the mini-mart opposite. They were armed with nothing more than a cheap-looking umbrella. Their makeshift shield lasted less than ten seconds before a strong gust of wind rendered it useless, leaving them to face the elements unprotected.

'She always wanted to be a nurse, you know, Poppy, she always wanted to be a nurse,' Dean said, his comment aimed at a motionless figure in the bed behind him. 'She was always dressing up her bloody dolls with bandages and sticky plasters when she was little, the silly mare,' he added.

Looking down at his wristwatch, he adjusted the fake alligator skin strap that was beginning to itch away at his skin. Checking the time, he peered up at the large silver clock on the wall to confirm that it was nearly twenty past eleven. Dean sighed as he peered through the misting windows to see if the nurses had completed their mission. 'I have been coming here months now, bloody months!' he said. The man snuggled up in the warm bedsheets said nothing. 'Got better bloody things to do than be here every night,' Dean added, but his words once again seemed to fall on deaf ears.

The downpour continued outside. Small streams were forming at both sides of the kerb. The pavements were now in danger of flooding. There was no respite. These atrocious conditions seemed, if anything, to be getting worse. Catching a glimpse of himself in the glass of the window, Dean's image portrayed the stark reality of forty years of hard drinking. His wayward lifestyle had not been kind to his features. The dark shadows under his eyes told their own story. His hair had turned a silvery shade of grey and his eyesight was fading. He had long lost the battle with his ageing years. He sighed again as his reflection became clearer. 'I get so bloody tired these days,' he said. 'So bloody tired.'

Dean had spent so much time in this hospital room it had become like a second home to him. This comfortable setting, however, was a vast improvement on his registered address. Time stood still for him within the confines of these four bright white walls, as if he somehow belonged there. He glanced down at the figure wrapped up in the fresh bedsheets. He looked so peaceful. Despite the array of tubes and brightly coloured machines surrounding him, he looked as if he didn't have a care in the world. There were no pictures on his bedside cabinet, no token bowl of decaying fruit by his side. All he had for company was the constant bleeping noise of a small white monitor to his side and of course the man that stood over him. Dean knew the limited number of features in this room so well he could have made his way around blindfolded. But he had to be here, every day, every night, hoping that the silent figure in the bed would wake up. He needed to speak to him, there were so many important things he needed to tell him before it was too late.

The drowning man looked back up at the clock on the wall, as if the minute or so that had passed would have made a difference. It didn't of course. He sighed again and continued to share his woes. 'I tried to contact her, you know, Poppy, I tried to contact her.' His words were still lost on the statue-like figure in the bed, but he carried on regardless. 'I got her mobile number from that black guy in the probation office. He said it would be a good idea for me to make contact, you know, to support her, after everything that happened. He was a nice fella, I liked him.' Dean looked down at his watch again. He started to scratch away at his itching wrist. 'I must have tried her a hundred times or more, phone calls, texts, you know, at least a hundred times.' His well-practised voice of self-pity kicked back into action. 'Never wanted to speak to me, blocked my number in the end. Don't suppose I can blame her, left it too long really.' He wasn't finished, despite the lack of an audience. 'The black fella says she was doing OK for herself, got off the drugs and everything while she was inside. Learned to drive as well, on some bloody rehab scheme they have. Can't imagine my little Poppy driving, all grown up, you know, driving her own car.'

A sudden burst of thunder roared above the rooftops causing Dean to turn his attention back down to the mayhem below. There were no pedestrians to be seen now and the flow of traffic was sparse. 'I tried to see her, when she was inside. I wrote a couple of times, you know, when she first went in there. But she wouldn't send me a visitor pass. Couldn't do anything without that! I was so pissed off with that newspaper, you know, all that shit they wrote about her. They made her out to be some sort of devil, like she was possessed or something. I went there, to the *Gazette*, told them, I did, told them I would burn their fucking place down if they carried on writing all those bad things about her.'

It was not unusual to hear Dean use bad language, it was however unusual to hear him talking with such passion about his troubled daughter. They were strong words indeed from the man whose waterfall of self-despair was slowly filling up around him. But if Poppy Jarvis was here now she would not entertain this show of belated remorse, she would tell it as it is, that he was talking bullshit! She would certainly not shy away from letting her estranged father know exactly what she thought of him.

It is strange how Dean's memory could be so selective, now that he was cast adrift, destined to end up at the bottom of his ocean of fake tears. He was desperate to find some consolation on this dark and dismal journey. Maybe that man in the bed could help him make sense of his life, maybe he would understand that it wasn't all his fault, despite what Poppy might think. Dean was still hoping for salvation, hoping that someone would throw him a life jacket to help him through these stormy waters.

The lights below were becoming dimmer by the minute. The atrocious weather conditions were winning the battle of the streets below. Dean felt an unusual chill run through his body, almost as if an ice cube had found its way into his veins. He continued with his tales of woe. 'I wish I had never found out about the boy,' he said. 'I should never have typed her bloody name into the computer. I should have left the past in the past. Damn that bloody Facebook thing! I would have been better off not knowing.' The man in the bed would probably agree with him on that point, feeling that Dean had already tormented enough lives over the past two decades. The drowning man would, however, never get to play out a scene with the boy he was talking about. He didn't know it that time, but it was too late for that now, far too late. His ramblings took him back to the child he did manage to spend time with, some would say quality time, others, who knew Dean, would say time of convenience. 'No, it wasn't a nurse, it was a vet, Poppy always wanted to be a vet,' he said.

His comment had no impact whatsoever on the man wrapped up in the bed. He was past caring. As another crack of thunder rumbled overhead, Dean's thoughts turned to a happier time in his life. For some reason it was a place he frequently visited in his head, it was a place where he could escape the gritty sewer of his life, a place where he felt safe from the depths of the dark and gloomy sea of his destiny. Maybe his curiosity had finally got the better of him that day he had typed her name in to the search engine on the computer at the internet café. His selective memory would take him back more than twenty years, to a time when he had a chance to feel more alive than he had felt at any other time in his life. 'She was beautiful, you know, she was so perfect. The most beautiful creature I ever saw in my life. I knew from the first time I saw her that I loved her.'

It would be a testament to a doting father to think that Dean might be thinking of his daughter at this time, but Poppy was far from his thoughts. Ask Dean Jarvis to remember when his daughter's birthday was or the date his wife left him, he would probably struggle to find an answer. But he could always remember that day when he first met Krista. He could never forget the moment no matter how close he was to his final calling.

It was the middle of April. It was warm, very warm. It was unusually humid for that month. He didn't want to wear a tie when he went to the Imediacom offices in Neasden, but he knew that the company's owner, George Penning, was best friends with his own boss. He thought it best not to give anyone a chance to bad-mouth him. Reluctantly, he buttoned up his shirt and tied an angry knot in his tie, cursing the sweltering heat as he left his vehicle in the car park. Maria, the pretty young receptionist, did not like him, in fact she really disliked him. Not just for his brash manner and his sexist remarks, but she also cared little for the cheap aftershave he wore. So they were at it again, him and the feisty receptionist, arguing about the collection of sample alarm systems he was expecting to pick up that day. He was shouting, as was Dean's way. She was more controlled, but rapidly losing her composure. Halfway through this heated encounter he felt the presence of another person standing behind him. He turned to find the petite figure of a woman, a well-dressed blonde woman holding a pale blue folder. She was staring up at him, a look of contempt etched on her face. He wanted to speak, to carry on his rant, but before he could open his mouth he was brought crashing down to earth by the tiny creature in front of him.

'You need to calm down,' the woman said, in a broken kind of English that he immediately found enchanting. 'You need to calm down or I will ask security to escort you from the building.'

His mouth became dry. He struggled to speak for a few seconds before he retaliated. 'Do you know who I am?' he asked. 'Do you know who you are talking to?'

The fresh-faced woman below his line of vision seemed unperturbed. 'I neither know, nor care, who you are. If you can't control your temper with the staff you will be thrown out of here, is that clear?'

Dean wanted to do so many things at that point. He wanted to throw his paperwork across the reception area and storm out, he wanted to shout back, much louder than this tiny girl could ever shout, but when he looked deeply into her smouldering eyes, all that Dean wanted to do was to grab her tiny frame and kiss her soft lips.

He did his best to fight his urges and found some words, hoping to get his point across. 'These samples were ordered three days ago, they should be ready for me. You shouldn't keep me waiting.' The expression on the woman's face remained unchanged as he continued his rant. 'My company spend a lot of money with you lot, we should take priority.'

As she looked upwards, a small smile cracked across her face as she addressed the unruly visitor. 'Three things,' she said. There were those beautiful tones again, Dean thought. 'Three things you need to know.' He wanted to respond at that moment, but his brain just stopped working. 'One,' she said, 'you don't own your company, you are just one of their salesmen and a very rude one at that.' His facial expression began to change to one of surprise. 'Two,' she continued, 'if you had phoned ahead and spoken to the product department, you would have found your sample units waiting for you. You didn't call, because if you had, you would have spoken to me and I certainly would have remembered speaking to someone as ill-mannered and pig-ignorant as yourself.'

Maria released a small laugh from behind the reception desk, which took Dean's attention away from the beautiful vision in front of him, but not for long. He was soon back staring into her eyes, those piercing spheres of enchantment, full of danger, like a burning wildfire. 'And three,' she said, 'brown shoes with a grey suit! Do you not look in the mirror before you set off for work in the morning?' The receptionist could not contain herself anymore and let out a huge roar of laughter.

He was angry now. His face had started to turn red, both through embarrassment and rage. 'And who the hell do you think you are?' he asked.

The beautiful creature brushed back her silky blonde shoulder-length hair before calmly pointing at her name tag. 'I am Krista, Krista Nylund, the new head of production here.' With that she turned and walked slowly along the corridor, moving gently away, her hips swaying, her head held high. She had serenity in her stride, as if a hundred ancient slaves were throwing flowers in her path as she was leaving.

Dean was mesmerised, rooted to the spot as if the sight of her had turned him to stone. He hardly heard Maria's voice calling out to him, 'The samples are here now, Mr Jarvis, your samples are here.'

And that's where it began, the fantasy, on that hot spring day in 1995. He would remember that moment forever. But it was a moment he should have taken back to his car and thrown out of the window on his way home. It was a meeting of two people that should never have been, it was a destiny that would be the start of a journey where the tides of the sea that surrounded his existence would start to rise

\* \* \*

The drowning man looked down from the hospital window. He could see that the lights in the mini-mart windows had been turned off now. Only the craziest of drivers were brave enough to run the gauntlet of the stream running through the soaking streets below. His temporary reflection on a better time in his life had been short-lived, but the wry smile on his ageing face told its own story. He may be sinking fast, but he knew that he could always go back to that place in his mind, to that sanctuary, to that fantasy.

He felt a chill run through his bones again as he turned to check on the figure behind him. He wasn't sure what he expected to see, the bedridden man was unlikely to be performing cartwheels. Suddenly, a thought crossed his mind, a dark thought. Maybe it was that thought that had sent that chill down his spine. 'No! It wasn't a vet,' he said. 'I knew that Poppy would never have been a vet, not after what she did to poor Snowball. Why would a little girl do that to a tiny rabbit?'

# CHAPTER THREE

J oseph Manning had, in layman's terms, been around the block
more than a few times with his delinquent clientele. Nothing
they ever told him seemed to shock him these days. But there
was something he found very unsettling about Poppy Jarvis. He
was never quite sure what it was, but it gave him constant cause
for concern. Despite his many years of dealing with convicted
criminals from all walks of life, this had been the first time he
genuinely felt uncomfortable during his one-on-one sessions.

A tall and softly spoken black gentleman in his late fifties,
Manning had a real passion for fine dining, a fact that was borne
out by his portly figure. He wore smart designer suits and spoke
with an educated and authoritative voice, a gift he acquired
from his days at Oxford University. Some people said he more
resembled a banker or a high-flying accountant than a probation
officer.

Manning enjoyed his role within the court service though and
had built up a real rapport with most of his visitors. In the seven
years he had spent working at the court in South London, he had
been physically assaulted just once. Even then the larger-than-life

official made valid excuses for his assailant and refused to have him prosecuted. He was a firm believer that every person had the chance to redeem themselves, his statistics certainly confirmed that. During his lengthy career in this sphere of work he had successfully steered many habitual offenders onto a path leading to a stable and crime-free life.

Manning preferred his visitors to call him 'Joe'. He felt it made things easier for them to discuss their day-to-day issues, as if they were talking to an uncle or a friend. The only negative observation that any of his clientele ever made was about his overbearing references to the Bible. He really did take his religious beliefs to the extreme sometimes.

Poppy treated these meetings as a real chore, an hour stolen from her life each week, as part of the deal that saw her gain an early release from prison. She would consciously look up at the large clock on the wall each time she entered his office, mentally counting down the minutes until her ordeal was over. She didn't really feel uneasy in Manning's presence but found herself very much 'going through the motions' during their sessions. Poppy would avoid eye contact with her would-be mentor during these arduos meetings and would only speak when she had to. The less she said, the better she would feel when each dreaded hour was over.

She often found these sessions confusing, one minute, Manning would be discussing her previous criminal actions, the next he would be reciting quotations from the bible. She found this extremely irritating to say the least. She often referred to him as 'The Reverend Joe', feeling that he would be better suited to reading a sermon in the local church. In truth, she was probably right. He would not have looked out of place at the head of a large gospel choir, spreading his ideas of righteousness to a colourful, all-singing, all-dancing congregation.

The clock indicated it was three minutes past ten when the session began. 'Good morning, Poppy, how has the week been for you?' Manning asked, the same introduction he had greeted her with for the past thirty-odd weeks.

'Not too bad,' she replied, probably the same response she had given over that time. *Small talk over with, time for him to start prodding*, Poppy thought.

'Are those new shoes?' Manning asked as he opened her case folder to review her notes.

'No, I found them at the back of the wardrobe and cleaned them up a bit,' she replied.

Poppy looked around his office as he wiped his spectacles. It was always so tidy in there, nothing was ever out of place, nothing ever looked different. It even smelled clean. She glanced over at a photograph on his desk, the one of Manning and his family. They looked like they were on holiday somewhere on a sunny beach. Poppy thought that it was a terrible picture. He looked extremely overweight in his ill-fitting T-shirt, and his wife had a sinister and evil sort of smile. Not that Poppy would have ever told him that.

'How is your job at the restaurant?' he asked.

'Fine.'

'No problems there?'

*What problems could you possibly have serving food to people in a bistro?* she thought. 'No, no problems.'

'Are they giving you plenty of shifts?'

'It's long hours, but I don't mind that. The money is alright.'

Joe looked closer at his notes. 'Oh, it is that Chez Blanc place, the bistro up in Welling High Street. My wife wanted to try that out. A friend of hers said they do a nice salmon teriyaki on their lunch menu.'

Poppy said nothing. The last thing she wanted was him being a regular at her workplace. One sermon each week was more than enough for her, thank you very much.

He began to flick his way through the growing number of pages in her folder. 'Don't worry,' he said, 'just got to update some of your information today.' Poppy looked back up at the clock on the wall. Not even ten past yet. *God, this is going to be a long hour*, she thought.

'Are you still at the flat in Stonely Parade in Eltham?'

''Yes.'

'You share that flat with your boyfriend?'

'Yes, with Cameron.'

Poppy saw Joe's eyebrows rise. 'Oh yes, Mr Turner, isn't it, Cameron Turner?'

'Yes,' she replied. *Keep it brief*, she thought, hoping he would move onto another topic. Cameron was well known to Manning and the courts, and they had discussed him at length in the past. He had been 'in the system' longer than she had, starting with car theft and burglary at the age of fourteen and working his way up the criminal ladder. He was twenty-seven now, a couple of years older than her. His crimes had progressed to dealing class A drugs and grievous bodily harm. However, two lengthy spells in Wandsworth prison had, in the court's eyes, finally straightened him out.

They had met on the Marfield estate in Woolwich, when she was sixteen years old and had just been released from the Medway Young Offenders Centre. Cameron had something of a 'bad boy' reputation on the estate. His six-feet-plus frame and bulging muscles meant that few people argued with him. He had 'respect', wherever he went. He had taken a shine to Poppy and she became part of his small clique of teenage dropouts. Cameron soon introduced her to his best friends, Ketamin and Ecstasy. She liked these companions, they took her to places she had never been before. Poppy never knew at the time whether it was Cameron she became addicted to, or the drugs he used to feed her. Either way the two of them became much more than friends before he was locked up for three years for a racially aggravated assault.

'Is Mr Turner working?' Joe asked. 'Does he have a full-time job?'

Poppy never liked this type of questioning, she was always afraid of giving the wrong answer, but she did her best to respond.

'Sort of,' she said. 'He is trying to get into the building trade.' Joe scribbled away in the folder. He knew full well that there was little or no chance of seeing Cameron Turner plastering walls or laying down bricks at a building site any time soon. Another glance up at the clock told Poppy that this was going to be one of those 'awkward' sessions.

'When was the last time our team paid you a home visit?' Manning asked.

'Just a few weeks ago,' Poppy replied, even though she knew it had been nearly three months.

'I will ask them to organise that,' Joe said. 'Just to make sure everything is OK there.'

Poppy knew that the word 'visit' was really court code for 'look around the flat for signs of drug use', but she had little say in the matter. The last time they came to 'inspect' her flat, she had to spend over £10 on fresh-air sprays and cleaning products just to nullify the potent smells of cannabis in the home. Fortunately for her, the overwhelming stench of rotting meat and chip fat from the kebab shop directly beneath her living room became more of a talking point for the court-appointed visitors than the solitary joint they discovered, so the money had been well spent.

Joe continued his interrogation. 'And I see here you are due for another test soon, at the Verney Centre.'

'The ninth of April,' Poppy replied. 'I have made a note of it.' She knew the consequences of missing her regular drug tests. The establishment would come down on her like a ton of bricks if she failed to turn up there. Besides, she had been clean for over four years now, an amazing feat, considering that, thanks to the habits of her boyfriend, her flat often resembled a 'crack den'.

Joe continued to scribble down his notes, but suddenly became sidetracked by a yellow sticker on the top of the folder. He asked her another awkward question. 'Have you called Mrs Bishop about the anger management course yet?'

Poppy took a deep breath. 'No, not yet.' Joe stared at her, waiting for an explanation. 'I haven't had any credit on my phone. I will call her this week.'

The probation officer frowned as he took off his glasses to give them another wipe. 'You know it is compulsory, Poppy, you do know that, don't you? It was a condition of your release programme. You have been out nearly eight months now. They will take a very dim view if you don't start soon.'

'I thought it was a voluntary thing,' Poppy said, a poor excuse that she had used several times before.

Manning shook his head. 'No! You need to take a full four-month course, Poppy, that's what it says in your notes, a full four-month course. You could have finished it by now.'

Poppy thought for a few seconds. She wanted to move on from this subject. 'I will call her this week when I get some credit on my phone.'

Joe's pen went back to work and the questioning continued. 'You don't seem to have a next of kin listed here. I can see here in your notes that you have never given us a next of kin, is that right?'

'I don't really have one. You can put Cameron.'

'What about your father? I thought you two were back in touch.'

'No!' Poppy snapped, almost immediately regretting it. She swiftly lowered the tone of her voice. 'No, we are not in touch, you need to put Cameron.'

'You know that I met with your father, Poppy, did he tell you that?'

Poppy said nothing. She had been seething with anger since he had taken it upon himself to let her estranged father have her mobile number. The man had never stopped calling and texting her, for weeks and weeks until she finally worked out how to block his number. What the hell did the Reverend Joe think he was doing? He may act like a preacher sometimes, but he shouldn't be playing God with her life. It was just that, her life, and she would decide. She had nothing but contempt for the man who had not been around for more than fifteen years. She wanted it to stay that way.

Joe rested the folder on his lap and pondered for a moment before he started one of his well-rehearsed one-liners. 'You know it says in the old testament, 'he will turn the hearts of fathers to their children and the hearts of children to their fathers'. Sometimes, Poppy, we have to…' Her mind just switched off at that point and she looked back at the clock. *Not even half past yet,* she thought, *and Joe is off on one of his bloody biblical journeys.*

As Manning continued his latest sermon, Poppy reflected on his comments about her next of kin.

*So, you want to know why I have no family, Joe,* she thought, *you really want to know why I would not want that waste of space father to be my next of kin? Maybe we should go all the way back to when he could be bothered to be present in my life. Let's start with a time when I first started school, when I made some friends, but I was afraid to invite them to my house in fear of what they might witness. Not just the screaming rows between him and my mother, no they were an everyday occurrence, or the piles and piles of empty wine and vodka bottles littered around our front garden, no, surely everyone's parents like a drink every now and then! No, let's talk about the violence, Joe, the fights they had, the bruises he left on her face, the time the ambulance came at three o'clock in the morning because my mother had stopped breathing. She was OK of course, a bottle of cheap 'voddie' and some of those anti-depressant pills she used to take made her feel better.*

*When my schoolfriends would be out with their parents, visiting theme parks or having trips to the seaside, I was stuck in my tiny room with a pillow wrapped around my head, desperately trying to escape the shouting and the arguing around the house. Sometimes, Joe, I would stay in there for a whole weekend, not eating or drinking, just frightened to come out. He hit me a few times, Joe, with the buckle on his belt. He used to say that I was getting 'too big for my boots', so I suppose he had every right to do that. But it was different for my mum, he would hit her for no reason at all sometimes.*

*The only time I did have my friends come to my house was my sixth birthday. I didn't get much that year from my father, but my mother did – two black eyes and a broken nose! I can't get that out of my head, Joe, that crazy woman dancing around the living room with a half-bottle of vodka in her hand, looking like she had fought ten rounds in a boxing ring. He did one of his disappearing tricks of course, went on the missing list for a week. He was good at that, Joe, running away from his guilt, hiding his shame.*

*Oh, don't get me wrong, Joe, there were some good days. I did go to the beach once, with that nice couple from Social Services. I was so embarrassed, I had to pretend to my friends that they were my aunt and uncle. I think I secretly wished inside that they were. I couldn't tell you where the beach was, but we had some fun. I went on roundabouts and a few fast rides, we even had candyfloss and ice cream. I felt, I don't know, I suppose I felt good about my life that day. I was just like my schoolfriends, feeling, well, just like any normal seven-year-old girl should feel. I didn't want to go back home. If you had lived in my house you would know what I mean.*

*It was there, Joe, there at the seaside that I bought my dad that keyring. I had emptied out all the coins from my money box at home and had taken them with me. I didn't spend them at the arcade like most kids would do, no not me, not me. You see, Joe, I was very naive back then. I looked for ages in that gift shop, trying to find the right present. It had to be special, you see it was his birthday the following week, so it had to be the perfect present. I found it, Joe, the perfect gift, it was a lion-shaped keyring. You see, that was his star sign, Joe, and it had the words 'best dad in the world' sitting underneath the lion's head. Now that was the funniest thing of all, I can laugh now, but to ever think of him as the best dad there could be has been the biggest joke of my life. I never saw that keyring after his birthday, I think he just put it in a drawer somewhere or maybe just threw it away, just like he threw me away. Did I ever tell you that, Joe? Did I ever tell you that he threw me away? I was just eight years old when he got rid of me. Just as if he was throwing out an old sofa or worn-out mattress, he just threw me away.*

*Hey, the time is moving on quite fast now, Joe, it is almost quarter to eleven, nearly time for me to go. I can still hear you dribbling on, you are back on that crap again now, about 'oldest sins and longest shadows', but I don't get it, Joe. I am so sorry, but I really don't understand any of this biblical bullshit at all. We haven't got long now, so why don't I tell you about why I have no next of kin? Before my dad – and God that word is so hard to say – threw me away, I had a mother, Joe. I wouldn't say a caring and loving mother, in fact, sometimes I think she was so out of it she never even knew that I existed, but she was my mother.*

*I was only eight years old when she left, Joe, just eight years old. It was a Thursday, I know that because that was the day the bin men came to collect the rubbish. It was raining, it had been pouring down all morning. I was not at school, it could have been half term or something. Or maybe – and there were plenty of days like that – nobody was bothered to take me to school. Anyway, I was watching the television. I wasn't worried that I was missing lessons. No eight-year-old would be, would they? She was blind drunk, Joe. It was half past ten in the morning and she was steaming. She told me she was going to the shops. I said she should take her coat, she would get wet if she didn't take her coat. She put the brown one on, the one with the fur collar. She liked that one, I didn't. There was no hug or kiss, Joe, but she did smile at me. I remember that smile. She looked funny. One of her teeth was missing at the side of her mouth, probably another gift from 'the best dad in the world'. So she smiled that funny smile at me and left. I watched her from the window, Joe, I watched her swaying all the way down the road. I remember that a young couple laughed at her as she passed them by. And that was the last time I ever saw her. I was eight years old, Joe. Was that fair, was that really fair?'*

*So, when she never came back, the 'best dad in the world' took me to the boating lake. He said that he wanted to talk to me, that he needed to explain why she had left. I used to like the boating lake. In truth I used to think that anywhere away from my house was good. But I didn't understand him, Joe, I didn't get what he was saying. He probably thought to himself, Let's give the little brat a few spins around the island, buy her a nice ice cream and tell her that it was all her mum's fault, she will feel better then. But I never did feel better, Joe, I never did feel better.*

*And so, some days I wish him dead and some days I don't think about him at all. Those are the better days for me, Joe, those are much better days for me. So let's just put Cameron's name down as my next of kin. I know he is not perfect. Yes, he can be violent. Yes, sometimes he hits me. There I have said it! So he would not be my first choice and God knows I know he would not be yours. But Cameron is all I have, Joe, he is all I have in this shitty little world, so he will have to do.*

*I know you are not a bad man, Joe, I will try my best to forgive you for giving my useless father my phone number. You know, I really wish sometimes that I could tell you all these things, but you are not a psychiatrist or psychoanalyst or whatever they call it nowadays. To be honest I would not want to burden you with the story of my life. In truth, Joe, I don't think you would be able to handle it. You see, you still believe that I can be saved, you really think that God would forgive me for what I did to Billy Keyes. But he wouldn't, Joe, trust me, he wouldn't! He knows that I have not been very good in my life, he knows that I am not sorry for the things I have done. It is far too late for me to read that big book that you keep banging on about and try to make my life better. Let's not kid ourselves, come the day of judgment, Joe, we both know which way I will be heading.*

*But I do wish that you would stop prodding at me every bloody week, prodding me, trying to get a reaction. You see they did that in Bronzefield – I am sure you have seen that in my notes – the people at the assessment unit at the prison. That is all they did, prod, prod, prod at me, all the time. Those men in their fancy suits and that strange American woman with the funny glasses, peck, peck, peck at my head.*

*Hundreds, no, thousands of questions. Maybe the newspapers were right, Joe, maybe they should have locked me up for longer, maybe even forever. No offence, Joe, but maybe we should simply skip these weekly meetings, forget all this nonsense about rehabilitation and you should just let them have me sectioned. That is, after all, what you all want, isn't it?*

At two minutes past eleven Manning called a halt to the session. Poppy let out a sigh of relief. *Only eighteen more bloody hours left to go*, she thought.

\* \* \*

Poppy exited the probation office much quicker than she had entered it, enjoying a much-needed cigarette on the way to where she had left her car. Her head was still spinning from her recent inquisition, but she had ticked off another visit and in her mind that was always good. She had an hour to kill before her shift started at the restaurant. She could have gone back to the flat, but Cameron had been in another one of his foul moods the previous night, so she thought it might be best to stay out of his way.

Back at her car, she lit up another cigarette and counted the money in her purse. She had just over £11. She needed tobacco, phone credit and at least £5 of petrol in her car, so realised that she was going to be short. The tobacco was her priority. She couldn't get through a day without her fix of nicotine, so the call to the anger management unit would have to wait a few more days. Poppy was confident that she would earn some tips from her job over the coming days, so she knew that she would be OK.

Poppy loved her car. Her silver Omega 2.2 offered her a lifeline she had never previously enjoyed. Danny Riordan, the owner of Chez Blanc, had helped her to buy the car when she first started working for him. With the vehicle priced at £800, she would never have been able to afford the purchase, but he had bought the car for her and was deducting £60 each month from her wages, until the full sum was cleared. He had even helped her to arrange a cheap motor insurance plan with one of his many 'contacts'. He justified his offer of assistance in simple terms. 'You have some freedom to roam around the roads and I get a bloody good waitress who is never late for work.'

Poppy had hated being locked away in prison for so long, but she would always recognise that she achieved two things at Bronzefield that changed her life. Firstly, their rehab team had got her completely clean of drugs for the first time since she was fourteen. Years and years of poisoning her body on a frequent basis had taken its toll on her, so the staff at the prison did not have an easy task. But she had been completely clean for over four years now and had found the resolution to stay that way, despite being around her boyfriend's substance abuse on a regular basis.

The second thing she benefited from was the prison's 'back-to-work' initiative, aimed at helping inmates find meaningful employment when they leave prison. She managed to enrol in a scheme where part of the course involved teaching novice road-users to drive. When she put her name down for the course, she envisaged herself making a fast getaway in the dual-controlled vehicle the first time she saw an open road. However, she enjoyed the freedom that the experience gave her so much she knuckled down and became only the third inmate to complete the whole course and obtain a full driving licence. The first week she sat in her Omega, she drove for miles and miles, going everywhere she knew, just to see what she had been missing. Her random journeys even took her to the old boating lake that she had visited as a child, but she didn't stay there for too long, she did not want the ghosts from her past to catch up with her.

She liked Danny, her boss, a small wiry man of Irish descent. He had been in the restaurant trade for more than thirty years. He took a shine to Poppy when she arrived for her interview several months earlier. He admired her honesty. She had told him about the time she had spent in prison and given him chapter and verse on the reason for her incarceration. Poppy guessed that her new boss had been a guest in one of 'Her Majesty's' establishments at some time in his life, not that he ever confessed to it. They would often have long conversations after work hours. He would offer her support when she was at a low ebb and she would listen to him talk about his ex-wife. Danny had told her that she had left him when she felt his excessive drinking had got out of hand. Poppy understood that, of course, having lived with violent alcoholic parents herself. Her boss had been completely teetotal since the day his wife had left him, hoping that his transformation would result in her returning to him one day. The standing joke in the restaurant was that he would often recite the exact amount of days he had given up the 'demon drink', regularly adding that the 'ungrateful bitch' had still not returned.

As she sat in her car, her mobile made a familiar noise indicating that there were messages on her voicemail. These messages were never good news, but she felt that it was better for her to know than not to know. The first was Mr Rahwaz, her landlord, chasing rent arrears. This was a regular message, left most weeks. Her and Cameron were always behind on their rent, mainly because most of the benefits her boyfriend received were spent fueling his unhealthy habits. Poppy did not earn enough to cover all the bills, so Rahwaz would always play second fiddle to everything else, including the drugs. Her second message was from a company trying to sell her life insurance. That one was deleted halfway through. The final voicemail recording, which had only just been received, was from Mrs Bishop from the Fallon Counselling Project, another name for the anger management unit. 'Thanks for that, Joe,' she muttered under her breath, knowing that 'The Reverend' had contacted this woman within seconds of her leaving his office. 'Don't you realise that all this shit about anger management is what makes me so fucking angry in the first place!' she said, rewarding herself with a smirk at her half-baked attempt at satire. Poppy finished her cigarette and headed for the restaurant. She knew she would be early, but the coffee was free there and she could find something to eat to make up for skipping breakfast.

# CHAPTER FOUR

Parking her Omega in the private car park at the rear of the building, Poppy entered Chez Blanc to the sound of a wolf whistle from the young chef Matt Jameson. 'Looking hot, lass! As always!' he shouted in his distinct Geordie accent. 'Just look at that great arse wiggle across the room.'

Poppy was in no mood for banter today. 'Fuck off and die, Matt,' she replied, in a bid to stop him from making any more sexist comments. Her brutal put-down worked instantly, and the chef got back to his duties. She headed inside the dining area and found Danny rearranging the tables. 'You are early,' he observed and then realised why she was there. 'Oh, it's Wednesday. How was the Reverend Joe today, still bringing down the wrath of God on all those sinners?'

Poppy laughed. 'Something like that,' she replied. 'At least that's another bloody week over and done with.'

Danny passed her a handful of dirty table cloths. 'Make yourself useful, love,' he said. 'Throw these in the wash for me, love.' Poppy took the linen and headed for the utility room.

It was strange, Poppy felt more comfortable at work than she did anywhere else. Danny was like the uncle that she had never really had. He knew her situation better than most and did his best to make sure that she always had plenty of shifts at the restaurant to help her with her finances. Unlike others, he saw Poppy as a hard-working and trustworthy employee and a valued member of his small team. Matt, the head chef, despite being something of an irritant, with his childish smirk and constant sexual innuendos, was harmless. She ignored his incessant flirting, knowing that he would probably run for miles if she ever gave in to one of his sexual advances. Poppy worked long hours, she had to, to make up for Cameron's lack of contribution to the bills. But she felt as if she was part of something at Chez Blanc, it was almost like an adopted 'dysfunctional family', and to her it was the closest thing she could remember to stability for some time. Poppy never took things for granted though, she knew that these 'good things' in her life never lasted for long. But for now, things were OK for her. She would settle for that, she would settle for things in her life being 'OK'.

Within an hour, the main doors of the restaurant were unlocked and Chez Blanc was open for business. The reasonably priced menu and the recent closure of the pizza parlour in the high street guaranteed a brisk lunchtime trade. Matt was true to form and flirted with Poppy on almost every occasion she entered the kitchen, while Danny spent most of the day promoting the forthcoming Mother's Day special offers with his patrons. Matt had told him that this was not a great idea as the restaurant was likely to be full on the day, but Danny did not want to leave things to chance. 'Tell me that when the schedule shows that we are fully booked,' he would tell his right-hand man. 'And I will stop making a nuisance of myself with the customers.'

Poppy did not go back to her flat during the time between lunchtime and evening shifts, she wanted to let Cameron's temper tantrum simmer for a little longer. Besides Matt had gone for a workout at the nearby gym and Danny was visiting the cash and carry to top up on bottles of spirits, so she was alone and had some time to reflect on her session with Joe.

Sometimes, when there was no one around, Poppy would go to the staff bathroom and look in the mirror, simply staring at her image for ages, as if she was looking to her reflection for advice. In truth though, if the mirror could speak, it would not want to tell Poppy what it really thought, in fear of retribution. After all, that reflection would know exactly what she was capable of!

Poppy Jarvis was twenty-five years old, but, as a result of her teenage drug abuse, looked several years older. You could not describe her as a beauty queen. Pretty, yes, in a quirky sort of way, but by no means stunning. Her shoulder-length brown hair was almost always tucked up neatly on top of her head, whereas it might have been better placed covering the two scars she had on the side of her neck. Her features were always pale and her skin somewhat blotchy. Despite the heavy application of concealer, you could still make out the dark circles beneath her eyes, tired and tested eyes that had witnessed more than their fair share of harrowing violence and abuse in their time.

Poppy knew that she was no catwalk model. At five feet nine she was probably only an inch or two short of the usual requirement, but her stocky size twelve frame would not have attracted many fashion designers. She spoke with a coarse and aggressive South London accent and used the 'F' word, without realising it, in almost every other sentence. Not the sort of girl that most men would want to take home to meet their mother. Maybe when she was spending all that time studying her reflection in the mirror, she may have been wondering what attracted good-looking, athletic guys like Cameron and Matt to her. Whatever their fascination, both men would probably agree that it wasn't her warm and sensitive nature.

Before the start of the evening shift Danny introduced his new part-time waitress, Chantelle Banks. She was sixteen years old and still finishing her exams at school. She would be helping in the restaurant at weekends and one or two nights each week, more if the schedule was busy. Poppy did not believe the scrawny teenager's claim. The skinny waif had badly concealed acne and a very immature manner, giggling loudly at almost every rude word used in the kitchen. Poppy thought she may have only been fourteen years old, fifteen at most, but as she was the daughter of one of Danny's regular 'contacts' and was being paid the minimum allowed wage, cash in hand, she decided not to share her thoughts. Poppy preferred her to the grumpy Romanian woman that Danny had employed previously. The two waitresses had almost come to blows several times, mainly arguing over who had served most customers and how the tips should be shared. Poppy Jarvis would have had no doubts as to who would have won any sort of physical altercation between the two of them. After a huge argument had erupted behind the restaurant one night, Danny had shown where his loyalties truly lay by dismissing the volatile Eastern European girl on the spot.

The evening was steady. There were only sixteen covers in the restaurant, but it gave Poppy the chance to show Chantelle what would be expected of her. The young girl, however, seemed more interested in her Instagram messages and the attention of a good-looking male customer than the advice offered by her senior. Nevertheless, Poppy persevered, feeling something of an obligation towards her employer.

During that evening a minor altercation had taken place, when some regulars had complained about their overcooked meat. Danny dealt with the fussy duo, giving them complimentary drinks and taking twenty percent off their final bill. After they had left the restaurant, he vented his anger at the petty-minded couple, by updating the staff on his static relationship status. He seemed to do this each and every time he became frustrated and felt he might need a shot of alcohol to calm his nerves. 'Three years, three months and twelve days!' he shouted at the top of his voice. 'God, I really hate that fucking woman sometimes!'

Although it had become a source of regular amusement for Poppy and Matt, they both wished he would find someone else to fill the void in his life. They shared a mutual respect for the fiery little Irishman and thought he deserved some real happiness. The pair had recommended dating sites to him, but Danny had laughed that off as a 'crazy' idea, still believing, somewhere deep down, that the woman he had been with for more than half of his life would come back to him one day.

Despite the fact Poppy was not a fan of Matt's crude comments and childish behaviour, she still thought he had a charming way about him. The fair-haired northerner was always immaculately dressed and well presented. He seemed to take an extreme pride in his appearance. Poppy often wondered how a man who spent most of his time grilling fish and cooking meat could always smell so fresh. He was a good listener too. He had started to become a regular addition to the after-service 'wind-down chat', where she and Danny shared their personal thoughts. Whether Matt was truly attracted to her or not, she wasn't sure, but he did not seem put off when she reminded him, almost daily, that her boyfriend was a very jealous bodybuilder.

As soon as the evening shift had finished, Poppy took the fifteen-minute drive back to her flat on the edge of the rundown council estate in Eltham. It was far from a desirable residence. Young kids, some of them no older than eleven or twelve, were still roaming around the shops beneath her home, a couple of drunks were perched up against a wall, trying their best to roll a joint, and two women were shouting obscenities at each other across the balconies of the flats. This was home for Poppy, somewhere to hang her clothes, somewhere to eat her meals and somewhere to sleep. She didn't have to be woken up at seven o'clock each morning to be let out of a locked cell, facing another day of mindless boredom, constantly looking over her shoulder for the next 'psycho-bitch' who wanted to take her on. No, this was not a desirable residence, far from a 'dream house', but it was a home, of sorts.

As she sat in her car, she lit up a cigarette and looked up at the grubby window of her flat above the takeaway. The illuminated images from the television screen were dancing across the curtains, loud sounds were still blaring out from her living room above. She sighed as she took the last drags of her nicotine roll-up, hoping that when she entered her flat through the tatty brown front door, that Cameron was asleep, sound asleep. She hoped he was laid out on the sofa in his usual resting place, out for the count, having taken a little too much of some fix or other. Poppy was late home again and the last thing she needed that day, after the verbal battering from the Reverend Joe, was another confrontation with her boyfriend.

# CHAPTER FIVE

t was silent, the sort of silence you usually find in the early hours of the morning, when the world rests in deep slumber and only the twitter of a lone blackbird or the alarm clock of the local postman might disturb your sleep. But this was not the break of another day, it was mid-afternoon. Bree lay motionless in Jamie's bed, her eyes open, the signs of deep despair etched on her weary face. Clutching his pillow tightly, as if it was a life jacket, a million salty tears now sunken into the fading patterns of the pillowcase, she breathed in the smell of his presence and felt a small morsel of solace. She was alone now, she knew she would always be alone now. There in the pit of her stomach, an overwhelming pain, a sharp numbness that would never leave her.

The long brown curtains were fully closed. Complete darkness was Bree's choice of company in her cocoon of sadness. The only sounds that made any sense to her were those of her own sobbing. She stared at the back of his bedroom door, maybe holding onto a crazy thought that it would open, and that he would suddenly appear before her. The real world might be happening somewhere out there, but this was her life now, she never wanted to leave this bed again.

It was nineteen days since they had buried him, nineteen long painful days and nights. Everyone had told her that she would feel better when the funeral was over. Everyone said that the healing process could only start when she had said her final goodbye. But everyone was wrong, everyone had lied to her.

A half-filled coffee cup was perched precariously on the corner of Jamie's bedside cabinet, a thick film of brown skin hanging over its edge. It had not been touched for days. On the floor to the side of her, twenty or more small white pills made an unlikely pattern on the carpet. She wished that she had followed her plan, she wished she had taken them, all of them. She knew it was the only way she could be with him again. But even in these dark hours of torment, she could not summon the energy or the courage to go through with it. She hated herself for being such a coward. Maybe this was her punishment, maybe this empty existence was the punishment she deserved.

She was wearing her brother's favourite grey T-shirt, the one he had bought when they visited Camden the previous summer. She had been wearing this treasured garment from the moment she had returned from the cemetery. She told herself that she would never take it off, but in truth it no longer smelled of him. She had begun to inhale the stench of her own sickly body odour which was now seeping through the precious top. It was rancid. Bree had not bathed for those nineteen days, she had barely eaten anything either. But she cared little about her personal hygiene or malnourishment. Why should she? She had nothing to live for now.

The sombre silence of her tomb was suddenly broken by the ring tone of the telephone downstairs, its constant ringing echoing through the hallway and up to where she lay. She wrapped Jamie's pillow tightly around her head and waited for it to go away. This was the third time it had rung that day. *Why can't everyone just leave me alone?* she thought. But this time it did not stop, it kept on, ring-ring, ring-ring, ring-ring, getting louder and louder by the second. She knew that it would not go away this time, she knew that she had to make it stop. Swinging her legs out of Jamie's bedclothes she found her feet crushing half of the discarded pills as she stumbled across the floor. When she opened the bedroom door, the bright lights from the outside world blinded her for a few seconds, causing her to clutch the stair rail for support. As her shaky legs made their way downstairs, she almost lost her balance and fell over before making it to the living room and the offending ring tone. 'Hello,' she said in a croaky voice that she barely recognised.

'Brianna is that you?' came the reply.

There were only two people in the world that ever used her full name. She knew instantly who it was. 'Hello, Mother,' she said, angry with herself now for making the effort to answer the phone.

'I have been trying you for days. Where have you been?' her mother asked in a harsh but concerned manner.

'Nowhere, just here, trying to sleep.'

'Have you been to the doctor's yet?'

'No.'

'You really need to see the doctor, Brianna. He will give you something to help you.'

*Will he give me Jamie back?* Bree thought. *That is the only thing that can help me.* She offered her mother an answer that she hoped might end the call prematurely. 'I will be OK, I just want to rest now.'

'No!' her mother responded in a sharp tone. 'You are not OK, I can tell.'

'Mother, I will make an appointment with the doctor if it makes you happy.'

'I know there is something wrong, Brianna. Do you want me to fly back? I can be back there tomorrow.'

*Why,* Bree thought, *if you know something is wrong, are you making this call from the comfort of your comfy sofa some fifteen hundred miles away? Of course, there is something wrong, my beautiful brother has been taken away from me, my whole world has stopped. I miss his smile, I miss his touch, I miss his voice. God, I miss his voice so much!* Not wanting to provoke her mother into making that journey back to England, Bree's response was aimed at simply pacifying her. 'I will get something from the doctor's. I just need a bit more time.'

'Are you eating? Has Kayleigh been there to help you?' More questions from the absent matriarch.

'Yes,' Bree replied, knowing that her answer to the first part of her question was a lie. She could not remember the last time she had eaten a proper meal. As for Kayleigh, she could not really keep her away. Her mother had given her best friend the keys to the house and asked her to visit her at every possible opportunity.

The inquisition continued. 'Is Kayleigh with you now?'

'No, she is coming today, after work.'

'You shouldn't be alone, Brianna, I don't like the idea of you being alone.'

Once again Bree thought to herself, *If I shouldn't be alone then why is my mother calling me from her new home overlooking the lake in Tampere?* She kept her answer brief. 'Kayleigh can't just give up her job. She comes round most days. She is doing all the cooking and cleaning, she is looking after me.' As soon as the words left Bree's mouth she looked around at the chaotic mess in her living room. The place looked as if it had been ransacked by burglars. But that was her fault. She had insisted that her friend, cleaner and part-time cook not touch anything, fearing that some small remnant of her brother's existence might be thrown away in error.

'Have you spoken to the people at the office?' More insensitive questioning from her mother. *Maybe she really has compiled a full list of things to ask me*, Bree thought.

She suddenly found herself answering her mother's questions, like a zombie reading their lines from a movie script. 'They are fine. They told me to take my time.'

'You don't want to lose that job!' her mother said firmly. 'You could get a really good career with them.'

The last thing on Bree's mind was her job prospects. The creature from the horror film spoke again. 'I will be back to work soon.'

Her mother seemed to be running out of things to ask, unless of course she had another page of questions she needed to fetch. 'Per wants a quick word with you,' she said and handed the phone to her father.

A small smile broke on Bree's face as she heard his distinct voice. 'Hey, baby girl, we have been worried about you.'

Tiny tears appeared in her eyes and ran down Bree's cheeks, as the zombie's voice was replaced with that of a grieving young girl. 'Hey, Dad!'

'I know things are tough for you, baby girl, but it will get better. I promise you, it will get better.'

Bree's eyes were now filled with tears. She so needed a massive hug from her father at that moment. 'I will be OK, Dad,' she said, rubbing her eyes. 'It just hurts so much, but I will be OK.'

'We can fly back if you need us, you know that, Brianna, we could be there tomorrow morning.'

'No, there is no need, Dad. Kayleigh is around here most of the time, she is looking after me.'

'OK, baby girl. You have my cell phone number out here. You know you can call me anytime, don't you?'

'Yes,' Bree replied, wiping the tears from the side of her face. 'Miss you!'

'Miss you too, baby girl. I will pass you back to your mother now. Love you.'

'Love you more!'

Her mother's voice returned. Bree hoped she hadn't found that second page of questions, she desperately wanted to return to her tomb of sorrow now. Even this short conversation with her parents had drained her energy.

'Why did you take so long to answer the phone?' her mother asked. 'I have been trying to reach you since Saturday.'

'Sorry. I have just been trying to rest.'

'And what about your mobile? I have called you on that at least twenty times. Have you lost it again?'

There was complete silence. Bree was dumbstruck. 'Brianna, Brianna, are you there?' her mother asked. Her daughter was there. She was shaking violently, as if she was going to have a seizure.

Suddenly Bree threw the landline onto the living room floor. 'My phone! My phone!' she screamed in her croaky voice. 'I have to find my phone!'

Bree could still hear her mother calling up to her. 'Brianna, what is it, what has happened?'

Immediate mayhem ensued as Bree flew around the living room in a state of complete panic, throwing cushions off the sofa and opening and closing drawers. 'Where is it? Where is it?' she yelled. 'Where is my phone?' The rampage continued as she raced through to the kitchen. Cupboards were flung open, cutlery on the draining board was brushed aside as her search continued. 'Where is my bag? Where is my bag?' she screamed.

As she returned to the lounge, Bree could still hear her mother's faint voice from the telephone on the floor. She lifted the handset and simply said, 'I need to find my phone, I will call you tomorrow,' before slamming it down onto the receiver.

Her frantic mission continued. The shouting had by now turned into screaming. Bree flew up the stairs, all but missing the last step and falling headfirst onto the landing. She dragged herself to her feet and pushed open her bedroom door, immediately throwing open the doors to her wardrobe and chest of drawers. She was resolute, like the first police officer arriving at the scene of a drugs raid. 'Where is it?' she screamed. 'Where is my fucking phone?'

Those terrible noises came back to haunt her again, as the landline began to ring downstairs. She knew it would be her mother. 'Go away!' she screamed down the hallway. 'Go away and leave me alone!' Maybe her mother had finally accepted that her daughter wanted to be left in peace, or maybe she had just found something better to do with her time. Whichever it was, the phone stopped ringing.

Now she was back in Jamie's room, she pulled the bedclothes off the bed and kneeled down. She began to search underneath, crushing a few more of those scattered pills with her knees in the process. 'Where is it? God, please let me find it!' she pleaded, as her search became frantic. Suddenly, it came to her. As she remembered where she had left it, she stood up sharply. 'The bookcase!' she said under her breath. 'The bookcase!'

Her weak legs were suddenly replaced with those of an Olympic sprinter. She raced down the staircase and ran to the back of the living room. There it was, her brown Mulberry handbag, the place where she always kept her phone. 'Please God, let it be in here!' she said and then repeated it more loudly. 'Please God, let it be in here!' She pulled down the bag and all at once a beaming smile of satisfaction shone across her face as she saw her mobile phone. Snatching the handset, she switched it on and waited an agonising thirty seconds for the lights to appear and that familiar noise to tell her that it was ready.

Her back slid down the wall and she sat down on the floor, cradling the phone in her arms, much like a mother would hold onto a newborn baby. 'Thank you,' she said, looking at the ceiling, but probably aiming her appreciation at some place much higher. When all the lights had appeared, she pushed the video replay button and sat in eager anticipation, waiting, waiting for the recording to start.

Her chin trembled as he appeared on her tiny screen. 'Do you think I look like a film star?' he said. 'You know, like that actor in the new Bourne film.'

'No,' she replied in the video, but now wished she had said more. Maybe, 'No, Jamie, because you are more beautiful than any film star I have ever seen.' He was wearing that smart grey suit with the waistcoat and that bright pink silk tie. She had tied his knot that morning when they got dressed together in her room. She wanted him to be the smartest one at his friend's wedding that day, and he was. Lewis was in the background, he was with Tia, they had just cut their wedding cake. Suddenly, the music started up, the DJ spoke. She hated these old soul songs from the 1970s. Jamie didn't. 'I love this tune!' he yelled directly into the camera. 'I bloody love this song!'

Bree's eyes lit up and a smile beamed across her face as he started to move around. He was dancing to the music. Now he was doing those funny moves he used to do, his actions imitating the words of the song. He was back, Jamie was back, he was here in the room, he was with her now, where he belonged. Her smile grew bigger and her head bobbed in time with the music as she watched her brother dancing in front of her on the small screen, but then suddenly, it stopped, the screen went blank, he was gone, Jamie was gone again.

'No!' Bree yelled, instantly pressing the replay button.

Her smile returned as he reappeared, he was back with her. 'Do you think I look like a film star?' He was talking again, he was singing again, he was dancing again. Her and Jamie were back together again. She took the phone up to his room, her head bobbing along to the sound of that old song that her brother liked so much. Falling onto his bed, Bree pulled the duvet covers over her head so that she could be alone with him.

The song played over and over. There were small signs of motion under the covers as Bree's head swayed in time with the music. After a short while, her heavy eyes began to tire and although she did her best to keep her eyelids open, she found herself fighting a losing battle. With the familiar tones of her sibling still ringing in her ears, she slowly succumbed to the trials of her emotional turmoil. Her mobile phone finally slipped from her vice-like grip and landed amongst the remains of the crushed tablets on the carpet.

It was the first time she had found some peace in her head in a long time. Her sleep would be deep. Images of her brother's singing and dancing raced through her brain. A thousand whispering voices seemed to be reaching out to her. She could hear the echoes of tiny waves as they crashed against a deserted shoreline. They brought a soothing melody into her head. The images of Jamie were becoming cloudy and his dulcet tones began to fade away.

* * *

The dimly lit streets ahead of her gave Bree an uncomfortable feeling inside, but that did not stop her feet from moving forwards. The pavements were wet, as though a recent downpour had yet to be washed away. It was cold, extremely cold. A swirling wind brought the sounds of angry waves crashing up against the harbour wall. A single lamplight seemed to be beckoning her down to the water's edge. It flickered wildly, throwing all manner of dancing shadows into her pathway. She felt a compulsion to be nearer to the light. It was calling out to her. She wasn't frightened, she was curious. She began to walk towards the lamp, her tiny feet splashing through some small puddles on the way.

A figure appeared from her right. It was a large figure. She could not see his face, but she recognised that long grey trench coat. He had bought it the previous year. It was her brother's. 'Jay,' she called. 'Jay, I am over here.' The man kept walking, as if he hadn't heard her. He was heading for the lamplight. She called out again, this time much louder. 'Jay, it's Bree, I am over here.' There was no response. The figure kept moving forward. She knew that walk, she would know it anywhere. It was Jamie's walk.

As the large figure reached the light, the dancing shadows seemed to gather as one and form strange shapes on the stone pavement. Bree picked up her pace, walking much faster, desperate to catch up with her brother. She called out to him again, but he seemed oblivious to her presence. As the shadowy figure ahead of her reached the water's edge, he began to walk down some slippery-looking stairs beneath the slime-covered walls of the harbour. There was a small boat, rocking gently in the dark water. He looked as if he knew that it would be there. Bree yelled out loudly, 'No, Jay, don't leave me here!' Her cold feet scurried along the pathway in the direction of the waiting vessel.

As she made her way down the rain-drenched stairs, she noticed that he had moved to the front of the boat. Why was he not speaking to her? she thought. Bree was now becoming slightly anxious, but still held no fear. She needed to be close to him. As she entered the boat, it rocked violently, as if they had been angered by her intrusion. Suddenly, she lost her footing, falling backwards and landing on her back amongst some heavy ropes. The large figure stood rigid at the front of the boat, motionless, unconcerned by her fall. She called out his name again. 'Jamie, it's me, it's Bree. Jamie, please say something.'

Suddenly, just as Bree began to drag herself to her feet, the boat began to move, the steady waves beneath them carrying the vessel away from the lamplight. As the boat picked up speed the sudden change in motion sent Bree crashing back down to the floor again, causing her to hit her head on the ropes. There was a tone of concern in her voice now as she called out to the figure ahead of her, 'Jay, please say something, you are scaring me.' The large shape at the stern of the boat did nothing and said nothing.

As the small wooden craft glided through the dark waters, she called out again, this time with a tiny tremble in her voice, as the fear inside her began to grow. 'Jamie, it's me, it's Bree!'

Suddenly the boat came to a halt. The waves were much calmer now. A beam of moonlight shone across the sea ahead of them and an eerie silence followed. Bree pulled herself to her feet. This time she held her balance. She had a much clearer view of her surroundings now. She was standing directly behind her brother. Slowly and with caution, she moved one foot in front of the other and began to move towards the figure wearing Jamie's coat. She stopped, less than two feet behind him. She was shaking now, but she knew that she had to see him, she had to tell him that she wasn't frightened, she wanted to stay with him, if that was what he wanted. Slowly she raised her arm and found herself touching his shoulder. He was real. She was so sure now that she was touching her brother. In an instant the figure swung around to face her, startling her and almost causing her to fall over again. He was the same height as Jamie and had the same colour hair, but this was not her brother. The head above the trench coat had no face, nothing, just a blank canvas shaped like a face. It looked like a glove puppet. Bree stepped back, she struggled to catch her breath. Half of her was terrified, the other half disappointed. She was so sure she would see her brother's face at that moment. Before she could work out what was really happening, the moonlight disappeared from her view and the boat was thrown into total darkness. The hairs on the back of her neck stood up as the small vessel began to rock gently backwards and forwards. Bree suddenly became disorientated and felt queasy. She was finding it hard to keep her balance. And then, as the moon reappeared, and the beams of light returned to the boat, she could see he was gone, the man in Jamie's coat was no longer there. She desperately wanted to believe that it was her brother that had been standing there, but now she was confused, she didn't know what to do. She shouted his name loudly, hoping he might return. 'Jamie, come back, don't leave me!'

Had he fallen over? Was he in the water? She had to know. She moved forward, very slowly, feeling much more scared than she had been before. A dark mist seemed to follow her as she reached the front of the boat. She could not see him, but she could make out a shadowy figure, lurking in the water. She didn't know what to do. Maybe it was Jamie, maybe he needed her help. She reached down, slowly stretching out her arm in a bid to pull him back into the boat. She began to tremble, her heart was pounding, faster and faster. 'Jamie!' she cried. 'Let me help you!' She leaned further forward, her hand now half-submerged in the icy cold sea. 'I am here, Jamie, I am here for you.' But before Bree could call out again, she saw a flash of bright yellow and a small hand appear from beneath her. It grabbed her arm and dragged her head first into the depths of the murky water. She took in a sharp breath as her whole body became submerged in the freezing cold sea. The first thing she saw was the shiny coat, that bright yellow coat. She recognised it immediately, it frightened her. Bree began to panic. She could see her face now, it was as clear as it could be. It was the girl, the small girl she had seen before. Bree began to struggle as she felt the girl grab her tightly by the arms. She couldn't breathe, she needed to get out of the water. But her opponent was winning the battle, she was holding Bree's wrists, squeezing them tightly so that she couldn't move. She was pulling her deeper and deeper into the dark abyss.

As her body plunged further into the freezing sea Bree tried again to free herself from the grip. She gyrated her body and kicked out at the girl, but it was all in vain. The girl's arms were small, but they were strong, they were very strong. Bree began moving her shoulders, kicking her legs, twisting her whole body, but she could not break free. And then, as they sank even deeper, they finally came face to face, they were just inches apart. Bree could see the twisted torment in the eyes of her opponent. Those eyes were black, a deep, soulless black, they were lifeless. In one last desperate bid to free herself Bree pulled one arm free and pushed at the girl's head, grabbing her jet-black mane and pulling it for all she was worth. But she was still fighting a losing battle, she could not break free. She closed her eyes tightly, she could feel her lungs slowly filling with water. A buzzing sound started inside her head and began searing through her brain. It was getting louder and louder. She wanted to scream, but she could not open her mouth. The girl pulled harder on Bree's tired and helpless arms as the pair sank further down. She could feel the reeds of the seabed beneath her. They were close, almost close enough to touch. Just as they neared the bottom, she heard the buzzing noise in her brain again, so loud it was almost deafening. It was all around her, it was ripping her in half. And then, in a split second her eyes opened, the girl had gone, Bree was no longer in the freezing water, she was in another place, a safer place. The buzzing sound started again, only this time it was less distant. Bree knew that sound, it was the bell on her front door. She was home, she was in Jamie's bed. She looked across to see that the coffee cup was now lying empty on the floor, the contents running, like a tiny brown stream, down the bedside cabinet. Bree pulled her legs out of the bed and made her way across the landing to the window in her mother's old bedroom. 'It can't be Kayleigh,' she mumbled under her breath. 'Kayleigh has a key.'

Peering through the curtains she looked down to see that it was Preston. She recognised him by his curly brown hair and his stocky frame. He was one of Jamie's friends from the gym. He was carrying a sports bag. She knew that bag, she had bought it for Jamie when he first left home to go to university. She noticed that Preston's attention had been drawn to someone calling his name. Looking backwards towards the end of the path she could see that Kayleigh was parking her car. Bree's best friend seemed to be tidying her hair as she approached Preston, a very common habit that she had developed. Bree moved behind the curtain to make sure she could not be seen. The couple met below and began to chat. They were talking about a mutual friend of theirs. They started to laugh. *Why are they laughing?* Bree thought. *How can anything be funny? My brother is dead, how can anything ever be funny ever again?* This made Bree angry, but she was in no mood for an argument today. 'Don't let him in,' she whispered to herself. 'Get rid of him, Kayleigh.' At that point Preston handed the sports bag to Kayleigh and Bree's request seemed to have been heard. 'Now tell him to go, Kayleigh,' Bree said to herself. 'We don't want him coming in here.' The two of them seemed to be discussing other matters now. Bree watched closely as Preston passed something in to Kayleighs hand, something small. The laughing stopped for a second or two and both or her visitors seemed to be in deep thought. When their conversation continued they began discussing the inquest into Jamie's death. 'What the hell has that got to do with him?' Bree said to herself. 'Get rid of him, Kayleigh, get rid of him!' Bree tried to make out what they were saying, but their conversation had changed again, they seemed to be laughing about something else now. Bree looked on as her friend reached into her coat pocket for a pen and wrote down her mobile phone number. 'You are such a slag, Kayleigh Hardy!' Bree muttered under her breath. 'Such a heartless fucking slag!'

As soon as Bree heard the keys at her front door, she sprinted back to the sanctuary of her brother's bed, those athletic legs returning just in time to save her from having to entertain her best friend. She did not feel like cleaning up the mess caused by the overturned coffee cup, but she did throw a pillow over the remains of the tablets on the carpet. The last thing that she needed now was Kayleigh thinking she had done something stupid. She knew that her friend would probably call for an ambulance, or far worse call her mother and give her chapter and verse on the unstable condition of her daughter. The idea of her mother returning to England to babysit her would be more than enough for her to scoop up the remains of those pills and end things once and for all. Retrieving her phone from the floor, Bree wiped off the coffee stains and huddled up underneath Jamie's warm duvet. She found the video, that one small morsel of comfort she had left in her empty existence.

Kayleigh should have been alarmed, when she entered the living room. The place looked as if it had been hit by a small bomb of some sort. But by now she was so used to Bree's strange and unpredictable antics, she simply turned the table back onto its legs and closed all the drawers in both the lounge and the kitchen.

She began thinking that she would have to spend an extra hour or so that night tidying up Bree's mess. But then she remembered that her best friend would not appreciate her touching anything that was remotely related to her lost brother and decided that she would just cook Bree a meal instead.

Kayleigh made her way upstairs and gently pushed open Jamie's door. The room smelled of stale sweat, but she had become accustomed to the foul odours by now. 'Hi, babe, are you still sleeping?' she asked, in a tone not much more than a whisper. Bree played a game of 'silent statues' under the covers. She wasn't ready for any conversation, not just yet.

'That was Preston at the door, you know, from the gym. He came to drop off some of...' Kayleigh cut her sentence short, not wanting to mention her late brother's name. 'He has gone now,' she added. 'He said that everyone there is thinking of you.' Bree's eyes moved from side to side under the covers. *Can't this girl take a hint and just leave me alone?* she thought.

Looking around the room at the coffee-stained carpet and assortment of bits and bobs scattered around the floor, it was obvious that Bree had been searching for something that afternoon. Kayleigh thought it best not to say anything. Bree didn't take kindly to her friend asking her personal questions anymore. 'I have bought some nice tuna steaks for dinner,' Kayleigh said. 'I will put them on a bit later, when you are feeling up to it.' Just as Kayleigh was about to leave the room, she noticed small signs of movement from under the covers. 'And maybe you will feel like a soak in the tub, with that nice scented bubble bath,' she added.

Kayleigh decided to give up at this point and leave her friend to her solitude, pulling the door half closed on her way out of the room. As she reached the top of the stairs, she heard a noise, a strange sound, coming from Jamie's bed. She looked through the gap in the door and could see that those bedclothes had moved slightly to one side. Suddenly she could hear a muffled wailing noise, like singing, and a tune playing from under the covers.

Kayleigh stepped back to leave Bree to rest in her bed of sorrow. This was probably not a good time to disturb her friend. Yes, she was worried about her health, but she was reassured to think that, whatever it was under those covers, it was keeping her best friend alive.

# CHAPTER SIX

The drowning man was still in limbo. The images of his torrid existence on this earth were hurtling through his brain at a hundred miles an hour, but he still refused to accept that the end of his days could be near. The figure tucked up in the warm hospital bedsheets behind him had remained silent. He knew Dean well enough to know that he would never accept his fate. Why waste your last breath trying to convince a man of his destiny, when that man had never listened to anyone in his life?

It should have ended there, he knew that, she knew that, it should have ended on that humid day at the Imediacom offices, the day he was put firmly in his place by a woman half his size but twice his stature. But he couldn't let go, something drew him back there, some mystical force lured him back to the scene of this fantasy. He had to see her again, he didn't know why, he just had to see her again.

Dean returned to Neasden within forty-eight hours of his altercation with the woman whose image, by now, had become embedded in his brain. He thought that a lame excuse about missing paperwork would be enough to at least get him a rematch with the winner of their first bout. But he didn't need to cross the threshold of the Imediacom building that day. Whilst parking his car, he noticed her, the silver-tongued goddess that had been ever present in his thoughts for the past two days. Krista was sitting in her car, eating her lunch and singing along to some random tunes on the radio. As bold as brass, Dean jumped in the passenger seat and offered her his heartfelt apology, telling her that he had been a 'very naughty boy' on his previous visit, and if she ever felt the need to punish him personally, he knew of a shop that sold PVC outfits and real leather whips. This was the one thing that Dean always had in his armoury, his quick-witted one-liners, but he rarely got the chance to use them in those days. For some strange reason Krista fell for his charm. She declined his offer of creating her own homemade torture chamber, but she did let him share her packed lunch. Their conversation was light and bordered on gentle flirting at times. Before she returned to her office Krista could not help but berate his patterned tie. She asked him if his constant efforts to mismatch his choice of attire was to win a bet.

Their spontaneous lunchtime rendezvous had left an impact on them both. Before either of them knew what was really happening they had arranged to meet for a drink in London the following week.

* * *

Krista felt a nervous tingle rush down her spine when he finally appeared from the tube station entrance at Baker Street. She had been there almost an hour, not that she would be telling him that. Dean strolled across the road without a care in the world. He was dressed in the same suit he had worn the previous week when he was sitting in her car. You could hardly say that he had made any kind of effort. For Krista, this was something different. She had left work early that day to have her hair coloured and her nails painted professionally. She was wearing a smart grey designer top, one she had kept locked away in her wardrobe for special occasions, and she was sporting new leather boots which had cost her the best part of a week's wages. She started to feel very foolish inside.

'You are late,' she said, as he strolled nonchalantly across the busy road. 'I was just about to go home.'

Dean smiled and gave her a kiss on her cheek. 'No you wasn't,' he replied, in a most confident manner. 'You would have waited at least another hour.' Krista gave him a harsh stare, which he completely ignored. 'So, shall we have a drink in here first?' he asked pointing at the pub where they had arranged to meet. 'And then we can find somewhere to have a bite to eat.' Krista agreed, and the pair found an empty table inside.

The Castle Moat was just an ordinary London bar – simple wooden tables and chairs, a jukebox housing mostly out-of-date tunes and an assorted array of bar staff, many with Australian accents. The pub may have looked in need of a makeover, but that didn't seem to bother the hordes of suited business types and foreign tourists waiting to be served. The place was heaving with customers.

When Dean brought the drinks to the table, he sat as close as he could to his overdressed guest and set down a few rules. 'No work talk!' he said, to which Krista nodded. 'And no fashion tips!'

Her huge brown eyes had a glint of mischief in them as she smiled. 'Oh, you want to spoil all my fun, do you? I was going to ask if you had actually taken that suit off since last week or whether you sleep in it.' Her comment amused Dean. It was rare for him not to offer an immediate answer, but she had caught him off guard this time.

To the regulars of this busy establishment it was obvious that the two of them must be on a date, snuggled up together in the corner seat, permanent eye contact and constant chatting and laughter. Certainly not the traits of your average married couple.

They discussed everything from politics to the awful fake tan the new receptionist wore at Imediacom. Neither of them noticed the time as the drinks flowed and their light-hearted conversation turned to matters of a more serious nature. 'I know we said no office talk,' Dean said, 'but how the hell did you end up working for old Mr Penning? He is such an arsehole! I call him the 'tortoise man' because of those thick lines around his eyes.'

'Funny, that!' Krista replied. 'He told me that he didn't think much of you either.'

'And Dolly Daydream, your receptionist, all that fake tan, she looks like an advert for satsumas.'

'That name suits her. I am sure she loves you too, Dean. Tell me, is that why they say you are such a bad salesman, because you spend all of your time making up nicknames for everyone?'

'It is much more fun than you think.'

'So, come on then, funny guy, is there a name for me yet, or haven't I been there long enough?'

Dean laughed. 'Nylund, the monster from the chateau Imediacom. Yeah, Nylund, you have got your own nickname right there.'

'I like it,' Krista said. 'Not just brave and bold but deeply insulting with it. I don't think a ten-year-old schoolboy could have done better. Or maybe they could!'

Dean backtracked slightly. 'A beautiful monster of course.'

'Sure,' Krista said. 'Not all beauty is skin deep, maybe I am nice on the inside.'

Dean smiled. 'You know damn well that you are the most beautiful woman in…'

'Don't let me stop you,' Krista said. 'Us monsters need all the confidence building we can get.'

'In this bar! You are the most beautiful woman in this bar.'

Krista looked around the busy public house, scrutinising the female customers. 'Mmm,' she said. 'Hardly a compliment, there is not much competition in here.'

Dean could not resist a put-down. 'I don't know, the girl by the door with the tight jeans on would give you a run for your money.' His newly tagged 'monster' gave him a friendly dig in the ribs and they both laughed and carried on their conversation. He didn't want to tell her what he really thought at that time, that he was mesmerised by her beauty, spellbound by her mysterious eyes, her face, her soft skin, her silky voice, just about everything about her. And there was more. She got him, she was so on his wavelength, it was a frightening attraction. This was their first night out and he felt as though he had known her for years. He had to find out more, so much more about his 'monster'. 'So, Nylund, you didn't answer my question. How the hell did a Swedish girl end up working in London?'

Krista stared long and hard at him before answering, 'Firstly I am from Finland, I am Finnish and very proud of it. My mother and father were Finnish and their parents too. Don't make that mistake again or I will get angry, OK?'

Dean stood corrected. 'My apologies, carry on, Nylund, the Finnish monster.'

'My English has always been very good.'

Dean shrugged his shoulders. 'That is a matter of opinion.'

'As I was saying before 'Mr Dick-for-Brains' interrupted me…'

Dean attempted to copy her broken Scandinavian accent. 'My English has always been very good.'

'No!' Krista repeated. 'Can you tell your friend 'Mr Dick-for-Brains' that I don't sound like an Italian housewife eating a bowl of pasta, I am indeed very fluent in English.'

Dean laughed. 'Carry on.'

'I was the top student at my college in most subjects, so my parents paid for me to come to England, to study at Loughborough University. They said it would be better for my career.'

'Wow, that is amazing! So you Scandies can just come over here and steal the university places from one of our own kids. A poor student who has worked their socks off to get to uni and probably deserved it more.'

Krista ignored his observation and continued. 'So, I graduated from university with a 2:2, probably a little better than the poor deprived British student would ever have achieved. And after finishing at university I moved to London and voilà. That's French, by the way, for the undereducated.'

'So, you moved to the big city to steal a job that one of our hard-working millions was after?'

Krista gave him a knowing stare, as if she was disappointed at his attempt to belittle her. 'Really!' she asked. 'Is that the best you can do?'

Dean laughed. 'So you went to work for Imediacom?'

'No, that was about five years ago, but can you thank 'Mr Dick-for-Brains' for thinking that I look so young. I will definitely take that as a compliment.'

'How old are you?'

'Twenty-seven. Do you remember being twenty-seven, Dean, or has your memory faded over all those years?'

'Nice one!' Dean said. 'So where did you start out?'

'At Marshall's in Ealing. They manufacture alarm systems for commercial buildings.'

'I think I know it.'

'And then the job came up at Imediacom, so I thought why not?'

'Don't tell me, you had to sleep with old man Penning to get the job.'

Krista laughed. 'No, nothing like that, it was just a blowjob. It wasn't very pleasant, but at his age he didn't last very long, about ninety seconds. So less than two minutes of shame and I end up with £40,000 a year, a nice little company car, five weeks' holiday and an expense account.'

Dean laughed out loud. He loved her warped take on life, she was so confident in her own skin. 'And what about promotion?' he asked. 'What if you want to get promotion?'

Krista thought for a second or two. 'Well!' she said. 'I suppose I would have to blow the whole of the management team, except for Sean of course, that tall guy with the red beard, he is just gross. Well, you have to draw the line somewhere.'

Despite her earlier reservations Krista had found the evening to be most entertaining. She could not remember when she had ever laughed so much in her life. Their banter carried on, from the bar to the nearby brasserie where they both enjoyed a chicken dish. They learned a lot about each other that night, not everything of course, because that may have spoiled things, but enough for them both to want to do it again. When they parted company that evening at the Baker Street tube station, Dean lunged forward, expecting a full mouth-on-mouth kiss. But all he achieved was a tiny peck on the cheek and a few well-chosen words from his companion. 'Maybe some girls fall that easy for your bullshit, Dean, but it will take more than a few glasses of wine and a cheap meal to win over the monster of the chateau.' They did share a hug and a long-lasting smile before the two of them went their separate ways.

Maybe it would have ended there, that night, outside the tube station. It would have been over before it had begun. If only their conversation had been more open and honest, if only they had revealed the truths behind this spontaneous rendezvous, they might have travelled in opposite directions and stayed there. Dean could have told her that night that his journey would take him to his home in South London, the one he shared with his wife Hannah. He could have told Krista that he and his spouse had experienced many problems over the past few years, but they were happy together, happy enough to be expecting their first child later that year.

Krista had her part to play in all of this of course. She was a highly intelligent and sophisticated woman, she had a bright career ahead of her, a beautiful head full of dreams and aspirations. She should have known better. Her and her long-term partner had just completed the purchase of a beautiful two-bedroom flat in Highgate village and had been planning their wedding. To all that knew them, they were the perfect couple. Why would she want to wreck all of that for a sordid affair with a much older man, one working his way down the ladder of success rather than up? There was no logic to this liaison at all, but when has logic ever played a part in a tragic romance?

More than three million souls travelled on the London Underground on that day, many of them tired and disillusioned with their pitiful existence. But on that warm evening, two of those passengers were blinded by the promise of a twisted fantasy in those half-empty carriages, both caught up in a moment of madness that would last more than a thousand days. One travelled northbound, feeling that there was a new meaning to her life. Krista felt as if a pulse of electricity had shot upwards through her body and woken a spirit that had been dormant within her. Those beautiful brown eyes were sparkling like diamonds as she smiled at her reflection in the glass. The other happy passenger had a southbound destination. Commuters in his carriage must have assumed that he was extremely drunk or high on something. His beaming grin had not left his face since he waved Krista off onto her train. He closed his eyes tightly as he inhaled her exotic perfume that lingered on his collar. Those other passengers in his carriage may have been right, Dean was high, he was extremely high, but it was not an abuse of any illegal substances that had taken him there.

* * *

The drowning man was still lost in the rapture of his fantasy at he peered out of the hospital window. The panes of glass had misted over, much like Dean's recollections of his past. His eyes were still fixed on the streets below, but he was not paying attention to anything that was happening. That body beneath the bedclothes wasn't being much help. Maybe if he could speak he could have asked the drowning man why he never told Krista about his daughter until she was nearly three months old. Surely if his favourite 'monster' had liked him as much as he thought she did, she would have understood. But Dean was no risk-taker when it came to his love life. He hid the truth from the two women in his life, never realising how much it would eventually affect the third.

There had been no movement on the clock face, nor in the hospital bed, but it did not concern the drowning man anymore, he was gradually becoming more aware of the purpose of his surroundings. He frowned, as somewhere in his rambling mind he tried to justify some of the mistakes he had made. 'She was always different from the other children,' he said, his words still falling on deaf ears. 'Poppy, she was always different. She bit some little kid once, in the creche, she can't have been older than two. She sank her teeth into his arm, she wouldn't let go, not for anything. I told Hannah, but she never believed me, she was too busy popping her bloody pills and getting drunk to notice it. But I did, I knew she needed help, proper help, even back then.'

Dean closed his eyes. He didn't want his thoughts to travel too far down that dark corridor of his life, he wanted the pleasant pictures to return, he wanted to remember the better times. His mind was full now, of hazy images, of a sunny day, a happy girl in a brightly coloured T-shirt. She was sitting opposite him in a small boat, laughing, shouting, not a care in the world. He knew deep inside his bruised and battered brain that he should have done something, he could have made things better, better for everyone. But he chose to bury the truth away, hiding his failure beneath a hundred thousand empty bottles of alcohol.

'It frightened me!' he said, so quietly that the figure in the bed would not have heard him, even if he had been remotely interested in his latest tale of woe. 'I always thought that her bloody moods and temper tantrums were normal for young kids. But it frightened me, when I found the brick, covered in blood, behind the rabbit cage. It frightened me, because I didn't know what to do!'

# CHAPTER SEVEN

Poppy counted the money she had received in tips that night. She had done well, almost £40. She tucked it away in a safe pocket inside her bag, hoping that Cameron would not find her windfall. In her head she knew that she should be saving any extra money she earned. She had to find over £400 in rent arrears for Rahwaz, but she also needed some new work trousers too. Danny had been more than generous that evening, giving her Chantelle's share of the rewards for the busy night in Chez Blanc. The immature young waitress had got drunk on four glasses of house wine and been sick on the new carpet. Not only did Poppy have to cover for the heavily intoxicated youngster, but she had also spent half an hour on her hands and knees, cleaning up the girl's vomit.

Matt had been his usual self that night, telling inappropriate jokes and flirting with her to the point where she was forced to throw a soup bowl in his direction in a bid to keep him quiet. Once Chantelle had been whisked off by an unsuspecting taxi driver, the poor man somewhat puzzled as to why Danny had tipped him £5 in advance, Poppy was left to serve the diners on her own. She did not complain. If anything, she had been pleased to see the back of the youngster, who was rapidly becoming an irritant on Poppy's radar.

During the evening, a table of twelve local businessmen were celebrating the award of a large overseas contract and had already spent over £700, before Danny invited them to stay for a drink after normal hours. He moved them to a table in the corner of the restaurant, firstly to keep them out of the view of nosy passers-by, but mainly to get them as far away as possible from the stench of Chantelle's little 'accident'.

Danny's gesture was well received. The group were pleased to continue their celebration and added another £200 to their bill. So not only did Poppy clock up a few extra hours that night, she also earned the bonus sitting pretty in her bag. But it was half past two now. She knew that Cameron would be furious if he was still awake. Looking up from her car she could see the lights dancing merrily on the curtains in their living room. The television could be heard blaring out loudly through an open window. She hoped that he would be, as he was most nights, fast asleep on the living room sofa.

Poppy's hopes, however, were dashed the minute she entered the flat. A raging bull approached her in the shape of her boyfriend. Cameron was stripped down to his waist, as if he was about to enter a cage-fighting ring. 'Where the fucking hell have you been?' he screamed, grabbing her neck as she tried to squeeze past him. 'Working!' she yelled back. 'Where the hell do you think I have been?' She freed herself from his grip and took off her jacket.

He followed her as she made her way into the kitchen. It quickly became clear that he was in no mood for a civil conversation. 'I asked you a fucking question!' Cameron bawled. 'Look at the clock, don't tell me you have been working until this time!' Poppy picked up the kettle and half-filled it with water. She really needed a cup of coffee, not her jealous boyfriend bawling in her ear. 'Is it that fucking Geordie bloke?' he yelled. 'You are always talking about him.' Poppy ignored his comment, changing her mind about the coffee and throwing a tea bag into a mug she had just cleaned. 'I will ask you one more fucking time,' her boyfriend yelled. 'What the fuck have you been doing until this time?'

Poppy knew it was best not to ignore him, he was clearly angered by her late arrival home. Maybe telling him the truth would suffice. 'Danny asked a table of people to stay, they were spending big money, so someone had to serve the drinks. I made a few quid in tips. I will let you have some of it tomorrow.' Poppy hoped that the enticement of some cash to fuel his nasty habits might be enough to pacify him.

But she was wrong. As the kettle began to steam, she put her hand forward to fill her coffee mug but never reached it. Cameron grabbed her and forced her head down with a heavy thud onto the draining board. Twisting one of her arms behind her back and pinning the other to her side with his bulky frame, he began to vent his frustration. 'You're a lying slag!' he screamed. 'You have been with that northern cunt!'

Poppy began to twist and turn in a bid to get free. 'Let me go! Cam, I swear I will fuck you up if you don't let me go right now!'

Cameron grabbed her hair, pulling her head backwards before slamming it down onto the work surface next to the sink. He lowered his head and looked her fully in the face. She could see the rage in the pupils of his eyes and smell the stale tobacco on his breath. 'Let me go!' she screamed. She could feel the anger building up inside her, like a dormant volcano ready to explode.

'I should have fucking known,' her boyfriend yelled, forcing her head down again, this time much firmer, scraping the side of her cheek against the worktop. But as her body came back up, Poppy's hand slipped from his grasp and her clenched fist caught him directly between his eyes and hit the bridge of his nose. 'Fucking bitch!' he screamed, twisting her arm behind her back and regaining control.

'I swear, Cam,' Poppy bawled at the top of her voice, 'I swear that when I get out of this I will go sick on you! Let me go now or you will be fucking sorry!' Cameron grabbed her much tighter now, pushing her body over the draining board and landing a punch to the side of her ribs. He raised her head again and thumped it with force into the stainless steel surface, sending some undried cutlery crashing to the floor. She winced in pain. Her whole torso began to wriggle as she tried to get out of his grip. Suddenly, she felt his arm reach over her head and lift the handle of the boiled kettle. Small streams of steam were still escaping through its lid. Before she could say another word, Cameron had tipped the kettle forward, releasing several drops of scalding hot water onto the side of her head. Poppy hollered loudly, releasing a long cry of pain. It reverberated around the walls of the kitchen, sounding out like the echoes of agonising screams from a medieval torture chamber.

But he wasn't finished there, he raised the steaming kettle above her head and began to tip it forward. 'Go fucking sick on me, will you? You dirty slag!' he yelled, as the boiling water searched its target. Poppy pulled her head to one side, but not before she felt the burning liquid catch the back of her head and top of her neck. She screamed again, a howling cry of pain. Cameron finally freed her hands and looked on as her battered body fell to the floor. She rolled sideways, moaning in agony as she raised both hands to clasp the back of her head.

Cameron bent down as she cowered on the floor. There was still a burning rage in his eyes, he felt she had not been punished enough. He stood up swiftly and swung back his right leg, aiming a fierce kick at her body. It found its target in the small of her back. His second kick was not so accurate, she was turning at the time, but it still caught the side of her shoulder. He leaned down to survey the damage, a gloating smile of victory cracked across his face. There was no mercy in his drug-fueled mind tonight. In Cameron's head he thought that she had gone too far, he had to let her know she could not mess him around. 'Go sick on me will you, bitch?' he barked. Poppy turned her head away and raised her arms to protect herself, but he didn't stop. Cameron grabbed her hair and turned her face towards him so that she could listen to what he had to say. 'I am not a fucking mug. I am not like that fucking little weasel that you carved up on the Marfield!' he said. 'Don't think you can treat me like a fucking mug and get away with it!'

She badly felt the urge to retaliate, she desperately wanted to hurt him at that moment. But Poppy could feel her aching limbs and an intense pain in her neck. She knew she was beaten tonight. She closed her eyes and hoped he would leave her there. He did, but not before aiming one last kick into the side of her shoulder. She bit her lip hard as a sharp pain raced through her body. 'Fucking slag!' he yelled as he left the kitchen, turning off the light on his way out, as if he might somehow want to hide the results of his merciless attack. His last kick had really hurt her badly, she wanted to burst into tears, but she knew that she wouldn't. It had been many years since Poppy gave anyone the satisfaction of seeing her cry. No matter how much pain she might be in, tonight would be no exception.

As Poppy felt the remains of the scalding water trickle down her back, beneath her shirt, the sharp measure of pain began to sink in. Slowly moving her aching body sideways, she looked into the living room to see if Cameron had gone to bed. He hadn't, he had found her bag and was riffling through the contents. She watched on as he discarded her makeup pieces and moisturiser, finally finding her secret pocket and what he was really looking for. Screwing the money up in his hand, he threw her bag across the room, turned off the television and headed for their bed, slamming the bedroom door en route, as if to confirm that she would not be welcome in there that night. Usually, she would have bounced back up, she would fight back, an argument would ensue. But there was no fight left in her at this time, her battered and bruised torso had received enough punishment for one night.

Poppy clambered onto her knees and swung her legs around in a bid to reduce the pain she was suffering. She slid across the dirt-stained floor, to the corner of the kitchen, ending up in a fetal position. As she lay in the darkness, she touched her battered limbs, she was aching all over. Her neck was stinging as if it had been set on fire and she could feel her heartbeat throbbing through the back of her scalded neck, a thumping sound, like a slow-beating drum.

As she looked out of the heavily grease-smeared windows, between the tatty lace curtains, she could see the flashing lights of an airplane, high up in the dark sky. Her vision was somewhat distorted, but she followed the lights at the rear of the plane until it was almost out of view. It made her have strange thoughts, it made her think of Mr Houghton and of piano wire. It had been a long time since these thoughts had come back to haunt her, but she knew that if she had some piano wire, here, right now, that she would finish him. She would not let Cameron get away with his brutal assault.

\* \* \*

The plane's lights were distant now, but those memories were never distant, they were always there, a constant reminder of the daily hell she had suffered at the hands of others. She was ten or maybe eleven years old. Birthdays came and went without anybody noticing them during those first years in care. She did remember that it was a few months after the incident at the Bluebridge children's home. She had just been given a new caseworker, Laura, a pretty woman with short dark hair and a soft voice. She seemed nice when Poppy first met her.

The Houghtons were the third or fourth foster family to take her in. She had not got on too well with the previous ones, they had not liked Poppy at all. Laura had bought a new suitcase for her. It was pink with a grey trim. Her new caseworker had felt sorry for Poppy, having seen her carting around an old tattered sports bag that looked like it had been found in a rubbish bin. Laura had not been too pleased with the last family's treatment of Poppy. One of the foster carers had been heavy handed with her after she had refused to do chores around the house. Three days later, the poor girl still had traces of his hand marks at the top of her legs. As Poppy packed her new case, Laura told her that she would like the Houghtons, that they were a lovely elderly couple who had been waiting patiently to foster a child for a couple of years and that she would be happy with them.

They seemed nice, the Houghtons, they seemed like very nice people when she first met them. He was a retired music teacher, she was a heavily built bubbly lady who wore very colourful flowery dresses. Mrs Houghton took to Poppy from the first moment they met. 'I am going to call you Poppet,' she said. 'My little Poppet, I think it suits you better.' Poppy found the name quite endearing. She had been given many nicknames at her previous foster homes but most of those had been quite vile and insulting.

Mr Houghton seemed to like her too. He would often take her with him when he went to other people's homes to fix their broken pianos. She found it fascinating, watching the precision and the patience in his old fingers as he fine-tuned the wiring.

They could be very strict at times. Poppy had a set bedtime, nine o'clock, not a moment later. They warned her against using bad language in their home. Even the word 'shit' would not be tolerated. The old couple did not like her to put her elbows on the table during mealtimes and they would check her toothbrush every night to make sure she had brushed her teeth. The Houghtons also controlled the type of programmes that she would be allowed to watch on the large television in the lounge. Cartoons and children's entertainment were OK, but nothing with nudity or bad language, that was a definite 'no-no'.

He taught her to play some simple tunes on the piano in his 'special' music room. She liked that, but when he had tried to teach Poppy to play the recorder he became quite angry when she told him that she thought it was boring and was just for 'little kids'.

She guessed that the couple were in their late fifties or early sixties, but despite his wiry frame, Mr Houghton was very strong. He would often carry large boxes of music books around and once she had witnessed him lifting one side of the large piano all by himself, to retrieve a missing songbook. He wasn't as friendly as Mrs Houghton, she always did her best to make Poppy feel special. During the first few weeks at their home, the larger-than-life lady took her to a big shopping centre a few miles away. It was massive. Poppy had never seen so many shops in one place. She bought her some new colourful dresses and skirts, telling her, 'We can't have such a beautiful young lady wearing those scruffy jeans all the time, can we, little Poppet?' Poppy had only ever owned jeans and trousers before then. She did remember wearing dresses when she was very small. She found it strange to start wearing them again. Mrs Houghton also showed her a special trick, one she had learned when she had worked for a dry-cleaning company many years before. When her clothes had been washed and dried, she showed Poppy how to fold them away, neatly and carefully, so that there would be no creases when she took them out of her drawers. The clothes always smelled so fresh too. Mrs Houghton was forever washing them, even if they didn't seem to need cleaning.

When she was not busy cleaning clothes or sewing, Mrs Houghton was cooking. She loved cooking, not just meals, she loved baking cakes. Poppy's favourite was chocolate brownies. They tasted so good she could have eaten a hundred of them, not that Mr Houghton would have been too pleased if she did. She allowed Poppy to help when she was in the kitchen, letting her lick the mix from the bowl to confirm that they tasted good enough, before baking them in the oven. Poppy's attempts at trying to make them herself were amusing to say the least, but the large round lady of the house, with a big smile and a loud laugh to match, would assure her that with plenty of practice she would get better. Poppy often thought that all that cooking every day was probably the reason that Mrs Houghton was so big and so round. She never told her that of course. Her new foster parent would forever be saying to her, 'We will make a chef out of you yet, little Poppet, you wait and see.' But Poppy never did learn to cook.

That's what she became over the first few weeks in their home, Mrs Houghton's 'little Poppet'. Her new foster mother would forever be on the telephone to her friends saying things like 'my little Poppet baked some biscuits today' or 'I bought a lovely little yellow dress for my little Poppet'. The only time she ever saw her angry was when Poppy had found a photograph of her and Mr Houghton's daughter. It was hidden in a cupboard that was usually kept locked. Mrs Houghton snatched the photograph out of Poppy's hand and told her that her daughter was a most ungrateful girl, who moved away to a place called Canada. It was very far away, too far for them to visit her. Because of this, her and Mr Houghton no longer spoke to their daughter and said that Poppy should never mention her again. Poppy never knew their daughter's name, but she wondered at the time why she would ever move so far away from such nice people.

The house was large. It had a long garden at the back with a fishpond and a neatly kept hedge. It must have been near an airport because the planes that flew over were very low. Poppy could hear their engines clearly as they would take off and land. She would often sit in their beautifully kept garden, watching those planes flying overhead, wondering if she would ever be brave enough to be in one of them, so high up in the sky.

And she had a friend too, his name was Skittles. He was a large ginger cat, with lumps of fur missing from his back and tummy. He was nearly fourteen years old and was blind in one eye. Sometimes he would fall over for no reason, but Poppy never laughed at his mishaps. She did not want to upset the Houghtons.

Skittles was the 'king of the house'. He had a large purple pillow in his basket with his name engraved on it and all his meals were freshly cooked. He was never given anything out of a tin. He even had his own cushion on the sofa, in between Mr and Mrs Houghton, and he would sit there in the evening watching the television with the couple, usually once Poppy had gone to bed. According to Mrs Houghton the cat had his own favourite TV programmes, something which Poppy found bizarre to say the least.

Most nights when Poppy was supposed to be in bed, she would creep to the top of the stairs and look down at the three of them sitting cozily on the sofa, watching the television. Mr and Mrs Houghton always seemed to be laughing. Poppy never knew what they found so funny all the time. Skittles would simply lie there having his balding tummy tickled, no doubt waiting for one of his favourite shows to start. Poppy often thought that her foster carers were both a little strange around the ageing ginger cat.

So those first couple of months were good at the big house near the airport. Poppy had some new clothes, she had learned to play four tunes on the piano and they had enrolled her to start at a local school once the summer was over. Every day was good. She would make cakes, learn a new tune on the piano, play silly games with Skittles. Every day was good at that house, every day, but not Sundays, Poppy hated Sundays.

Each week when the loud bells at the end of the road would welcome the locals into the old church for Sunday service, Mr Houghton would be hurrying his wife to make sure she was not late for her journey. Every Sunday he would take her to the local station, so that she could catch the 10.16 train to London to visit her mother. Every week, without fail, he would make that trip, taking him less than half an hour to get there and back. Every Sunday Poppy waited nervously for him to return, and then it would start, the reason she hated Sundays so much.

Firstly, on his return, before it started, Mr Houghton would always make sure she was wearing a dress. She was never allowed to wear jeans or trousers on a Sunday. He used to say that it was 'out of respect for God's day of worship'. But it didn't take Poppy long to realise that there was nothing 'God-like' or 'respectful' about Mr Houghton.

It always started the same way. They would sit at the piano together in his special room and he would pretend to show her how to play a new tune. He would hold her next to him on the piano stool, squeezing her tightly so she could not move. His hand would then go up beneath her dress and inside her knickers. She never moved when he did this. She wanted to, but something about him frightened her. She remembered when Mr Donovan had done the same thing to her at the children's home at Bluebridge, and the staff there had not believed her, so why would anyone believe her now?

After a while he would place her hand around his private parts and make her rub him hard. His face would turn red and be all twisted and distorted when she did this. Sometimes he would make funny noises and he would be shaking as though his head was about to explode, but it never did. Her ordeal would usually last around half an hour, a little less if she was lucky. Afterwards he would give her a couple of packets of sweets he had bought on the way back from the station and let her help herself to the chocolate ice cream in the freezer. She never liked that ice cream anymore, she would pretend to eat it and simply let it melt in the bowl. Poppy would usually spend the rest of the day looking out of the skylight of her room, watching the planes going backwards and forwards. He would lock himself away in his music room, playing very old songs, very loudly. She didn't like those songs, she didn't like Sundays, she didn't like Mr Houghton anymore.

At exactly twenty past five, he would leave to collect his wife from the station, but not without a lecture for her. He would tell her that Mrs Houghton would always believe him over her and that she was nothing but a 'little wretch that been thrown into the gutter by her parents'. He reminded her that she was lucky to be living in such a lovely house with good people and that she should be thankful. Poppy certainly didn't feel very lucky at that time.

Mrs Houghton would return from the station with him, both laughing. Something or other always seemed to amuse them. Poppy would usually make herself scarce, sometimes pretending that she had a tummy upset or was exhausted from running around too much that day. In her bedroom she would look up at the skylight, watching the planes, until she fell asleep. Something told her that she would be brave enough to fly now, up there, high in the sky, to get away, far, far away. She sometimes wondered if her mother had flown on one of those planes and gone somewhere far away. Maybe she had gone to Canada, perhaps she had met the Houghtons' daughter. Maybe their daughter had told her that her father was not a very nice person, maybe her mother would come back for her, to get her away from him. But something in the back of her mind always told her that she was only fooling herself, her mother would never be coming back for her.

She wanted to tell Laura, each time that she visited the house to check how things were. She wanted to ask her if she could find another place for her to live. But she remembered how friendly she was with the Houghtons, often laughing at their silly jokes and spending most of her time stroking Skittles' tummy. She thought Laura might think she was making things up or being ungrateful. She didn't want to be sent back to the Bluebridge home, so she thought it better to say nothing.

When Laura did next visit, Poppy asked her about her parents. Laura had promised that she would do her best to get in touch with them. She made it clear, however, that there had still been no contact and promised to keep trying. Poppy began to believe that Mr Houghton was right after all, maybe she was just a 'little wretch whose parents didn't want her'.

Poppy never slept well on Saturday nights, she would lie on her bed hoping that Mrs Houghton would fall ill or find a reason not to go to her mother's the next day. Why couldn't her mother visit them? Or why couldn't her mother move far away, like her daughter did, too far for her to visit on a Sunday? Sometimes she would get on her knees and pray that Mrs Houghton's mother would die. If she was dead, there would never be any need for the woman to leave the house again. But, like most things Poppy prayed for in her life, her prayers were never answered.

On this warm Sunday morning they were running late for the 10.16 train. Skittles had been ill the previous night and Mrs Houghton was worried and wanted to find a vet that was open at weekends. But her husband was determined that she visit her mother that day. She reluctantly agreed. The lovely large lady still found time to put Poppy's hair into a neat ponytail, as she often did, and gave her one of her 'special hugs' before she left. Poppy had hoped that Mrs Houghton would see something was not right in her sorrowful eyes before she departed, but she didn't.

When they left for the station, Poppy sat next to Skittles on the long sofa and reached for the remote control for the television. 'And we are watching my favourite programmes today, stupid fat cat,' she said. 'Not yours!' Running through the channels she found a music station she had not seen before. She liked the music, she left it on. When she looked down at the clock on the DVD player, it was nearly half past ten. He would be back soon. Her mind began to wander as the music blared out in front of her. She started to move and then dance to the beat of the track playing. There on the screen was a handsome black man stripped to his waist. He was gyrating on the bonnet of a car. There were scantily dressed girls, dancing behind him. Just for that moment, Poppy was on that screen, she was in that video, she was one of those dancers. She swayed around the living room, the music was thumping out from the television, the man on the car singing out louder and louder, but then suddenly she stopped. He was there,

Mr Houghton had returned, he was watching her, she could see the anger in his face.

She knew what was coming. Her eyes began searching desperately for an exit route or maybe something to defend herself with. But he was quick. Before she knew what was happening, he had swept her tiny legs up into the air and had her under his arm. She screamed and shouted as he carried her towards the music room, her legs kicking out at him along the way. Once inside the room she watched him close the door and turn the key in the lock. She knew that this was it now. Her shouting stopped as he threw her feeble body onto the floor. He towered over her, a twisted smile on his wrinkled face.

Looking up at him, Poppy could see that anger was still there in his eyes. She had really upset him this time. She offered him a child-like smile. She hoped he might take pity on her. A smile that said, 'Please don't hurt me.' But there would be no clemency today, Mr Houghton was in no mood for forgiveness.

'So, you want to be a little whore?' he asked her in a calm tone, almost as if he was asking which cereal she wanted for her breakfast. 'You want to be a little whore, like all of those other whores on the television!'

Poppy wanted to speak, she wanted to defend herself, but she was frozen to the spot. She shuffled her legs to get away from him, but he had her move covered. Grabbing her ponytail tightly in one hand and her body in the other he lifted her up and moved her towards the piano. She didn't kick out at him, she knew that there wasn't much point now. He placed her facedown on the piano stool, her head hung over the edge and he pinned his body down on top of her. His heavy weight made her gasp for air. He moved slightly to one side and she felt that she was able to breathe again. Suddenly, she felt her dress rise and touch the back of her head. She could hear him breathing, more heavily now, next to her face. Poppy winced as she felt his hand slip inside her knickers. In a matter of seconds, they had been pulled down and were around her ankles. She closed her eyes and her body shook. She knew what was coming next. This is what had happened at her previous foster home when she had refused to clean her room. She gritted her teeth and waited for the large slap that would follow, but it didn't happen. She could now hear the zipper on his trousers and felt his skin touching the back of her legs. She began to panic, the music chair wobbled violently beneath her. He held her more firmly, one hand pushing her head down, so that she was unable to struggle, the other pushing her legs apart. And then he did it, he pushed it inside her, not where he usually put his fingers, but into her bottom. She screamed loudly, as she felt the excruciating pain as he pushed it further and further inside. Her eyes began to water, she bit her lip, her teeth biting so hard that her whole mouth began to bleed. It went on for what seemed to be forever, but in truth was probably less than a minute. Suddenly his head fell over the stool and his face was beside her neck. All at once he let out an enormous groan and his body moved violently on top of hers. All she could hear now was his heavy breathing and the sound of her heart racing inside her chest. She wanted to cry so badly at that point, she wanted to let go of a river of tears. Crying would surely ease this terrible pain she felt inside. But she didn't cry, she bit her lip even harder, swallowing her own blood as the cut opened wider on her side of her mouth. She was in so much pain, but she refused to give him the satisfaction of seeing how much he had hurt her. Instead, she moved out from underneath him, and reached for her discarded underwear. No words were exchanged. What could he possibly have said to justify what he had just done to her? Poppy felt a sharp pain in her backside as she put on her knickers and pulled down her dress. It was a pain she would remember for the rest of her life. She moved away from the monster beside her, still trying hard to regain his composure, and sat by the door of his 'special room', waiting for him to release her from his torture.

There were no sweets that day, no chocolate ice cream and no television. Poppy lay on her bed watching the planes fly past, praying that he would die now, instead of Mrs Houghton's mother. That would be much better, she thought, if he were dead instead. Her bottom felt as if someone had kicked her there, kicked her very hard. She touched it a couple of times, but it began to make her feel sick inside. She noticed that a button had come off her dress in the struggle. *Mrs Houghton will be angry*, she thought, *she will have to sew that back on. I will need to find that button for her now.*

Mr Houghton spent the rest of the day playing those old songs, very loudly, more loudly than she had ever heard him play them before. She didn't want to hear those songs again, she despised them now. She wanted to run away from the house, but she knew she would not get very far. She lay on her bed, trying to work out the best way of escaping her tormentor. In Poppy's head, she knew what she wanted to do now. He would be sorry for what he did to her. She didn't care now if she had to go back to the home. Nobody did what he had done to her at Bluebridge, not even Mr Donovan, nobody was that evil.

Something inside Poppy died that day, maybe it was the last shreds of her innocence. She felt different now, something happened to her at that moment in the music room. Her bitterness and helplessness had been replaced with an unequivocal feeling of anger, a burning rage that would stay with her for the rest of her life.

She bided her time and waited for him to leave, the plan for revenge was slowly formulating in her head. Mr Houghton came to her room before he set off for the station. He did not come to apologise for the vile act he had performed on her that day, his despicable crime against a defenceless child. No, he had entered her room to remind her not to say anything to Mrs Houghton about what had happened. He used those words 'unwanted' and 'gutter' again in his warning, but this time Poppy was not listening.

As soon as she heard his car leave the drive, she made her way downstairs to the music room, that terrible place where it had all happened. But she had not returned to the scene of his brutal act to find the missing button from her dress. Reaching up onto one of the shelves, above the music books, she found several strips of piano wire. She chose the longest one, about eighteen inches in length, then walked back to the living room. Skittles was fast asleep on the sofa, probably wondering what would happen in his favourite shows later that evening. Poppy did not want to disturb the big cat. He was stretched out, purring gently, his overweight tummy no doubt waiting for a friendly rub. Poppy toyed with the wire for a few seconds, bending it and stretching it, before wrapping it around her wrist, as if to make a bracelet. Sitting on the edge of the sofa she looked down at her furry friend, so peaceful in his slumber. She watched him for a minute, maybe two, then delicately slipped the wire underneath his big ginger head. She slowly pulled the cord through, feeding it across the ring she had created and waited a few seconds. The poor unsuspecting creature was blissfully docile, he had hardly stirred at all.

Suddenly, with one almighty yank on the wire, Poppy rose to her feet. Skittles screeched, an ear-piercing cry, as his body swung from the makeshift noose around his neck. A frantic struggle ensued as the animal's paws clawed desperately at the wire. Poppy pulled harder, tightening the wire's grip until it began to rip into the cat's neck. Skittles continued to struggle, shaking violently and spitting venom at his aggressor. Poppy was undeterred, stretching her arms wider to tighten the grip even further. Suddenly the cat's eyes bulged, wide and then wider, as if they were about to explode. Skittles lashed out at his attacker, hissing at her, his body began to gyrate, as if he was having a fit. Poppy stood firm, watching every strain of torment and agony on the poor animal's face. Finally, the struggle ended, the cat stopped fighting, he stopped moving, it was all over. Skittles was dead!

The silence returned to the living room. The furry creature with his personally monogrammed pillow was sprawled out on the carpet near the front door, one of his eyes was open, one closed, the piano wire wrapped firmly around his neck. Poppy looked down at the poor lifeless creature. She felt no remorse, if anything she thought that Skittles should be thankful. After all, Poppy had saved the animal from having to spend the rest of his days with that tyrant Mr Houghton. Skittles, she thought, in a strange way, might just understand why she had to do what she had just done.

Making her way to her bedroom, Poppy took off her dress and left it on the bed. She thought of writing a small note to let Mrs Houghton know that the missing button was not her fault, but she did not have time. She put on her comfortable jeans and favourite black top and began to pack her things in the nice suitcase that Laura had bought for her. She left the other dresses hanging in the wardrobe. She did not want any reminders of her time at that house. She didn't want to be a 'little poppet' anymore and she never wanted to wear a dress again in her life. Folding her clothes neatly, just as Mrs Houghton had shown her, she emptied her drawers as quickly as she could. She hoped her clothes would not be creased when she arrived at her next home, she would want to make a good impression there. Poppy walked calmly down the staircase and sat on the bottom stair with her little suitcase by her side. She looked down at the time on the DVD player. *Nearly time*, she thought, *nearly time*.

They were laughing when they came in, Mr and Mrs Houghton, they were laughing very loudly, but they did not laugh for long. At the sight of her precious Skittles on the living room floor Mrs Houghton let out the most earsplitting scream Poppy had ever heard. Mr Houghton shouted, directly at Poppy, he shouted very loudly in her face. He waved his arms around, while he was screaming at her, but it did not frighten Poppy. She knew he could not hurt her anymore.

Laura did not get to the house until past midnight. Her caseworker had struggled to find another placement for her, with it being so late and on a Sunday. Poppy had not moved an inch from the bottom stair, not to go to the toilet, not even to let Mrs Houghton pass as she retreated to her bedroom in tears. When Laura came into the house, Mr Houghton said very little to her. He had said most of what he needed to during their earlier telephone conversation. His wife could clearly be heard sobbing loudly in the upstairs bedroom. Poppy said nothing at all.

Poppy was convinced she would be going back to Bluebridge now, back to those evil Baxter brothers, and Mr Donovan's wandering hands, but at this moment in time she did not care. Laura sat Poppy in the passenger seat of her car, offering to put her small case into the back seat, but Poppy gripped it tightly and sat it on her lap, as though she thought it might offer her some form of protection. The journey seemed to take hours, the roads were dark. They drove a long way, much further than where the children's home would have been. Poppy sat in the passenger seat of Laura's car as her caseworker drove through the night. She was hungry, she hadn't eaten since breakfast. She was desperate to go to the toilet, but she was holding it in. The poor girl was tired. She fought desperately to keep her eyes open, but she said nothing, she said nothing to Laura for the whole of the journey. She could not understand why her new caseworker had let her stay in that horrible house with that evil man, so she said nothing to her at all. Poppy liked her new pink and grey suitcase, but she did not like Laura. She did not trust her anymore.

Eventually they stopped at a small cottage at the end of a dark country lane and Laura introduced Poppy to her new foster family, the Lockwoods. She did not know it at the time, but it would only be a couple of weeks before she would be packing her small suitcase to move on again.

* * *

Poppy shivered as she sat on the cold floor of the kitchen in her flat. Her eyes were still fixed on the dark sky between those grubby torn curtains. That plane was probably halfway to its destination by now, its passengers filled with eager anticipation of the holiday ahead of them. As she touched her scalded neck a strange thought crossed her mind, not for the first time. Why did the Houghtons' daughter move so far away from them? Maybe it was a handsome young man she had met or perhaps it was an exciting new job that took her all the way to Canada. Or maybe, she simply moved away because she knew the kind of man that her father really was. Maybe, like Poppy, she did not like wearing those dresses on Sundays either.

The sun could be seen rising in the distance. Poppy did not know how long she been sprawled out on the grease-covered floor, but she was sure that Cameron would be asleep now. So if she had some piano wire here, right now, maybe in one of those kitchen drawers, she knew what she would do. She would make him pay for all the pain she was suffering. She would wrap that wire so tightly around his neck and pull it so hard and for so long that his face would turn blue and his eyes would pop of his head. She would be too strong for him this time, she wouldn't let go, not until he was gone, not until she was sure he was dead. She knew if he was gone for good that she would not have to forgive him the next morning. Forgive him, like she had done so many times in the past. If he was gone, she could start again. Maybe, she thought, there might be a better life for her out there after all.

But there was no wire in those drawers. Poppy laid her head back down on the dirt-stained floor of her kitchen and closed her eyes.

# CHAPTER EIGHT

A tiny ray of sunlight peeped through a gap in the heavy grey curtains in the lounge. It sent a beam across the room, highlighting the food-stained plates and unwashed coffee mugs littered across the dust-covered table. Next to those dirty dishes lay a handful of sympathy cards, carefully worded thoughts from family and close friends of Jamie.

Bree sat on the sofa, a duvet, the cover of which was in bad need of a wash, was wrapped around her shoulders. The room wasn't cold, it was less than two weeks until the start of spring, yet Jamie's sister felt the need to be surrounded by the warmth of her brother's quilt. She was dressed in a crumpled brown T-shirt, another one of her twin's treasured garments, and a pair of jogging bottoms, which carried the stains of a spilt mug of coffee. Nobody would have recognised the girl that could turn heads wherever she went, the one that was often mistaken for a fashion model.

She sat in complete silence. Her unwashed hair was becoming matted, strands of her greasy mane dangled across her forehead. She looked pale and drawn. The lack of sleep and the river of tears she had shed over the past three months had done nothing for her once radiant complexion. In truth she would not have looked out of place with the small crowd of homeless people that were living under the nearby viaduct. It had been eleven weeks now, eleven painful weeks since her world had stopped. She no longer recognised her own reflection, she was living someone else's life now. Reaching across the table she lifted one of the cards, running her fingers delicately over the embossed wording on the front. She had memorised every word in every card on the table, but no words of sympathy would ever ease the hurt she felt inside. Bree was beginning to find it harder to picture his face, to remember his voice, his funny laugh. The only time she was reunited with him was in her sleep, but even then, she was always there to take him away from her, the girl, the girl in the raincoat.

Bree suddenly sat upright. Almost as soon as she heard them, the footsteps, they were coming down the path, they were heading for her house, it was him, she was sure it was him. The key turned in the front door, he was back, this wasn't real after all, he was here, Jamie was here. He would open the door now and she would hear his voice again. 'You see, sis,' he will say, 'I got you, you believed it all.' Yes, of course, it was just a prank, one of his silly pranks, Jamie was back. She would forgive him for his cruel joke, she would tell him that he was wrong to put her through all this misery, but she would forgive him, forgive him anything, just to have him back.

Bree swiftly pushed her hair back across her head. She had to look her best for Jamie. She raised her heavy head to greet him as the door opened, but her heart sank faster than a vessel full of holes as her friend appeared. 'Hi, babe, I just thought I would call in on the way to work, to see if you needed anything.'

Bree slumped back to her resting place, the feeling of prolonged numbness restored to her body. 'Hi, Kayleigh,' she said, in a muffled voice that hadn't been heard for days.

'Have you managed to get some sleep?' Kayleigh asked. 'Are those pills the doctor gave you helping?'

'Not really,' Bree replied, her usual voice starting to return. 'I am still having those nightmares.'

Kayleigh put down her bag and looked around at the messy room, wondering if Bree had been entertaining a group of vagrants. She reached up to pull open those big curtains. 'Leave them!' Bree screamed. 'I don't want them open.'

Not wanting to unsettle her friend, Kayleigh switched her attention to the floor around the table. 'I will give the place a hoover and clean these dishes before I go,' she said, not that Bree was paying any attention to her. It had only been a few days since her last visit, but the room had an air of uncaring abandonment about it. Kayleigh picked up some plates and cutlery from the floor, together with some half-eaten French bread and what looked like the remains of a bowl of spaghetti. She placed the unopened mail and some photographs on the table as Bree watched on.

'Why don't I run you a nice bath and maybe we can have a walk down to the shops together?'

'No!' Bree snapped. 'I don't want to go out.'

'But you haven't left the house since...' Kayleigh stopped herself mid-sentence, but she knew what was coming next.

'Since the funeral, Kayleigh!' Bree barked. 'Just say it, the funeral.'

'Some fresh air will do you good, babe, it will put some colour back in your cheeks.'

'Tomorrow,' Bree said, curling back up into her duvet. 'Let's do that tomorrow, I am too tired today.'

'What about a nice cup of coffee?'

'That would be good.'

Kayleigh's hand moved the cards on the table to reach the stained coffee mugs. 'Don't touch those cards!' Bree screamed. 'Don't touch them, they are all I have of him now.' Her friend simply smiled and retreated to the kitchen to clean the dirty cups and plates.

Kayleigh thought some small talk might be needed, she did not intend to open any sore wounds that day. She called out to her friend as she waited for the kettle to boil. 'I saw Luke Stevenson the other day, he was at the Esso petrol station.'

'Really!' Bree replied, not in the least bit interested, but making a small effort to give the impression that she was. 'Is he still with that girl, you know the one that looks Asian?'

'She is Turkish,' Kayleigh called back. 'Turkish-Cypriot I think. Yeah, they are getting married next year.'

Bree's effort to make idle conversation was short-lived. She pulled her cover tightly around her shoulders and slumped back into her usual resting position.

Returning to the room with two steaming hot cups of coffee Kayleigh made the mistake of asking her friend another question. 'Have you spoken to your mother?'

Bree looked up from her self-made pit on the sofa. 'No!' she snapped. 'And I don't want to.'

Kayleigh thought it best to park that conversation there and moved on. 'So are you still getting the nightmares?'

Bree nodded. 'All the time, the girl, the one in the raincoat, she always seems to be in them.'

Her friend was becoming concerned for Bree. It was clear that she was struggling to cope and the anti-depressants she had been taking did not seem to be helping her at all. Part of her wished that her friend would take up her mother's offer of counselling. It was becoming clear that she needed professional help.

'You must have seen her,' Bree said. 'The girl in that coat.'

'No. You have asked me that before.'

'That night, in the pub, in the Rising Sun.'

'I don't remember her.'

'You were there, Kayleigh, you must remember her.'

'It was busy. I left early, with Tom, remember?'

Bree shook her head. 'You must have seen her. Those eyes, you wouldn't forget those eyes.'

She really didn't want to revisit the subject, but her friend felt the need to discuss it. 'You should really speak to your mum, babe. She is hurting too, you should be helping each other now.'

'Hurting so much she fucked off to her hideaway in the snow!'

'I don't think she wanted to be here, you know, with all the memories. She is really hurting inside, babe, you know that, don't you?'

'Why are you always sticking up for my bitch of a mother, Kayleigh? Why do you always do that?'

'She asked me to keep an eye on you, you know, after…'

'Funeral, Kayleigh! Just say it, after Jamie's fucking funeral.'

'Yes, after the funeral. She was worried about you. She really didn't want you to be on your own.'

'Is that why she got the first plane out of Heathrow? She couldn't fucking wait to get away from all this mess.'

Kayleigh tried to find some words of comfort but everything she said seemed to be aggravating her friend that day. 'I don't think that's fair, babe. I think she was still in shock.'

The two friends looked across at each other, sipping their cooling coffee. An awkward silence ensued. Kayleigh was considering the best way to keep this conversation going without antagonising Bree further, but something told her that she would be fighting a losing battle. Bree was also deep in thought, but she was certainly not in the mood to hold back now the subject of her mother had been thrown on the table. 'She was jealous, Kayleigh, my mother was jealous.'

'Of you?'

'Of me and Jamie, of what we had, how close we were, she was so jealous.'

'I don't get it, babe, why would she be jealous? You are her kids.'

Bree sat forward. Her whole demeanour began to change. She seemed to be on a mission to make her friend understand her growing hatred for her parent. 'She hated everything we had together, how close we had become, everything. And now I hope she rots in fucking Finland. I hope she stays out there, I hope she dies out there, for all the shit she did!'

'No, babe, you don't mean that.'

'You don't understand, Kayleigh, that's why she sent him away, that's why she made him go.'

Her friend was startled. She wasn't sure what Bree was trying to say. 'It wasn't her fault that Jamie died, babe, it was an accident.'

Bree shook her head. 'You don't get it, you really don't get it. When she took him away from me, when she sent him off to that Holme Vale place.'

'The boarding school?'

'Yes, you see you do remember.'

'But that was a long time ago. She sent him there because he was struggling at school. He was always playing up, babe. She did it for his own good.'

Bree continued her rant. 'She was a fucking bitch. You see, Kayleigh, you do remember what she was really like.'

'But the school helped him. He would have never got the grades to go to university if he hadn't gone there.'

'It wasn't about his fucking grades, Kayleigh, she just wanted to take him away from me.'

'Why, babe, why the hell would your mother send him all that way to Holme Vale? It was in Middlesbrough, it was over two hundred miles away.'

Bree sank back into the sofa. 'Because she found us.'

'Found you?'

'She found us in bed.'

Kayleigh wasn't sure what to make of it. She struggled to understand. 'So you were in bed together?'

Bree began to think back to the day it happened. 'It was the weekend, she had gone out to some charity do or something. Dad was away on a location shoot in Norway. We were watching television in Jamie's bed, we always did that, he had a bigger screen than the one in my room. You know, munching midnight snacks and watching a horror film or listening to music or something.' Kayleigh nodded as Bree continued. 'Suddenly, she burst into his room like she was the fucking riot police or something. She dragged me out by my hair, all the way along the hallway and threw me on my bedroom floor. Who does that to their fourteen-year-old daughter?'

'Jesus!' Kayleigh asked. 'Why was she so angry?'

'She thought we were, you know, doing it. She thought I was having sex with my own brother.'

Her friend was now in total shock. 'Wow! That's mad, that is insane!'

'We told her she was wrong, both of us, but she wouldn't listen. She got on the phone to Dad and told him he had to fly back straight away. She lied, she told him she had found her disgusting kids naked in bed together, having sex.'

'Wait! You were naked?! You were both naked?'

'Yeah, we used to do it all the time. He was my brother, Kayleigh, my brother.'

'I know, babe, but that is still a bit strange. What happened?'

'Dad flew home, he always did what that bitch told him to do. They paid a lot of money to get Jamie into Holme Vale, just to get him away from me. She was so jealous, so fucking jealous. She knew how close we were, she just fucking sent him away.'

'Jesus, babe. It is a lot to take in.'

'The bitch made me do a pregnancy test. How fucking stupid was that? I kept telling her, over and over again, that we never did anything. And then she made me go see some woman at the counselling place, like I was a freak or something. All because we were watching television, all because we were watching fucking television.'

'So, they sent him to Holme Vale?'

'Yeah but that wasn't all. Every time he came home for holidays she would pack me off somewhere, to stay with dad in Tampere or to Auntie Millie's place. Do you remember the trip when she paid for you and me to go to Belgium?'

'Yeah, the Ardennes, wow that was amazing!'

'She only did it because Jamie was home on his school break. She only did it to keep us apart.'

'Shit, babe, I don't know what to say.'

'She did anything, anything to keep us apart from each other.'

'But you still saw him, Bree, we all used to go out together.'

'No, Kayleigh, it was never the same. We were never allowed to be alone together, to share anything together, she would always be there, right in the middle of us.'

'I never had a clue this was going on, babe, not a clue.'

'That's why he was going to Australia, it was her idea. She gave him the money, told him to go travelling, she even booked his flight.'

'No!'

'Yeah, she gave him five grand, enough to keep him away for a year. He would never have come back.'

'I thought that was the money he got for his twenty-first birthday. You got the same amount, babe. You both got five grand, you told me. That's how you paid the deposit on the Audi convertible.'

'You really are thick, Kayleigh, you are still not listening to me. You know that she is selling this house now, don't you? Getting rid of the scene of the crime. He would have had nowhere to come back to.'

'But she is your mother, Bree, she will always be your mother.'

'Not anymore, that bitch has been dead to me for a long time. And now he is gone, now Jamie is dead, she can get on with the rest of her life. I bet she is pleased he is dead, no more dark skeletons left in the family cupboard.'

It upset Kayleigh to hear her friend talking this way. 'Have you ever told her how you feel, babe, have you ever sat down with your mum and explained your true feelings?'

'I don't want to, I am finished with her. I hope she rots in Finland, I hope she never comes back.'

Kayleigh sat next to her friend and tried to put a comforting arm around her, but Bree pushed her away. 'The photos!' she shouted. 'The photos will show you everything.' With that Bree threw off her makeshift sleeping bag, rose to her feet and headed towards the drawers in the glass cabinet. She rummaged through them, throwing much of the contents onto the living room floor. 'Not here!' she said and quickly moved to the kitchen.

'The photos will prove what I am saying, you will see,' she yelled, throwing open the cupboard doors and drawers. Kayleigh stood at the door to the kitchen, worried that her friend might really be losing her mind. 'Where are those fucking pictures?' Bree shouted, emptying every cupboard in sight. 'I know, the wardrobe in her old room.' She pushed past her friend and made her way up the stairs. 'I will show you, I will show you just what a bitch my mother really is!'

Kayleigh followed her friend upstairs, half hoping that she wouldn't find these pictures that might be so damning. Bree's earlier revelations were still reeling in her head. She had already had enough shocks for one day.

'Got them!' Bree announced dragging down a large red box from the wardrobe next to her parents' bed. 'Now you will see.' Kayleigh sat on the uncovered mattress at the side of the bed and watched Bree as she opened the box and pulled out a handful of assorted photographs. 'That's one of Jamie at Beth's birthday party.' She showed her friend the picture and then tossed it across the floor. The next half dozen or so pictures ended up in the same corner of the room. 'Me and Dad at a barbecue, me at the prom, Jamie and Preston, Jamie with Lewis at a Halloween party, me with my bitch of a mother at Millie's birthday do, Jamie at Bristol Uni. One here of me and you at that summer fete.'

Kayleigh picked that photo up from the floor to have a closer look. 'God, I look rough in that one,' she said. 'I remember that day.'

Bree suddenly threw the box of memorabilia onto the bed. 'You still don't get it, Kayleigh! How fucking stupid are you?' Her friend looked puzzled. 'There are none of us together!' Bree bawled at her friend, as though she was telling off a young child. 'There are none of me and Jamie together.' Kayleigh began to sift through the rest of the photographs as Bree continued her rant. 'She never saw us as a two anymore, not after that night, it was always just him or me.'

Kayleigh continued to look through the box, turning over the pictures one at a time before showing one of them to her friend. 'Look, there is one here of Jamie with poor Jess,' she said. 'God, it was so sad what happened to her.'

Bree snatched the photograph and ripped it into small pieces, showering her friend's head with the tiny fragments. 'For fuck's sake, Kayleigh, you are still not listening. My mother has spent all these years keeping me and Jamie apart. She is evil, pure fucking evil. Now can you see why I hate her?'

Kayleigh shook her head, refusing to accept that her best friend's mother would be so cruel. 'There must be some here, somewhere, you can't be right. She wouldn't just throw all those old photographs away.'

Bree snarled at her friend's continuing defence of her mother. 'Burned them, on the bonfire, I swear she burned all of them.'

Kayleigh continued sifting through the box, hoping to prove her friend wrong, but she wasn't having much success. The sudden rush of mixed emotions had made Bree tired all of a sudden and she sat down at her mother's dressing table. Turning her head to catch a glimpse of herself in the mirror, a sense of sharp reality hit her as she looked closer at her reflection to discover what the strains of the past three months had done to her once beautiful features. 'Fuck, I look terrible!' she said. Kayleigh could not disagree. Bree reached in the drawer and found a thick hairband which she used to tie back the mangy mop of greasy blonde hair dangling across the top of her head.

'Who is that?' Kayleigh asked suddenly, producing a photograph of Bree's mother at an upmarket dinner evening.

'Who?' Bree replied, still angry that her friend was refusing to entertain her conspiracy theory.

'The man sitting next to your mother.'

Bree snatched the picture and looked more closely. 'I don't know,' she said. 'It looks like one of her charity events.'

'They are holding hands,' Kayleigh pointed out. 'Look, there, under the table.'

Bree studied the photograph much more closely. 'The bitch was probably cheating on my dad. I wouldn't put anything past her.'

Suddenly the doorbell rang, making both girls jump. 'Shit!' Bree said and then quickly lowered her voice to a whisper. 'I bet it's them nosy neighbours, the new ones. They keep calling round to see if I need anything.' Kayleigh stood up and began to head for the door. 'Don't worry, babe,' she said. 'I will get rid of them.' She left the room with Bree still scrutinising the strange photograph of her mother.

When Kayleigh opened the front door, the visitor was halfway down the path and walking away, but on hearing the door open, slowly turned and walked back. She was a large lady, tall and wide. She was wearing a long black coat, as if she had just come from a funeral. The expression on her face was very solemn and she seemed quite nervous. 'Bree is having a nap,' Kayleigh said. 'I have popped round to get her shopping for her, so I think she will be OK.'

The woman nodded but said nothing. Her face was very pale. Suddenly her chin began to tremble, she looked as if she were about to burst into tears. 'Are you alright?' Kayleigh asked. 'You don't look very well.' The large lady was finding it difficult to speak. 'I wanted to, I came to see if, I am sorry, you know…'

As Kayleigh stood trying to understand what the poor woman was trying to say, Bree moved to the window upstairs and looked down to see what was happening. She didn't know the woman, she didn't know why she would be there, but as her eyes moved towards the end of the path, to the street beyond her front gate, she recognised something that sent an ice-cold shiver racing down her spine. It was a sight that would be embedded in her brain until the day she died. It was the Shogun, it was that car. She dropped the picture as she felt a surge of boiling blood rush up through her body to her head. Hurtling down the stairs, she began screaming hysterically, as if she was trying to escape a fire. She thrust open the front door and headed straight for her target, knocking poor Kayleigh sideways and onto the ground in the process. Her clenched fist caught the woman full on the side of her head. It was followed by another. She continued pounding the startled lady who covered her face with her arms. Kayleigh rose swiftly to her feet and grabbed her friend from behind, one hand around her neck and the other catching her waist. 'Let me go!' Bree screamed at the top of her voice. 'Let me go.' Kayleigh held her friend tighter, but Bree was now lashing out at her too, kicking her legs and twisting her body as she tried to break free. 'She killed my brother, I will murder her!' she screamed at the poor woman, who was desperately trying to defend herself from the onslaught.

'Just go!' Kayleigh shouted at the large lady. 'For God's sake, just go! I can't hold her for much longer.'

The woman scurried down the path and headed directly to her parked vehicle, starting the engine before she had even closed her car door. Bree was still swinging her arms around and screaming at the top of her voice. 'She killed Jamie, it was her fault.' Just as the Shogun began to pull away Bree managed to break free from Kayleigh's grip. She chased the Shogun for a hundred yards or so before catching up and aiming several blows at the driver's window. 'I will kill you! I will find you and I will fucking kill you!' she yelled, as the car gathered speed and disappeared.

This quiet suburban road was not used to this type of commotion. Several of the neighbours' curtains had opened and a few bystanders in the street, who witnessed the event, stood together in total shock. 'What are you all looking at?' Bree screamed at them. 'What are you all fucking looking at?'

Kayleigh caught up with her friend and reached out to her, putting an arm around her waist and guiding her back to the house. The nosy residents of the usually peaceful close were still dumbstruck by the sudden outburst of their neighbour. Bree was ushered back into the dark and gloomy front room where Kayleigh sat her down amongst the scattered pillows and makeshift bedding. 'It is OK, babe,' she said wrapping her arms around her tightly. 'It is OK now.'

'No, Kayleigh, it will never be OK,' Bree replied. 'It will never ever be OK again.'

Bree pulled the duvet back around her shoulders and retreated to the position she had been in when her friend had found her earlier. Kayleigh held her hand tightly and looked at her, so fragile, so helpless, yet so angry, so full of venom. It was clear that she wanted to find someone to blame for the loss of her brother, but rationale had clearly deserted her. She seemed ready to lash out at anyone, including her mother. Kayleigh was beginning, with good reason, to be concerned about the sanity of her best friend.

'I will make us another drink, babe,' she said, straightening the pillows behind her friend's back to make her feel more comfortable. 'And how about I run a nice bath for you and do something about your hair?'

Bree nodded. 'Thank you, Kayleigh, thank you for being there for me.'

Washing the rest of the dirty dishes, thoughts begun to run through Kayleigh's mind, some of which had been with her for some time. That photograph, the one with Bree's mother sitting hand in hand with that unknown man – they looked so happy together, they really looked like they belonged together. She wondered if Jamie's theory had been right all along. He had confided in her several times to say that he believed that Per was not his real father, a fact he said he felt sure he could prove. He did not believe that, simply because Per's name was on their birth certificates, it meant that he was his and his sister's natural father. Kayleigh always thought that he had a point. None of their features were similar at all. Jamie had confronted his mother, looking for answers, a few months before his death, but she denied it, laughing it off as just another one of his 'crazy fantasies'. She would say to those people closest to her that his mind had been scrambled by an incident involving a girl that he had liked, and that he was in a state of delayed shock.

Per had been away for much of the past six months, working on the new house that he and Jamie's mother had bought in Finland, so there had been little chance to voice his concerns to the man he had known as his father for most of his life. He believed that Per would only side with his mother anyway, he always did, he never seemed to disagree with anything she said. Jamie had even considered buying a private DNA kit from a medical company on the internet and taking samples from Per's toothbrush the next time he returned to England. He had never told Kayleigh what prompted him to believe that his parents had been deceiving him for most of his life, but he seemed totally sure that his theory was right. When Kayleigh learned from Preston that a strange man had come looking for Jamie at the gym where he worked, the rumour started to gather pace.

Bree had told her that she did not share her brother's beliefs. She had always been a bit of a 'daddy's girl' and she idolised Per. She had even chosen to sit next to him rather than her mother at Jamie's funeral, saying that she found him a real source of comfort on that heart-wrenching day. One of Jamie's close friends had told Kayleigh that Bree had become very angry with Jamie recently, when he told her that he had discovered who their real father was and was arranging to meet him. But Bree made it very clear to him that the only father she ever wanted in her life was Per. The siblings rarely argued, especially in public, but the appearance of the unknown man who was looking for Jamie at the gym had created a massive rift between the two of them.

But somehow Jamie's theory had always made a lot of sense to Kayleigh and now the discovery of that photograph began to play on her mind. Bree's mother was much younger in that picture, at least twenty to twenty-five years younger. Kayleigh thought her mother looked stunning in the picture. She also realised how much Bree's mother looked like her daughter when she was younger. But she would never tell her friend that, knowing that her 'bestie' was desperate not to be associated with the woman she had recently been referring to as 'the bitch'.

Bree's mother had always maintained that her and Per had been together since their teens. It had been a college fling in their home town of Tampere that had blossomed into a fairytale romance. He even moved to England to be with her when she finished her studies at university. Maybe her mother had been lying, maybe she had met Per after they were born. Or maybe she had been having an affair behind Per's back. Now that really would give her friend more ammunition to fuel the growing hatred she seemed to have for her mother.

Whatever it was, Kayleigh thought it best to say nothing about that picture again. Maybe, when Bree was relaxing in her bath, she should find the photograph and hide it, better still destroy it. She promised herself to put today's discovery behind them and never mention it again. But as she placed the coffee cups on the table in her dining room, watching her broken friend sobbing as she stared out into oblivion from beneath the duvet cover, she was about to learn that she would never be able to keep that promise.

'Do you think,' Bree asked in a slightly croaky voice, 'do you think that the man in that photograph could be my real father?'

# CHAPTER NINE

I t had been two days since Poppy had ventured out of her flat. Her neck was still sore from the burning kettle water, her limbs still aching from the beating she had endured. The previous day she had rubbed after-sun lotion into the back of her head. The cream had soothed the throbbing in her skull, but now her hair felt as if it was glued to her scalp. Poppy was desperate to wash the makeshift healing solution out of her hair, but there was no hot water, the gas had run out, and Cameron had not felt obliged to put money on the key for the meter. So Poppy had to make do with several bowls of freezing cold water to wash out the shampoo she put in, her face twisted in pain each time she had to turn her head. She did her best to hide the scars left by the altercation, by brushing her hair down over her neck to cover the bright red marks. When she looked in the bathroom mirror she did not like the look of the girl staring back at her. She looked broken and dejected, she looked beaten. She took a deep breath and whispered under her breath, 'He will pay for doing that, Poppy, that bastard will pay for doing that!'

Having little credit left on her phone, Poppy had to text Danny to let him know why she had failed to turn up for her missing shifts. She told him that she had 'slipped' on the stairs outside her flat and had a sore back and behind. Danny did not believe her. He knew full well what was likely to have happened. He called her to assure her that he would pay her for the missing days but asked her to try her best to make it into work for that day. The restaurant was going to be extremely busy. He had a crowd celebrating a fortieth birthday due at Chez Blanc that lunchtime, as well as a number of regular bookings. She promised Danny that she would be there, she had to, she was desperate to get some cash for some tobacco. She had not had a cigarette for twenty-four hours and it was killing her inside.

Poppy had not eaten properly for two days. Cameron had spent her hard-earned tips on his own guilty pleasures. At least at the restaurant she knew that she could have a proper meal. She knew that her life could not get much worse at that point, but as she checked the text messages on her mobile she could see that Rahwaz was back on the warpath for his overdue rent. It was the first time he had ever mentioned 'eviction proceedings'. Poppy shook her head. She felt like giving up, but she never did, it wasn't in her DNA.

Cameron had, as he always had, apologised for his brutal outburst, blaming everything on the 'dodgy weed' that his friendly neighbourhood dealer had supplied him on that night. He did admit that he needed to find a solution to combat both his drug and anger problems. He knew that the two were related and even admitted that he could not control his jealous paranoia. But these were words, they were just words, hollow promises that she knew he would never keep. She often wondered why she never had the willpower just to get up and leave their flat. They were hardly a 'loving couple' these days, she struggled to remember the last time they had enjoyed sex together. But she felt a crazy sort of obligation towards him. He had been a constant in her life for more than ten years, even if one or the other of them had been serving time in prison for most of that period. He had been loyal to her, having defended her against the bully boys from the Marfield estate, risking an almighty beating in the process. But was that really a good enough reason to stay with someone?

When she arrived in the car park at the rear of Chez Blanc, Poppy tidied her hair, pulling it down as far as possible. She applied some fresh makeup to her pale and battered features and searched her car in the hope that she may have dropped a cigarette in there. She hadn't, she would have to face the day without that fix of nicotine.

'Nice of you to bother showing up, lass,' Matt said, as she passed him in the kitchen. 'Still looking as hot as ever!'

Poppy simply raised her middle finger towards the cheeky chef and mimed the words 'fuck off!' She was not in any frame of mind to suffer any of the Geordie's bullshit today. She made her way to the refrigerator and helped herself to some slices of fresh chicken to make a sandwich. She was famished.

'They will be here in about half an hour,' Danny said, as he entered the kitchen to collect some clean glasses. 'There are two extras coming, so there will be eighteen of them now. Did you sort the cake out, Matt?' The chef nodded. 'All done, boss, let's hope that none of them have any nut allergies.'

Danny suddenly noticed Poppy in the corner, a half-eaten sandwich in her hand. 'Thanks for coming in, love, it is going to be a bit manic today. We have that birthday bash, three tables of four and the walk-ins, so we needed you. Chantelle is out front. She is on her half-term holiday, so I gave her some extra hours this week. I thought we could do with another pair of hands.'

'I am fine now, Danny,' Poppy said. 'Just a bit sore, I will be fine.'

'Good girl,' he said rushing past her. 'Make sure you have plenty of white wine in the chiller, Matt, this lot sound like a right bloody bunch.'

'It's all women,' Matt said to Poppy as she finished her snack and started to prepare for work. 'Eighteen hot and horny lasses, some sort of hen-do to celebrate some woman's birthday.'

'Fuck me, Matt!' Poppy replied. 'Even you might get lucky if there are that many pissed women in the restaurant.' Matt's child-like grin beamed across his face. 'That is funny for you, Poppy, really funny. Maybe that fall you had has knocked a friendly personality into you.'

Poppy wrapped her apron around her waist. 'Don't bank on it, Matt, don't fucking bank on it!'

Danny had been right, within thirty minutes or so, a small cavalcade of taxis brought the group of women to Chez Blanc. The air turned blue as the rowdy bunch of forty to fifty-year-old ladies made their way to the tables that Danny had decorated with an assortment of coloured balloons.

'Get over here, girl!' shouted the largish women with her cleavage hanging over the top of her black dress. 'We need to get the bloody drinks sorted!' Chantelle stood still. She was clearly intimidated by the brash tone of the guest.

Danny intervened. 'I will take your drinks order, ladies. Poppy and Chantelle will look after your food requirements.'

The young waitress seemed noticeably nervous as she was joined by Poppy to oversee the diners' orders. 'Have you ever seen such a bunch of ugly old dogs in your life?' she asked her senior.

Poppy laughed. 'Just smile at the bitches,' she said. 'Don't let them get to you.'

When Danny had made a list of the drink requirements, he asked Chantelle to assist him, leaving Poppy to face the hen party alone. The group had settled in now, a sea of fake tan, vulgar fashion jewellery and oversized breast implants on view across their table. The women's conversation was coarse to say the least, but for Poppy this was nothing new. It was highly unlikely that anyone sitting at this table was going to unnerve her. A chubby woman, dressed in an ill-fitting leopardskin top, with badly bleached blonde hair and a strange piercing in her nose, seemed to have taken an instant dislike to Poppy and did nothing to hide it. 'Don't you ever smile, darling?' she asked, as the waitress passed around the menus. 'You have a face like a smacked arse!' Poppy ignored her comment and gave the woman one of her well-practised stares, the 'you wouldn't want to fuck with me!' stare that had served her so well in prison. The woman with the red stud on the side of her nostril was braver than most though. 'Moody bitch!' she said, returning Poppy's stare with one of her own. Poppy soon realised that she was going to be tested to the full today. The throbbing pain in her neck wasn't helping matters much either. She left the women chatting as they looked over their menus and walked away. The less time she spent near that woman, the better, she thought.

As Poppy returned to the kitchen Matt was busy showing his new sous chef, Anton, the best way to prepare courgette fritters. The northerner was proud of the way his dishes were served and liked everything to look just right. He caught Poppy's eye as she passed him. He could sense that she was in a bad mood by the look on her face. 'How is it looking out there, gorgeous?' he asked. 'How hot are those ladies?'

Poppy smirked, having studied the rough and rowdy crowd of women in the restaurant. 'Right up your street, Matt, right up your street!'

As Poppy reached to the top shelf to get some clean serviettes she felt a sharp stabbing sensation rip down her back. It shot through her like a hot needle. She tried to hide the pain on her face, but it had not gone unnoticed. 'He has hit you again, hasn't he?' Matt said. Poppy carried on with the task in hand before Matt asked her again. 'Your bloke, he hit you, didn't he?'

Poppy brushed past him and headed back to the ever-growing din coming from the hen party. 'It is none of your business, Matt!' Poppy said bluntly. 'So keep your beak out of it!'

The restaurant was alive now. Smutty innuendos and dirty laughter filled the air as the group of women became more intoxicated. The large woman in the leopardskin top still seemed to be targeting Poppy. She had her fully in her sights now, imitating her serving manner and sullen look, much to the amusement of her fellow party guests. Poppy heard the phrases 'grumpy-faced bitch' and 'chavvy skank' aimed in her direction several times from the newly formed 'Poppy Hate Club' but still managed to retain her composure. It would take more than a few insults from some middle-aged harpies to set her off on this day, despite those ever-growing pains tormenting her beaten limbs.

Danny was pleased to see his restaurant so busy at lunchtime. The birthday group were taking up half of the dining area and the rest of the tables were now full. Poor Chantelle was struggling to keep up with the pace that day, leaving most of the work to her senior, a fact that had not gone unnoticed by the owner of Chez Blanc. He made a mental note to reward her efforts with a larger share of any tips that night, something he often did to show his appreciation for Poppy's efforts.

With the birthday party tucking into their main courses and Danny taking care of the drinks, Poppy decided to take a cigarette break. Luckily for her, Anton was a smoker and gave her a couple of ciggies. The new assistant chef probably did not realise it at that time, but he had become her saviour that day. Matt had noticed how hard Poppy had been working with very little help from her junior. 'I think the young lass is out of her depth today,' he said.

'She is just a lazy bitch!' Poppy replied. 'Danny should get rid of her, she is fucking useless!'

As Poppy began to riffle her bag in search of a lighter, she noticed a shape in the kitchen doorway, a large shape. It was the leader of the 'Poppy Hate Club'. 'The toilets are down there,' Matt explained, pointing down the narrow corridor. 'You can't come in here, you know, health and safety and all that.'

The woman eyed Matt up and down and grinned. 'You are a fine-looking young man,' she said, as she squeezed his arm in search of his muscles. 'Why don't you come and join us at the table? Come and have a drink with the girls.'

The cheeky northerner let out a nervous laugh. 'You really shouldn't be in here,' he said, taking a step back from her grasp. The woman with the pierced nose was persistent. She smiled at the chef and ran her hand up his trouser leg in the direction of his groin.

Suddenly Poppy reacted to the woman's unwelcome intrusion. 'Are you deaf as well as stupid?' she asked. 'He told you that you shouldn't be in here, so fuck off! The toilets are down the corridor to the left.'

Suddenly, the woman moved her hand from Matt's leg and fixed her eyes on Poppy. She swiftly sidestepped the chef to vent her anger. 'Who the hell do you think you are?' she asked the waitress.

Poppy put down her handbag to face her enemy full on, looking around the kitchen area to assess the battleground. Something told Poppy that she needed to take a deep breath and find some soothing colours in her head, but the pain in her neck and side and the presence of the tyrant in front of her was making that increasingly difficult. The women were barely two feet apart now, eyeball to eyeball. Poppy was smaller in stature than her opponent, but that never bothered her. She bit the corner of her lip hard. It seemed now as if both women were resolved to conflict. Matt tried his best to defuse the situation. 'Come on, girls,' he said, 'it is only a silly mistake, I am sure it is not worth arguing over.'

The kitchen intruder was not for backing down. 'You have been a mardy bitch all day,' she said. 'I should teach you some fucking manners.' Poppy said nothing, her eyes fixed firmly on her target. The woman tried a little harder to intimidate her opponent. 'Trust me, girl, my bite is much worse than my fucking bark!'

Matt knew that it was time to act, the tension was growing, this confrontation was destined to escalate further. He tried one last time to reason with the duo before they locked horns, but his effort was short-lived as the angry woman took another step towards the stubborn waitress. In the blink of an eye Poppy had reached down to the table by her side and produced a knife, a long, sharp carving knife that was now pointing firmly at her aggressor, the shiny blade resting just a few inches from her startled face. 'Come anywhere near me, you bitch,' Poppy snarled, 'and I will cut one of those fat fucking chins off your face!'

There was a few seconds' silence. The woman with all the bravado was in complete shock. Her feet slowly began to backtrack. Matt wanted to speak but had been struck dumb by the sudden turn of events.

'She is a fucking headcase!' the woman said as she moved back to the safety of the kitchen doorway. 'She is a fucking loony!'

Matt felt like agreeing with her, but also felt it his duty to support his co-worker. 'She has had a really tough day,' he said. 'She wouldn't really hurt you, would you, Poppy?' The waitress said nothing, her outstretched arm still pointing the weapon in the direction of the shaken diner. Poor Anton was shell shocked. He had already retreated to the relative safety of the rear entrance.

Danny walked in at that point, complaining that one of the group of women had spilled half a bottle of claret onto the carpet. He walked past the shaken woman and Matt and headed for the washbasins. 'Put it down now, love,' he said, firmly but calmly, as if the object in Poppy's hand was a potato peeler, rather than a ten-inch carving knife. 'Put it down and give me a hand with the birthday cake.' She followed his instruction but maintained full eye contact with her enemy who was still perched in the kitchen doorway. Finally, the woman with the bad hair and leopardskin top decided to return to her table with a parting shot at the restaurant owner. 'She is a fucking psycho, that one, you should keep her on a leash.'

Danny laughed it off and began adding the finishing touches to the birthday cake with some bright candles, mumbling quietly under his breath, 'Three years, six months and four days, God, that ex-wife of mine is a bitch, a fucking bitch!'

The storm in the kitchen had calmed and now it was the turn of Chantelle to be on the receiving end of the rowdy hen party. She started by complaining that the women, now extremely intoxicated, had been dishing out non-stop abuse. 'She said I looked like a boy,' she moaned. 'That woman with the pink streaks in her hair, she said I looked like a little boy, because I don't have any tits.'

Matt did his best to hide his laughter and carried on preparing some desserts for some of the other customers. 'Can I take a break now?' Poppy asked the restaurant owner. 'I have been flat out since I got here.'

Danny nodded. 'They are starting to leave now anyway. Take a couple of hours, we can manage here. I am going out this evening, there are not many in, so it will just be you and Matt.'

Poppy grabbed her bag and jacket and headed for the back door. She was followed swiftly by the chef who called out to her. 'Why don't you go back to my flat? It is just around the corner. You can use the shower and stuff and chill out for a while if you like.' This is usually the point where Poppy would tell the Geordie lad to 'get lost' or words to that effect, but she found his mention of a hot shower enticing, after all it had been more than four days since her body had seen the bathtub. The well-meaning chef scribbled down his address and gave her brief directions. 'No point taking your car,' he said, 'it is only a five-minute walk. The security number for the main door is at the bottom of the address.'

Poppy wanted to show her gratitude in some way, but it wasn't in her nature. She simply took the keys and the address and started walking. 'Ta,' she said, as if she was doing him a favour. As she was about to leave, Matt mentioned that there was some cocoa butter in his bathroom cabinet which might help the swelling on her neck. Lighting up a cigarette to accompany her on her short walk, Poppy checked her mobile for messages. None of them were good, so she switched her phone off. *Fuck you all!* she thought.

Poppy was surprised when she entered Matt's flat, everything looked so prim and proper. The place had a distinct smell of lilacs, probably down to the number of air fresheners scattered around the living room. The wooden floors shone as though they had been polished that morning and the array of pictures on the walls looked as if they had been organised by a professional photographer. The flat resembled a show home, something you might find in a magazine. She decided to have a look around before taking her shower. She was curious to see if the squeaky-clean chef, who was always so clean-cut and well mannered, had any dark secrets hidden in his home.

The living room was spacious. An expensive-looking red leather sofa sat facing the large television screen mounted on the wall. There was a glass table in the middle of the room, with a neatly arranged assortment of fruit staring at her from a shiny bowl. Nothing was out of place. Pushing open the door to Matt's bedroom, she had a browse through his wardrobe, three sets of dazzling bright chef whites on one side, a dozen or so smart jackets and shirts on the other. Everything was neat and tidy and well laid out, somewhat different to her own abode, which often resembled a section of a landfill site. She noticed that the top drawer of his bedside cabinet was slightly open. Maybe this is where she could find something sinister, she thought, maybe he secretly wore frilly knickers or had leather thongs tucked away in there for secret sex parties. Her curiosity got the better of her and she opened the drawer. There was no erotic underwear, there were some expensive-looking underpants sporting a fancy label, but certainly not erotic. As she looked closer she could see that tucked away in the corner of the drawer was a large bundle of cash, £500, £600, maybe £700 in £20 notes. Something in Poppy's head told her that he wouldn't miss a few of those and she scooped up three of them and tucked them inside her trouser pocket. She completed her examination of his room before heading into the bathroom, where she was met with the aroma of jasmine and lavender. The shiny bath and toilet were spotless, even his toothbrush looked as though it was waiting to be photographed, as it sat at an angle in its holder. *He must have a cleaner*, Poppy thought, *nobody is this clean!*

The steaming hot spray from the shower hit Poppy full on. She stood there for a full two minutes before reaching for the shower gel. It felt so refreshing, as if the water was cleansing her inside and out. She covered herself with streams of soapy lather. They rushed over her bruised and battered body, bringing some much-needed comfort to her aching limbs. Her hair got the full treatment now. She was more than generous with the application of shampoo she ran through her greasy mane. She recognised the shampoo bottle as an expensive brand she had once stolen in her shoplifting days. It took a full ten minutes to get all the sticky traces of after-sun out of her tangled locks of hair. It felt good, she felt good, she felt as if she had come back to life.

Wrapping herself in Matt's large fluffy white bathrobe, Poppy made her way into the living room and headed for the kitchen area at the back. After opening the refrigerator in search of some refreshments she suddenly noticed something familiar. There perched nicely on the wine rack beside the fridge were four bottles of Moobuzz Pinot Noir. They were identical to the ones that Danny served at Chez Blanc. A coincidence? Poppy didn't think so. 'Who's a naughty boy, Matt!' she said, as she bent down to look more closely at the contents of his neatly organised shelves in the refrigerator. Poppy suddenly noticed a small amount of fresh salmon. She could swear that it was the same type of wrapping that Danny's fish supplier used. 'Matt! Matt! Matt!' she said, realising that she had found a chink in the friendly northerner's armour. 'You really are a dark horse!' She poured herself a large glass of the fruity wine and helped herself to some ham and cheese to make a sandwich.

When she had eaten, Poppy fetched the cocoa butter from the bathroom cabinet and began to apply it to her neck. She didn't stop there, pulling out large scoops of the soothing cream and covering whole areas of her yellowing skin. Cameron's hefty kicks had certainly done their job, the bruises had covered most of her body. Her aches and pains felt slightly better when she had finished. The mental scars of her beating, however, would never fade.

It was time for her to have another look around. Poppy had uncovered one of Matt's hidden secrets, maybe she would find some others? It amazed her just how immaculate everything was laid out in his flat. Did he have a cleaner or maybe a secret girlfriend that he had never mentioned? Back in the lounge she studied the photographs standing proudly on the long glass cabinet beneath the television. There were several of him with an older couple. One of the pictures seemed to be a graduation. Matt was wearing one of those funny gowns. It did not take a genius to know that the older man in the picture was of his father, the two of them sharing the same large ears and inane grin. Poppy opened a few more drawers and cupboards, not quite sure what she was looking for. She didn't know why, but she was becoming more curious about the lifestyle of the man she had belittled for the past eight months. When she had finished her investigation, she concluded that she had been wrong about him all along. Yes, he was a lecherous chancer, full of sexist remarks and smutty innuendos, but in her small friendless world, who else would have trusted her with the keys to this place?

A feeling of guilt, an unusual emotion for Poppy, suddenly struck her, and she realised that she should not abuse her colleague's generosity. She replaced the £60 she had taken from his drawer and cleaned up the crumbs she had dropped onto his shiny floor. If nothing else, Poppy learned that day that she did indeed have a friend 'of sorts' in Matt.

\* \* \*

By the time Poppy had returned to the restaurant everyone had left, apart from the Geordie lad, who was busy preparing some vegetables for the evening sitting. She still felt no obligation to offer her thanks for the use of his shower and flat but did at least offer him something of a small smile as she entered. 'I see you found the shampoo,' Matt said smelling the side of her head. 'It's really nice that one.' Danny had left an envelope with £30 inside. He was aware that his waitress had little or no money to her name that day so gave her a share of the tips from the busy lunchtime session. Strangely, the woman running the 'Poppy Hate Club' did not contribute to the gratuity left by the hen party.

Chez Blanc was quiet that night, so Danny had picked a good time to take an evening away from his place of business. There were only ten customers served during the whole evening – two couples, a mother and daughter and a table of four women, who, despite being slightly drunk when they left the restaurant, had behaved like nuns compared to the lunchtime gaggle of hens at the birthday bash. By ten thirty the restaurant was empty. Matt locked the doors before pouring himself and Poppy a large glass of wine.

'Wow! What a day!' the ever-smiling chef declared. 'I really thought you had lost the plot earlier.' Poppy downed a mouthful of the refreshing wine and sat herself down at one of the tables that had yet to be cleaned. She would have loved a post-service cigarette to enjoy with her drink, but she had smoked the other one given to her by Anton on the way back from Matt's flat. Making his way to the CD player located at the side of the bar, Matt sifted through some of Danny's collection before settling on an R&B compilation. 'Where do you think Danny has gone tonight?' he asked. 'Maybe he is out on a date, maybe he has been on dating websites and we don't know.'

Poppy was not impressed with his comment. 'Don't take the piss, Matt, just because he doesn't try to chat up the women that come in here, it doesn't mean he has to find someone. He still misses his wife, he would take her back in a heartbeat.'

Matt laughed. 'Calm down, lass, I was only saying. I like Danny, I like him a lot.'

Poppy made it clear where her loyalties lay. 'Well don't take the piss out of him then or maybe I will have to tell him how much you also like his special wine.'

The chef looked puzzled for a few seconds and then his boyish grin reappeared as he realised what she meant. 'Danny and I have an arrangement,' he said. 'He lets me have a dozen bottles each month at cost. It helps him get a bigger discount with the supplier. It's a win-win for both of us.'

Poppy was not convinced. 'Yeah, yeah, sure, Matt, whatever you say!'

It was not often that the two of them were left alone together. Matt hoped that his earlier act of kindness would have helped break down a few barriers between them. He thought that this time alone would be a good chance to get to know Poppy a little better. 'So, tell me more about you, tell me about the real Poppy.'

Poppy frowned and poured herself another glass of wine. 'What are you, Matt, a therapist? You sound just like my probation officer.'

'So, there is one thing, let's start there, you are on probation. What is that for?'

'Fuck off, Matt!'

'Tell me something else then, something that no one else knows about you.'

Poppy thought for a few seconds before giving her response. 'OK, my boyfriend is over six feet tall and very violent. He hates Geordies, especially pervy ones!'

Matt laughed. 'That's funny, that's really funny. Tell me, why do you let him get away with it, hitting you I mean, why do you put up with it? There, that's another question.'

Poppy shook her head. 'It's none of your business, Matt, keep your beak out, OK?'

'OK, calm down, lass. What about that woman today, what pushed you over the edge?'

'I was nowhere near the edge, Matt, trust me, you wouldn't want to see me pushed over the edge.'

'For Christ's sake, Poppy! You went from nought to psycho in a split second, you pointed a carving knife in her face.'

'She deserved it, she was a bully.'

'Bully?'

'I met her type in prison, they think they own the fucking world, but when push comes to shove they are just all talk and no action.'

Matt was shocked. 'You were inside, you were really in prison?'

Poppy ignored his question. Checking the clock on her mobile phone, she decided it was time to go home. Despite the application of the cocoa butter, her body still ached. She thought an early night might be a good tonic for her. In the back of her mind she didn't want to give her boyfriend any reason to punish her again. She finished the remnants of the wine in her glass and made her way to the staff toilet. Matt was still stunned by her revelation and thought it best to end his questioning there. Poppy stood looking into the bathroom mirror, turning her head slightly. Beneath the bright lights, she could make out the red marks made by the boiling water. She pulled her hair down slightly to hide them. Suddenly Poppy became aware that she was not alone. Matt had followed her and was watching her from the shadows in the corridor. Within a few seconds he had made his way into the small bathroom and was directly behind her.

'Fuck off, Matt!' Poppy said. 'I have had enough of your silly questions for one night.' The chef ignored her. Moving a little closer, he was right behind her now. She could see his reflection clearly in the mirror. There was that smile, that confident yet extremely irritating smile. Before she knew what was happening, Matt had put his hands on her waist. Poppy swiftly pushed them away. 'Matt, stop fucking around! I swear you will be sorry.' But the Geordie lad was going nowhere, his hands returned to her waist before slowly moving upwards. He began cupping her firm breasts. Poppy started to wriggle her way free from his grasp. She turned around to face him.

Matt had a sickly smile, the one she hated. It was beaming all the way across his face, it was making her blood boil. 'Come on,' he said, 'I know you like me.'

Something began to snap inside Poppy's head, she felt her anger slowly rising. 'So what is this then, Matt?' she asked. 'You let me use your shower and shampoo and expect a fuck in return?'

Matt's hands slowly moved down and held her wrists tightly. 'Come on, Poppy,' he said. 'Just one kiss.' With that he leaned down and aimed his mouth towards hers. She turned her head before he could connect with her lips and he caught her cheek.

Poppy was getting angrier by the second. 'Matt!' she barked, her tone becoming louder and more direct. 'Do yourself a favour and let me go, I swear, Matt, you will be sorry, you will be very sorry!'

The jolly northerner ignored her comment. He had a look of stealthy determination in his eyes. He lunged forward in another attempt to kiss her. Poppy's head began to spin. She didn't want to find any calming colours passing through her thoughts at that second, all she wanted to do was break free and kick this big lump in front of her in his testicles, as hard as she could. But Poppy chose another weapon, one that would completely degrade the chef and leave him in no doubt what her feelings truly were for him. As the Geordie lad towered over her, Poppy rolled around as much spit in her dry mouth as she could. A small smile cracked on her lips, before she swung her head and delivered the full ball of messy phlegm directly into his face. *That will teach him*, she thought, *that will teach him to mess around with me.*

There was a brief silence, apart from some heavy breathing, then, suddenly, Matt's smile returned and one of his hands released Poppy's arm and moved upwards towards his head. His fingers caught the ball of spit and he rubbed it down his cheek and across his face into his mouth. Poppy's breathing became heavier. The look of rage on her face had been replaced with one of confusion. *What the hell is he doing?* she thought. But something strange began to evolve inside Poppy's head. The venom had gone, she wasn't angry, she wasn't anything, anything except extremely turned on by his crazy reaction. She felt a tingle rip through her body, she was excited, she could sense something strange was happening to her. Suddenly her head lunged towards him and her lips met his with a mighty force. Her tongue entered his mouth and rolled around inside, reclaiming some of her own spit, which she swallowed. Matt squeezed her tightly as they shared the embrace. She was aching for him now, she wanted him, she wanted him badly. Within seconds her trousers were undone and lying on the bathroom floor alongside his chef whites. The strong northerner lifted her from the floor and perched her bottom firmly on the basin. It wobbled slightly as she moved her frame to get more comfortable. His hands ran over her body and reached up inside her top, unbuttoning her bra with one click of his finger. His began grabbing her breasts firmly and tugging hard at her erect nipples. Poppy could feel herself down between her legs, she was moist, she was wet, she wanted him inside her now. She did not have to wait long. His hands reached down and ripped at her knickers. They came apart like sheets of cheap kitchen tissue. Poppy moaned loudly as first one and then a second of Matt's fingers found their soaking target. They were still kissing, a deep sensuous all-engaging kiss, when he moved forward and entered her, thrusting his whole manhood inside her. It felt huge, it hurt her, but in a good way. Her eyes began to roll as she bit hard on her lip. As Matt's tool began to move inside her wet cavity, Poppy's scalded head hit the mirror repeatedly as she rocked backwards and forwards. She could feel those bruises on her body now, they were stinging, but she felt no pain, just pleasure, pure pleasure. A bead of sweat appeared on Matt's forehead, as his body jerked back and forth. Poppy let out another groan as the thrusting continued, still in a state of erotic confusion. Half of her wanted to cut him, to stab him, to slice him up, rip him to pieces, but the other half of her just wanted him to carry on, not to stop, never to stop. It did carry on, for what seemed to be an age, but was probably no more than a few moments. His thrusts became deeper and much harder, Poppy's moans became louder and much longer. 'Don't stop!' she screamed. 'Don't fucking stop!'

Suddenly the basin beneath Poppy's bottom began to shake and tremble as if it was going to fall off the wall. Matt's movements became more rapid and his noisy panting became much heavier. Poppy let out another scream of passion. Finally, just as Poppy's nails ripped into Matt's fleshy back, his whole body jerked violently and moved upwards as he reached his climax, letting out a screeching yell as if his team had scored a winning goal in a cup final.

The pair of them remained locked together for a few seconds, entwined in a mess of flesh and body fluids. The moment of madness was over. They were both breathing heavily. Neither one could find the energy to speak. Poppy's legs still quivered beneath her as Matt slowly pulled himself away from her body. When she moved down from the basin Poppy grabbed the chef tightly fearing that her legs might give way. She was finding it very hard to hide the smile of satisfaction on her blushing face. Matt was red-cheeked and still breathing hard. He pulled up his trousers and stood over his shell-shocked colleague, waiting for her to break the silence.

Finally, as Poppy began to recover the feeling in her legs, she looked up and gave the sweating Geordie a harsh stare. 'You are in big trouble now,' she said. 'Do you know what they do to rapists in prison?'

'Rape?' Matt said, still trying to catch his breath. 'You enjoyed that as much as I did.'

Poppy shook her head. Her voice was weak, but she made her statement very clear. 'That was just wrong, Matt, that was just so fucking wrong!'

The Geordie buttoned up his trousers and left the waitress in a state of both bewilderment and complete ecstasy, a strange mix for Poppy to come to terms with. As he walked away toward the kitchen area, he shouted back at her, 'That was incredible, I need a drink!' Poppy, still shocked by the episode, slipped on her bra and did up her work shirt as fast as she could. Her head told her a hundred things to do next. She decided that leaving the restaurant as quickly as she could was without doubt her best option.

As Matt arrived back in the corridor with a bottle of wine and two glasses, he caught a glimpse of Poppy's green bomber jacket as she exited Chez Blanc through the back entrance. He thought about calling out her name, but something told him that it was better to just let her go. Neither he nor Poppy knew why what had just happened had indeed happened, but strangely, neither of them felt guilty for their behaviour. If anything, they both felt a warm glow inside their bodies, something that would last for at least a few hours.

# CHAPTER TEN

Poppy lay back in her steaming hot bath of foamy bubbles, her headspace fully occupied by the crazy events of the previous night. She was pleased that she gone into work the day before. The money she had earned in tips had helped her to get the heating and hot water back on in the flat, not that Cameron had shown any real appreciation for her efforts. Poppy replayed her encounter with the Geordie chef over and over in her head but could not come up with any logical reason for having had sex with him. She didn't fancy him, God, she didn't even like him, why the hell did she have sex with him? It wasn't like she was that vulnerable teenager anymore, the one that would be so high on pills, the one that might end the night with some random guy who happened to be paying her attention. No, this was different, very different. Despite the fact she felt no shame for what she had done, she was worried that things might be awkward for her now at the restaurant. Worse still, she feared that Matt would have got the wrong idea and now thought that she had wanted him all along.

Her train of thought was broken by Cameron entering the bathroom. She covered her soapy breasts with her hands, she didn't know why. Maybe she should stand up and wipe the suds down from her body to reveal the bruising he had inflicted on her earlier that week, shame him, on the spot. But she couldn't be bothered, she felt relaxed that morning and not in the mood for any form of conflict.

'I am going over to see my mum this afternoon,' he said. 'It is her birthday tomorrow. I thought I would buy her a card and take her some chocolates or something.' Poppy had been on the receiving end of this line of conversation a hundred times before, she knew what was coming next. 'I don't suppose you have a tenner that I can borrow until pay day.'

That expression always angered Poppy, him constantly referring to the day he received his benefits as 'pay day'. She often felt like saying to him, 'It is not pay day, Cameron, it is not your wages, you have not done any work to receive wages. No one would pay you to sit on your fat lazy arse all day, smoking weed and watching daytime television. It is not a job, Cameron, you don't get paid wages, you are just a fucking benefits scrounger!' But today she had no energy. She pointed him at her work trousers lying on the living room floor. 'There are two fivers in the front pocket,' she told him. 'Don't take the change, Cam, I need to get some milk and bread before I go to work.'

Her boyfriend left the flat with a smile on his face and the £10 in his pocket. She was pleased that he had gone and left her with her thoughts. It was worth that money to get him out of her way for the morning. If only he knew, she thought, what had happened at the restaurant the previous night. She shuddered to think what kind of damage he would inflict on the softly spoken northerner. The poor chef certainly wouldn't have that sickly grin left on his face by the time Cameron had finished with him.

Poppy had more than an hour before she needed to set off for the restaurant. She turned on the hot tap to top up her bath water and lay back. She enjoyed a good long soak in the tub. It always reminded her of her friend Nikita and the crazy days in the tower block at the side of the Marfield estate. The local council had given Nikita the flat after she won back custody of her son Zain. The high-rise block of flats, Rutland Towers, was very modest to say the least. The walls of the outer building were in a state of decay and were covered in badly spelt graffiti. Young children would be playing games beside the abandoned dog faeces which often littered the path to the entrance.

Inside the flat there were small cracks in the walls, a grubby carpet that looked as if it had been there for more than thirty years and a cooker that was heavily lined with a film of thick grease. There was a terrible smell in the place too, a sort of musky stale smell that seemed to have an immunity to normal air fresheners. But it was a place to stay, a dry place to stay, a better option than living rough on the streets or in the confines of a prison. The flat was sixteen floors up in the air. The lift, when it wasn't out of order, often bore the strong stench of cannabis, puke and fresh urine. By the time you arrived at the sixteenth floor you either felt physically sick or on the way to a happy place for the day. When the lift was out of use the girls would have to brave the stairway where they would often be confronted with an array of used condoms and syringes, abandoned by addicts from the estate. Yes, it was bleak and dirty, a 'shithole in the sky', but it was their 'shithole in the sky', and for a while it felt like a real home.

There were a thousand ways you could describe the effervescent Nikita Pearson. The girl was barely five feet in height, but the kooky pixie with glowing emerald green eyes and an enchanting smile stood out like a sore thumb wherever she went. She had long dark hair that was always wrapped in two messy buns on her head, a dozen tiny rings covering the lobes of each ear and a tattoo bearing the name of her son emblazoned on her neck. She was extremely hyper-active, an untamed fireball of unbridled energy, often talking at one hundred miles per hour. She had a head full of torrid stories from her past and strange one-liners about her views on life.

Nikita and Poppy had met at the Medway Young Offenders Centre shortly after Poppy's release from the segregation unit following her altercation with Meghan Masters. Poppy had been something of a loner during her spell in Medway, but despite her notoriety, following the incident with Meghan, she had no time for the inmates queueing up to be her friend. Poppy trusted no one, not, that is, until she met Nikita. The other girls in the institution had taken an instant dislike to the pint-sized girl with the 'Minnie Mouse' hairstyle, seeing her as an easy target for their bullying. But Poppy liked the tiny waif with a look of mischievous craziness in her eyes and the two of them became instant friends. Any thoughts that the other inmates had of intimidating Nikita vanished the minute Poppy declared, 'You mess with her, you mess with me!'

The two sixteen-year-old girls found that they had much in common, having been placed in some of the same foster homes in the Kent area and both having spent time at the infamous Bluebridge children's home. Poppy soon discovered that she had not been the only target for the sexual predator Mr Donovan at Bluebridge. Her new friend had also endured his sexual harassment. Nikita had been sent to the young offenders centre for possession of a large quantity of cocaine, coupled with a string of offences for shoplifting. She had owned up to her robbing spree from more than twenty department stores, but felt she received rough justice when it came to the possession charges. Her boyfriend, a well-known dealer, had left her to face the police when they raided his hotel room in Thurrock. Unfortunately for Nikita, she had been high on mamba and was in the grip of some form of hallucination at the time of the raid. For some unknown reason she owned up to everything. The state she had been in at that time she would have probably claimed that she also killed John F. Kennedy and planned the Great Train Robbery. But Essex police were keen to make an example of her, and they succeeded, the district judge handing her a nine-month sentence for her misdemeanours. Her 'so-called' boyfriend was never caught, he was last seen hitchhiking on a motorway, somewhere near Manchester.

The girls shared an experience at Medway which would create an unbreakable bond between the duo. It was a day that neither would ever forget. It was also an experience that brought home the stark reality of how tough life could be in those dark surroundings. The pair had skipped a workshop programme to share a cigarette behind the canteen building. The centre was short-staffed at the time, so it was unlikely that they would be missed by any of the warders. When the girls moved to the back of the building they noticed what they thought was a bundle of clothes hanging from one of the windows. They were amused at first, both agreeing that it was a crazy plan to escape from the place, when the makeshift ladder would only take the escapee into the prison courtyard. But when the pair moved closer to see the bundle swinging in the morning breeze, it revealed the dangling body of one of the girls from their wing. Even though her face was twisted and had turned a deep shade of mauve, they recognised the hanging figure instantly as Chloe Beaumont. She was swinging backwards and forwards above them, hanging by her neck from what looked to be a thick white wire. The girls had completely different reactions to the horrifying spectacle, Nikita heaving up the contents of her breakfast in shock, while Poppy simply stood there, studying the tormented look on the hanging girl's face, seemingly fascinated by the tragic event. It was the first time that Poppy had ever seen a dead body close up, but even then, something told her it would not be the last. The girls raised the alarm, but the warders were unsuccessful in their attempts to revive poor Chloe. She was pronounced dead almost as soon as the paramedics arrived. The rumours began to circulate around Medway that Chloe had taken her own life because she had found out that her boyfriend had been cheating on her. Other inmates were sure that it had been the fact that her stepfather was responsible for impregnating her fourteen-year-old sister. The more astute girls at the institution worked out that her boyfriend and her stepfather were, in fact, the same person.

Chloe may, or may not, have been clever enough to work out the act of treachery for herself. She was, however, clever enough to convert an extension cable she had stolen for the television room into a makeshift noose, and she had done a bloody good job of it too! Medway received a barrage of negative press coverage following the incident. Staff shortages and a lack of psychiatric support at the centre were highlighted as the main reasons for the tragedy. It later transpired in a national newspaper exposé of the youth offenders centre that this was the third suicide in as many years at Medway. An independent inquiry was promised but there were no noticeable changes made to the place in the years that followed.

Poppy was released from Medway the month after Chloe's suicide. She would not see Nikita again for more than two years. The circumstances of their reunion would hardly be described as ideal. Both girls had moved up a level or two in their search for a 'happy' place in their heads. Poppy had become a regular user of crack cocaine, while her impish friend was now injecting heroin. Poppy had found her friend sleeping rough beneath a viaduct in Thamesmead, on a bitter cold February evening. She would not have recognised Nikita had it not been for the messy buns, which were now coated with a thick film of grease and were scruffier than ever. The sparkle in those emerald eyes had been replaced with a look of despair, her gaunt, pallid face bore the blotchy marks of self-neglect. She had lost weight, not that she had had much weight to lose in the first place. The little pixie's bright smile had been replaced with an array of yellowy rotting teeth. She resembled a walking corpse.

Poppy took her friend back to the hostel room she stayed in and did her best to support her. Nikita confessed to Poppy that she had recently turned to prostitution to find the money to feed her habit, but a couple of beatings from other street workers and a nasty dose of chlamydia had turned her off the idea. She had turned to begging as a final resort but barely raised enough money each day to pay for her fix. This was a deeply traumatic time for Poppy, watching someone she cared for 'on the rattle', unable to find any blankets of comfort to keep her safe from the demons inside her head. One morning Poppy woke to find that her friend had gone, simply vanished, as if she had never been there at all.

Poppy thought that she might never see Nikita again. She feared that she might have gone back to working the streets and simply become another sad victim of the lifestyle she had chosen. But she was wrong. Two years on from their brief reunion in Thamesmead they met up again. Poppy had just served her first term in an adult prison, a massive learning curve for the girl who couldn't keep her temper under control. She had received a fifteen-month sentence for handing out a severe beating to a drunken youth and his girlfriend outside a takeaway restaurant. The argument had been over nothing more than queue-jumping, hardly a valid reason to lose your liberty. Try telling that to Poppy!

On her release from HMP New Hall in Leeds, Poppy returned to South London and stayed in a halfway house paid for by the government. Her new home, if that is what you could call it, was a dilapidated bed and breakfast hotel. It was just a stone's throw away from 'The Marfield', the run-down council estate on the outskirts of Woolwich.

The Marfield estate was a place full of crackheads, single mothers and rudderless teens with no direction in life, a purpose-built fortress of degradation and depravity for those at the bottom of the social ladder. It was there that she bumped into her favourite 'little fireball of mischievous mayhem' again. Poppy had gone to the estate hoping to team up with her old boyfriend Cameron but discovered that he had recently been incarcerated himself for assaulting two police officers and wouldn't be back on his old stomping ground for many months. It was that crazy head of hair that caught her attention again. The vivacious little 'pixie' was back. Poppy saw her entering the tower block at the edge of the estate and screamed her name at the top of her voice. Within hours she had abandoned her bed at the sheltered housing address and moved her small bag of belongings into Nikita's flat. This was a new beginning, a new start, on the sixteenth floor of Rutland Towers, in their very own 'little shithole in the sky'.

Nikita had been through a turbulent couple of years – the death of her older brother, a victim of an unsolved knife crime, a four-month spell in a residential rehab centre and to top it all, childbirth! The tiny-framed girl now had a son. Zain was Nikita's world. His arrival had brought back lots of the endearing qualities that Poppy had seen in her friend during their Medway days. Those sparkling green eyes had returned to their rightful place, her moments of mischief and madness and crazy ideas about the true meaning of life were there too. The real Nikita was back in the land of the living and her friend was over the moon. Poppy never found out who Zain's father was, her tiny friend refused to talk about it. It might have been that Nikita never actually knew herself, but it didn't seem to bother her at all. She told Poppy that her son had been a gift from a heavenly place and that her destiny was to love him, protect him and make him a better person than she had been in her troubled life.

The day after Poppy moved into her new abode she received a payment from the local council, money that was meant to help her buy new clothes for job interviews and for living expenses. She decided that those luxuries could be shelved for a few weeks, there were other priorities, much more pressing priorities. Half of the money was spent at a seedy tattoo parlour, where the girls had their nicknames for one another inked inside a purple heart-shaped tattoo on their right thighs. Both 'Nixie Girl' and 'Popsy Girl' were more than happy with the results, even if they did both suffer from the experience for several days after. The remainder of Poppy's rehabilitation money was spent with a dealer she knew on the estate, mainly on skunk and some 'Molly' pills. It wasn't what Poppy had hoped for, but it transpired that the supplier of crack cocaine was apparently having an 'unexpected' holiday at Her Majesty's pleasure.

The friends would often share bubble baths together, not just to save on the gas bills, but because it was the place where the two of them could dare to dream. Their bath nights would usually start when Zain was tucked up in bed and the only noises that could be heard were the thumping reggae beats rising from the flat below. The girls would lie back, at opposite ends of the bathtub, sharing a large joint and a bottle of cheap vodka, as the world simply turned around them. Their conversations could sometimes become quite intense, when they would talk about their pasts and discuss their hopes and fears, not that Poppy held many fears. Nikita always had her own take on life. She had captured a million one-liners, many of them could have come straight out of a philosopher's handbook. 'All those people with money,' she once said, during bath night, 'the ones who look down their noses at us, they forget, they forget that we are all born equal. Two arms, two legs, a head and a heart, we all have those. Some may think that having money makes them a better person, but while we are asleep and when we die there is no difference between us, we are all equal.'

One night in their bathtub of bubbles and dreams, the girls created a list, a simple list of the names of all the people that had wronged them during their time in care. The bullies and the heavy-handed ones were marked at the bottom of the list, with the vile perverts and sexual predators nearer the top. Mr Donovan was very high up on both girls' calculations, but Mr Houghton was at the top of the list, he would always be at the top of the list for Poppy. It started as a 'Hate list' but ended up being a 'Kill list', the girls adding different ways that they would murder each of their tormentors if they had the chance. It turned out that Poppy knew quite a few different methods that could be used to end a life.

She didn't know why, but Poppy loved her little friend's free spirit and her crazy outlook on a society that was often too quick to shun girls like them. Something that the little pixie often said would came back to Poppy in moments when she might be feeling low. 'We will be famous one day, Popsy girl! Trust me, one day we will both be famous!' Poppy never forgot those words. She would later spend many nights on a hard pillow inside Bronzefield prison, remembering Nikita's prediction, and wishing that her friend had been wrong.

The girls celebrated Nikita's twenty-first birthday with a shoplifting spree which earned the little pixie some smart designer babywear for the favourite little man in her life and Poppy a green bomber jacket with air force badges emblazoned on the sleeves. Zain soon grew out of the babygrows and brightly coloured romper suits he had been gifted, but Poppy never let go of her prized jacket, the one she wore every day, the one that always reminded her of a better time in her life, however short that time was!

The water in her bath was cold now. Poppy's sidetrack through the foggy corridors of her past life had left her with strange thoughts in her head. She looked down into the bath water and touched the tattoo on her thigh, running her fingers across the tiny lettering which spelled out her affectionate nickname for her absent friend. It had been more than five years since those crazy days and nights in the high-rise, more than five years since she had felt the warmth of Nikita's arms around her in the double bed they shared in the flat. More than five years since someone truly cared about her. Poppy so wished that her kooky friend was there with her in that bath, sitting opposite her, foamy bubbles sitting proudly on top of that crazy head of hair, her sparkling eyes shining brightly like beautiful diamonds. She would be telling her crazy stories and reassuring her, as she always did, that everything was alright. But she knew that she would never see her friend again or hear her infectious laughter. The 'little pixie' had, like everyone else in her life, gone, left her alone.

Poppy felt very sad at that moment.

Suddenly, her memory of that distant dark place was disturbed by three loud knocks on her front door, followed by four more. They were not the knocks of a friendly visitor. Poppy grabbed a towel and wiped herself down as the banging on the door continued. An immediate thought came into her head as she pulled on one of Cameron's T-shirts which was lying on the carpet in the hall. *Dealers*, she thought, *I bet it is fucking dealers, I bet that bastard Cameron owes the bagman!* Poppy knelt down and crawled along the floor into the bedroom, hoping that she would not be seen. The first thing she looked for was some trousers or jeans to put on, the second, something sharp or heavy to defend herself with. The knocking continued and was now accompanied by a voice. She felt slightly more at ease, it was a voice she recognised, it was Mr Rahwaz, the landlord. She no longer needed a weapon.

He was still there, ten minutes later, her angry landlord, outside her front door, but now the knocking and the shouting had stopped. Poppy was sitting on the floor of the bedroom applying some makeup. She was less bothered by her visitor now, more concerned about getting to the restaurant in time for her shift. Her thoughts turned back to the previous night and how she would face Matt. She decided that she would make it clear to him that day that their sexual encounter, however good it was, was a one-off, a mistake that they should bury and never mention again.

An envelope was pushed through the letterbox of the tatty brown front door to her flat and landed on the grubby carpet in the hall. When she was happy that Rahwaz was no longer outside, Poppy picked up the letter and opened it. The text messages she received from him never brought good news, so she wasn't expecting this to be any different. She was right. The letter was an eviction notice. It stated that unless the tenants paid £520 of rent arrears by the tenth of August they would be evicted.

# CHAPTER ELEVEN

He was late again. Krista wondered sometimes if Dean did it just to see how far he could push her. She had been waiting outside Reigate train station for three quarters of an hour. *Why say eight o'clock*, she thought, *when you know damn well that you will not be here until nine?* She tried his mobile again. It went straight to voicemail. She was not happy, in fact she was livid. She would tell him tonight, she would tell him to stop taking her for granted.

But she didn't, he was forgiven, the minute she saw his smile and felt his face next to hers. 'Sorry, Nylund,' Dean said, hugging her tightly. 'I had to sort out some things for a big meeting tomorrow. I have got that new sales director on my back.'

Krista wanted to berate him for his poor time-keeping but instead found herself lying. 'I only just got here myself,' she said, before the two shared a long and lingering kiss. Anyone passing would probably have guessed that these two adults must surely be having an affair. People of that age don't usually behave like teenagers in the street, touchy-feely and slobbering all over one another. Neither of them would have cared, though, what any of the people passing them were thinking. They had not seen one another for nearly two weeks. Krista had been feeling the strain.

'Have you been drinking?' she asked, recognising the strong taste of whisky in his kiss.

'I had a few while I was waiting for the train,' he replied, adding, 'I had a skinful lunchtime too, which is why I couldn't drive.'

This was also becoming something of a bone of contention with Krista. He was rarely, if ever, sober when she saw him. She felt concerned that he may have a drink problem, but never brought it up for fear of ruining the limited amount of time they were able to spend together. 'Tequila!' Dean said out of nowhere. 'Let's get a bottle of tequila and head for the lake.'

Krista never argued with his choice of alcohol, but she was curious about the destination. 'Lake?' she asked. 'What is that, is it a restaurant or a bar?'

Dean simply grinned. 'It's a lake, Nylund, it is just a lake, lots of water, probably a few fish swimming in there, it is just a lake.'

She was slightly confused, but to her it did not concern her where they might be going. He was there, they were together that night, that is all that really mattered. 'Two minutes,' Dean said, leaving her side and running across the road to a small mini-mart.

He returned a few moments later carrying nothing but a large bottle of tequila. 'Neat?' Krista asked. 'Are you expecting me to drink that neat?'

Dean's all-knowing smile appeared on his face. 'It's the only way to drink tequila,' he said.

As she drove off, away from the small town centre and into the dark country lanes, Dean navigated Krista through a series of small roads, which he suggested would be a shortcut to their destination. 'Won't it be cold?' she asked, now realising that the venue was going to be nothing more than just a lake.

'That's where the tequila comes in,' he pointed out. 'You see, always prepared, that's me, always prepared.'

He seemed to be in a buoyant mood, he even sang a few bars of a song playing on the car radio. Krista didn't know if it was the fact that she was there that put him in this frame of mind or the excessive volume of alcohol he seemed to have consumed that day. As they approached a badly lit roundabout, his mobile phone made a sound indicating that he had a new text message. He ignored it, as he did a few others on their journey. Their conversation was light, but there were some questions that Krista felt she needed to ask him that night. 'How is she?' she said.

Dean knew exactly who she was referring to and kept his reply brief. 'Still the same.'

Krista waited for more information, but it was not forthcoming. She tried a different approach. 'Where does she think you are tonight?'

Dean shrugged his shoulders. 'Out with some clients. Turn left when you get to this junction.'

She followed his instruction, but his silence had given her another reason to wonder what this relationship, if that's what this was, was all about. Why did he never talk about his wife, what was there to hide? Maybe he was lying about her medical condition, maybe she was not ill. Her heart did not want to process what her brain was telling her. *What if he is happy with her and this is just one big game to him?*

When they reached the small road leading to the lake, Dean told Krista to veer off onto a dirt track just before the locked gates. It led them over the neatly cut grass and within twenty feet of the water's edge. Krista felt slightly uncomfortable and overdressed for this excursion. She glanced down at her newly bought skirt from the latest Dior range. 'I had better not get stains on this,' she said. 'It was very expensive.'

Dean asked her to leave the headlights on in her car. Their beams shone brightly and seemed to dance on the still waters ahead of them, creating a mystical and enchanting setting for the evening. Another call on Dean's mobile went unanswered and a subsequent text was left unread. Dean could see that the constant bombardment of unwanted attention on his phone was beginning to aggravate Krista, so he switched his mobile off.

The evening was very mild, the warm and humid air cooled by the gentle breeze escaping from the lake. Dean took off his suit jacket and spread it out for Krista to sit on. Maybe her comment about her designer skirt had struck a chord with him. 'Why here?' Krista asked. 'I mean, it is nice and everything, but I would have preferred a Chinese restaurant or a country pub.'

Dean inhaled, filling his lungs with the fresh countryside air. 'It just feels so good to get away from the town, all those car fumes and people rushing around everywhere. This place is just so, well, it is just so peaceful.'

'I am not complaining,' Krista said. 'I love peace and quiet, but it is a bit out of the way.'

Dean smiled, the cheeky smile that always put Krista at ease. 'No one can hear you scream,' he said. 'Nobody can hear you shout out here, however loud you holler, no one will hear you.'

Krista played along. 'Oh so you have brought me here to kill me?' she asked. 'Can I at least have a shot of that tequila before you do it?'

Dean passed her the bottle and then kicked off his shoes and undid his tie, throwing it backwards towards the parked car. 'Is that the only time that you scream?' he asked. 'When you are being murdered?' Suddenly it dawned on Krista what he may really be talking about. She smiled.

The two of them sat in silence for a few moments, taking in the tranquil setting and watching the bright rays from the car's headlights flicker across the ripples on the lake. They sat close together, Krista's hand clutching his, their legs touching. It was so peaceful they could almost hear each other's heart beating. 'I love this place,' Dean said. 'Here, away from all the shit at work, all the shit at home. I could be anywhere on the planet sitting here right now.'

Krista nodded and added her take on the setting. 'Yes, I agree, it is amazing, but I would have brought a picnic if I had known, I am bloody starving. I thought we were going for a meal tonight.'

Dean laughed. 'How can you think about food or anything like that? The whole universe is here, right in front of us.'

Krista looked puzzled. 'What, in a lake, in the middle of nowhere?' she asked.

Suddenly Dean kicked off his socks and began to unbutton his shirt. 'Let's go for a swim,' he said. 'Come on, Nylund, live dangerously for once, let's get naked and go for a swim.'

Krista was taken by surprise. 'Are you kidding me? I would have to be mad to strip off and get in that dirty water.'

Her negative response did nothing to dampen Dean's enthusiasm. Within seconds his shirt was thrown sideways onto the grass, followed by his trousers. He made his way down towards the lake wearing only his polka dot boxer shorts, the strange image bringing a grin to Krista's face. He walked into the lake until the water rose above his knees. It was still lukewarm, it felt refreshing. 'This is real!' he said. 'This feels so real. God, it makes you feel so alive!'

Suddenly, the shining lights from the headlamps seemed to darken as the shadow of a moving body passed in front of them. Dean could feel a presence behind him. He turned his head slowly and his body stood frozen, as if he had been trapped in Medusa's line of vision. She was standing there, she was naked, she was completely naked, one arm outstretched across her small pert breasts, the other nestled at the join between her legs. It was a perfect vision, a sublime beauty, an eighth wonder of the world had suddenly appeared at the side of a lake in the middle of the Surrey countryside. It was extremely rare, but Dean Jarvis was completely lost for words. Krista moved closer to the edge of the lake, her tiny feet trembling as they tested the still water ahead of her. Finally, Dean found his voice. 'I thought you said that you wouldn't get naked and get into the...'

Krista stopped his sentence by moving her hand and putting it firmly on his lips, her action fully exposing the firm nipple on one of her breasts. 'I didn't say that I wouldn't do it, I just said I would have to be mad to do it. Well, maybe I am mad, I must be mad to be here with you, right?'

Dean nodded. 'Completely mad, as mad as a box of frogs.'

'Shit!' Krista said, seemingly alarmed. 'There won't be any frogs in there, will there?'

Dean shook his head. 'No, of course not.'

Krista could not help but notice that a bulge had grown in those polka dot boxers. It was desperately trying to burst its way out. She placed her hand on his naked chest and ran her fingers down his torso until she found her target. Rubbing it gently, she watched as his eyes closed tightly and he released a small groan. 'You had better get these off if we are going in,' she said, slowly manoeuvring both of her hands to relieve him of his underwear. Dean kept his eyes closed for a few seconds, taking in a moment that would live with him for the rest of his life.

The pair held hands and walked slowly forwards into the lake, tiny ripples moving around their naked bodies as the water reached their waists. Dean pulled Krista close to him and kissed her on the lips before moving his mouth to caress her tiny nipples. She began to realise now just what he had meant before, at that moment in time they could have been anywhere in the universe. This wasn't just a lake, it wasn't just a green field, it was paradise. They shared a long lingering kiss and said nothing to one another. There were no words that could possibly describe how they were both feeling at the precise moment, so why try to find any?

The beams from the headlights began dancing once again on the lake as that moment they had both waited for since their first meeting had finally arrived. Dean led Krista by the hand to the water's edge and pushed her gently down onto her back. Their lips met again, each devouring the other's hungry mouth as their eager anticipation began to build up inside them. Dean's hand moved slowly downwards and pushed her trembling legs apart. She closed her eyes as his fingers found her pleasure zone. His head moved away from hers as she lay motionless. He licked across her nipples, moving from one breast to the other, feeling her tremble slightly each time his mouth found the spot that made her tingle inside.

As Dean moved his body on top of her, to lie between her legs, Krista opened her eyes and looked up at the darkening sky. She could see a thousand stars or more, they were bigger and closer than she could ever remember. She let out a small cry as she felt him enter her, followed by a long groan of sheer pleasure. Their bodies moved up and down as the stars in Krista's line of vision seemed to draw nearer and nearer. Dean moved slowly at first, each penetration being met with a moan of satisfaction from Krista. As she wrapped her legs tightly around his body, she felt something stirring inside her, a feeling she had not felt before. She didn't want it to end, it was a burning feeling, as if the inside of her body was on fire. She let out one scream followed by another, as his movements became more rapid. Her breath began to shorten as she gripped him tighter, her fingernails digging deeply into the flesh on his back. His hands were now beneath her bottom, squeezing her buttocks tightly as the momentum of his thrusts became even faster. Krista moved her glance from the starlit night to Dean's eyes. They were full of passion, he was staring deep into her eyes, deep into her soul. She wanted to let out a huge scream, but found her teeth sinking deep into his shoulder, like a bloodthirsty vampire. The headlights from the car shone brightly, projecting a shimmer of light across the silhouettes of their writhing bodies. Krista could feel the fresh breeze from the lake running gently across her body as Dean's thrusts became faster and faster, each penetration being met with a groan of unequivocal pleasure. Their bodies had moved closer to the edge by now. They could feel tiny streams of water gently caressing their skin. Dean began to sweat slightly as the motion of his strokes became more rapid. Krista's nails were digging deeper and deeper, cutting into the flesh on his bare back.

Suddenly, she let out a small scream followed by a much louder one as her ecstasy reached its peak. Her body gyrated from head to toe. She wrapped her mouth around his shoulder blade and bit hard, hard enough to draw blood. Suddenly, Dean's breath began to shorten as he neared his climax. Krista clenched her legs tighter around his back, as if she was trying to squeeze the life out of him. His mouth switched backwards and forwards from her mouth to her nipples, and then, just as he became aware that he was at that point of no return, his head moved upwards and he looked into her eyes, those amazing brown spheres of indescribable beauty. They were on fire now, flames dancing across his reflection, like a raging inferno. He pushed harder and harder and finally his body erupted, sending his bodily fluids deep into her aching loins.

They lay at the edge of the water, wrapped in a tight embrace for a full five minutes before either of them found the strength to speak. Suddenly, Dean decided that there was something that they both needed. 'Tequila?' he asked Krista.

'Tequila and a stretcher,' she replied. 'I don't think I am going to be able to walk for days now.'

Dean leant down and scooped up her tiny frame in his big strong arms. 'Come on,' he said. 'It is a well-known fact that tequila is the best known cure for everything.' Dean laid her down gently on his jacket and sat close beside her. Neither of them felt the cold at that moment, despite the fact the temperature was falling rapidly.

They both swigged mouthfuls from the bottle of Mexico's finest export and Krista wrapped Dean's jacket around her shoulders to keep off the breeze from the lake. 'Can you get my bag from the car?' she asked Dean. 'I need to check my phone.' Dean obliged her, checking his own mobile en route. It showed he had missed four more calls and had three unopened text messages. He threw his recently purchased Nokia C16 handset onto the passenger seat of Krista's car. He was in his own world now, he had no intentions of seeing what those messages were going to tell him.

'It looks expensive,' Dean said, passing Krista her blue leather handbag.

'It is new,' she said. 'I bought it last week, it's a Hermes.'

Dean sat back down beside her and laughed. 'Hermes,' he said. 'The son of Zeus, the bringer of dreams, a prowler in the night.'

Krista was confused. 'What the hell are you talking about?'

'It's not important, you wouldn't get it anyway.'

'Try me, I may not be as thick as you think I am.'

'Hermes, he was the son of Zeus, the god of wealth.'

'How do you know all of this? I wouldn't have you down as a history buff.'

'It's not history, it's mythology, Greek mythology.'

'And there is a difference?'

Dean nodded. 'A big difference. Greek mythology was all about the parallel world that existed centuries ago, another world full of brave heroes and monstrous demons.'

'Wow, you are really into this stuff. Where do you get all this from?'

'My dad, well, not my real dad. Peter, the guy that brought me up. I suppose he was my dad really.'

'OK, sorry but you have lost me now. Would you like to explain?'

'Not really, it's not that important.'

Krista was not happy with his response. 'I know nothing about you, Dean, nothing about your wife, your family, nothing at all, you keep everything so close to your chest.'

Dean took a large swig of tequila and breathed in the night air, but Krista was still keen to learn more about the man she had just shared such an incredible experience with. 'Are they dead?' she asked. 'Are your parents dead?'

Dean looked across the lake. It was obvious that he didn't really want to have this conversation, but he felt that her owed her some sort of explanation. 'He is, my dad, he died in a fire at our house, when I was three years old. My mother…'

Krista pressed her fingers against his lips and put her arm around his shoulders to hold him closer. 'I am sorry,' she said, 'if it is too painful. I am sorry I asked.'

Dean took a deep breath and continued, he was anxious now for her to know the whole story. 'She was in hospital after the accident, she has been there ever since. I don't even know if she is still alive.' Krista squeezed him a little more tightly. It gave him the courage to continue. 'I was saved, the night of the fire. A neighbour broke through my window and rescued me, but my dad died.' Dean struggled with his words. 'He was locked in the bedroom, nobody knew why. They said that she started the fire, my mother. They said she started the fire after the two of them had argued. She told the police that he had hit her, beaten her black and blue and she wanted him to suffer, like she had suffered. Apparently, after the court case, the doctors found her to be...'

Dean stopped himself. He had always hated the professional description that the court gave his mother's condition, so he substituted 'clinically insane' with a kinder explanation. 'That she was ill, they said that she suffered heavy bouts of depression and that she wasn't safe to be living in society.'

Krista listened intently, maybe realising now why he had never spoken about his family. 'God, Dean, I am so sorry. So you have never seen her since?'

'No, I did, until I was about eleven or twelve. Peter used to take me there, every couple of months. It wasn't like a prison or anything, it was alright there, it was like a big country house. I still remember her, sitting in that huge armchair in the big white room. God, it was so bright in that room, so white, a bit like how I would expect heaven to be. She never spoke, she never ever said a word to me when I visited her.'

Krista didn't know if she should keep asking questions, but she was curious. 'So you never saw her after that?' Dean shook his head. 'Peter, my dad, Peter said that it was not good for either me or her. She wasn't getting any better, she was never going to be let out. He was trying to be honest with me, to save me any further hurt. It was Peter that first brought me over here, to the lake. We used to go rowing. They have small boats over there by the pavilion. Him and Diane, that was his wife, they brought me up as their own. They couldn't have kids themselves, so I suppose it worked for everyone. I used to call them Mum and Dad, but it never felt right.'

'And do you still see them, Peter and his wife, are you still in touch with them?'

Dean shook his head. 'Not for ages, they moved to Scotland about fifteen years ago. I went up there a couple of times, but it was a long way to go. We just sort of lost touch.'

Seeing that he had been affected by his disclosures Krista thought it best to lighten the mood. 'So, you were saying, Hermes, not just a fashion accessory, a god too.'

Dean laughed. 'Hermes was the messenger for his father, Zeus. You must have heard of Zeus, he was the top banana of mythology.'

'OK,' Krista replied. 'I am mildly interested in your fantasy world, but only mildly. So you and your Uncle Peter, tell me more about him.'

'We used to watch all the movies together, I must have seen some of them a hundred times – *Jason and the Argonauts*, *Ulysses*, *Clash of the Titans*. Peter, my dad, Peter always saw himself as being like Neptune, probably because he was such a strong swimmer and he loved boats. I used to read up on all the stories about the gods and the warriors that would fight all the terrible demons, they were the only books I ever enjoyed reading. I wanted to be like Ulysses, a true warrior, searching the earth for treasures and destroying all the monsters.'

Krista was amazed to see him so passionate about something. He rarely spoke at all about his early life. 'I just wanted to be a fashion model or an air hostess when I was growing up,' she said. 'Sounds pretty boring now!' Dean laughed. 'No, I could never have been Ulysses, he was fearless, the bravest of them all. I used to sleep with the light on in my bedroom until I was in my teens.'

'So who would I be in this crazy made-up world in your head?' Krista asked.

Dean smiled, a huge smile. 'Persephone, without a shadow of a doubt, you would be Persephone, the daughter of Zeus and Demeter, goddess of the underworld.'

Krista grabbed the bottle of tequila nestling in Dean's lap and took a large mouthful. Her face screwed up tightly as the undiluted alcohol hit the right spot. 'OK,' she said, 'tell me more about this amazing Persephone girl. Was she really fit, like me?'

Dean looked deep into those beautiful eyes. *No point lying*, he thought. 'Fit, yes, one box ticked.'

'Beautiful?' Krista asked, hoping for a positive response.

'The most beautiful creature in the universe.'

'Intelligent?'

'Tick.'

'Sexy, you know, like everybody thought that she was just 'sex on legs'?'

'Another tick for the modest woman sitting next to me.'

'And could she be, you know, a bit of a bitch at times?'

Dean nodded. 'Double tick, she could be a bitch most of the time.'

'So, who did she get off with, this goddess? She must have had all of the men after her.'

Dean laughed. 'Hades, she fell in love with Hades.'

'But that is like, well, that is like the devil, isn't it?'

'He was the god of the underworld. He took her away from her mother and her family, he took her to the depths of the earth and made her his bitch.'

'Nasty! What happened next?'

'They did a deal, Zeus and Hades. He got to keep her for four months of the year and her mother got her back for the rest of the time.'

'Bastard!'

'Her mother was well pissed off. Every time she went off for her four months with Hades, she sent a frost and heavy snow to stop all the plants and flowers growing on earth.'

'So does that make you Hades then? If I am this Persephone girl, does that make you Hades, does that make you the devil?'

'Yeah I suppose it does. But I would probably send you back sooner, maybe after three or four days rather than months. I would be bored of you by then.'

'Total bastard, Dean Jarvis! Total bastard! And you were doing so well until then.'

'So that is why we have a winter, it is all down to Persephone's mother, Demeter. The frost and snow that we get every year is all down to that mad bitch.'

'OK, I will buy that. Tell me though, what did this Hades fella do for the other eight months of the year, when this Persephone was back with her family?'

'I don't know, probably read a lot of books and spent his time wanking.'

'That is a hell of a lot of wanking,' Krista said and started to laugh. 'You see what I did there, hell and Hades?'

The two of them fell laughing into each other's arms, both feeling that they had found something very special that night. Any doubts that were in Krista's head had now been erased. She liked this vulnerable side to Dean, she loved the fact that he was just a big kid at heart. She would be his Persephone now, she would be his exclusive goddess. Something that night told her that this was going to be more than just a fling. She hoped desperately inside that he felt the same way.

As dawn approached, Dean and Krista lay together on the crumpled and badly grass-stained suit jacket, wrapped in a tight embrace with a small smile of satisfaction etched on their faces. The tequila bottle was empty. It had served its purpose though and was now redundant to their requirements. The sun began to rise slowly in the sky, welcoming the start of a new day, maybe bringing a new chapter to the lives of these two lovers.

At around four forty, the last of a long series of texts was received by Dean's mobile phone, still perched on the floor of Krista's car. It had been sent by a midwife at St Luke's Hospital. It revealed that at exactly 3.56 that morning, Poppy Louise Jarvis had entered this world. She weighed just four pounds and ten ounces, not uncommon for a baby born five weeks premature. She was lying comfortably in an incubator in the special baby unit at the hospital, and was, in the words of the nurse on duty that day, 'doing just fine'.

The newborn's mother, Hannah Jarvis, was not faring so well. She had endured several problems during the delivery of the child and was now in the hands of specialists in the intensive care unit. If possible, could her husband make his way to the hospital as soon as possible?

Dean Jarvis was an absent father at the birth of his daughter. Baby Poppy could not have known it at the time, but it would set a precedent for most of her life. When those bright hospital lights blinded her as she first entered this world, she may have been thankful that she had been finally released from the relative security of her mother's womb. Maybe she had taken for granted the fact that she had been warm, nourished and protected from harm inside that hollow cavity. It is probably true to say that on numerous occasions in the years that followed, Poppy Jarvis may have wished that she had never left that safe haven at all.

# CHAPTER TWELVE

Bree arrived at the cemetery gates, dark cobwebs still clouding over the corners of her mind. It was a day of firsts for her. The first time she had driven her new car, a mid-range Mercedes. She had loved her old Audi, but after the incident she felt that she could never look at that model again. It was the first time she had come to the cemetery alone. Kayleigh had always accompanied her before, treating her as if she was an invalid or small child. And it was to be the first time that she would see Jamie's newly laid headstone. Her mother had made a fleeting visit from Finland with Per to watch the stone be erected, but Bree had avoided meeting up with her mother by pretending that she was attending a grief recovery support meeting. In Bree's troubled mind she wanted to put as much distance between her and her parent as she possibly could. They may be separated by a thousand miles or so of icy cold sea since her mother had moved to Finland, but they were a million miles apart in their broken relationship.

It was early summer. The long, dark and dismal nights may have gone but those ever-present nightmares were still haunting Bree. The frost covered weeds in the grounds of the cemetery had, by now, been replaced with colourful displays of brightly coloured flowers, blossoming everywhere, making her brother's final resting place seem a little less daunting. As she passed a small group of elderly people, huddled around a newly laid grave, she noticed the inscription on the adjacent headstone. The woman buried there was eighty-eight when she passed away. How fair was that? Bree thought. How fair was that for someone to live all those years when her brother had barely had a quarter of that time in this cruel world?

Bree needed to come here today, not just to see his new headstone, but to remind him of things that he may think she has forgotten. To remind him that she still hears his strange laughter echoing around the hallway of the house and that she plays his video at least one hundred times every day. To tell him that his toothbrush still sits beside hers in the holder, they would never be separated. She did not want him to think her foolish for sleeping on his pillow, but it made her feel as if he was still with her when she went to sleep each night, and again when she woke each morning. She would never ever wash that pillowcase.

It was over six months now since he had left her, but she felt no respite from the numb pain which lay dormant in her body. Every morning, when her eyes opened, still felt like the first morning after the accident. She did not sleep well anymore. It was strange, those reoccurring nightmares began to feel more comforting to her, as if she felt the need to be tormented.

Bree dragged her feet along the hard ground which led her through the cemetery. A bright ray of sunshine appeared through the clouds as if it was leading her to him. As she reached the path which took her to her brother's graveside she could see that there were two figures there – one large, one small, a child. They seemed to be studying the new stone. Bree stopped for a few seconds and watched. The small figure had her mousy coloured hair tucked up in a small ponytail. She was wearing a bright red coat, with black trim. She remembered seeing that coat before, the previous time that she had visited the cemetery. The young girl had passed her in the car park that day. Bree stood at a short distance and observed. She didn't recognise either of them. They might simply be admiring the new gravestone, she thought. As she moved nearer, she watched as the young girl walked forward a few steps carrying a small posy of flowers. Bree was puzzled, until the large figure turned her head and she caught a glimpse of the woman's face. It was her, it was that woman that had been at her front door, the one who drove the Shogun, it was the woman she held responsible for Jamie's death. A searing rage tore at her insides as she stomped forward to confront her. 'What the hell are you doing?' she roared at the large woman. 'Get away from there now!' The figure reacted to the full force of Bree's harsh tongue and moved swiftly away from the graveside, grabbing the arm of the small child and pulling her with her. The little girl looked frightened, almost dropping the spread of fresh ivory lilies in her hand.

'How dare you come here!' Bree yelled, causing the large figure to move further away and bow her head in shame. The woman's mouth opened, as if she wanted to respond, but nothing came out. Her chin began to tremble.

Suddenly, a tiny voice came up from beneath the badly shaken woman. 'We come here every week,' the small child said. 'We come here to say thank you to Jamie. We always leave some flowers for him. We bring these ones because they are pretty. My mum said he would like them.'

'Your mother doesn't know him,' Bree said, now lowering her voice, so as not to frighten the child any further.

The small girl looked puzzled and glanced up at the woman clutching her arm. 'Come on,' the woman said. 'We need to go now, Maisie.'

The little girl looked at the small bouquet in her hand. 'But what about Jamie's flowers?'

The woman moved her hand down and placed it into the palm of the confused child. 'No, Maisie, we need to go now, right now!'

Looking over at the panic-stricken lady and the bemused child, Bree suddenly realised how intimidating her outburst must have been. 'Wait!' she said and moved closer to them. She crouched down to where the tiny girl stood and offered her a small smile. 'Maisie?' she said. 'That's a nice name.'

The girl smiled back. 'I was named after my nan, the one who lived near the seaside. She had lots of cats, didn't she, Mum?'

Bree felt her raging anger begin to subside. 'Those are nice flowers,' she said. 'I am sure Jamie would love them.'

The girl released her hand from her mother's and offered it to Bree. 'Would you like to help me put them in his pots?' she asked.

Bree nodded. 'I would like that very much, Maisie.'

The two of them made their way back to Jamie's resting place, leaving the large woman, still shaking slightly, to watch on. 'You seem very angry,' the little girl observed. 'Was he your boyfriend?'

Bree shook her head. 'No, Maisie, he was my brother, he was my twin brother.' As the child began separating the bottoms of the stems from the lilies, it was obvious to Bree that the small girl had done this before. She decided to take a small step backwards and leave the girl to her task. As she did she caught her first sight of the new black marble stone, the beautiful engraving standing out in bold gold. Bree looked at the bottom of the headstone. *'Loving son and brother'* – hardly a fitting description, she thought. There were a thousand more appropriate words they could have used, words, sentiments that truly described the irreplaceable soul that rested here now.

Maisie was also reading the wording at the head of the stone. 'It says that he is sleeping with the angels. Will he ever wake up?' she asked. 'Will we ever meet Jamie?'

Bree choked on her reply. 'No, Maisie, no we won't see Jamie again.'

The small child seemed so mature for someone so tiny. She only seemed to be around five or six years old but spoke like a young adult. She was a little surprised at Bree's answer and explained why. 'My mum says that Jamie was the bravest man ever, for what he did, you know for saving us that night, from the train. She said that he was braver than all the superheroes put together.' Bree said nothing. She had just realised what the tiny child had said. It was her, that crying in front of the Shogun that night, this little girl had been in there with her mother.

'If that is true,' Maisie continued, 'and he has superpowers like all the other superheroes, why can't he make himself come back? He could help lots of other people then, just like he helped my mum and me.'

Bree could not bring herself to answer Maisie's question. She felt a pain rip through her insides at that moment, as the reality of that terrible night came back to haunt her for a few seconds.

Feeling slightly unsteady on her feet, she left the girl to finish arranging the fresh flowers. She seemed to be doing such a fine job, she didn't need any help. She walked back to where the child's mother was standing. This time the expression on her face was one of a more compromising nature. The large woman was still lost for words and had to wait for Bree to start the conversation. 'She was in the car, that night, Maisie was in your car?' she asked. The woman nodded but said nothing. It was clear that the anguish and pain from that experience still lived inside her too.

Maisie joined the two women, after neatly placing the broken stems from the lilies and the remains of the dead flowers into a convenient litter bin. As her mother produced a couple of wet wipes to clean her hands the little girl made a heartfelt observation to Bree. 'I like Jamie's new stone,' she said. 'It's like he has a proper home now.' The two women looked at each other but said nothing, not sure if the tiny child's innocent comment brought any comfort to the other.

'So do you have the same birthday as Jamie?' Maisie asked.

'Yes, the twenty-fourth of August,' Bree replied.

'I don't know your name,' the little girl said, now feeling much more comfortable in Bree's presence.

'It is Brianna, but everyone calls me Bree.'

Maisie gave a cheeky grin. 'My mum's name is Caroline, it is a very old-fashioned name. I always call her 'Mum' though. 'Mum' or 'Mummy', because, well, she is my mum, I suppose.' Bree let out a small laugh. She could not help but be amused by the small child's view of the world.

Caroline finally joined in the conversation. 'We will have to be going soon, Maisie, the centre is open now.'

'Can Bree come, Mummy? Can Bree come with us?'

Her mother shook her head. 'I am sure Bree has other things she needs to do. Maybe another time.'

'Oh, please, Mummy, she might have some fun there.'

Bree was curious. 'What is it, Maisie, where do you go?'

'Cheeky Charlies.'

'What is that?' Bree asked.

Caroline explained. 'It's like a big adventure indoor playground. It is about two miles from here. We go there after we come here. I just think Maisie needs something to, well, you know, make her feel happy if coming here has made her feel sad.'

Maisie jumped in with her own take on the place. 'It is full of ropes and slides and thousands of plastic balls. You can't hurt yourself, there are all these special soft mats.'

Bree smiled. 'It sounds like a lot of fun.'

'You have to come,' Maisie said tugging at Bree's coat. 'If I have been good, Mum always buys me a chocolate smoothie there.'

'And if you haven't been good?' Bree asked.

'Oh, I am always good, aren't I, Mum?' the little girl replied. 'Apart from that time I broke the glass cabinet.'

Caroline buttoned up her daughter's coat. 'Come on, you, let's get going,' she said.

'Is it OK?' Bree asked Caroline. 'Is it OK if I tag along?'

'Yeeeessss,' the small child yelled. 'Bree is coming with us, Mummy. Jamie's sister is coming with us.'

As the three of them made their way back to the car park area, Caroline gave Bree directions to the Cheeky Charlies play centre. Maisie was excited, talking at a hundred miles an hour as she described the different types of apparatus at the venue. As they walked and talked, Bree began to find some small crumbs of comfort in the fact that Jamie had saved the lives of these two people. But she still felt slightly uncomfortable in Caroline's presence. If it had not been for her then Jamie would still be alive. She needed to find out more about that evening, why they had broken down on the railway tracks, what the hell a young child was doing out at that time of night and why Caroline never opened the car doors. She needed to try to make some sense of it all, that terrible twist of fate that had led to her brother's death

\* \* \*

The play area at Cheeky Charlies was bustling with the screams and shouts of hyperactive children. Caroline could hardly hear herself speak. 'We go over there,' she said loudly, pointing to a cafeteria. 'We can still see what is happening and the kids can't get out once they go past the barrier.' Maisie was impatient, kicking off her shoes and throwing them at her mother's feet, before sprinting to the secure area. Somewhere amongst the din of the overexcited youngsters was her mother's plea for her to 'Be careful'.

Bree joined Caroline in the queue for refreshments as Maisie disappeared into the ball park. She could not help but comment on the clamorous atmosphere. 'Wow! It is crazy in here,' she said. 'Has Maisie gone in already?'

Caroline pointed at her daughter's tiny feet as they disappeared at the top of a rope ladder. 'She loves it here,' she said. 'She can get a bit emotional about what happened sometimes, so I find that this place helps her to remember that she is just a kid. I forget myself at times that she is only six years old.'

Bree nodded in agreement. 'She seems much older than her years, she seems very astute.'

Caroline smiled. 'She is very forward for her age. I bring her here after we visit the cemetery to try to take her mind away from what really happened. She may seem very resolute, but I know it must have been a shocking experience for her. She just seems to take everything in her stride.' Bree pondered on those words for a few seconds, maybe wishing that she had half of the resolve that Caroline's daughter had.

'Tea or coffee?' Caroline asked as the women reached the front of the queue. 'Or do you want to join Maisie and have a chocolate smoothie?'

'Coffee will be fine,' Bree answered with a small smile.

The two women took their drinks to a table close to the entrance of the ball park area. Caroline removed her coat and made herself comfortable. 'It is a lot easier getting her in here than getting her out,' she said. 'She never wants to leave this place.'

Both the women seemed to sense that there needed to be an uncomfortable conversation. Bree got things started. 'I didn't see your car, you know, at the cemetery.'

'I sold it, just after I came to your house, I suppose it just, well, you know, it brought it all back.'

'How did you find out where I lived?' Bree asked.

'It was a local newspaper, they printed the name of your road. I just sort of knocked on a few doors and someone gave me your house number.'

'Was that *The Herald*? I can't stand that paper. I hated what they printed. Everything they published seemed like it was made up.'

'Oh, I didn't read it that way, but then in truth I didn't really take much in for a while after it all happened.'

Caroline paused for a second, she wasn't sure what to say next, but her comment did not go down very well. 'I thought everyone was OK. I never realised that someone was still in your car.'

Bree was angered by her comment and raised the tone of her voice a notch or two. 'What the hell were you doing on the tracks in the first place? How on earth did you get stuck?'

Caroline looked down at her coffee cup, trying to avoid Bree's eye contact. 'The car ran out of petrol,' she said, her voice filled with remorse. 'We just ran out of petrol.'

'How?' Bree asked. 'How the hell does a grown woman with a child in her car put herself in danger like that? You ran out of petrol? Who the hell ever runs out of petrol these days?'

Caroline tried her best to explain. 'I had taken Maisie to the hospital that night. The nearest A&E was in Epsom. She was ill, she had a temperature of 105. I didn't call an ambulance, I just panicked and put her in the car. Halfway there I realised that the petrol light had been on most of the day. I didn't want to stop I just wanted to get her there.'

'What was wrong with her?' Bree asked.

'It was just flu, a small chest infection. We were there for hours before they told me to go home. They told me just to give her some Calpol and keep an eye on her.'

Bree was still seeking answers. 'Why not then?' she asked. 'Why not stop on your way home? There must have been petrol stations open.'

'Before I knew it,' Caroline said, 'we were coming back through Oxley. The rain was bucketing down. I thought the petrol would get us home. The main road was flooded, so we had to go through the level crossing.' A tear or two appeared in the large lady's eyes as she continued. 'The car just stalled, as soon as we passed the barrier, it just stopped. I am so sorry, Bree, I can never ever tell you how sorry I am.'

Sipping her coffee, Bree mused over Caroline's answer. She still had more questions. 'I banged on the side of your window, I told you what was happening, why didn't you just get out of the car?'

Caroline was becoming visibly upset. 'I panicked,' she explained. 'I looked at all that rain. I thought, because Maisie was ill, I shouldn't get out of the car. I didn't know what to do. I just panicked.'

'I tried to open your door, you had locked it.'

'It just jammed. I didn't know what was happening. I didn't realise the danger we were in.'

'You must have seen the train coming?'

'When I looked back at your car, after it pushed us off the track, I thought I saw someone get out, I thought everyone was safe.'

Bree shook her head. 'No, I got out before that, Jamie was hell bent on getting you off the railway lines.'

Caroline was shaking now, clearly remembering that awful night. 'The train, it just came out of nowhere. It just all seemed so surreal, it just seemed to happen so quickly.'

Bree nodded. 'I don't think the driver had a chance, he couldn't have seen anything in that weather.'

'He quit his job,' Caroline declared. 'The train driver, he was in shock for weeks. I read somewhere in one of the newspapers that he held himself responsible for what happened.'

Bree turned up her nose at Caroline's mention of the press. She hated the stories that the newspapers had written about the incident. 'Probably that *Herald* rag again,' she said. 'Just scum, those reporters, evil scum!'

Caroline agreed. 'I know, I still have to live with what happened every day. To know that someone has given their life to save yours, that is not a burden that you can carry easily.'

Bree tried to show some empathy. She could see that the woman was clearly still suffering from the events of that night. 'You have to think of Maisie. You need to remember that she would not be here either. Maybe, I don't know, maybe in some twisted way, you two are meant to be here and Jamie is not. I really don't know. But what is the point of you punishing yourself and Maisie for the rest of your life?'

'It just won't leave me though, Bree. I have been offered counselling and stuff like that, but, I don't know.'

'You should speak to my mother. She would have you booked in at the psychiatrist's like a shot. I am sure that is her answer to bloody everything.'

'Your mother?' Caroline asked. 'You should support each other through this, it must be so hard for her too, losing her son.'

'We don't really see eye to eye, Caroline. I have even stopped telling her about my nightmares now. She will have the men in white coats pick me up and keep me locked away if I am not careful.'

The two women shared a small laugh, a real laugh. It had been a very long time since Bree had heard that laugh. That was a good moment for Maisie to arrive back for a break. The two women were getting on well and all the animosity on Bree's side seemed to have evaporated. Clutching several small plastic balls from the play area, an out-of-breath Maisie spoke. 'I just want a quick drink then I have to go back in,' she said. 'That boy in the red jumper keeps chasing me, so I need these balls to throw at him.' She took an ample mouthful of her smoothie, leaving a large brown beard of chocolate around her mouth.

'Come here,' her mother said. 'Let's clean you up.' Reaching for a wet wipe Caroline wiped away all traces of the drink, shaking her head at the amount of mess one mouthful of her drink had produced. 'Why is he chasing you?' she asked.

Maisie gave her mother a knowing look. 'He obviously likes me, Mummy, that's why boys chase you, if they like you.' The two women both smiled at her observation. 'But he won't catch me,' Maisie added. 'I am too fast for him.' With that she turned and sprinted back towards a large yellow slide in the play area, dropping half of the plastic balls en route.

'I don't know what I would do without her,' Caroline said. 'She is just so full of energy, she drains me sometimes, but I wouldn't change her for the world.'

'What about her father?' Bree said, not knowing why she had asked such a personal question.

'He works in Iraq, we don't see much of him, just once a month, if we are lucky. He flew home the day after…' Caroline suddenly paused in fear of upsetting Bree. 'He flew back the day after it all happened. He said he would quit his job if I wanted him to. But we really need the money, so he is back out there.'

'Is he in the forces?' Bree asked.

'No, he left the military years ago. He works in close protection, it is sort of doing bodyguard work. He has gone from a simple life as a security guard in a supermarket to risking his life to protect some rich oil tycoon. He said that the money was too good for him to turn down.'

'So Maisie doesn't get to see much of him?'

Caroline shook her head. 'I think he actually enjoys it, playing at being James Bond. I sometimes think that me and Maisie and all his responsibilities come second to his ego.'

Bree changed the subject, realising that their personal life really was none of her business. 'Did that reporter, the one from the *Herald*, come to see you? Did he do an interview?'

Caroline nodded. 'He made Maisie feel like she was a pop star. He took hundreds of photographs. They only ever used one. He called her 'The miracle girl' in the paper, but most of what he printed was just made up or he twisted things to make it all sound much more glamorous than it was.'

'You were not happy about it?'

The large woman sighed and shook her head. 'They don't print things that are real. The anxiety it causes, the pain, the guilt, all the sleepless nights, they don't print all that stuff. I never even kept a copy of the newspaper when it came out. I try to forget that night, as if it never happened.'

'He did the same thing to me.'

'What, that Scottish fella? Kerr, that was him, David Kerr.'

'Yeah, he came knocking on my door just two days after it happened. I didn't want to let him in the house, but he was persistent. He asked me if Jamie had been depressed at the time, he asked me if I thought it might have been suicide.'

'No!' Caroline barked. 'What a bastard!'

'He told me he had spoken to one of his friends and they had told him Jamie had mental health issues. What a crock of shit that was, nobody loved life more than my Jamie!'

'Did you find out which friend it was that told him that?'

'No, I think the reporter just made it up or twisted the person's words. He even asked me to call him first if I found a suicide note.'

'Did you throw him out?'

'I didn't have the energy, I just sat there and let him ask me all that crap. I couldn't really take in what he was saying.'

'They are so out of order. He should be locked up, that Kerr fella, inventing stuff like that. Those scumbags will do anything to get a sensational headline.'

'I am stronger now,' Bree said. 'I would tell him what I really thought of him if he turned up again.'

A small silence followed, both women reflecting on the conversation. Bree started to realise how the events of that night at the Maple crossing had affected other people's lives more than she could ever have imagined. She looked over at Maisie, rolling around in the playpen, teasing the young boy in the red jumper. If her and Jamie had not driven home that way that night or if they had gone to the Shallows club that night, that poor child would not be here now. Caroline and her daughter would be lying in the cold cemetery and not her brother.

Bree decided it was time to leave the two of them to some quality mother and daughter time, giving a red-faced Maisie a friendly smile and a wave on her way out of the place. She felt so much better than she had done when she set out that morning. She reassured Caroline that if they did meet up at the cemetery again, that she would be much more welcoming than she had been earlier. It was not exactly an apology from Bree, but Caroline understood that her intentions had been well meant and the women parted on good terms.

When she arrived back in the seat of her car, she felt as if she could finally start to move on now, not from the numbness that ran through her body and her mind, no, that would last her a lifetime. But she would try to stop blaming other people for what had happened. Maybe if she could accept that it was just a tragic accident that took the life of her brother, then the nightmares she was having might finally end and she could close her eyes without fear of dreaming.

Before she set off for the short journey back to Oxley, she switched on her mobile to retrieve any calls or messages she might have missed. She thought that her mother would have probably called her in a panic again, because she had switched off her phone, but she was certainly not in any mood to deal with her today. As she looked at the entrance to Cheeky Charlies adventure playground, she smiled again, remembering the comment that young Maisie had made about Jamie being a 'superhero'. It warmed her inside to think that someone would remember him that way.

As her phone came back to life, she pressed the message button, fully expecting to hear the overexaggerating tones of her worried mother. But the only voice she heard was that of Kayleigh. 'Call me as soon as you get this message, babe. I think I have found him, I think I have found the man in the photograph.'

# CHAPTER
# THIRTEEN

Most people would be excited about a trip to the seaside, but halfway through their two-hour journey to Bournemouth, it was obvious that Matt was looking forward to the day out a whole lot more than Poppy was. The restaurant was closed. Danny had returned to his native Ireland for a family funeral at short notice, leaving the staff with a day off. Matt had talked Poppy into taking this excursion, telling her it would be a real tonic for her to get away from all the stress in her life, even if it was just for one day. After all, Danny was still paying them for their day off, so in Matt's words it was a 'win-win situation for everyone'. Poppy's solemn expression, however, told its own story. She began sniping about everything from the length of the journey to the unsettled weather. Matt had begun to have second thoughts about his invitation.

Since that encounter at Chez Blanc, they had repeated their secret sex trysts three times. The first move would always be initiated by Matt, but the sex most definitely enjoyed more by Poppy. They had christened the food preparation table in the kitchen once. On the other two occasions they had returned to the scene of their first encounter in the staff toilets. Poppy had refused to go back to Matt's flat, saying that to do that would make it seem that it was more than it really was. 'A fuck, Matt!' she would say. 'It is just a fuck!' What she didn't tell him was it was a 'good fuck', and that she thrived on their steamy episodes in unusual places. They had almost been caught in the act the previous week, when Chantelle had returned to the restaurant unexpectedly, looking for her purse. They both knew that what they were doing was bad, but also, that it felt so good.

The warm-hearted Geordie persevered with her sullen mood and self-indulgent attitude and spent most of the journey attempting to find out more about his passenger's past. 'I can't believe you have never been to the seaside,' Matt said. 'Fresh fish and chips, the amusement arcades and sticks of rock. You can't beat it.'

Sitting with her arms folded and her mouth twisted, Poppy responded. 'I went once,' she said. 'It was cold. I didn't like it.'

The cheery northerner wasn't giving up. 'I love the seaside, I used to go to Whitley Bay every month when I was a kid. You will see, Poppy, it will be fun!'

Her enthusiasm was still somewhat lukewarm. 'Whatever you say, Matt. Now how much further is this bloody place?'

Poppy was impressed with the cruising speed of Matt's perfectly polished BMW five series, but not his choice of music. She had ejected several of his CDs from the player, throwing them onto the back seat, with a scathing attack on the choice of artists. 'That one is shit, never heard of them, this one is alright if you are twelve years old, I suppose.' Eventually they both agreed on a national radio station to keep them company for the rest of the journey. Even then Poppy complained that the DJs talked too much.

That morning, Poppy had left her precious Omega parked outside Matt's flat. Her only concern was that one of Cameron's friends might be sober enough to identify the vehicle. Her body was still recovering from his last violent outburst and the last thing she needed was another beating from him.

Arriving in Bournemouth, their first task was finding a parking space. The unusually hot June day had brought swarms of families to this popular seaside town, all wanting to take advantage of the sunny weather and inexpensive attractions on the famous pier. As the long queues of traffic moved slowly through the town centre, all the drivers looking for an elusive parking space, Matt prodded his ungrateful passenger. 'Look at all of them people in the sea,' he said.

Poppy's response was less than enthusiastic. 'They must be mad!' she replied. 'That water looks fucking freezing to me.'

Matt finally found a space and parked the car at the rear of a hotel, a good half a mile stroll to the coastline, giving Poppy yet another reason to complain. His face lit up as they walked down past the pier. He began grinning like a small child, pointing out every landmark en route. His companion was far from impressed with his knowledge of the town, she seemed more interested in other matters. 'Can we eat soon?' she asked. 'I am starving!'

When the couple finally reached the seafront, Matt reached for Poppy's hand. 'Let's have a walk down the beach,' he said. 'We can walk in the sea.'

Her response was still rather frosty. 'Get off me, Matt,' she said, pulling her hand away. 'It is too bloody cold down there.'

They made their way to where the pavement met the golden sand and Matt kicked off his trainers and rolled up his jeans. 'Come on,' he said, grabbing her by the arm. 'You will enjoy it.'

Poppy decided that her overenthusiastic companion was not going to let her rest until she did what he wanted. Taking off her shoes and slipping them in her bag, she joined the smiling northerner and headed down towards the sea. 'I can't believe I am doing this,' Poppy said. 'I will not be happy if I catch fucking pneumonia, I can tell you!'

'I really can't believe that you never came here before,' Matt said. 'It's brilliant when the weather is like this.' Poppy shrugged her shoulders. 'It's a walk on a beach, Matt, it's not a walk on the moon.'

'Best days ever, the sands at Whitley, when I was a kid,' Matt said, reaching out for Poppy's hand again as their toes touched the sea. Once again Poppy declined his offer. The two of them walked a few feet into the Channel. The fresh sea air filled their lungs and the cool breeze brushed through their hair. Excited young children ran backwards and forwards around them, filling their buckets with water for the moats around their sandcastles. As they began to stroll away from the pavilion, tiny waves rolled inshore, soaking their jeans bottoms on their route. Finally, Poppy relented and pushed her hand into the Geordie's palm, bringing an immediate grin to his face.

'So you never said,' Matt asked. 'You never told me why you never went to the seaside.'

'Once,' Poppy replied. 'I told you I went once, I didn't like it.'

'I don't believe you,' Matt said.

'We can't all have wealthy families that just pack up the car and head for the beach every weekend, Matt.'

'You don't need money to have fun, not at places like this.'

Poppy shrugged her shoulders, but she started to feel that Matt had made such an effort, he was working so hard to make this day a memorable one for her, that she owed him something. She began to open up. 'I never really had proper parents, not since I was eight years old.'

Matt's painted-on grin all but disappeared. 'Oh, what happened?' he asked.

Poppy explained. 'They put me into care. After my mum left, my dad put me into care.' Matt said nothing, he wanted her to continue. 'I went from home to home, children's care homes, foster homes, you know all those lovely do-gooders willing to look after me,' she said, with a tinge of sarcasm in her voice.

'But none of them took you anywhere, like the seaside or anything.'

Poppy shrugged her shoulders. 'I never really stayed anywhere long enough, they kept moving me, from place to place, so no one ever got to know me that well.'

'Maybe that was a good thing,' Matt said, in a joking kind of way.

'The truth is, Matt, when I went that one time to the seaside I didn't hate it. I just hated that all the other kids there, they were just normal kids with their real mums and dads and I was with two people from Social Services that I had only ever met once before. How can you say that you are having fun when it is like that?' The friendly Geordie didn't really have an answer for her.

Suddenly a large wave found its way inland and caught the two of them by surprise, almost knocking Poppy off her feet. Matt grabbed her tightly to stop her slipping and she ended up wrapped tightly in his arms. 'You can't keep your hands off me now, can you?' he said, that irritating grin resurfacing across his face.

'In your dreams, Matt,' Poppy replied, pulling herself out of his grasp. 'Only in your dreams!'

As they continued their walk along the coastline, Poppy spoke briefly of her spells in the youth detention centre and how much she had hated being in Bronzefield prison. She drew the line at discussing the crimes she had been punished for. She had to do that soul searching every Wednesday morning with the 'Reverend Joe', that was more than enough for her. Matt was intrigued. He had started to see a more vulnerable side to the moody girl now and began to understand why she always seemed to be so angry with the world. Matt shared some of his own insecurities, mainly the problems he had endured when he first moved to London. He often felt homesick, living nearly three hundred miles away from his family. Poppy showed little interest in his career history and family life. Instead of asking him any questions, she made several poor attempts to imitate his strong Geordie accent, something he pretended to find amusing.

When they walked back to the pavilion area, Matt's face lit up once again. 'Arcades!' he shouted. 'We must go into the arcades.' Poppy's reaction was not exactly one of enthusiasm, but she followed him. Matt changed up £20 for coins, eagerly looking around for something he thought might tempt his sour-faced companion. 'Dance-off!' Matt yelled. 'The dance-off machine, over there.' Once again Poppy showed little interest but felt an obligation to humour the overenthusiastic northern lad. Kicking off his trainers he invited Poppy to a challenge. 'Loser buys lunch,' he said, helping her onto her side of the machine.

When the music started Matt was like a young kid at a school disco, bounding around on the small platform as if he had played on this machine many times before. It took a few seconds for Poppy to realise that this was a competition and the numbers on her counter still showed zero. Poppy finally jumped into action and began to copy the dance moves on the screen in front of her. Her pace picked up and it soon became obvious that she was both quicker and more accurate than the Geordie. Whether that was really the case or not was debatable. Matt seemed to be more interested than her in the scores, he was probably not trying to beat her at all. As the results flashed up, Poppy had turned out to be a resounding winner, showing her contempt for Matt's poor effort by raising her middle finger in his direction. 'Beginner's luck,' the smiling lad said. 'Table football next.'

The time seemed to fly by as the couple played game after game in the noisy arcade. The car racing turned out to be Poppy's personal favourite, beating the man who usually drove a speedy BMW by constantly ramming into him and knocking him off the circuit. It was clear to Matt that Poppy was making up for lost time. She seemed to be trying to squeeze twenty years of missed opportunity into one afternoon. The couple spent a few pounds on the fruit machines to round off their visit to the arcades and decided it was time to eat. Poppy seemed to have found a new personality that morning, a less abrasive, less defensive one. Matt liked this side to her, but he didn't say anything for fear of spoiling things. He thought it would round off a good day if Poppy ended up in his bed that night. He was starting to realise that he was beginning to like this girl more than he should.

'Fish and chips?' he asked, as the two of them finally agreed that Poppy had just edged him out in their competition to pay for lunch.

'Sounds good,' Poppy responded, asking her opponent, 'What does it feel like to be a loser, Matt?'

He took her hand again and they walked up towards the town centre. This time she didn't resist and clutched his palm a little tighter than before. As they neared the top of a small hill, Poppy suddenly stopped, her attention drawn to something on the other side of the road. It looked familiar to her, despite the fact that she had never been to the town before. 'Can we go in there?' she asked. 'It will not take long.'

Matt looked a bit puzzled. 'The gift shop?' he asked. 'You want to buy something?' Poppy seemed to be mesmerised by this quaint-looking store. She felt an urge to be inside there. 'For Danny?' Matt said. 'You can't really take something back for your boyfriend, can you?'

Poppy was not really listening to him. She crossed the road and made for the shop's large window. Walking along slowly, she scrutinised all of the rings, bracelets and small trinkets in the display cases before declaring, 'It is not here, let's go inside. The curious Geordie followed her into the store, not sure exactly what she was looking for.

The inside of the gift shop was littered with everything from banners carrying funny slogans to sticks of rock embedded with the name of the town. There were only a couple of people browsing inside the store – a heavily pregnant woman who was telling off a young boy who seemed fixated on a selection of risqué postcards, which in truth should really have been placed on a higher shelf. Poppy headed for the cabinets filled with assorted fashion jewellery, scrutinising each tray until she found some items resembling the one that she was searching for. The elderly man behind the counter offered some assistance. 'Is there something particular you are looking for, young lady?' he asked. Poppy said nothing. She walked slowly, closely studying the contents of the cabinets housing the assortment of trinkets until she came to the end.

The shop assistant was about to ask her if she needed help in her search again, when she grabbed Matt's arm. 'It is not here!' she said abruptly. 'Let's go!' The elderly man shook his head as the two of them left the shop, knocking the small boy sideways as they brushed past him. Matt wanted to ask, but he didn't. Whatever she was looking for, it was something personal to her. *The day has gone well so far, let's keep it that way*, he thought.

Most of the seafront restaurants looked as if they would benefit from a lick of paint, but somehow their decaying frontage added something special to their appearance. The couple found two seats in a busy diner, the unmistakable smell of fresh fish in batter escaping from the nearby kitchen area. Poppy agreed with Matt about one thing that day: the sea breeze and the smell of fish and chips was something special.

They both ordered the traditional dish, Matt opting for the large haddock while Poppy played safe with the small cod. By the time their food arrived they had both built up a healthy appetite and little conversation had been made at their table. Matt's table manners intrigued Poppy. She was bewildered as he emptied no less than six sachets of mayonnaise onto his meal. The salt and vinegar followed, again in massive quantities. He then proceeded to add four large spoonfuls of sugar to his cappuccino, stirring the drink soundly for at least a minute. Her attention was now drawn to his eating habits. He seemed to be attacking the haddock on his plate as if the fish was still alive, devouring large mouthfuls without realising that small portions of the batter were falling down his chin. 'Hungry?' she asked. He could not answer. His jaws were working overtime on his mouthful of food, so he simply nodded. Maybe, Poppy thought, she had finally found a fault in the personality of her squeaky-clean work colleague. His chef qualities were never questioned, he certainly knew how to cook good food, but as for eating it, he seemed to have fewer table manners than a wild pig.

Poppy was barely halfway through her meal when she noticed that Matt's plate was already empty. He began to look around the restaurant before calling to a waitress for directions to the toilet. She pointed to the rear of the diner and he made his way there, giving Poppy an opportunity to test his resolve. She called over the same waitress and they spoke for a few seconds before exchanging some paper. When Matt returned, Poppy was busy looking over the bill. 'That's expensive for shit food,' she said. 'We are not paying that.'

Matt was taken aback by her comment. 'What!' he said. 'Give it here.'

'We are not paying that bill,' Poppy said, her face screwing up slightly. 'The fish was not cooked in the middle and the chips were soggy.'

Matt tried to laugh off her comment. 'The food was OK, Poppy, what are you talking about? It is very reasonable, you would pay double that price in London.'

Poppy turned her head around as if to see if anyone was listening to their conversation. 'Let's do a runner,' she whispered, just loud enough for the Geordie lad to hear her.

Matt's face changed to one of concern. 'What! No, Poppy! I will pay.'

Poppy pulled Matt closer to her and stared deep into his eyes. 'What are you, Matt, a pussy? Come on, follow me.' With that she rose to her feet and began to walk towards the exit, beckoning him to join her. Matt was in two minds what to do, but suddenly found his feet following in her footsteps. As they reached the main door, Poppy took one long look over her shoulder and grabbed her bewildered companion's hand. 'Run!' she screamed. 'Just run!'

They exited the diner and began to sprint away, gathering pace as they ran downhill. Before they knew it, they were a hundred, then two, then three hundred yards away. 'Keep running, Matt!' Poppy shouted. 'Keep running!' She yanked his hand, pulling him along, further down the hill, towards the beach road. He wanted to look over his shoulder, but the fear that someone might be following them stopped him. What was he doing? he thought. He had never broken the law, he had worked so hard to become a senior chef, why did he listen to her? Why was he still running? Poppy was like an excited schoolkid, screaming at people as she ran past them. Poor Matt kept running, slowly watching his life go down the drain before his own foolish eyes. He felt bad, but strangely good about himself. He felt ashamed, but this was so exciting, it made him feel alive. Suddenly, Matt felt his legs tire, he began to feel sick and he came to a halt. The pair were blowing hard, both fighting to catch their breath, their hearts were racing. Poppy's face was bright red, beads of sweat dripping from her brow, a clear indication that she did not go in for this running lark very often.

The lights of the pier seemed more distant now. They must have run for a half a mile if not more. As the pair began to regain their composure, Poppy began to giggle, like a little girl. Her snigger got louder and turned into a roar of laughter. 'You were so funny, Matt, you were so fucking funny.'

Matt was still doubled over, he felt a pain in his side as if he might have a stitch. 'What do you mean?' he asked. 'What was so funny?'

Poppy let out another loud chuckle. 'You, Matt, you were fucking priceless!'

He still didn't understand. 'It's really not funny, we could be in big trouble.'

Poppy was still laughing loudly. 'I paid them, Matt, I paid the waitress when you went to the toilet.'

'What!' he said, his face a mixture of anger and relief.

'You don't think I would risk going back to prison for a plate of fucking fish and chips, do you?'

The confused Geordie was still trying to see the funny side of things. 'You bitch!' he said. 'You are such a mad bloody bitch, why did you do that?'

Poppy stopped laughing and her tone became much more serious. She moved closer to Matt and their eyes met. The only sound that they could hear was the gentle movement of the waves in the sea behind them. 'I wanted to see if you could be a bad boy, Matt. I wanted to see if you could really be a bad boy.'

The child-like grin which irritated Poppy so much began to return to Matt's face. 'Bitch,' he said again, shaking his head. 'And did I pass?'

Poppy's face moved closer to his, their lips almost touching. Her hand reached down and rubbed gently against his crotch. 'Not yet, Matt, not yet. Now you have to take me back to your flat and show me what a bad boy can really do.'

The couple stood in silence for a few seconds. A large bulge began to appear in the front of Matt's tight jeans. 'Now?' he asked. 'Are we going now?'

Poppy placed her hand into his. 'Of course now, before I change my mind.'

The two of them headed back to the BMW, hand in hand. No more words were said on that walk, none were needed. The large beaming smile seemed to be fixed on Matt's face as they reached the car. *This*, he thought, *is going to be such a perfect day after all.* As they reached the car Poppy still felt the need to impose one or two rules. 'I will pick the music on the way back,' she said, to which Matt nodded. 'And get rid of that stupid bloody grin, it really does my fucking brain in!'

\* \* \*

Poppy ran a shower and helped herself to some of Matt's expensive shampoo. Her greasy locks were certainly not used to this kind of treatment, she was determined to make the most of it. She was more familiar with the layout of his flat now and knew where to find the freshly cleaned towels. She certainly felt a lot more at ease than she had done during her last visit. The journey to the beach and their hour and a half session of torrid sex had worn Poppy out. She badly needed to refresh her aching body. She felt slightly unstable on her feet, having enjoyed three orgasms in such a short space of time. Her legs wobbled slightly as the invigorating hot water rushed over her body. A small smile cracked on her face, she felt strangely satisfied. She closed her eyes and let the foamy lather run down her body, forgetting, for the shortest of time, about reality.

Poppy could hear Matt talking on the telephone as she dried herself off in front of the bathroom mirror. He was clearly in high spirits and his boyish laughter echoed through the hallway. As she brushed through her freshly cleaned hair, she wiped over the steamy mirror. An image appeared. It was an unusual reflection, one she did not see too often. She looked content, she looked almost happy. It had been a good day for Poppy, a rare experience, a very rare experience.

As Poppy entered the lounge she could see that Matt had opened another bottle of wine. The first one had been devoured almost as soon as they had entered his flat, the empty bottle lying somewhere amongst his sheets on the floor of his bedroom. She knew she would have to drive back to the flat that night and she already had more alcohol in her system than she should have done. But she felt at ease, so accepted Matt's offer of a large glass of his prized Moobuzz Pinot Noir. It would round off a perfect day. Now those were words you would not find too often in Poppy's diary.

'Your hair smells nice,' Matt said stroking some of the falling strands of her mane back behind her ears.

'I used your shampoo,' she replied. 'The one in the red bottle. It was very rich, I used it all up. It is all gone now.'

Matt was not fooled. 'I only bought that last week, not even you would use that much shampoo in one go,' he said. Poppy enjoyed a large mouthful of her wine. 'Mmmm, I always think this wine tastes better when it's stolen,' she teased.

Matt was quick to defend himself. 'I told you before, Danny and I have an arrangement,' he insisted.

Poppy was in a playful mood. 'If you say so, Matt. Oh, and I suppose that fresh salmon in your fridge is part of the same arrangement.'

Matt laughed. 'I like seeing you like this, Poppy. You know, relaxed, laughing, cracking 'unfunny' jokes.'

'Are you saying I am usually a mardy bitch?'

'Definitely!' Matt said. 'Boy oh boy you can be one stroppy cow when you want to be!'

Poppy shrugged her shoulders and grabbed the bottle to fill her glass up. 'So, I am just a moody bitch in your eyes now, is that right?'

Matt laughed, he was in a playful mood. 'I did think I saw you smile once, but that was probably just indigestion or something.'

Poppy sneered at his attempt at sarcasm and gave him a playful punch in his ribs. 'Watch it, Matt, you don't want to upset me now, do you?'

Matt felt his side. 'Mind the bodywork,' he said. 'You may want to use this again later.'

After running her brush through her hair, Poppy decided she needed a cigarette and opened the side door leading onto the balcony. She emptied the remains of the fine wine supplied by Chez Blanc into her glass and sat on the small chair outside. Matt busied himself, tidying up the trail of mess that she had left in the bathroom, before joining her. The sun was setting in the distance and it was peaceful. The happy-go-lucky northerner did not want the day to come to an end. 'Are you pleased you came to the beach today?' he asked. 'I told you it would be fun.'

'It was OK, I suppose,' Poppy replied, not wanting to share her real take on their trip to the seaside. 'It was OK if you like that sort of thing.'

'It didn't take long for the moody bitch to return, did it?' Matt asked. He knew her well enough by now to know that her ungrateful tongue was somehow a cover for her insecurities. She rarely let her guard down.

'Are you like this with, you know, with your boyfriend?' Matt asked. Poppy said nothing, she took a long drag on her cigarette. The Geordie lad was not finished with that subject. 'Why do you put up with it, you know, the beatings? Everyone knows he hits you, Poppy, we have all seen the bruises.'

She took a large mouthful of her drink. 'I suppose that I must deserve it sometimes,' she said. 'Other times, I don't even think he knows what he is doing.'

Matt was determined to give her his opinion on her violent boyfriend. 'I think he is nothing but a bully, a thug, I don't know why you just don't leave him.'

Poppy let out a loud laugh. 'And what?' she said. 'And move in here with you?'

Matt immediately began to backtrack. 'No! I didn't mean, I meant, you know, just…'

She laughed at the sudden hint of panic in his voice. 'Don't worry, Matt,' she said. 'I think you are an OK sort of guy, but I won't be packing my bags and turning up on your doorstep just yet, you can relax now.'

Matt smiled at her comment. 'You know what I mean, Poppy. He is a sick fucker, you can do better than him, you can have a better life than that.'

Poppy thought carefully before speaking. 'He is not really that bad, Matt, he can be alright at times. It's all the gear that fucks him up. I don't even think he knows what he is on half of the time.'

'So, that is not your problem, leave him, there are plenty of places where he can get help.'

'It's not that easy. He was there for me, when I came out of prison, he looked after me. There were some nasty people that...'

Poppy changed the direction of her conversation mid-sentence. 'I guess I sort of owe it to him, to be there, maybe try to help him if I can.'

'But not to let him beat you black and blue,' Matt said. 'That is not helping anyone.'

Poppy refilled her almost empty wine glass. 'You don't understand, Matt. You really don't understand.'

She was right, Matt struggled to comprehend why she would defend her boyfriend's violent outbursts. She tried to explain the best she could. 'I have been there, just like Cameron. Years ago, I was hooked on everything. I know what it is like.'

'But you got clean,' Matt said. 'You sorted yourself out, didn't you?'

'It was not easy, you can't stop just like that. You don't just wake up one morning and find that life is so easy that you can get yourself through it without any help.'

'But you did?'

Poppy pondered for a few seconds. She wanted to share a chapter of her life that she rarely discussed with anyone. 'I had a friend, she looked after me, when I came out of prison for the first time. I had nowhere to go, I would have been on the streets, she took me in, she let me stay at her place.' Poppy smiled as an image of Nikita appeared in her head. 'She always had this crazy thing going on with her hair, and she was a funny girl, like a little pixie, she was so funny. She had her own thoughts about life, she used to say the craziest things, but I got what she meant, it all made sense to me.' Poppy thought for a few seconds and took a long sip of her wine. 'She had been on smack since she was sixteen, but she had got clean, she needed to get off that shit to get her little boy back.' Matt was intrigued, he had never heard Poppy talk about her past. He let her continue. 'Her sister had looked after her little boy while she was in rehab. She had to prove she could stay clean before she could have him back.' Poppy looked at the setting sun as it disappeared into the distance.

'Go on,' Matt said. 'So was it her that got you off the drugs?'

Poppy bit the corner of her lip, very hard. It was obvious that this was not an easy conversation for her. She took another large swig of her wine and sat back in her chair to continue her story. 'Zain, her son was called Zain, cute little fucker, he was just one year old. One day the Social Services turned up at the highrise where we lived. Nikita had gone to the shops, to do a bit of thieving, we had no money. But I was there, I was looking after him. They were very angry, the social bods, angry that Nikita had left him with me. I wasn't even supposed to be living there. I told them she wouldn't be long, I told them that, but they were still angry.' Matt thought he knew the reason why, but still asked the question. 'Were you on something, is that why they were angry?'

Finishing her drink and swiftly filling her glass again, Poppy answered, 'I was on sunshine or some sort of methadone shit, I can't really remember, I was sort of halfway down. He wasn't in any harm, Zain, he was playing with some toy bricks or something. God, she had fought so hard to get him back and I fucked it up for her, it was all my fault.'

Matt was intrigued now. 'What happened?' he asked.

Poppy looked down into her glass. She could see a reflection of Nikita's angry face looking back at her. 'They took Zain away, put him into care until they had a chance to assess her again. She was in bits, he was her whole life. She blamed me, told me that I should never have opened the door. I had never seen her so upset, so down. She wanted to score that night, she needed to get rid of the pain. I told her not to go to the Marfield.' Poppy looked down at the floor, her lip became to tremble. 'I fucking begged her not to go there.'

There was a long pause, this was clearly hard for Poppy, but she continued. 'Some joggers found her the next morning, in an alleyway at the back of the estate.'

'Dead?' Matt asked.

Poppy nodded. 'She overdosed, she overdosed on brown and it was all down to me.'

'Shit! That must have been really tough.'

'So I did things that…' Poppy clearly didn't want to finish the story, but she did. 'So I ended up back in prison. You don't really need to know the rest, Matt. I got clean in prison and stayed clean. You didn't really have much choice in Bronzefield. I haven't taken anything, not even weed, for nearly five years.'

'But that's a good thing. You should be proud of yourself for that.'

'She was twenty-one years old, Matt, she was only fucking twenty-one years old, she was just a little kid herself, in a woman's body. I can never forgive myself, never!'

He felt like putting his arms around her to comfort her, but instead, Matt opened another bottle of wine and topped up her glass. Poppy was still in deep thought. No doubt remembering that painful experience had played on her emotions.

'But you did the anger management course in there as well. I remember Danny said you used to have, well, like, problems. They helped you, there in Bronzefield, didn't they?'

Poppy laughed. 'Anger management, more like dig out the fucking psychos!'

'What do you mean?'

'The colours, Matt, you must have heard about the calming colours bullshit?'

'Colours?'

'So, every time you lose your rag and you feel like you want to belt someone, you think of other things to take your mind away to a better place.'

'Colours?' Matt asked again.

'Yeah, you know, the sky is so blue, the sun is warm and yellow, the grass is so fucking green, the water is so calming. The bods in white coats tell you to think of a place where you feel safe, then think of the colours and 'Hey presto!' you don't feel angry anymore.'

'Did it help?' Matt asked. 'Did you remember a safe place?'

Poppy thought for a few seconds and then shook her head. 'No, I have never really felt safe anywhere. Everywhere I have ever lived has been like a house of straw.'

Matt didn't understand. 'A house of straw?'

'You know, like the first little pig, I was always in the house of straw, just waiting for the next big bad wolf to come and take everything away.'

'So, there was no safe place at all?'

The conversation was now beginning to take its toll on Poppy. The excessive amount of wine she had consumed in such a short space of time was beginning to affect her emotions. Matt could see she was becoming a little agitated by his questions now and decided to lighten the conversation. 'So, in true gung-ho Poppy style, you told them to shove their colours up their arse, and that there was no safe place.'

'The boating lake!' Poppy replied, shaking her head. 'I told them that the boating lake was my safe place. I had to tell them something.'

Matt looked puzzled by her remark, but Poppy explained. 'If I had said there was no safe place they would have done more of their crazy tests, so I told them that it was the boating lake. My 'dad', if that's what you can call him, he used to take me there, every month, when I was six or seven years old. I told the assessors at Bronzefield that I could see the lake and that it was very peaceful there. I could see all of their fucking calming colours, right in front of me.'

'And did they believe you?'

'Yes, of course they did. They patted themselves on the back. They thought, *Hey, she gets all the shit about the colours and the safe place, don't put her in a straightjacket*, not just yet anyway.'

Matt laughed. 'If I didn't know you better, Poppy, I would think you really were insane.'

Poppy pulled a couple of faces at him and finished her drink. 'I have to go for a wazz,' he said. 'There are some snacks in the fridge if you are still hungry. Let's keep talking, Poppy, I want to hear more about you and those men in the white coats.'

Poppy checked the time on her mobile phone. 'I will have to go soon,' she said.

'Sure,' the cheeky northerner replied. 'I guess you will need to get some rest after today.'

Poppy was quick to respond. 'Ha fucking ha,' she said. 'You really think that you are some sort of stud, don't you, Matt?'

The beaming smile returned to his face as he headed for the bathroom. 'I don't get many complaints!'

Poppy could not resist the chance to bring down his ego a notch or two. 'Five out of ten, Matt,' she shouted. 'Six at best!'

\* \* \*

Alone with her thoughts Poppy began to regret talking so openly to Matt that evening. Maybe it was the excessive alcohol or the fact that she had just felt so at ease after such a good day out. The sex had been incredible. Maybe she trusted him with her darkest thoughts because he had made her feel so good in bed. A crazy notion went through her head for a few seconds – maybe Joe Manning should try that technique, giving her an earth-moving orgasm before each weekly session. That might loosen her up, she would finally answer all those awkward questions he kept asking her. But then an image appeared in her head, a picture of an overweight and ageing black man clambering up and down on top of her whilst reciting verses from the Bible. Suddenly, that idea did not seem like such a good one after all.

She was pleased that Matt had left the room, she had been finding it impossible to find the pause button to lock in her emotions. She felt that she had already said far too much, she began to feel slightly vulnerable. Deep down she knew that she had not been lying about the boating lake, that it really had felt safe there. She thrived on those regular trips with her dad. He had been a proper father in those days. The sun was always shining when they visited the lake. The sky was always blue when they were floating around in their small boat, sometimes for hours and hours at a time. He would make up funny names for the people in the other boats. 'Captain Stripey' and 'Captain Hooknose' were her favourites. Those two characters always seemed to be at the lake when they were there. Their boat would race against every other vessel on the water. Her dad's big strong arms and determination meant that they never lost a race. At the end of the day they would always go into the pavilion at the side of the lake. She would laugh loudly at his crazy impressions of the ladies serving in there. 'Treats for the winners,' he would shout when they entered the pavilion and she would be allowed to pick any ice cream she wanted. She always chose the same flavour, mint, smothered with chocolate sauce and covered with hundreds and thousands. They would laugh all day at the lake. She felt she could have stayed there forever. Yes, at the boating lake the sky was always blue, the sun shone all day, everything was peaceful, she really did feel safe there. But now that all seemed like it was so many years ago, she never knew why everything had to change.

When she was first placed into the care home he promised her that everything would be OK. He told her that he needed a week or two to 'sort himself out'. There were always excuses: he had a new job lined up, he would be getting a new house for them to live in, he had a hospital appointment. He assured her that her mother would come back home and soon they would all be a happy family again. She was only eight years old, he was her dad, she believed every word he said. But he never kept that promise, it was one of a thousand promises he never kept. He visited her, every week at first, then a couple of times each month. He was always late, but that was her dad, she knew that he never turned up on time for anything. But before long he only visited every other month and then just on her birthday and at Christmas. He usually brought gifts, a few badly wrapped cheap bits and pieces that he had found in a discount store, usually meant for a child much younger than she was. She often asked, but was never allowed, to stay with him. He used to say that things were 'complicated'. He always said it was best to wait until he had sorted out the new home, then everything would be good again.

As time went on Poppy realised that there was no new home, she realised that there would be no more trips to the boating lake, no more ice cream, and as for her mother, she was afraid to even start thinking about what had really happened to her mother. The clearest memory of her childhood would always be the day that the Baxter brothers locked her in that small dark cupboard in the kitchen at the Bluebridge home. How she thought she would never get out, she thought she was going to die in there. She screamed and screamed so loudly, but nobody heard her. She remembers being so frightened, terrified of dying, that she wet her knickers. All she wanted that day was for her father to come, to grab her in his arms and take her out of that terrible place. They could go to their boating lake and he could use those big strong arms to row and row and keep rowing. To row to the other side of the world, just anywhere, but not that place. She never ever wanted to go back to that cupboard, never to go back to that home, not to that life, ever again. But he never came, and soon after that day, he never came back at all.

That was the last time Poppy could ever remember crying. What was the point of getting upset and shedding all those wasted tears when there is nobody there to hold you tight and tell you that everything would be alright? After her terrible experience at Bluebridge, Poppy knew that her life would never be alright again.

By the time Matt had returned to the living room, Poppy had collected her things, made her way out of his flat and was halfway back to her car. She knew that she shouldn't drive back home that night, but she felt the need to be somewhere else, anywhere else, just not there. Her hidden emotions were unravelling far too fast for her liking. She felt like she had opened some painful wounds that evening and now needed to go back into hiding. Cameron was not a great listener, in truth he never really asked her anything to do with her past, or the way she was feeling. He was always happy for her to bury her thoughts somewhere deep in her fragile and scrambled mind. Something told Poppy that, in truth, that really was the safest place for them.

# CHAPTER
# FOURTEEN

Krista had finally plucked up the courage to tell her partner of ten years that she no longer had feelings for him. It had not been an easy conversation for her and all the things she had planned to say just came out wrong. He had accepted that their lack of physical contact over the past few months had put something of a strain on the relationship, however he put this down to the workload created by her recent promotion and his own hectic schedule of work commitments. He had left their house with a large suitcase and a sports bag full of his personal belongings. He did not leave in a fit of anger, but if she had told him the whole truth this may well have been the case. He believed that if he gave Krista some time to think things over that they may reconcile, as they had done on several previous occasions over the past decade. He had no idea of the double life she had been leading for the past couple of years and had no reason to think that, given time, they would work out their differences again. Krista had told him she hoped they could remain friends. They had come to England together all those years ago and had shared many highs and lows during that time. But something was now missing in their relationship. She wanted to tell him that she now thought of him more as a brother than a lover, but she decided to spare his feelings and instead blamed the breakup on the day-to-day pressures of their jobs.

He had moved his belongings into a work colleague's house in central London. The man in question was going through something of a messy divorce himself, so her boyfriend would have someone he could relate to. Krista was in his thoughts, morning, noon and night, and he often hoped his phone would ring and it would be the sound of her beautiful voice, telling him that she had made a mistake.

Tonight, however, Krista was not thinking about him, she was not thinking about work. Tonight Krista was only thinking about one thing, Dean. She would be seeing him in less than two hours and she wanted to look her best. She had been into London that morning to visit her favourite clothes shop in Bond Street. She needed something special for the glamorous event they were attending together. After much deliberation, she found the perfect dress for the occasion. Costing more than £300, the black strapless dinner dress came with a novelty clip in the shape of a small padlock. The key for the padlock was tiny, so she put it in a small pocket in her purse. She intended to have a lot to drink that night to celebrate her first night of real freedom. The last thing she needed was not being able to get out of that dress. She had spent more than two hours in the hairdressers during the afternoon. Her flowing blonde locks bore tight curls at either side of her head and her nails were a painted a shocking shade of purple. She applied a final coat of lipstick before admiring herself in her bedroom mirror. 'I hope that bastard appreciates it,' she said, the bastard, of course, being Dean Jarvis.

Her best friend Millie had called her, just as she was about to set out for the evening. She warned her, and it wasn't for the first time, that Dean was 'playing' her and she would end up being hurt. She wasn't happy at the way that Krista had ended her relationship and begged her to rethink the situation, before jumping in 'too deep'. Krista decided to ignore her friend's advice. She knew how she felt about Dean and was sure that if she remained patient, things would work out for them in the end.

The *Southern Gazette* annual awards dinner was a 'must-attend event' on the calendar of every self-respecting local businessman in the North Surrey area. Usually held in the function suite of respectable hotels in either Croydon or Sutton, it was a tribute evening to the successes of local businesses and charity organisations. It was not necessarily the prospect of winning an award that got everyone excited about this particular event, it was more the opportunity to dress up in a tuxedo or evening gown and get completely inebriated at your company's expense.

The previous year Krista had sat three tables away from Dean. He had been the guest of a rival company. The two of them made eye contact through the whole of the evening and managed the odd couple of minutes of conversation during their frequent visits to the bar area. There was no touching, that was the rule last year, no touching in public. They managed to keep to their agreement at the event but almost as soon as the function had ended they were wrapped up in one another's arms. Dean had booked a cheap, but not so cheerful, bed and breakfast hotel, less than a mile from the venue. They both headed there in separate taxis after the event had finished and nobody was the wiser to their sordid affair. The Regal Deluxe hardly lived up to its name with a stained carpet and burn marks on the duvet spread. The bath towel smelt of stale tobacco and the shower didn't work properly. However, neither of them had been worrying too much about what they might write in a Trip Advisor review for the place, as they enjoyed a two-hour session of animalistic sex. They also did not seem to be bothered that they both had small insect bite marks on large areas of their legs, as they made their way back to their respective partners in the small hours of the morning.

In Krista's mind, tonight would be different, public showing of her affection could be allowed. She was a single woman now and everyone at Imediacom knew it. What she did not realise was that everyone at her workplace had also worked out that her and Dean had been something of an 'item' for more than a year, but in truth, nobody was really that bothered. Their suspicions were rubberstamped when Krista had invited Dean to be her guest at their table at the forthcoming function. George Penning had given each head of department at Imediacom the chance to invite one client along as their guest. Only he, being the boss of the company, would be allowed to have his partner there. So when it was announced that Dean Jarvis, a mere salesman of one their smaller clients, had been invited, he knew that there was more than just a working relationship between the two of them. The company owner respected his employee enough, however, to say nothing on the subject, but his staff all knew that he was not a fan of the cocky sales rep.

In Krista's mind, it would be different tonight. There could be touching, maybe dancing. Kissing, however, would be a definite 'no-no' in front of her work colleagues. But in truth, if the night ended with Dean inside her, she did not care where it happened. Whether that was in a five-star hotel or that disgusting Regal Deluxe place, it would not worry her at all.

Krista met her work colleagues in the main bar area of the Britannia hotel, many of them passing comments on her unusual evening dress. She was never one to compliment herself, but Krista thought that she looked 'hot' tonight, a fact borne out by the countless men who stared in her direction on their way to the bar. But the much-talked-about outfit, the expensive cut and blowdry and her perfectly manicured nails were all for the benefit of just one person, but he was nowhere to be seen. She tried hard not to, but she found herself looking over her shoulder every thirty seconds or so, expecting to see Dean's face.

As the toastmaster indicated loudly and clearly that guests should be seated, Krista reached for her mobile to call Dean. *Not tonight*, she thought, *please don't be late tonight.* Before she could make the call, however, George Penning had started to chat to her about his forthcoming cruise around the Mediterranean. She felt obligated to walk with him into the main hall, turning her head around a few times hoping that Dean was behind her. He wasn't. Those damning comments from her friend Millie came back to haunt her as she took her seat at the Imediacom table. Maybe she was right, maybe nothing would ever change, maybe she was just kidding herself that she could ever have him to herself.

Dean finally arrived, somewhere between the serving of the starter and the introduction of the compere for the night. 'Sorry, sorry, sorry,' he said as he approached the only empty seat in the banquet room. He acknowledged everybody at the table with a small handshake. 'Dean Jarvis from Galaxon,' he said to them all, leaving the final gesture of a small kiss on Krista's cheek to last.

'Bastard!' she whispered as he neared her face. 'I really hate you sometimes.'

Dean ignored her comment completely. 'Really good to see you too, Miss Nylund,' he said and perched himself down next to her. Nobody at the table from Imediacom was fooled by the formalities, a couple of them expressing their disapproval with a shake of the head. Dean's hand found Krista's knee and gave it a small squeeze under the table. 'You look fucking amazing!' he whispered, before pouring himself an overgenerous glass of the house wine.

'You had better make up for this later,' she replied softly, not that anyone at the table would have been bothered by her comment.

Dean had hired his tuxedo, shirt and tie for the event from a local tailor. It was nothing too fancy, but he looked sufficiently smart to convince the other guests that he was more than comfortable in his surroundings. In truth though, he wasn't. Dean hated all this dressing up palaver for the sake of watching a self-indulgent newspaper editor hand out a few cheap trophies. He resented paying out over £100 of his hard-earned wages to pretend to be someone he wasn't. Many of these people enjoyed six-figure salaries and spent at least four weeks each year sunning themselves on faraway exotic beaches. He, on the other hand, was a journeyman, a salesman with no real talent. In truth Dean would have starved if he had to rely solely on his commissions, and only endured the job at Galaxon because of the half-decent basic salary they paid him. But he did not want to upset Krista any more than was necessary. She had been somewhat strange with him on the telephone over the past week or so and he felt she might be growing tired of him. He didn't want that, he had found his 'Persephone', his golden goddess. She made him feel special inside, not that he told her that often enough. So he was here, he would pretend to laugh at the guests' jokes and listen to them drone on about islands to visit in the Caribbean. He would, however, be taking full advantage of the free bar that night. Dean had every intention of making sure that his presence was rewarded with both sex with his goddess and consuming enough alcohol to make him feel that wearing this uncomfortable suit for the whole evening was worthwhile. He emptied the remains of the last bottle of house wine into his glass and ordered some Chablis.

The general table conversation seemed to be centred around the rapid development of modern technology and the publicity behind the tribute band that were performing that night. Dean's input to both conversations was limited. He seemed to have other things on his mind. Getting drunk and inside Krista's knickers that night were very much at the forefront of his thoughts. The pleasant and somewhat innocuous table conversation, however, was about to take a twist in a different direction.

'How is that lovely Norse god of yours, Krista?' Mr Penning's wife asked. Obviously, no one had made her aware of the recent change in her personal circumstances.

'Oh, we are not together anymore,' she replied, her comment receiving a look of bewilderment from Dean's direction.

'Oh, I am sorry,' the uninformed woman said. 'You were together for a long time, I believe.'

Krista blushed slightly as she became the centre of attention at the table. 'About nine years, but it was always on and off. I guess we had just passed our sell-by date.' Dean said nothing, he looked as surprised as Mrs Penning.

Melanie Sharp from the finance department suddenly got in on the discussion. 'No kids though, Krista, it is good that there are no kids.'

Still embarrassed at being the topic of conversation, Krista laughed. 'God no!' she said. 'The last thing I want in the world is kids!' She was now holding court at the table, so felt obligated to carry on. 'I can never imagine me wiping someone else's bottom. No, definitely no kids on the radar for me.' Her response startled Dean somewhat and he gulped down at least half a glass of wine in one go.

'What about you, Dean?' Melanie asked. 'Have you got kids?' A comment that made Krista realise that the woman from accounts was stirring the pot.

'Just one,' Dean replied. 'Poppy, my beautiful little girl.'

It was now George Penning's wife's turn to poke her nose in again. 'How old?' she asked.

'Almost two and a half,' Dean said. 'She started playschool last week.' There were a few token 'Aaahhhs' and 'Bless hers' bandied around the table, but not from Krista, she was seething inside. She made a mental note to make life hell for the prim and proper Ms Sharp from now on. But before she could formulate any plan to exact her revenge, something else began to irritate her. Dean was deep in conversation with the big-chested lady with striking red hair, to his left. The woman was clearly flirting, those large bosoms thrusting over the top of her silk dress and pointing directly in the eyeline of 'her man'. *What are they talking about?* she thought. What was so fascinating that she had his full attention?

Krista decided to fight fire with fire. She turned to the well-spoken man on her right and indulged him in a pointless conversation. 'You look like an actor,' she said. 'The one off that New York cop series.'

The man thanked her for her kind observation. 'I get that all the time,' he replied. 'God, I wish I had his money.'

Krista continued her attempts to draw Dean's attention away from the heaving bosom of the woman beside him. 'I like men with rugged looks,' she said loudly. 'Not guys who look like they spend more time getting ready than I do.' She didn't know where it was all coming from – the drink, the jealousy, the anger she was feeling towards her so-called soul mate. But she was not yet getting this strange man's undivided attention and Dean certainly didn't seem too bothered about her flirting. Krista knew she had to up the ante. 'Everyone has been trying to guess if the padlock on my dress has a real key or not,' she said, now gaining a grin from the well-heeled gent and the undivided attention of a couple of the male guests sitting at the table.

'Well?!' her newfound friend asked. 'Does it?'

Krista took a long drink from her glass and said, 'I hope the bloody key fits, otherwise I will be wearing this for work on Monday.' The man laughed and was joined in his laughter by the two curious men and Melanie, who had been listening in on the conversation.

The drinks continued to flow at their table, bow ties were being loosened and the tone of the conversation began to drop. The blonde middle-aged woman, who was the guest of the sales manager, had been quiet for most of the evening, but suddenly came to life and had some raunchy tales to tell about some of the sexual shenanigans that went on at her office in North London.

Before long she had begun to share with the table her intimate fantasy involving clowns and custard, bringing a roar of laughter from most of the guests, most that is, but not Krista. The well-spoken man, who had been flirting with her, had now turned his attention to Melanie. The two of them seemed to have a mutual interest in horse riding and sailing. Dean and his new flame-haired friend had stopped laughing by now and were both considering their dessert options. The bubbly blonde parked her sordid office tales and decided that she needed to relieve herself of the full bottle of red wine she had just necked. Dean's new chatting buddy decided to follow her, leaving him looking aimlessly at the other guests. But, no sooner had the large-breasted lady disappeared to go to the toilet, Dean was at it again. He was clearly flirting with the waitress. Krista couldn't quite make out their conversation, the noise of the tribute band was covering their words, but she could tell that it was more than friendly banter by their body language. She may have been wrong about 'Miss Big Tits', Krista thought, but she could see that Dean was definitely chatting-up the hired help. She wanted to scream at him at that moment, but something told her it was not the right thing to do. Instead she bit hard into her thumb and made the decision that she would make him suffer for the rest of that evening.

A range of desserts arrived at the Imediacom table, accompanied by envelopes, marked up for voluntary, but obviously meaning compulsory, charity donations. The guests began to lower their voices as the toastmaster asked for some silence in the hall. The speaker for the evening was Brian Needham, the managing editor for the newspaper. He took his place on the stage and announced that he would shortly be revealing the winners of the 1997 awards. Dean now came into his element. Having been there the previous year he realised how laborious the next hour or so would be, so he added his own brand of entertainment for the table guests. He began mimicking each recipient of an award, with his own take on their mannerisms. His impressions were certainly more entertaining than the actual award winners. Even the usually sour-faced Melanie was amused by his comic routine. Her and the other table guests laughed loudly at his antics, attracting much attention from other attendees, who asked them to respect the efforts of the compere.

Krista felt slightly more at ease now. The woman with the exposed chest had moved seats and was chatting to her boss on another table. She seemed to have Dean back to herself. But now another new threat had appeared in the shape of a slim brunette waitress serving at their table. She was much younger and prettier than the other one. His eyes were all over her. The waitress and Dean were exchanging some amusing anecdotes and he seemed to be enjoying the attention of this much younger girl. Krista's face screwed up as she watched their banter continue. *Why the hell is she still at the table?* she thought. *She is just a waitress, she is just the bloody hired help, she is here on minimum wage, to serve food and drinks, not to chat to all and sundry.* Was he doing this on purpose, to wind her up? *Why doesn't she just fuck off and leave him alone?* A moment later the young girl moved away from the table leaving Krista to give Dean a stare that would have killed off one of his mythical heroes at thirty paces. Millie's warning was sounding out louder than ever in her head now, Krista was livid.

The interval arrived. A mass exodus from the tables ensued, many heading for the toilet area or the bar, others to the smoking platform outside. Dean opted for a walk to the bar at the far end of the hall. He was still hell bent on getting his money's worth for hiring out the tuxedo. The drinks were still free, so there was something of a queue at the bar. He suddenly felt a presence behind him and turned around to find Krista. The stare was still there. He knew instantly that he was 'in the doghouse'.

'Having a good time?' she asked in a sarcastic tone. 'Having a good time making me look stupid?'

'What?' Dean asked, turning away to avoid her glaring eye contact.

'You, with everyone at the table. You pretending to be 'Mr Perfect'. I am starting to see the real you now.'

Dean looked back at her and shrugged his shoulders. 'This is me,' he said. 'I am not the one putting on an act.'

'What was all that shit about?' she asked, mimicking his voice. 'She is only two and a half, she started playschool last week.'

'I have a daughter,' Dean said. 'You have to learn to deal with that, Nylund.'

Krista raised her voice a little louder. 'I have been dealing with it every day for more than two years. Could you not have just given it a rest for one night?'

Dean seemed to be avoiding this confrontation. He raised his arm to get the attention of the barman. 'Drink?' he asked her.

'Shove your drink!' was her immediate response.

At that moment Mrs Penning and one of the table guests walked past them, looking for her husband. Dean and Krista both raised a smile and nodded as if everything was fine between the two of them. Dean was handed a large Jack Daniels by the barman. He seemed happy. Krista was far from happy. 'You were all over that slutty ginger woman. I saw you, you couldn't take your eyes off her tits,' she said.

Dean seemed bemused. 'What the hell are you talking about? I was just making conversation.'

'Shame that fake tan can't hide her freckles,' Krista pointed out. 'She looked really ugly when the lights went up.'

Dean sighed. 'Here we go again, here comes the psycho!'

Krista's rant continued. 'And that teenage waitress, is that the type of thing you like, Dean, or do you just do it to wind me up?'

'You are so paranoid, Nylund, you need to chill out, you are making a fool of yourself.'

'Paranoid?!' she said. 'Paranoid?! Are you not fucking surprised that I am paranoid?'

Dean was taken aback, he rarely heard her use the 'F' word unless they were having sex. He started to realise how upset she really was.

Krista was now in full swing, she needed to get everything off her chest. 'You turn up late, again! You spend half your time chatting up some ugly ginger bitch and the hired help and the other half pretending how blissful things are with you and your daughter at home. No, Dean, I am not paranoid, I am angry, I am really angry!'

'I can hardly sit there holding your hand, can I?'

'Maybe not, but you could start to appreciate what you have. Half the men in here would love to be sitting where you are tonight and to have what you have with me.'

Dean snapped back at her. 'I'm here, aren't I? I made the effort. It was over a hundred quid to hire this bloody monkey suit. I am sitting there listening to them all drone on about the best place to eat when you visit Marbella and all that shit. Isn't that enough?'

'If you didn't want to come tonight you should have said so.'

'Oh, what and have you on my case, telling me that I never make any effort to be with you.'

'Well, you don't, not really. It is always me these days, Dean.'

The bubbly blonde from their table, clearly a little drunk, walked past them at that moment and their heated conversation came to a halt. They both offered her a polite smile as she waddled off to find the toilets. 'That will teach her to hog the red wine to herself all night,' Krista said, now seemingly having an axe to grind with most of the guests on their table.

It was Dean's turn to vent now and he did not hold back. 'So what was all that shit about you and your boyfriend not being together anymore? Or was that just for other people's benefit?'

'He has moved out. We are finished now, for good.'

'Oh what, like the last time and the time before that?'

'No, Dean, he has really gone now. It didn't feel right, sneaking around behind his back all of the time.'

'So now you expect me to do the same thing with Hannah?'

'No, Dean, I never said anything because I didn't want you to feel under any pressure.'

Dean shrugged his shoulders. 'No pressure on me!'

'No, of course not, Dean, why would there be? Everything is great in your life, everything is so bloody rosy in Dean Jarvis's little world!'

'Here we go again, let's spoil a perfectly good evening.'

Krista's anger began to escalate. Dean could see she was almost at breaking point. 'You don't get it, Dean, you really don't get it. I don't ask for much out of what we have, but you just take the piss, you take me for granted all of the time.'

They broke off their argument to let a couple of stumbling party revellers get nearer to the bar. 'I see you once, maybe twice a week,' she continued. 'It is always when you want to meet. Everything has to work around you.'

Dean didn't like home truths, but he knew he was in the wrong this time, so he let her continue. 'You are always late or cancelling at the last minute. You were even late tonight.' He started to explain the reason, but she spoke over him. 'Is it too much to ask for a bit more? To ask you if this is really what you want?'

'You know I can't leave her, not at this moment. Hannah is not stable, I have told you about her problems. I can't leave her with Poppy, I told you what she said she is capable of, what she might do.'

Krista looked him in the eye. She had heard this so many times before. 'I don't believe you, Dean. I don't believe that you think she could harm her own daughter. Jesus, you make her sound like she should be locked up in an asylum. If you were really that worried you would report her to Social Services or something.'

'And risk losing Poppy?'

'You wouldn't lose her, Dean. If your wife is really ill, like you say she is, they will give her help. But I am sorry, I just don't believe you, I think it's all bullshit. I think you will keep using her illness, if she really is ill, as a reason for staying with her. I don't know, maybe you still love her. Do you, Dean, do you still love her?'

'No of course not,' he said. 'You can believe what you want.'

The two stood in silence for a few seconds, both regretting some of the things they had just said. Krista began to shake a little, as if she was about to cry. 'Maybe we should just finish it, Dean. Maybe that would be best for both of us.'

'No!' Dean snapped, grabbing her hand and pulling her closer to him. 'I can't lose you!'

And then it happened, as they stood at the crowded bar, face to face, they were close enough to feel one another's breath, both desperate to taste the other's lips. He gripped her hand so tightly he almost crushed her tiny fingers. Dean looked deep into her eyes, those mesmerising whirlpools of unbridled temptation. They drew him back in, they sent his ship sailing on towards the dangerous waters, back towards the rocks and the sirens. He knew it was wrong, he knew he shouldn't say it, but he knew he needed to, the words just left his mouth. 'I love you, Nylund,' he said. 'I can't lose you, I love you.'

Krista was dumbstruck, she was completely stunned. A dozen or more voices were sounding out behind her back, but she heard nothing, nothing but those three words, a simple sentence that she had never expected to hear that night, or maybe ever. She blushed. In that moment they seemed to be alone. They were surrounded by hundreds of partying revellers, there was loud music piping out from the speakers, but they heard nothing. It was as if they were on a small island, somewhere else, somewhere magical. Krista immediately thought of their visit to the lake.

Dean began to open his mouth to say something, but Krista's finger stopped him, sealing his lips closed, so she could let those few words linger in her head, words that she had waited almost three years to hear. 'Don't say anything else,' she said. 'Just don't say anything else.' In her mind she wanted those three words to be the last she ever heard. If the world were to end that night, those words would still be resounding in her head. Her heart raced, and she felt slightly giddy. 'Let's go back to our table,' she said, grabbing his hand and dragging him through the crowd of smart suits and dinner dresses. She was not bothered about any rules they may have. So what if this was a display of public affection, she no longer cared, he had said he loved her, he had said he loved her and that was enough for her.

As they took their seats and shared the remainder of a bottle of Chablis, the toastmaster asked guests to return to their tables for the remainder of the awards ceremony. The constant flash of a busy photographer's camera could be seen moving around the room, snapping shots of drunken guests, some pulling strange faces, others taking his artistry more seriously. Arriving at the Imediacom table he shouted over to the couple that had exchanged less than a dozen words since that moment at the bar. 'Smile!' he said as they faced the camera. 'Try to look like you are really having fun.' They didn't need to try very hard. Krista and Dean looked like a couple that had won the lottery. Their eyes shone like sparkling jewels, their fingers wrapped tightly together. The photographer probably didn't know it when he took that photograph, but he captured an embrace that would live for all eternity.

The tribute band had received a very mixed reception. They may have dressed like the original artists but sounded nothing like the band they were imitating. Those who thought their covers of one or two classic songs were worth singing along to were either very drunk or had hearing difficulties. Brian Needham gave a closing speech, thanking all for attending and their continued advertising support to the *Gazette*, the latter being the more important of the two. All that was left was an hour or so of music and dancing, which Dean and Krista decided to watch rather than join in. Dean, as was his way, ridiculed most of the guests' moves on the dance floor, not that any of them seemed too bothered. The topics of conversation had been limited since Dean's declaration of his love, but there were no more mentions of Hannah or Poppy and no further shows of jealousy from an ever-smiling Krista. Their hands parted just once, when Dean raced across to steal a half bottle of wine from another table as its guests were departing.

As the night began to wind down the happy couple's attention was drawn to the man who had been sitting next to Krista at the table. He was dancing very closely with the busty redhead. They seemed to be whispering in one another's ear, his hands, at the time, placed firmly on the woman's buttocks. 'I wonder if they will end up fucking,' Dean said. 'Maybe we should give them the number for that Regal place we stayed at last year.' Krista thought about his comment for a few seconds. 'The Regal Deluxe rooms,' she said. 'Oh my god! That was such a disgusting shithole, Dean. I wouldn't recommend that to anyone.' She suddenly started scratching her arms. 'It makes me itch just to think about that place.'

Dean smirked and then a large smile appeared on his face. 'But it was a great night there though. I wouldn't have changed that night, would you?'

Krista's eyes lit up and her beaming smile matched his. 'Not for anything in the world,' she replied.

George Penning and his wife said their farewells to their employees and guests, George giving Dean a hard stare as he shook his hand. 'He has never liked me,' Dean observed. 'Your boss, the tortoise man, he has never really liked me.'

Krista smiled. 'Not many people do at our place, Dean. In fact, I think I am the only one at our offices that tolerates you.'

He saw the funny side of her comment and was lost for words for a few seconds. Suddenly he spotted something which had clearly amused him. 'Look, Nylund,' he said. 'Over there in the corner,' pointing out that their table guests had gone from smooching on the dancefloor to fully locked lips. 'Lucky bastard!' he added, a comment which Krista showed her contempt for by giving him a hefty dig in his ribs.

'Wait 'til he sees her in the lights,' she said. 'He will run a mile.'

As the bar finally closed and flocks of staggering revellers started to search for taxi numbers, Dean clutched Krista's hand tightly. 'So,' he asked, 'if it is not the Regal Deluxe and it is too far to get to the lake, where are we going tonight?'

The answer was instantaneous. 'Back to mine of course!' she said.

Finishing the remains of his drink he pulled her close to his chest and gazed directly into her beautiful eyes. 'Is that a good idea?' he asked.

Krista nodded. 'Yes, but you will need something when we get there, otherwise we might have a problem.' Dean looked slightly puzzled by her remark, until she produced a tiny key for the padlock on her dress and slipped it into his hand. 'And I love you too, Dean, with all my heart.'

It was an evening that had brought them closer together, closer than they had ever been before. Dean spent the whole night with the tempestuous siren of his dreams, totally unaware of what the consequences of this stolen night away from his wife would bring.

# CHAPTER FIFTEEN

The smell of the probation office always reminded Poppy of the butterscotch sauce they served in Chez Blanc. It was clean and fresh, like pine. She assumed that Joe cleaned his room vigorously every night after seeing off the last of his criminal delinquents that day. Maybe, she thought, in a strange way, he really did believe that cleanliness was next to godliness. The room never looked any different to her. The blinds were always half drawn, the comfy black sofa and matching chairs never moved. That awful photograph of his family on his desk was staring out at his visitors. Maybe it was his way of showing his children the type of people that they would become if they strayed onto the path of evil. And there looking down on her from the wall behind his desk was that large clock, the symbol of the time she had spent inside that small prison.

They were more than halfway through their session. As usual Joe had done most of the talking, throwing in the odd biblical parable along the way. It had all been going well until her probation officer began studying a new folder with Poppy's name on it. She hadn't noticed this one before, it looked very official.

He seemed to be focused on one section of the folder. His facial expressions gave her the impression that something in that report was bothering him. When he left the folder open to refresh his glass with water, Poppy noticed a photograph of herself on the inside cover and quickly realised that the file was something to do with Bronzefield prison.

When he returned to his chair, Manning got straight to the point. 'I have noticed that you have still not arranged the anger management course, Poppy, the authorities are not very happy about that.' Poppy did not respond, she knew there would be more to come. 'You have been telling me for months now that you were going to call Mrs Bishop. I believe she has also tried calling you, without success.'

Poppy knew that her lies had finally caught up with her. She tried a slightly different tack. 'I think we just keep missing each other. She always calls me when I am busy at work and I didn't want to call her late at night.' Her would-be mentor wasn't really listening, he was still engrossed in the fresh folder. Poppy looked up at the clock. Twenty-five minutes to go and only five sessions left. *Take your time with that report, Joe,* she thought. *Read the whole bloody thing from cover to cover and then read it again, read it ten times if you want, read it until it gets us past eleven o'clock.*

But Manning had more questions, he always had more questions. Wiping his glasses, he gave her a stern but friendly stare. 'It says here that you spent some time at the assessment centre attached to Bronzefield.'

Poppy couldn't deny it, she hated hearing that word 'assessment' again. She simply nodded. 'They did lots of tests there.'

'They looked at ways that you could deal with your anger issues,' Joe said. Poppy didn't know if that was a question or a statement but nodded again. 'What sort of tests were they, Poppy?' Manning asked.

She didn't have to think hard, she remembered it well, the loud-mouthed American woman and the two softly-spoken staff with painted-on smiles, all of them asking her a million awkward questions and doing all those crazy tests with the colours. She certainly wasn't going to share any of that with him today. 'Just tests,' she said. 'Just like questions and things.'

Joe was still pawing through all the new reports he had received but there was no let-up in his line of questioning. 'The report says that the anger management course was a condition of your release, Poppy, that you had to complete a minimum four-month course.'

She had to tell another lie. She hoped it would get him off the subject. 'I am sure they said it was voluntary, that I could choose. They said I only had to do it if I thought I needed it.'

Manning shook his head and tapped the folder with his pen. 'No! No! It definitely says that you had to attend.' Poppy remained silent, she was good at doing that. She had told her lie, she thought that would buy her some more time, but it didn't, Manning was still on the warpath. 'Do you remember the first time you lost control of your temper, Poppy, do you remember the first time you lashed out at someone?'

Time seemed to have come to a standstill. 'I don't remember,' Poppy said, willing the big hand on the clock to move faster. 'I really don't remember.'

But that was another lie, another untruth that she had used to avoid reliving her past. Poppy did remember, she remembered everything, torrid times in her life she had chosen to lock away in her troubled mind. She was nine years old, she had been in care for over a year. Her father had stopped coming to see her by then. She had argued with a foster family that she had been living with and had been moved to the Bluebridge children's home in Crowborough. The first few weeks were hard. Nobody spoke to her, nobody seemed to like her. The staff there were very strict, they would punish her severely if she misbehaved. In the modern day and age, the thought that children could still be physically beaten to teach them manners is almost unthinkable, but at Bluebridge it was commonplace. She was smacked soundly on her backside for her insolence by two different carers during those first few weeks at the home. She soon learned to keep her thoughts to herself. None of the children seemed to ever be visited by their family at that place, so the staff could get away with almost anything. If there was no one for the children to tell, the care workers felt safe dishing out punishments and putting their hands and other parts of their bodies in places that they shouldn't. In her first month at the residential home, Poppy was touched inappropriately on more than one occasion by Mr Donovan. He was a lanky man with a lop-sided moustache, he had crooked teeth and always smelled of alcohol. One of the older girls had told Poppy that he was 'sick in the head' and that he had forced her to give him oral sex. When Poppy reported his behaviour to the manager of the home she was called a liar. They said that she was simply an attention seeker. He was never even questioned about her allegations.

She felt very scared and alone at Bluebridge, but Mr Donovan was the least of her problems. The staff there were very strict with all the children, all the children that is, except for the Baxter brothers. The evil siblings could get away with anything. Lewis Baxter was thirteen years old and had a scar on his forehead and wild demon-like eyes. His brother Callum was two years younger. He seemed to be the one with the more vicious streak. They bullied everyone, stealing any treats kids had earned and implementing a non-stop campaign of intimidation and violence. Many of the staff seemed to be afraid of the duo and chose to pass off their behaviour as 'just kids being kids' rather than confront them.

During her early days at Bluebridge, Poppy had been mostly left alone. The odd punch and kick here and there and the brothers spitting in her dinner was just something she had to accept. But as time went on their campaign of violence towards her began to escalate. In the space of one week the brothers had burned her legs with a lighter, placed dog excrement on her pillow and covered her hair with eggs and flour. They laughed when she cried and hit her when she threatened to report them to the staff. She hoped that they would get bored of terrorising a young defenceless girl and that they might move their attention to other residents at the home, but she was wrong. Poppy will always remember that warm summer day. Most of the staff and other children were in the back garden. She didn't want to go outside, but surely would have done had she known what the brothers had planned for her. First, they grabbed and covered her mouth to stop her screaming, they then dragged her into the utility room behind the kitchen area and forced her into a tiny cupboard where the pots and pans were usually kept. The cupboard was so small they had to bend her knees to get her all the way in. Poppy kicked out and screamed as if she was in fear of her life. The brothers laughed loudly as they shut the door closed behind her and pushed a heavy table in front of it to make sure she could not get out. Inside the coffin-like cupboard she could hardly move at all. She shouted and screamed and cried out for help, but no one came. Surrounded by the eerie darkness, her tiny frame began to ache as she tried to stretch her legs. In her panic-stricken state she struggled to catch her breath, she wet herself and was sick down the front of her top. At some point she stopped struggling and her screams were replaced with a mellow sobbing. In Poppy's mind, she thought that this was it, this was where her misery would finally end, that this was where she would die.

It was over two hours before the staff came back into the house and moved the table away to release her from her prison. She expected sympathy for her plight and retribution for the brothers on her release, but instead she received a scolding from the head care worker, Mrs Keane, for playing dangerous games. Poppy wiped away the traces of her tears and headed for her room. She made no mention of who the culprits were, she knew that there was no point. But something happened to Poppy Jarvis in that cupboard that day. A twisted bitterness took over both her body and her mind, a bitterness that would stay with her for the rest of her life. Her abuse from the vile siblings continued for a few more weeks. She suffered in silence, almost accepting her beatings as part of her daily life.

It was a week or two before Christmas and the home had recently lost several of its long-term residents to foster homes. Lewis Baxter was next on the list, and suddenly, out of the blue, he had been bundled into the back of a caseworker's car and carried off for a one-week trial stay with a family in Kent. His brother was furious that they had been separated, letting everyone know that others would suffer until he returned. Poppy was always an easy target for him and while she was sitting on her bed he caught her from behind, wrapping his hands around her neck as if to strangle her. He may have only been playing, but he left her with red marks around her neck and a cut on the side of her face. But Poppy said nothing. In her head, she knew that it was time, time to bring a stop to her torment. He was alone now, there was no big brother to protect him.

In the early hours of the following morning, Poppy crept downstairs and made her way into the kitchen. As quietly as she could, she opened the drawers to find the weapon of choice, a fork, a simple dinner fork. She ran her fingers across the edges of each of them until she was happy she had secured the sharpest one. She slowly made her way back upstairs and into where Callum lay sleeping. The other bed in the room, his brother's, was empty. She remembered clearly how the beam from the lamppost light outside seemed to be guiding a path to him across the floor, leading her directly to her target. She watched the unsuspecting bully for a few seconds, wrapped up tightly under his bedsheets and heavy duvet cover. He looked peaceful, no doubt dreaming of some more sick and twisted ways to torment her and the others at Bluebridge. All at once Poppy raised her arm and brought the fork down with an almighty force, the object splintering his skin as it cut deep into his cheek. Callum moved sharply and let out a cry of pain, but Poppy had not finished, her arm went up again and brought the makeshift weapon crashing down. This time it pierced his face much deeper and shots of blood flew up into the air. His moans had now become screams as he struggled to free himself from the covers, but a third blow was already on its way, this one barely missing his left eye and gouging a much deeper gash into the softer skin on his face. There was blood everywhere now, his pillow turned into a sea of soaking claret. As Callum struggled to free himself from the bedclothes, the fork cut him for the fourth time, this time piercing the side of his nose. Suddenly the bedroom light went on, a startled Mrs Keane rushing in to see what all the commotion was. She entered just in time to see the bloody object in Poppy's hand raised again. She screamed out loudly, 'No, Poppy, no!' But her shouts went unnoticed as Poppy swung her arm downwards, this time catching the side of Callum's neck. Luckily for the panic-stricken boy, the blow missed his jugular artery.

By now most of the staff were on the scene of this bloody carnage, Mr Donovan grabbing Poppy's arm and forcing the object of destruction from her grasp. There was screaming, there was shouting, there was blood everywhere, it was pandemonium. As one of the staff rushed to Callum's aid with some towels to help stop the bleeding, it happened, that moment of realism. Poppy stood there, in complete silence, looking at the mayhem she had caused. But there was something strange. She felt nothing inside, she simply felt numb. Poppy was not worried about retribution, either from the staff or Lewis Baxter. She felt no sympathy for the boy whose face would now be disfigured for life, she simply felt nothing at all.

Poppy was removed from Bluebridge a few days after the incident and relocated to a rundown children's home on the Sussex coast. The staff at her previous home had apparently 'hushed up' the incident in a bid to protect the ailing reputation it already had. Apart from the severe telling-off and some brutal manhandling, Poppy received no punishment at all. In her mind she wondered if this was because the staff there may have thought that the brothers might have needed bringing down a peg or two, and that this was some sort of rough justice. Some years later, a former resident at Bluebridge told Poppy that the brothers were sent to foster homes at opposite ends of the country. They believed that Lewis ended up serving a ten-year prison sentence at a maximum-security prison in Yorkshire and that his younger brother had turned his life around and was now serving in the armed forces.

Despite there being no retribution for her act of violence, the stigma followed Poppy around for years to come. She was moved five times before the following Christmas – two children's residential homes and three foster families. It seemed that nobody wanted to keep this 'damaged' child in their presence for long. Her constant disobedience and violent outbursts certainly did nothing to help her cause.

* * *

'I don't really remember, Mr Manning, I mean Joe,' Poppy said. 'I really don't remember.'

The probation officer wiped his glasses again and began to scribble some more notes in her folder. This always irritated Poppy. *Why is he doing that?* she thought. *If I told him I don't remember, why bother making a note of it?*

'You really don't give me much to work with, do you, Poppy?' Manning stated. 'I am here to help you, but I can't help you if you don't talk to me.'

'It was a long time ago,' Poppy replied. 'I can't remember everything from back then. She glanced up at her timekeeper on the wall. *Nearly time*, she thought, *not long now.*

But this morning he was not satisfied with her stubborn silences. Manning tried to dig a little deeper. 'The assessment report, Poppy, the one they sent to me from Bronzefield, they said that your anger issues were related to your childhood. Would you say that was where your anger issues first started?'

Poppy sighed and looked back up at the clock. Manning's inquisition was definitely taking its toll on her today. 'It could be,' she said. 'I don't really know.'

Manning tried again. 'Have you ever worked out what the triggers are? The assessment team would have told you that there might be certain triggers that make you lose control of your temper.'

Poppy's mind drifted off again as Joe began to drone on about the virtues of anger management courses and how everyone can change. She sat in silence, nodding, as if she understood him, but she didn't. She just hated the idea of other people messing with the thoughts that were inside her head. *And now here he goes again*, she thought, *he is back droning on again about that bloody road to Damascus and the nasty bloke who became Mr bloody 'Goody Two Shoes'. What the hell has all that nonsense got to do with me?*

As her probation officer took her through his idea of her possible road to redemption, Poppy mused over his earlier question. *Triggers*, she thought, *what would he know about triggers? Meghan Masters, now there is a trigger, one big fat nasty bitch of a trigger. Is that what he means?*

Poppy was barely sixteen years old when she had met Meghan Masters at the Medway Young Offenders Centre in Gravesend. The magistrates had finally lost their patience with her repeat offending and had decided that six months' incarceration might teach her right from wrong. Most of her juvenile crime sheet had been reasonably minor offences up to that point – shoplifting, possession of drugs and striking one of her foster carers. But this time she was back in court for a serious assault on a security guard who had grabbed hold of her when he caught her stealing groceries. The fact that she had hit him in the face with a can of baked beans, causing him to lose one of his front teeth, was bad enough, she was due to lose her freedom. Her original sentence of sixteen weeks, however, was increased to six months, when she told the magistrates in no uncertain terms what she really thought of them and their ideas of justice.

Meghan Masters was an enigma, a brutal force of twisted nature. She was a one-girl, walking, talking, fighting army, who ruled the North Wing of Medway by the power of fear. She was followed around by a small group of feral teen girls, purely for the fact that they would rather be her friend than her enemy. Meghan was stocky, some would say chubby, but certainly not to her face. She had a mop of blazing red hair, often held back with a tartan hairband. She was hardly softly spoken and ladylike, you could hear her strong Welsh accent bellowing out from over a hundred yards away when she was angry. She had been in the detention centre for several months, so knew all the ins and outs of the terrain she controlled. She didn't have many fights there, she didn't need to. In her early spell of incarceration, she had beaten two girls so badly that her reputation was such that everybody did their best to keep out of her way. One of her victims, an African girl, had dared to look at her in a funny way when she was having a shower. The poor inmate was left with three broken ribs and a bulging eye socket. The girl never returned to North Wing after her brief spell in the local hospital. Neither the victim nor the dozen or so witnesses had reported her to the warders in fear of retaliation, so Meghan's growing reputation was enhanced.

Poppy did her best to avoid this ogre for the first few weeks at the centre but rumours began to circulate that the fiery Welsh inmate had taken a dislike to her. Their cells were on the same landing of the institution, so it was going to be extremely hard to avoid her for long. Sure enough, one evening, just before dinner was about to be served, Poppy felt a tug on the back of her hair and an oversized hand dragged her into the small corridor where the lockers were. She had finally come face to face with Meghan Masters. The first thing that Poppy noticed was her wild stare. Her eyes were wide, her pupils bulging inside her eye sockets. She looked deranged. Poppy was around the same height as her aggressor but had much less meat on her. 'You have been bad mouthing me, you bitch,' Meghan said, a statement, not a question from the red-headed fireball. 'I need to teach you a fucking lesson.' Poppy showed no fear. She was somewhat unsettled by the female tyrant, but she stood her ground. Looking behind her menacing aggressor she could see three girls, all part of the regular 'Masters possee'. One of them seemed to be keeping watch, the other two there as backup for their self-appointed leader. The red-headed dragon began to breathe fire, raising her finger and prodding it into the side of Poppy's head. 'Can't you fucking talk, are you some sort of fucking retard?' she asked her. Poppy was aware of her predicament, but not scared, she was certainly not going to be intimidated today. So Poppy simply stared back, and for a few seconds the two girls stood toe to toe, eye to eye, like female warriors sizing up their opponent. Suddenly, a call from Meghan's lookout broke up the altercation. 'Warders!' she cried. 'Warders on the way.' Meghan stepped back a few inches from her opponent, maybe a small look of surprise in her eyes. This new girl seemed to be braver than most. Rolling around a mass of slimy spit inside her cheek Meghan opened her mouth and released a large ball of phlegm straight into Poppy's face. Poppy clenched her fist tightly and bit the corner of her lip, but did nothing more, as the shiny spit rolled down the side of her cheek. 'This ain't finished, bitch!' the Welsh girl said. 'This ain't fucking over!' Meghan walked away, laughing with her crew of followers as Poppy wiped her face. She knew that Meghan was right, this was not finished, it was far from finished.

Maybe there was a slight twist of fate that week. When Meghan was forced to spend three days in the segregation unit, it gave Poppy time to think, it gave her time to plan her move. The redhead's temper had earned her seventy-two hours in isolation because she threw her dinner at a fellow inmate. The argument had more to do with the girl not sharing her tobacco than the Welsh girl's dislike of the food. During those three days Poppy realised that she was alone. No one would stand by her side if she took on her nemesis. She had more than four months left inside these walls, there would be no way that she would be able to avoid the confrontation for much longer. But Poppy had been in the care system for almost seven years now, she was much harder than she looked. Maybe in a one-on-one fight Meghan would wipe the floor with her, but if that was going to happen it needed to be on her terms. Her mind worked overtime for those three days. Time was running out.

It was a bright morning and most of the inmates were in the outdoor recreation area. Meghan had been out of the segregation unit for almost a week and nothing had happened. She was sitting with a couple of her usual followers when Poppy approached her. 'What do you want, retard?' the hard-faced redhead asked.

'I need to speak to you, in private,' Poppy said. 'It is important.'

The Welsh girl laughed at her. 'Fuck off!' she said. 'Fuck off and stare at someone else, you weird bitch.'

Poppy persevered. 'It's about a stash. I thought I'd tell you where there is some hidden.' Meghan lifted herself up off her seat and approached her. The word 'stash' had appealed to her. 'Stash' was, in simple terms, tobacco. It was currency within those four walls, much more valuable than anything else. 'I know who is hiding a stash, their boyfriend smuggled it in on visiting day. I know where it is hidden.'

The fiery girl with man-sized fists suddenly seemed interested. 'I ain't sharing it,' she said.

Poppy shook her head. 'No, no, you can have it. I just want to make the peace, I just want you to get off my back.'

The menacing redhead laughed out loud. 'Not so fucking brave after all then, are you, retard?' The girls seemed to have reached an understanding. 'Where is it?' Meghan asked, wasting no time at all.

'Follow me, I will show you,' Poppy replied, still doing her best impression of a humbled opponent. 'It's under Darcy Brown's bed, I saw her hiding it.' The girls walked side by side, much to the amazement of many of the other inmates. Could this new girl be a recruit for Meghan's gang?

'I hate that fucking Darcy!' Meghan revealed. 'She is such a dirty skank!'

Poppy nodded in agreement. 'She is such a sneaky bitch, there is loads there too.'

Meghan smiled as the two of them entered the room where Darcy Brown slept. 'Over there,' Poppy said. 'She sleeps in the corner bed.' As Meghan moved forwards, Poppy gently closed the door behind them, so they would not be disturbed.

'Where?' Meghan asked. 'Where has that bitch hidden it?'

Poppy pointed at the bed. 'She has cut a hole underneath the mattress.'

Meghan fell to her knees and slid her arm underneath. 'Where?' the Welsh girl asked again.

Poppy leaned over her enemy. 'Further over,' she pointed out. 'Right over there, in the corner.'

The Welsh girl was on her knees, her arm fumbling around beneath Darcy's mattress. She had no idea what was going on inside her enemy's head at that moment. In the blink of an eye, Poppy grabbed a firm hold of the chubby girl's mop of bright ginger hair and pulled her head backwards. The unsuspecting inmate just about caught a glimpse of the rage in her attacker's eyes before her face was thrust with great force directly into the metal frame supporting the bunk beds. Before she knew what was happening her head was pulled back again. She could see the lights above her spinning before Poppy smashed her head full on into the frame for a second time. Meghan cried out at her attacker. She was completely disorientated now, desperately trying to free her arm from under the mattress. Poppy was not for stopping, dragging her enemy sideways and yanking on her thick locks again. This time her skull was thrust into the corner of the radiator, the sound of bone crushing against metal was sickening. The Welsh girl's arms were moving backwards and forwards as she desperately tried to break free. Poppy smashed her head once more into the side of the radiator. This time the force of the impact caused the Welsh girl's nose to split open, sending a huge splatter of thick blood up the wall. Meghan's screams now turned to a whimpering moan. She was barely moving, she had had enough, for her this fight was over. But for Poppy this was far from finished. Straddling her opponent tightly so her arms could not move anymore, she systematically pulled the flailing girl's blood-soaked mane backwards and forwards, hitting her head on the hard floor in front of her. The Welsh girl offered no resistance now, she was completely unconscious.

Poppy never heard the alarms sounding, nor the jeers of the crowd of onlookers that had gathered in the bedroom. She did, however, feel the warder's heavy hand strike her head, as he pulled her off her badly beaten opponent. Within seconds she was dragged to her feet and surrounded by the whole prison team. A second blow landed on the side of her cheek as the staff did their best to contain her. There was lots of shouting, even some cheering, the place was in total chaos, but her mind was in a distant place at that moment. With her arms wrapped tightly behind her back, Poppy looked down at her beaten opponent. Blood was still flowing from a wound on the side of her head, her battered face, was barely recognisable. And then she felt it again. Poppy felt that numbness, that emptiness. She stood in silence, feeling no compassion, no remorse, no fear, she just felt nothing at all. It was as if she had watched all of this unfold from a different room or on a television screen.

As her arms were twisted behind her back, one of the warders gave her a couple of well-aimed elbows to the side of her face to stop her from struggling. Cheering inmates shouted out her name as she was dragged along the floor in the direction of the segregation unit, many of them finally plucking up enough courage to voice their honest thoughts on the oversized Welsh bully. It seemed that Meghan's reign of tyranny had been brought to an abrupt end.

Poppy served ten days in the segregation unit before she was hauled before the governor of Medway and a magistrate from the local court. Meghan could not attend to give her side of the story, she was still recovering in hospital. An additional four months were added to Poppy's sentence, with no chance of any remission on her original term. Poppy served her time at Medway without any further harassment from any of her fellow inmates. In her final month there she would meet Nikita, a chance meeting that would lead to a strong friendship and mark out the path of her destiny. Meghan was transferred to a London-based youth offenders institute when she was released from hospital, her broken nose and facial scarring a permanent reminder of the time she chose to cross Poppy Jarvis.

As the clock in Manning's office finally told her that this week's ordeal was over, Poppy thought she might share that story with the Reverend Joe, finally give him something worthwhile to write in that folder. Maybe she would tell her probation officer what her take might be on some of those clever scriptures from that big black book, such as 'do unto others' and all that stuff. In Poppy's world you live by a far different set of rules. 'Do unto others before they do unto you, only do it fast and do it fucking hard, so fucking hard that they don't get the chance to do it to you at all.' Maybe Meghan Masters had learned something from Poppy's personal bible that day at Medway.

As usual Poppy said nothing and instead listened to his usual parting comment of 'We didn't get very far today' and his reminder for her to call Mrs Bishop. But this week, the overbearing, oversized probation officer made a comment which would dampen her spirits for the day and set her mind reeling back into a direction she had chosen to ignore. 'I see it is your birthday on Friday,' he said. 'I hope you enjoy it, whatever you do.'

When Poppy had left his office, Joe Manning revisited her folder. There was something in that paperwork that did not sit easy with him, he needed to study it more closely. The assessment unit analysis from Bronzefield prison contained detailed reports from the three professionals who had spent time with the troubled girl. It was the findings of one of those that had captured Manning's attention. He had to study it again, just to make sure he had read it correctly.

Professor Camilla Fitzgerald, a senior and well-respected forensic psychoanalyst who had published several books in America, was fascinated by her study of Poppy. The woman was something of a renowned expert on human behaviour patterns and had worked with many inmates on Death Row in the United States. She had met with Poppy several times and made her own findings on her state of mind very clear in her report. The whole case study was over forty pages long, but it was her summary of Poppy's case that the probation officer found so disturbing.

In the first half of the document Ms Fitzgerald referred to her extensive research into Poppy's ancestry. She was a big believer that the genes that cause psychotic behaviour are hereditary. The professor had found that there was a history of mental imbalances running through Poppy's family. Her grandmother had spent more than twenty years in a psychiatric unit in Worcester, after she had locked her husband in a room in their house and set fire to the building. During her incarceration she had tried several times to take her own life before successfully slashing her own throat with the sharp edge of a lid from a tin can.

Her expert research also highlighted the actions of her father. The unexplained disappearance of his wife and two nervous breakdowns, which led to him being diagnosed with several mental disorders, covered more than five pages of the report.

Her extensive studies on the connection between a small number of genes and malfunctional chromosomes made her something of a leading light in this field of analysis. During her studies into the case she identified the gene that may be present in all three members of the family, a strand of MAOA-L. Her findings led her to believe that the gene was twenty times more likely to cause psychotic behaviour in females than males.

Joe Manning understood most, if not all, of the information in her report, but it was not that part of the document that concerned him. Ms Fitzgerald was asked to assess Poppy as a candidate for early release from prison. She had served nearly four years inside Bronzefield with only one noticeable incident and was now completely clean of drugs for the first time since she was fourteen years old. The panel of experts, of which Fitzgerald was one, were asked to consider if they felt she could be rehabilitated on the outside, subject to continued behavioural and drug monitoring.

Three of the panel thought that Poppy would be a good candidate, providing she adhered to a strict period of either probation or wearing an electronic tag after her release. Camilla Fizgerald was not as enthusiastic. Her final summary of Poppy's state of mind was something that Manning found most alarming:

\* \* \*

*'I have spent more than four months working with Poppy Jarvis and have found her to be one of the most interesting case studies in my forty-plus years in this field.*

*Poppy has an extremely low empathic nature and finds it hard to relate to other people. It is well documented that she has shown psychotic traits from a very early age, some reports suggest ten years old. I believe them to have been there from early childhood. Many of the carers at the fifty or so foster homes and child care institutions where she was housed have put her violent outbursts down to ADHD or having come from a dysfunctional family background. It amazes me that in all that time, she was never recommended for psychological analysis.*

*Since the age of sixteen, Poppy has spent around eighty percent of her life inside prisons and reform institutions without receiving any professional evaluations relating to the state of her mental health. She has simply been branded 'The girl with the violent temper' without anyone ever wanting to find out the reasons for her pent-up anger.*

*She has shown no remorse whatsoever for her crimes and in truth I found her not to have any remote sense of conscience whatsoever when it comes to her victim or his family. She seems to be completely immune to any kind of compassion.*

*I made several breakthroughs with Poppy, mainly with the anger suppressant schemes involving colour-safe recognitions. It showed that Ms Jarvis can indeed control some of the psychotic tendencies that she has.*

*However, I would warn the committee that releasing Poppy into society at this stage would be premature to say the least. In my opinion she needs extensive psychotherapy sessions to help unlock the demons still present in her head. The level of psychiatric care needed to help her with this is not available at this prison or indeed many others. There are, however, several institutions around the country that cater for this type of treatment. I fully recommend that Poppy spends the remainder of her sentence at one of those establishments.'*

Before inviting his next visitor into his office, Manning wiped his glasses and pondered on that uncomfortable reading. It didn't shock him, he knew all along that there was something not right with the girl who never gave him straight answers. But it wasn't the thought that he might never be able to break down the barriers that the troubled girl put up in his presence that concerned him. No, Manning was asking himself if Poppy Jarvis should really be free at all.

Poppy sat stone-faced in her car. She was halfway through her second cigarette. *Why did Manning have to say that?* she thought. Why did he have to remind her? She never celebrated her birthday. Friday would just be another day, like a Tuesday or a Thursday. This Friday would be just another day. But he had reminded her. She knew now that she would be turning twenty-six this week. It was exactly twenty years ago exactly that she had that party. Poppy was in deep thought, the images of her mother waltzing around their old living room sporting two black eyes and a bloodied nose, swigging from that bottle of vodka in her hand. The laughter of her schoolfriends, the looks on all their faces. She could not remember any of their names, but those laughing faces still haunted her. To top it all, her parents had bought her a rabbit, a big pure white rabbit, like the one in *Alice in Wonderland.*

A rabbit! A fucking rabbit! She hated rabbits! She didn't like animals! Why the hell couldn't she have had a games console or the Hello Kitty backpack she had asked for. No! That was too much trouble for them. Buy her a rabbit, give it a silly name and shove it in a cage at the back of the garden, that will keep her quiet! But even the rabbit didn't want to live there, not with all the shouting and screaming. Even 'Snowball' the bloody rabbit left her!

Poppy was angry with her probation officer now. Why did the Reverend Joe have to open his bloody mouth and ruin her day? She had intended to have a rummage through the charity shops that morning, but now felt sick inside. She needed to talk to someone, not Cameron, she thought, he would neither care nor understand. She finished her cigarette and made her way to Chez Blanc, hoping Danny would say something crazy that would make her laugh and take her mind off things. She needed to forget what Joe had said, forget about her birthday, it wasn't her birthday this coming Friday or any other day for that matter.

*  *  *

Matt was on the telephone when she entered the restaurant. He turned his back as if to say his conversation was private and not for her ears. Danny was sitting at a large table in the dining area, a laptop, a calculator and a bundle of paperwork in front of him. 'Fucking VAT!' he said, as she approached. 'I hate the fucking VAT man!' Poppy realised that it was not a good time to disturb him, but as she turned away Danny could sense that his waitress was slightly uneasy. 'Did the Reverend Joe give you a hard time this morning, love?' he asked. She turned back and nodded. 'Just a bit.'

Danny gave her a sympathetic smile. 'Get Matt to make you some coffee and croissants, you will feel better after that. We can catch up and have a chat later.' Poppy nodded and made her way to the kitchen area. Danny was wrong, coffee and croissants would not change her mood today, the shrieks of those giggling schoolchildren were still being played out in her head.

As she made her way towards the kitchen, Matt grabbed her by the waist and tried to kiss her on the cheek. 'Fuck off, Matt!' she said as she pushed past him.

He could tell by her tone of voice that she was not for playing with at that moment. 'What's up?' he asked, genuinely concerned.

'Just leave me alone today, Matt.'

'Fuck, Poppy, you can be one moody bitch sometimes. What have I done wrong?'

'Nothing, Matt. I just want you to leave me alone, is that too much to ask?'

Matt shook his head and carried on with his preparations for the lunchtime sitting. Poppy helped herself to some toast and coffee and sat in the corner, pretending to be busy checking texts on her phone, hoping that Matt would not disturb her.

The lunchtime shift came and went. Little was seen of Danny, although his shouts of despair could clearly be heard bellowing out from his small office next to the toilets. The 'fucking VAT man' had now been replaced with a more damning description, much to the amusement of Matt, who laughed loudly each time the 'C' word was heard.

Chantelle joined them for the evening session. The restaurant had over twenty covers booked, a good number for a Wednesday. The evening seemed to fly by. This was good for Poppy, it gave her less time to hold court with her demons. She pocketed a cash tip of £10 for herself when Chantelle was on one of her many toilet breaks, feeling fully justified that she did not share it.

By half past nine there were only six diners left in the restaurant and Poppy was planning on an early exit. She was angry at the antics of Matt and the ditzy waitress. They had spent most of the evening throwing food at each other and playing childish pranks. The highlight of the unlikely duo's evening had been the invention of a new game they had called 'Danny's Cunt Counter'. In simple terms every time they heard the word bellow out from his tiny office next to the storeroom, they would add the number to a chart on the wall and take a sip of wine. Poppy was no fan of the new waitress, feeling that the skinny waif would seize any opportunity to skive for the evening. When Chantelle wasn't checking her social media accounts on her phone or calling her friends, she would encourage the chef to join her in an array of childish antics. Matt, being Matt, always played along. Their immature behaviour irritated Poppy but not enough for her to complain to her boss. Danny had enough on his plate with the upcoming VAT inspection, she thought, the last thing he needed was her bleating about the behaviour of his staff.

The final count on the 'Cuntometer' was seventeen, probably not a world record for a five-hour shift. Danny's ex-wife, however, would not have been impressed to know that his not so affectionate comment was used in reference to her absence in at least three of the final tally. Fortunately, the unknown VAT man had received the rest.

As it was more than likely that they would all be finishing earlier than usual that night, Poppy was half hoping that Matt would invite her back to his flat. She was not in the mood for another sexual encounter, she simply wanted the pleasure of turning him down. But Matt had been far from impressed with her constant mood swings that day and had said little to her, preferring to follow the childish instructions of his new sidekick.

Poppy drove back to her flat and parked beneath her window. Lighting up a cigarette, she stared at the dark silhouettes dancing on her curtains. She could hear some music blaring out from the television. Cameron would be in there, as usual, sprawled out like a zombie on the sofa. Was he asleep? She hoped so.

Inside her head was a tangled mess of images from her sixth birthday party. She wanted to close her eyes, to fall into a deep sleep, to forget the cruel laughter and the faces of her schoolfriends. She hoped that if he was awake that Cameron would not be in one of his foul moods. She had endured enough punishment already that day.

# CHAPTER SIXTEEN

The tube station was deserted, echoes of tiny footsteps fading into the distance. Bree looked both ways and suddenly felt an uncomfortable swelling in the pit of her stomach. It was so quiet on the platform, she could hear the ticking of the clock on the wall at the end of the station. Above her, the illuminated noticeboard was clearly showing that the next train was due in two minutes. It felt as if she had been standing under that same sign for hours. Bree shuffled her feet as she felt an eerie chill run up her spine. 'Come on! Come on!' she said. 'I need to get home!'

A sudden gust of wind blew from the tunnel and carried a small heap of crisp packets and confectionary wrappers past her. She looked on anxiously, but there was no sign of the overdue train. Bree was feeling more uneasy by the second. The ticking of the clock seemed to be growing louder now. Staring hard at its face she could see the time was a quarter past eleven. The platform seemed to be colder than before. She moved her feet again and rubbed her hands together. 'For God's sake, come on!' Bree said, hoping her small prayer would bring the tube train to her aid. She looked around again and felt a growing unease. It felt as if she was not alone, there seemed to be another presence on the platform, she sensed that she was being watched. All at once a large clanking sound above her head made her jump. It was the noticeboard, it had finally changed. Just one minute for the train to arrive now. Bree's attention was drawn back to the end of the platform. She could see some movement. Two shapes slowly appeared from the shadows, one quite large, one petite, wearing a bright red coat that she had seen before. They began to walk towards her. Bree turned her head the other way and looked down the tunnel, hoping to see the train's bright headlights.

The figures drew closer and closer. Bree turned back and was surprised to see who was standing next to her. 'Hello,' came Maisie's tiny voice. 'We hoped we would see you here today.'

There was a sudden look of bewilderment on Bree's face. 'Hello, Maisie, what are you doing here? It is a bit late for you to be out, isn't it?'

Maisie looked up at her mother, but something in her expression told her that she did not want to speak, so the little girl continued the conversation. 'We are going to see Jamie, of course. Do you want to come with us?'

Bree looked first at Caroline and then down at her daughter. 'But it is too late to see him now, the cemetery gates will be closed.'

Maisie smiled, that sweet enduring little smile. 'We need to see him, to say thank you.'

A small gust of wind rushed out of the tunnel and distracted Bree for a few seconds. She turned back and hoped for some sort of explanation from Caroline. 'What are you doing?' Bree asked. 'She shouldn't be out at this time of night, she should be in bed.'

The large lady raised her head to look Bree squarely in the face. 'But this is the right time,' she said. 'It is nearly twenty past.'

Not sure what the woman was talking about Bree looked at the large clock at the end of the platform. She could still hear the loud ticking. The clock's hands showed that it was nearly twenty past eleven. 'The cemetery will be closed,' Bree insisted. 'The gates will be locked.'

As she looked again at the clock Bree noticed something else, another figure, lurking in the shadows. It looked like the girl, the one in the yellow raincoat. She was moving in and out of the small side passages, as if she was playing a game of hide and seek. Suddenly, to Bree's relief she could hear a noise coming from the tunnel behind her and the sound of electricity charging through the tracks. *Finally*, she thought, *finally the train is coming!*

Holding her mother's hand tightly Maisie looked up at Bree, her small voice struggling to be heard amongst the growing sounds of the oncoming train. 'No,' she said, 'you don't understand, Bree. We are going to see Jamie for real today. We need to see him, to thank him properly for saving us.'

Bree was alarmed. 'What do you mean, Maisie?' she asked. The little girl said nothing. She looked at Caroline, squeezing her mother's hand tighter as a large gust of wind gathered in the tunnel. 'What does she mean?' Bree shouted at Caroline. 'What does she mean?'

The little girl in her bright red coat looked up and offered Bree her spare hand. 'Do you want to come with us, do you want to see Jamie?' she asked. Bree's attention turned back towards the tunnel as the beams of the train's lights appeared in the distance. When she turned her head back the two figures had started to move away from her. The ticking of the clock was growing louder again, the rushes of wind began howling through the tunnel. The girl in the raincoat was still there, she was on the platform, she was watching from a distance. Bree began to panic, her heart pounded in her chest. Suddenly another large clank echoed out above her head. It was the noticeboard, it now spelled out the word 'Time'. Bree was confused, she didn't know what was happening. Maisie started to speak, but her words could barely be heard above the cacophony of noise. The headlights of the train suddenly became much larger. The sharp scraping of brakes against the tracks could be heard. Suddenly Maisie's words became clearer as Bree watched her and her mother start to move forwards, towards the edge of the platform. 'We will tell Jamie that you will always love him. We will tell him that you are sorry.' Caroline grasped her daughter's hand tightly and the pair continued walking.

'No!' Bree screamed loudly. 'No, Maisie!'

All at once the headlights of the tube train had become a mass of silver carriages as it pulled into the station. Bree turned her head away and shut her eyes tightly just as Caroline and Maisie stepped off the platform's edge, their bodies disappearing beneath the wheels of the train's screeching underbelly. The scraping noises of the tube's brakes ripped through Bree's body. She covered her ears, hoping to block out the orchestra of torturous sounds that surrounded her.

As the shades of silvery metal finally came to a halt in front of her, she opened her eyes, slowly, but what she saw alarmed her. There in the glass of the tube train's window she could see her reflection. It was the girl from the bar, she was standing behind her. Bree's heart pounded harder and harder. That bright shiny coat was so close to her she could feel its dampness. She knew that she had to face her nemesis. She didn't want to, but there was nowhere to run now, nowhere for her to hide. She trembled inside as she slowly turned around. The girl was less than a foot from her, her eyes dark and lifeless, her face pale, it was wet, it was without expression. The girl began to raise her arm and a tiny hand appeared from the sleeve of her raincoat. She raised it until it touched Bree's face, moving her slimy fingers across Bree's cheek, which sent an ice-cold chill all the way through her shaking body. And then she spoke, softly, not in an angry tone as Bree had expected, but like that of someone she knew. 'It is me, Bree, it is only me.' Bree tried to raise her arm to move the girl's cold hand from her quivering cheek, but she couldn't, it was as if a strange force was holding her arms, stopping her from moving, stopping her from fighting. She felt helpless. The girl repeated her statement. 'It is me, Bree, it is only me.'

Bree began to feel pressure, as if her head was being squeezed. She couldn't breathe, the clammy hand on her cheek seemed to be draining all the life out of her. Suddenly she found her voice, but her words came out as no more than a whisper. 'No!' she said. 'Go away!' She tried again to move her arms, her whole body began to gyrate, she wanted to scream out loudly, but nothing would come out of her mouth. She closed her eyes hoping that the evil fiend in front of her would disappear, leave her alone, but she could still hear her voice, it was clearer than ever. 'It's me, Bree, it's me, it's Kayleigh.'

Bree opened her eyes to find her best friend looking over her. She was at home, she was laid out on her sofa. 'It was just a nightmare!' Kayleigh said. 'Just a bad nightmare!'

Bree began to sob uncontrollably. 'Maisie and Caroline, they were there, they were under the train. God, it was all so real!'

Kayleigh pulled her friend closer and hugged her tightly. 'It was just another nightmare, babe, you are safe now.' The two of them held their tight embrace for a few minutes. Bree did not want to let her friend go, she feared that she would be back on the platform if she did. 'Kayleigh, it is so frightening,' she said. 'I keep seeing them, the girl in the coat, the man without a face!'

Kayleigh could not offer her any explanations for the recurring dreams she was having, but she did offer her friend some fresh coffee. 'You haven't forgotten about this afternoon?' she asked. 'The newspaper.'

Bree hadn't forgotten. 'What time is it now?' she said. Kayleigh showed her the time. It had just turned midday. 'Shit!' Bree said. 'I have lost all track of time.' Her friend helped her up from the sofa which had become more like her second bed these days.

'What don't you get your arse into the shower and freshen up, babe. I will make you some lunch,' Kayleigh said. Bree nodded and made her way upstairs. Kayleigh began to ponder on the events of the past half an hour or so, when she been watching over her friend. Bree, not for the first time in her sleep, had called out a name, a name that no one mentioned these days. She began to wonder if it was time for her to call Bree's mother. Her best friend was clearly in need of professional assistance.

* * *

Kayleigh made some poached eggs for their lunch before the girls set off for the forty-five-minute journey to the *Southern Gazette* newspaper in Sutton. There was not a great deal of conversation on the way. Maybe both girls were hoping for different results from the visit. Bree appeared to be desperate now to find out more about the man holding hands with her mother in that old photograph. It seemed to have given her a fresh impetus. Kayleigh, on the other hand, was hoping that this would be a wild goose chase. It had been her that had taken the photograph to one of her friends at work and had the detail of the picture scrutinised with the aid of a powerful magnifying glass. They had established that an award on the table next to where Bree's mother had been sitting had an inscription from the *Southern Gazette* newspaper. The year inscribed on the trophy was 1997, the year before Bree had been born. Yes, it made perfect sense that the man in the photograph could be her father, however she wondered how her best friend would really react if that was confirmed. She already seemed to hold a bitter resentment for her mother and this would fuel her hatred even further. It also meant that Jamie had been right all along and that the man who was so desperate to get in touch with him had made no such efforts to find her. In Kayleigh's mind the best result today was for the newspaper to have no record whatsoever of that night and that would bring an end to the matter. Neither of them could possibly have predicted at this time, however, how this day would end.

Sutton town centre had limited parking spaces available, so the girls had to walk a fair distance from a multi-storey car park to find the *Gazette*'s offices. Bree took a deep breath as they approached the reception area. 'God, I am shaking,' she said. 'I am so nervous.'

Her friend grabbed her arm. 'Don't worry, babe, I will do the talking.'

The well-dressed receptionist finished what seemed to have been a personal call and asked the girls what they were there for. 'We need to see someone about an old photograph,' Kayleigh said, producing the picture from an envelope in her bag. 'Do they have someone in charge of events and stuff, someone who might know about this picture?'

A male voice called out to them from the end of the reception area. 'Gary Marshall,' the man said. 'He deals with all that stuff, you need Gary Marshall.'

Kayleigh gave the man a pleasant smile. She was immediately attracted to his rugged looks and his bright multi-coloured tie. 'Thank you,' she said. 'That's really helpful.'

The man returned the smile with a small glint in his eye. 'Anything for a pretty lady,' he replied.

The receptionist tried ringing Gary Marshall's internal line a few times before reaching him. Within a few minutes, a stocky middle-aged man carrying a black folder arrived at the reception area and ushered the girls into a glass-fronted office at the side of the building. They sat down at a table which was littered with the last dozen or so issues of the *Southern Gazette*. 'It is a bit more private in here,' he said closing the door behind him. 'OK, so I am Gary Marshall, I believe you need some assistance with an old photo or something?'

Bree was still visibly nervous, so Kayleigh produced the photograph and did all the talking. 'It is from quite a long time ago,' she said. 'I think it was taken in the late nineties, maybe 1997.'

The man studied the picture, both front and back. 'It does look like the sort of do we have. It is our annual awards dinner by the looks of things. This is a bit before my time though.' The girls' faces both dropped as he seemed to have little interest in the image, but then he pulled out his mobile phone from his jacket pocket and called for a colleague to join him. Kayleigh glanced out of the window to see if the young man who smiled at her was still at the reception desk. He was. He looked back at her and indicated a thumbs-up sign, as if to wish her 'good luck'.

An elderly man, dressed in an ill-fitting jacket and sporting a rather large beer belly that hung over his trousers, entered the room and offered a handshake to the two girls. 'Brian Needham,' he said. 'Gary tells me you need help with an old photograph.'

The girls both nodded. 'It is quite old, I think it was from 1997,' Kayleigh pointed out.

Needham made himself comfortable in the chair next to Bree and took out his glasses. 'I can't see a thing without these nowadays,' he declared.

Kayleigh explained why they were there. 'The man sitting at the front, he was a friend of the family, but they lost touch with him. We are sort of trying to reunite them.' Bree gave her friend a harsh stare, wondering why she needed to hide the real reason for their visit.

Needham looked closely at the picture and then directly up at Bree. 'Is that your mother?' he asked. 'You look so alike.'

Kayleigh saw Bree snarl at his comment before answering him through gritted teeth. 'Yes, that is my mother.'

The newspaperman lifted the photograph to study it more closely. 'I know this man, but I am not sure where from. He wasn't one of our advertisers, I am sure of that.'

Kayleigh could see the disappointment in her friend's face and thought she might need to push Needham further. 'Don't they keep a log of all the people that they photograph?' she asked. 'Maybe his name would be somewhere in there.'

Gary Marshall had some input to the conversation. 'It could be in archives. We usually file copies of all of these pictures in the archives room upstairs.'

Needham nodded. 'Yes, it might be in there.'

Bree was anxious now. She badly felt the need to know more about the man in the photograph. 'Can you look for us, we don't mind waiting.'

The elderly man laughed. 'It could take hours,' he said.

'Please,' Bree asked. 'It really is important.'

Needham was no fool, he didn't believe a word of the 'long-lost friend' story, but he felt an obligation to help her find further information, whatever she was really looking for. 'Tell you what,' he said, 'you leave me your number and we will take a copy of this on the scanner. I will get one of the team to trawl through and find the details later today.'

His remark brought a small smile to Bree's face. 'Thank you so much,' she said, before squeezing Kayleigh's hand tightly below the table.

The two men led the girls back to the reception area and scanned a copy of the photograph while an excited Bree found a pen in her bag and scribbled her name and number on a page from her pocket diary. As they said their goodbyes and were just about to leave, Kayleigh snatched the pen from her friend's hand and made her way across to the man wearing the eye-catching tie. He smiled at her as she grabbed his arm and scribbled her mobile number on his wrist. 'That's my number,' she said. 'Just in case they lose that piece of paper.' As she walked back to join Bree, she shouted back at him, 'My name is Kayleigh, by the way.'

The young man laughed as the girls headed for the exit. 'Wow!' he said. 'Now that really has made my day!' The receptionist shook her head, as though she disapproved of the forward antics of the visitor, giving her colleague a look of disgust, before answering an incoming call.

No words were exchanged on their walk back to Kayleigh's car. There was a strange feeling in the air, as though something exciting was about to happen. Bree broke her silence as they reached the parked vehicle. 'Fucking unbelievable!' she said. 'You are fucking unbelievable sometimes, Kayleigh Hardy!'

Her friend shrugged her shoulders. She knew how much Bree disapproved of her forwardness with men. 'But,' she replied, 'you have to admit, babe, he was fit.'

Kayleigh checked her car mirror and blew a small kiss at her reflection, before starting the journey back to Oxley village. The beaming smile on Kayleigh's face told its own story. This may end up being a dead end for Bree in her search for the truth about her real father, but it was certainly not going to be a wasted trip for her.

Little was said in the first half of their journey back, but something more than Kayleigh's moral compass was bothering Bree. She had to get it off her chest. 'I don't really look that much like my mother, do I?' she asked. Her friend could not resist a sly dig at her 'bestie's' uncanny resemblance to the woman that she was desperate to disown. 'You are the spitting image, babe, the absolute spitting image!'

Bree screwed up her face and gave her friend a nudge in her ribs. 'You bitch!' she yelled. 'You are a total fucking bitch!' Almost at once both girls let out a huge howl of laughter, making their homeward journey much less tense than their trip there. In a war of wits, Bree began reminding her friend of the countless one-night stands she had encountered and revealing the truth about some unpleasant graffiti that had been written about her on the back of a toilet door at their old school. Kayleigh retaliated by repeatedly mimicking Brian Needham's comment about her and her mother looking so alike. She even dared to suggest that she might enter the two of them in a 'mother and daughter beauty contest'.

It had seemed such a long time since the two of them had shared so much banter and laughter together, Kayleigh wished it would never end. She loved seeing her friend smiling and joking again after everything that had happened. Maybe this would be the start of her road to recovery, she thought. Something told her however, that her friend's mood swing would very much depend on the result of the call from the newspaper.

The call came at exactly 5.46pm. It was a brief conversation, but it was a call that would change Bree's life forever. Kayleigh held her friend's trembling hand tightly as the phone rang.

'Hi, this is Bree.'

'Hello, Bree, Brian Needham from the *Gazette*.'

'Hello,' she replied and took a deep breath as her heart pounded in her chest. Kayleigh sat closer to her friend, crossed her fingers and smiled. Bree switched her phone to the speaker, so they would both be able to hear the conversation. 'Did you manage to find out anything about that man in the photograph?'

'Dean Jarvis,' the newspaperman said. 'His name is Dean Jarvis.'

'Dean Jarvis?' Bree asked, seeking his confirmation one more time. Kayleigh squeezed her 'besties' hand more firmly and said to her shaking friend, 'I know that name.'

Brian Needham continued. 'Yes, his name is Dean Jarvis, we found his name on the file photograph. There was no company name for him though.'

'Oh,' Bree said slightly disappointed.

'But he did come in here a few years back. One or two of the staff on the news desk remembered him.'

'He came into your offices?' Bree asked.

'Yes, he came in here ranting and raving about the article we ran on his daughter. Did you know that he is the father of Poppy Jarvis?'

'Poppy Jarvis?' Bree asked as if she should know who that was.

'Yes,' came the reply. 'You know, *the* Poppy Jarvis. She may know where you can find him, she is out now.'

Bree didn't understand and was a little lost for words. Kayleigh was slowly getting the gist of what was being said to her friend and sat closer to her with her mouth wide open.

'Hello,' the newspaperman said, not sure if Bree was still on the line. She tried to speak, she wanted to ask him so many questions, but the words never left her mouth.

'She works in a bistro in Welling High Street,' Needham revealed. 'Poppy Jarvis, I saw her there myself a few weeks back.'

Bree was still stunned, she felt as if she was having one of her nightmares, waiting for someone to wake her up. She finally responded with a few jumbled words. 'Restaurant, High Street, Poppy, Poppy Jarvis.'

Brian Needham could be heard calling out to one of his colleagues before providing her with further information. 'Chez Noir or Chez Blanc, it is one or the other. It is opposite the Marks and Spencer store.'

Both girls now sat open-mouthed. Was this really happening? Was it a dream? Bree had to pinch herself to make sure it was all real. Needham seemed to have finished dropping this huge bombshell in her lap, so Bree cleared her throat to speak. 'Thank you, Brian, thank you so much for your help,' she said.

She was about to cancel the call when the man from the newspaper left her with a friendly but firm warning. 'Just be very careful with Poppy Jarvis,' he said. 'She is, well, she is a nasty piece of work, she is not a very nice person at all.'

The call ended at 5.51pm.

Neither of the girls wanted to speak first, they were both in a state of shock. Kayleigh was the one to break the silence. 'You have a sister, if he is your dad, then this Poppy girl is your sister.' Bree nodded, but was clearly still dazed by the revelation. The two girls reached out and hugged each other. A small tear left Bree's eye and rolled down the side of her cheek, she didn't know why. Bree was still confused, she was trying hard to digest all of what she had just been told.

Their embrace lasted a whole minute before Bree broke free with a slight look of concern on her tearstained face. 'What did he mean when he said she is out now?' she asked.

# CHAPTER
# SEVENTEEN

B ree did not sleep a wink that night, she was afraid to. It was
not because of her recurring nightmares, but because she was
worried that the events of the previous day would turn out
to be nothing more than a dream. As she sat on the bed, clutching
Jamie's pillow, she began to piece together what she now believed
to be true facts and how her brother had turned out to be right
all along.

Before her friend had left her the previous night, she had
remembered where she had seen the name Dean Jarvis previously.
They had found it, her and Kayleigh, the business card, it was at
the bottom of the sports bag, the one that Preston had brought
them from the gym. It had taken half a bottle of wine for Bree to
pluck up enough courage to call the mobile number on the back of
the card, entering the digits at least a dozen times before actually
pressing the call button. The number they were calling, however,
seemed to be disconnected.

Kayleigh had advised her friend to let the news of her sister's existence sink in for a few days before making any decisions on her next move. But despite the fact she agreed, she couldn't wait to meet Poppy and within minutes of her friend leaving the house, Bree had checked the postcode and opening times of Chez Blanc online and had already entered the location in the sat nav in her car. The journey would take her less than an hour.

As the sun began to rise, Bree's anticipation rose with it. There were a million and one questions she needed to be answered. 'What would her big sister look like? Did Poppy know that she had a sibling? If she did, why hadn't she tried to find her? Why did her real father only want to contact Jamie and not her?

Brian Needham's words were still sounding small alarm bells in her head. 'She is out now. She is not a very nice person.' What had she done? Bree thought to herself. What could her sister possibly have done that would make him say what he had said?'

There was another conundrum for Bree. What should she wear? She didn't want to look too formal, too smart, so casual, but not jeans, she wanted to make the right impression. In the end she decided that her red Gestuz top and her black Armani trousers gave her the right balance. She was shaking, she couldn't stop fidgeting. Why was she so nervous? she thought. She should be excited, she had a sister, a real sister.

Suddenly her mobile rang, it made her jump. She thought it might be Brian Needham again. Maybe there was more information about her father. But it wasn't, it was her mother. She was certainly not in the mood for one of her question and answer sessions today. She ignored the call and began to apply a light layer of makeup to her face.

Her mobile rang again and once more remained unanswered. Bree knew what was coming next and sure enough the landline rang in the living room. Bree tried to carry on with her preparations for the day, but that constant ring tone began to make her skin crawl. 'Fuck off, you evil bitch!' she shouted from the top of the stairs, but it was the turn of the phone to ignore her this time and it carried on ringing. By now Bree was infuriated with her mother's persistence. Maybe, she thought, it was time to give 'the bitch' some home truths.

As she lifted the receiver, that all too familiar voice sounded out the name she had been born with, but never used. 'Brianna, is that you?' her mother asked.

Bree shook her head, wanting to ridicule her parent by saying, 'No, it is a fucking burglar! I just broke in through the window and I heard the phone ringing, so I answered it!' But she decided against flippancy, it would only be wasted on her mother. 'Hello, Mother,' she said. The all too familiar pattern followed, her mother telling her how many times she had called her, how worried she had been because she hadn't answered her phone and her concerns that she might have starved herself to death that week. As Bree listened, an anger built up inside her. She did not feel like having a civil conversation this morning. She couldn't care less what the weather was like in Tampere or whether her mother had found a buyer for the house, she had much more important things on her mind. Her mother was halfway through her one-way sermon when Bree simply said it. 'Who is the man in that photograph, the one taken at the awards night?' Her mother started to talk over her, swiftly trying to redirect the conversation. *Maybe she didn't hear me*, Bree thought. She asked again. This time it was more to the point. 'Who is the man holding your hand at the dinner table? Is that Dean Jarvis?'

The silence was deafening, it seemed to last an age, but in truth was surely no more than a few seconds. It was not often that her mother had been cut short in a conversation. Bree asked the question one more time, but her mother interrupted her halfway through. 'How dare you!' she barked. 'How dare you go through my personal things.'

Bree knew that she had touched a nerve. She suddenly found a new resolve as she looked for answers. She got straight to the point. 'Is that my real father?' she asked. 'Is Dean Jarvis my real father?'

The silence returned, followed by a heavy sigh at the end of the line. 'Throw the photo away,' her mother said in an agitated voice. 'Rip it up and throw it away, it's not important.'

Her mother was on the ropes now and Bree was in fighting mood. 'Jamie was right, wasn't he? Per is not our real father, this man is, this Dean Jarvis is my real father, isn't he?'

Bree could now sense that her mother was fighting back. She would seemingly do anything to avoid discussing this subject. 'Is this Kayleigh?' she snapped. 'Is this your friend Kayleigh stirring things up, putting crazy thoughts into your head? Doesn't she realise what you have been through, Brianna? Doesn't she know how much you have suffered these past few months? She can be poisonous that girl, poisonous!'

Bree wanted to answer her mother's condemnation of her best friend by saying, 'That's funny, she was the salt of the earth the last time you called me and now she is poisonous. No, Mother, it is you that is poisonous, a lying, scheming, poisonous bitch.' But she didn't have time for those words, she wanted a straight answer and she wanted it now. 'I asked you a question, Mother. I have the right to know the truth. Is Dean Jarvis my father?'

She didn't know why, but she was hoping that her mother would just answer 'Yes'. Maybe then, she might just give her the chance to explain. All she needed to do was simply say 'Yes'. But her mother was off the ropes now, refusing to give her any straight answers. Now it was the turn of Bree's medication to be blamed for this crazy notion she had. 'Those tablets, the blue ones, are you still taking them?' her mother asked, now angering her daughter even more.

'It is not the fucking anti-depressants, Mother, and you know it. I just want the truth.' Bree wasn't sure where her outburst had come from, she had never sworn directly at her mother before that moment, but there was no holding her back now. This conversation had taken a turn way beyond the concept of family respect.

Her mother tried one last time to dismiss her daughter's attack on her. 'So, the photograph, Brianna, I want you to tear up the photograph and never ask me any more nonsense questions like this again.'

That word was still missing, why could she not just say 'Yes' and tell her the truth, Bree thought. Maybe, just maybe, she could try to understand why she had hidden this from her for all these years. Bree was not prepared to let her mother off the hook. The sparring was over, the boxing gloves were thrown onto the floor, she was fighting dirty now, she had a new choice of weapon. She pushed a dagger deep into her mother's heart and twisted it around. 'And were you ever going to tell me that I had a sister?' she asked. 'Were you ever going to tell me about Poppy?'

There was a sharp intake of breath heard down the phone line, as reality finally smacked her mother full on in the face. Her daughter knew, her daughter knew everything! The blade in her mother's heart twisted one more time as Bree finished the conversation. 'I am going to meet her today, Mother,' she said. 'I am going to meet Poppy, I am going to meet my fucking sister that you have kept from me for all these years.'

As the line went dead, Krista Nylund fell to her knees and held her chest. Her breathing became very heavy, she began to sweat, her body started to shake violently. Slumping forward onto the floor of her living room in her brightly decorated home in Finland, she held her head in her hands and sobbed uncontrollably for at least an hour.

\* \* \*

The skies were clear over Tampere on that bright sunny morning, but a dark cloud would hang over Krista's head for an eternity. She would never forget that telephone call. Word for word, she would remember every heartbreaking moment of agony that her daughter had put her through. She had not heard Poppy's name for more than twenty years. That name alone scared her, it had been everything that held her and Dean apart. But Krista knew that she would not have been having that conversation with her daughter had she carried out her plan all those years ago. In fact there would never have been a Brianna or a Jamie Nylund at all.

Her mind took her back to the car park of that private clinic in North London. It was very cold outside. Christmas was less than a week away and normal people were preparing to celebrate. But there was nothing normal in her thoughts that day and she was far from ready for any type of celebration.

She thought he might be on time, just this once, but Dean Jarvis stayed true to form and was nowhere to be seen. The appointment was for three thirty. Why didn't she tell him that it was an hour earlier? She had tried to reach him, but once again his phone was not switched on. That seemed to be happening more frequently now, ever since that day she had told him. Why did she bother to tell him? she thought. How did she ever find the strength to tell him? It would have been far better to simply book the termination herself and he would have been none the wiser. Now he seemed to be treating her like a leper, like she had some toxic contagious disease that he might catch. The previous week, when she was desperate to see him, he had told her that he had been on a sales training course somewhere in Yorkshire. But she didn't believe him, she wanted to call his company and check if what he had told her was true, but she had been more worried about being proved right than wrong.

At three twenty she dragged her feet into the reception area of the clinic, looking over her shoulder, hoping that she would see his car turn into the car park. It didn't. She had confided in Millie who had offered to leave work early to meet her there. Why did she say no? She should have known this would happen. She so wished that she had asked her friend to come now. She would support her through this painful experience and give her the strength to see it through to the end.

She was a friendly woman, the consultant inside the clinic. She explained everything to her in full detail. She told her how the first tablet would terminate the pregnancy, and the second, to be taken the following day, would deliver the fetus, as if she was having a heavy period. She would need a couple of days off work, to rest, and may have some bouts of nausea, but they would wear off. The kindly consultant seemed to wonder why Krista was constantly staring at the door. She could probably have told her that he was not coming, that he had let her down, that Dean Jarvis was just a selfish bastard that had had his fun and dumped her when she needed him most. The whole staff at the clinic could have told her that she was better off without him. Krista, of course, would not have believed them.

She had been sitting in the small consultancy room for nearly twenty minutes. Why did they allow her so much time to think before giving her the first tablet? she thought. Jumbled images began to run through her mind. She thought back to the night of the awards dinner. She could still see his face across the dinner table. He had said that he loved her that night, he told that he really loved her. When they arrived back at her flat he told her again, he said that she would always be his 'Persephone', his goddess, that he could not live without her. He said that he would walk barefoot on hot coals to save her from danger. Her head began to spin as the terrifying ordeal in front of her became more real by the minute. So he would walk on hot coals to protect her, but he couldn't make a three thirty appointment at this clinic, when her needs were surely greater than any fallen temptress from those mythological creations he had created in his head.

There was still more time to think, to make sure she was making the right decision. No sign of his car in the car park. It would all be over soon. But her mind would not let her forget how perfect that night had been, how close they were, flesh to flesh, soul to soul, entangled in an embrace that would have stood firm against the strongest hurricane. It was not just passion, it was love, she was sure it was true love. So why would you kill something that came from true love? *No*, she thought, *there is far too much time to think, these thoughts need to be about how stupid it was to come off the pill or not make him use protection.* She had only ever used contraceptives to avoid having a baby with Per. Did something in her soul cry out for this, was this meant to happen? *God*, she thought, *please bring the first pill now before I change my mind.*

Twenty-odd minutes later Krista found herself dragging her feet back to her car. A frost was beginning to set on the windscreen of her car and large snowflakes began to fall around the wheels. It wasn't the arrival of Dean that made her cry that day. No, she accepted the fact that he was late because he had been collecting some Christmas presents for Poppy. He proudly pointed to them, sitting on the back seat of his car. So while she had been deliberating over the most heartbreaking decision she had ever made in her life, he had been queuing at the local toy store for the child that he did want to have in his life.

She held herself together for the whole three minutes he hugged her and told her it was the best thing to do. She fought back the tears as he waved her goodbye and set off to wrap those toys he had bought for his beloved daughter. But as his car left the car park of the clinic, Krista fell to her knees as if she had been struck by a bullet from a sniper rifle. She felt so cold, so isolated, as if she was stranded on an island of misery. She knew now that she was not, nor had she ever been, his true Persephone, she was far from it. She was just some dumb woman that had fallen madly in love with a man who she could never be with. She had never felt so alone in the whole of her life. The snow began to fall around her body as she picked herself up from the cold tarmac, pulling tightly on her coat to keep out the chill. Her emotions were all over the place. The tears ran down her face, she could taste them as they passed her dry lips. She knew that she would need to find an inner strength to carry her through. These tears were not for anyone else but herself now, herself and the beautiful creation that was still growing inside her.

Bree's mother sat on the wooden floor of her home in Tampere, remembering that cold December day in 1997, when her fantasy had ended and been replaced with harsh and frightening reality. She wondered if Bree would ever understand why she made the decisions that she did. She wished that she was close enough to her daughter to be able to tell her the truth. That it was not sordid, it was not just sex, it was love, real love. Even if it had only ever been in her head, she believed that it was true love.

Krista saw the ghosts of her past every day in the faces of her beautiful twins. It was a torturous pain that never faded. As Jamie reached manhood those images became almost unbearable. He looked so much like his father that she had called him 'Dean' on more than one occasion. Jamie may have had a striking resemblance to his biological father, but he was certainly more astute. Her son had been asking her from the age of eight why he bore no resemblance to Per. Why he had dark hair and matching complexion, while his father looked like a walking advertisement for natural Scandinavian yoghurt. Her son may have failed miserably at university, but in the end, he proved that he was smart enough to work it all out for himself.

Krista was terrified that the truth was closing in on her when he told her of the mystery man who had contacted him at the gym. Millie had also called to say that she had been approached by a strange old man asking questions about her son. Her friend had only ever met Dean once in her life and was caught off guard when he spoke to her. She felt that she may have given him too much information before realising who he might be. Krista had begun to fear that Dean might just turn up on their doorstep. Her twenty-two years of living a lie would finally be exposed, the twins would hate her forever, she would hate herself forever.

Bree had never bought into Jamie's theories, maybe because she had her mother's pale features and glossy blonde hair. Or it could have been because she idolised Per and had always been something of a 'daddy's girl'. Bree would always take his side in family arguments. The older she became the more distance she put between herself and her mother. It hurt Krista sometimes, to think that her own daughter could prefer to spend so much of her time with a man that was not blood related. She was sure that if her Bree had a choice, she would always choose Per to have been her natural parent, rather than her. Krista had, for some time, been deeply concerned about her daughter's erratic behaviour. She seemed to change from being a loving, attention-seeking princess to a cold and calculated loner. Over the past few years her daughter had shown that she would construct elaborate lies and constantly manipulate people in a bid to get her own way, traits that Krista believed she may well have inherited from her real father.

Since she witnessed the incident in Jamie's bedroom, she felt that she had no option but to separate the two of them. Despite the fact they had both denied vehemently that they were doing anything more than cuddling in bed, she knew what she had seen, and she did what any parent would have done. Krista had spent years protecting her twins from the real world, not just the bullying they encountered at their schools because they were so well spoken, or the jealous teenagers who isolated them from their crowds, simply because they wore nice clothes. She never in her life thought that one day, though, she might have to protect them from each other.

Bree refused the counselling that her mother had organised for her, dropping out after just three sessions. When confronted by her mother she would lock herself in her bedroom for days at a time to avoid any form of conversation. From that moment onwards, her relationship with her daughter became very strained to say the least. Bree never spoke to her the way she used to. There were no more intimate chats about boys and the hopes and fears she held for the future. She missed their shopping trips to the London and Bicester village, they never felt the same when she went with Per or Millie.

When Bree left high school and went to college she became a completely different person, using extremely bad language on a regular basis and experimenting with cocaine and ecstasy. Krista never knew from one day to the next what her daughter was feeling anymore. They were like strangers living together in the same house. It sometimes seemed as if her stubborn daughter wanted to punish her for the rest of her life.

Krista was still confused as to what had happened on the night of the tragic accident, but she did know that Jamie had been under severe stress. He had never really opened up about losing his girlfriend in the accident in Iceland, he even insisted that no one ever mention her name again. For a while she could not possibly perceive that he would have been in a bad enough place to have taken his own life, but his moods had become very dark and she thought that he might be capable of anything. Despite the fact that he had managed to mask his feelings with binge drinking and bouts of outrageous behaviour, she knew that deep down inside he was still tormented by the death of Jess.

When Jamie died, Krista's world seemed to collapse around her. She blamed herself for not getting her son professional help when he needed it. She should have insisted on counselling for him. She knew that she should never have booked his flight to Australia, letting him travel thousands of miles away from home when he clearly needed her and Per's support. But her intentions had been good. She thought if he went away for a while, travelling, meeting new people, it would take him away from all the hurt and pain, away from everything that reminded him of the tragedy in the Husavik Straits. But Krista realised that, selfishly, she also wanted him to be away, a long way away, from the things that could hurt him most. She didn't want him to meet his real father and she knew that it was bad for him to be back with his sister.

Krista knew that if it had not been for Per, she would never have got through these past few years. He had been a rock in her life, a solid rock – reliable, dependable, faithful and trustworthy, all the things that the twins' real father had never been. When she had ended things with Dean and was at her lowest ebb, he had taken her back without ever questioning her about her motives for separating in the first place. He even treated the large bump in her belly as his own, regardless of the fact that she told him the twins were not his. He was the best father she could have ever chosen for Jamie and Bree. Like her, he sacrificed everything to give the children the best life they could possibly have. He always treated the twins as if they were his own and loved them unconditionally.

Krista loved Per, she loved him in a special way, but she knew in her heart that no matter how hard she tried, she would never love him the way she had loved Dean.

# CHAPTER EIGHTEEN

Bree would certainly not be feeling any sympathy for the torment her mother had been through for all those years. In her mind, she deserved every heart-wrenching twist of pain she was now feeling. It seemed as if Krista's troubled daughter had found another reason to hate her mother now. Bree regretted nothing from her earlier phone call. If anything she wished that she had trusted in her brother more and believed his theory, which was not only true, but was coming to life at the rate of knots.

Sitting at the corner table of Chez Blanc, Bree sipped her coffee and waited for the first glimpse of her sibling. She began to practise her opening speech in her head but kept changing her mind about the best way to approach the situation. After all, you can't just say, 'Oh I will have the mushroom risotto and by the way you and I are related, we are sisters', can you?!

Bree had turned her mobile off, just in case her mother called and attempted to instil some form of emotional blackmail in a last attempt to get her to back out of this situation. Nothing and nobody was going to stop her from meeting her sister now, least of all her lying and deceitful 'bitch' of a mother.

Poppy was parked at the rear of the restaurant. She had driven the last mile into work with a flat tyre and Danny was helping her change it. The punctured tyre was proving to be somewhat difficult to remove, so her boss enlisted the aid of a large heavy-duty tyre iron, borrowed from his neighbour. His perseverance finally paid off and he prised the stubborn obstacle off the wheel of her car. He told Poppy that he would finish changing the wheel while she went into the restaurant to clean her dirty hands. 'I will leave the tyre iron in the boot,' he shouted to her as she left him. 'Just in case one of the others goes down.'

Matt grabbed Poppy's arm as she entered the kitchen. 'There is some posh bird in there,' he said. 'She is asking for you.' Poppy headed towards the sink and began soaping her hands. 'She looks a bit official,' Matt added. 'Maybe you have been a naughty girl and she has come to tell you off.'

Poppy screwed up her face as she ran her grease-covered hands underneath the taps. 'I bet it's that Mrs Bishop, I wish the Reverend bloody Joe would get off my case about all that shit.'

As Poppy finished drying her hands, Matt passed her a small brown envelope. '£400,' he said. 'It will get that landlord guy off your back. I was saving it for a holiday, but I would rather know that you are not going to be thrown out onto the street.'

Poppy smiled and tucked the envelope into her pocket. 'Do you know, Matt, you are OK, for a geeky northerner, you are actually OK.' She gave him a friendly peck on his cheek and headed for the corner table.

Bree looked up as Poppy approached. Her sibling looked much older than she had imagined. She must be in her late twenties or maybe early thirties, she thought. Her skin was covered in blotches and her hair looked greasy. She had a rough sort of look about her, even her walk seemed to have an attitude of its own. Bree's mouth dried up as Poppy sat down opposite her, but she managed to ask the first important question of the day. 'Are you Poppy, Poppy Jarvis?'

There was an immediate stare of arrogant disdain from the woman in front of her. She clearly did not want to be here, having this meeting. 'Yes, I am Poppy. Did Joe send you?'

Bree was puzzled. 'Joe?'

'Yeah, Joe from Probation, did he send you here? Do you work with Mrs Bishop, because I have been trying to call, but it's always late at night and no one ever answers the phone, so it's not my fault.'

Shaking her head Bree put Poppy in the picture. 'No, I am nothing to do with Probation or Mrs Bishop.'

'You are not a news reporter, are you?'

'No!'

Poppy felt slightly more at ease and sat back in her seat. 'Well, if it is nothing to do with my probation what do you want me for?'

Bree was becoming more anxious by the second. They were less than a minute into the conversation and this stroppy girl, who could well be her sibling, had already mentioned probation and reporters. What in God's name had her sister done? she thought.

'I am Brianna, Brianna Nylund, but everyone calls me Bree.'

Poppy wasn't really interested in her visitor's personal details. 'And?' she asked. 'What do you want?'

Still feeling a little nervous, Poppy felt it best to ease her way into the conversation. 'This place seems nice, they have a good choice of menu.'

Poppy stood up, as if she was about to walk away. 'So, order some food then. Are we done?'

'No, it is sort of personal and a bit complicated. Please, can you sit back down, I will try to explain.'

Poppy sat down and started to look around the restaurant, as if she was already bored with the conversation. 'Can you get to the point, I have to start my shift soon.'

Bree was unnerved by the brash attitude of the girl sitting opposite her and began to feel more uncomfortable by the minute.

As Poppy turned her head again to look around at the rest of the empty tables, Bree noticed something familiar in her features. Maybe she had been studying that photograph for too long, or inwardly had a deep yearning for this to be her real sister, but she could swear that the girl in front of her had some of Jamie's features, especially his nose. She was now more convinced than ever that the two of them could be related. Searching through her bag Bree produced the photograph from the awards dinner and placed it on the table in front of Poppy. It received an instant reaction as her sibling's eyes glanced down at the picture. Poppy certainly wasn't looking anywhere but the table now.

Bree's hand trembled, as she pointed to the man in the tuxedo. 'Is that, is that your father?' she asked.

Poppy simply turned her head sideways, as if her interest in the picture had only been temporary, but it was obvious that seeing the photograph had some effect on her. 'Who are you?' Poppy asked, the tone of her voice direct and far less welcoming than it had been previously. 'What are you doing here?'

Bree sensed that she had touched a nerve, a raw nerve. 'It is, it is your father, isn't it?' she asked again.

Poppy glanced back down at the picture, her eyes twitched slightly. Bree could tell that she really wanted to pick it up, to study it closer, but she didn't. She knew who the man in that photograph was but was somewhat confused about her visitor. 'He is a bit old for you, isn't he?' Poppy said.

It was Bree's turn to be puzzled. She looked down at the table. 'No! No! No!' she said. 'That is not me, that's not me in the picture.' *Why the hell does everyone think I look like my bitch of a mother?* she thought.

Bree took a small sip of her coffee to help clear her throat. This was not going the way she had planned it in her head that morning. She felt awkward and slightly intimidated in the presence of the woman opposite. She thought for a few seconds about walking out, but she was here now, she would say what she had come to say. 'I think that this man, the one in the photograph, is my father. I think that your father might be mine too.' Poppy said nothing, she simply stared at Bree as if her revelation had not been heard. 'He is your father, isn't he?' Bree asked again. 'I would like to find him, I was hoping that you might help me find him.'

There is no way that Bree could have known what was happening inside the brain of the girl sitting opposite her at that moment. She had no idea of the precarious position she had put herself in. Poppy's blood had begun to boil. A familiar humming sound had started inside her head. It was a sound that she had managed to keep at bay for some time. But now it had returned, and it was slowly getting louder. She was fighting inside to find those soothing colours, she could barely make out the green grass. The sun was in the sky, but she could feel no warmth. Her warped mind began to search. She knew that she had to find some calming colours, the lake, where was the running water? Where was the lake?

'Can you say something?' Bree asked her. 'I know it is a lot to take in.'

Suddenly Poppy did something that she knew she had to do. She rose to her feet to leave the table, her abrupt action causing the coffee cup to spill some of its contents. 'I don't know this man,' Poppy said, staring down at her visitor with a wild look in her eyes. 'I don't know this man, he is certainly not any father to me.' She walked away from the table and headed for the kitchen area, biting the corner of her lip sharply en route. But suddenly a comment from her startled visitor stopped her in her tracks and froze her to the spot. 'But if he is your father, that means we are sisters. That means that you are my sister, Poppy.'

The small traces of calm colours in Poppy's head began to fade. She bit her lip hard and then harder, clenching her fist tightly. Swinging around, she moved swiftly back towards her unwelcome guest. It quickly became apparent to Bree that her last comment had angered her would-be sibling and her face turned pale as the girl arrived back at the table. Towering over her visitor, Poppy picked up the photograph and tossed it into Bree's face, making her thoughts loud and clear. 'Listen good, missy! I don't have a father, do you understand? I don't have a father. If your mother was stupid enough to open her legs to that fucking waste of space, that is your problem. I don't have a father and I don't have a sister. You are not my sister, is that clear?' With that Poppy reached down and tucked her hand around her visitor's coffee cup, sliding it with great force across the table. Her shove was so hard, that the cup travelled several feet across the restaurant and hit a picture frame on the opposite wall, its impact shattering it into several pieces and leaving a trail of warm coffee stains across the carpet. Poppy stomped off with one final parting warning for the clearly shaken girl sitting at the table. 'Don't come back here again, do you understand me? Don't fucking come back here again!'

Grabbing her jacket and handbag from the kitchen, Poppy made her way out of the rear entrance of Chez Blanc. Matt followed her and grabbed her arm. 'What's up?' he asked.

'Not now, Matt,' she snapped, pulling her arm free. The caring Geordie reached out for her again but was brushed to one side as Poppy stormed out of the gate. As she exited through the back she heard Danny's voice call out to her. He had clearly seen that the girl was in a state of distress. Poppy completely ignored him and marched down to the end of the road.

The colours were appearing and disappearing inside her head. Poppy knew that if she had stayed in the restaurant it would have been worse, far worse, for her, for everybody. She had done the right thing. 'Keep walking, Poppy, keep walking,' she told herself. 'That girl will be gone when you get back, keep walking, keep walking.' When she was far enough away from the restaurant, she found herself behind some terraced houses, with just a dozen or so lock-up garages to witness her release her built-up anger. She aimed a kick at the first garage shutter door, denting it, somewhere near the bottom. Another kick followed and then another. 'Bitch!'

she screamed. 'Fucking bitch!' Her temper tantrum lasted a full minute. The garage door now looked as if it had been hit with a battering ram. She slumped down onto the floor and sat with her back to the brick wall between the garages, closing her eyes for a few seconds until the soothing colours began to reappear in her head. Reaching inside her handbag she took out her cigarettes and lit one up to calm her nerves. Two or three drags later, she felt more at ease and by the time she finished the cigarette her head was no longer clouded with dark obstacles.

In the restaurant Matt was busy cleaning the coffee stains from the wall while Danny was chatting with a trembling young girl. Bree was still in shock, she was lost for words, but still felt an urge to pursue her goal. Danny offered her a complimentary brandy, but she refused. She knew that she would only make matters worse if she was still there when Poppy arrived back. Bree reached inside her bag and found her small pocket diary. Ripping out a page she began to scribble her name and number on it. She handed it to Danny and gave him a very brief reason for her visit, as brief as, 'She is my sister, we have the same dad, I just want to talk to her.'

The restaurant owner assured her that he would give Poppy the number and made a valid excuse for her irrational behaviour. 'She has been through a tough time lately.' If only Bree knew how much of an understatement that really was, she would have probably asked for her number back there and then. Bree left Chez Blanc, looking over her shoulder as she exited, maybe in the hope that she could get a parting glimpse of her sister. But by that time Poppy was half a mile down the road and smoking her second cigarette, deciding whether or not to return to her duties later that day or simply to leave the job she enjoyed so much.

As Matt switched his attention to cleaning the coffee-stained carpet, Danny sat at the table trying to work out what had just happened. The Geordie felt that this might be the time to ask his boss some questions, some things that he wanted to know about Poppy. 'She is a real loose cannon, that lass, you never know what she is going to do next, do you?'

Danny shook his head. 'She has had a troubled past, Matt, she just wants to leave it all behind her.'

Matt wanted to know more. He knew she had always confided in Danny. 'Why did she spend so long in prison? What did she do that was so bad?'

The restaurant owner did not feel it was his place to tell him. 'You need to ask Poppy,' he said.

'Anyone would think that she had murdered someone or something,' the strapping chef said, laughing. His laughter, however, soon stopped, when he saw the solemn expression on Danny's face. Matt was shocked. 'Oh my god! She did, she bloody killed someone, didn't she?'

Danny shook his head. 'It is not my place to say, Matt, let's just leave it.'

'Shit!' Matt said. 'She really did, didn't she? She really did kill someone.'

The restaurant owner thought it might be better if he filled his chef in on the reason for Poppy's incarceration. The last thing he wanted was Matt quizzing his waitress all day. That would not be good for her in the state that she was in. 'It was about five years ago,' Danny said. 'She stabbed some drug dealer on the Marfield estate, you know, up in South Woolwich.'

Matt stopped his cleaning. He was all ears now. 'She stabbed him?'

'Twenty-odd times, or so the papers said,' Danny replied. 'Took four people to drag her off him apparently.'

Matt was truly stunned. 'Shit!'

'He was a scumbag, dealing to kids, thought he was a big shot. Billy Keyes, that was his name, that was him, Billy Keyes.'

'Why did she do it?' Matt asked. 'I know she had a problem with drugs in the past, she told me that.'

Danny felt bad recalling the event, but he thought it might be best to fill Matt in on all the details now. 'One of her friends overdosed. I think she said that the Social Services had taken the girl's little kid into care.'

Matt suddenly remembered the conversation after the trip to Bournemouth. 'She told me about that girl, she told me that they were close, that she had overdosed on heroin. I knew she was upset about it, but I never knew she had stabbed the dealer.'

'I don't know all the details,' Danny said. 'I just know that she got seven years for manslaughter and served her time in Bronzefield prison. The newspapers went mad when they only found her guilty of manslaughter. The jury had all agreed it was diminished responsibility or something like that.'

The chef began to piece things together in his head. 'That's why she did all them tests and stuff, that's why she has to go to Probation every week.'

Danny continued. 'The newspapers hated her, they painted a picture of this lowlife Billy Keyes as being some sort of angelic do-gooder. They said that he was just in the wrong place at the wrong time. One of the papers started a campaign to have her case reheard. They wanted her locked up for murder, locked away for life.'

The Geordie lad felt slightly uncomfortable now, realising he had become so close to someone so volatile, somebody capable of murder. 'I do feel for her, Danny, I know she has had a shit life.'

'You don't know the half of what that girl has been through, Matt, trust me.'

'What I don't understand is why she stays with that bloke. You know he hits her, don't you?'

'Cameron Turner?'

'That's him. Do you know him?'

'I know of him. He is really nasty bastard. She knew him before she got locked up, I think.'

'I feel like going round there sometimes, you know, to sort him out, when I see her bruises and what he does to her.'

'He protected her.'

'What?!'

'When she first came out of prison, he protected her. Billy Keyes' brother Nathan and a couple of his cronies from the Marfield turned up at their flat to get revenge for what had happened. Cameron is a big fucker, he can look after himself. He gave the three of them a good hiding.'

Matt was shocked again. 'Shit! I never knew all this was going on.'

'So she stays with him. I suppose she sort of feels safe there.'

'Just another big bloody bad wolf waiting to happen,' Matt said shaking his head. 'Poor bloody Poppy!'

Danny didn't understand Matt's remark. He wanted him to fully appreciate how vulnerable he felt his waitress could be. 'This girl, the posh one who came in today, she is apparently her sister. It's not good, Matt, she loathed her dad, she is going to hate him even more now.'

'I wondered why it all kicked off.'

'I ripped up the girl's phone number, Matt. Don't tell Poppy but I just binned it. If that girl comes back, just tell her that Poppy is on holiday or has left the job or something. She really doesn't need any more stress in her life.'

\* \* \*

Halfway through the lunchtime shift Poppy came back to Chez Blanc. She said very little to either Danny or Matt, who had covered the duties for their missing waitress. Fortunately for them the restaurant had not been over busy that day and they coped well. She accepted Matt's offer to have a coffee at his flat during their break before their evening shift. The coffee was steaming hot at the flat that afternoon, but their sex had been lukewarm to say the least. Poppy had changed her mind and stopped Matt halfway through the act. She couldn't get the images and words of her unwanted visitor out of her head, however hard she tried. As usual the big Geordie lad accepted her mood swing and did his best to offer her some comfort, not that Poppy really appreciated his efforts.

The evening was busy at Chez Blanc. Poppy worked hard to make up for her absence during lunchtime while the clumsy teen Chantelle was at it again, dropping two main courses into the lap of one of the regulars at the restaurant, costing Danny two free meals and a dry-cleaning bill. He threatened to deduct the money from the infantile girl's wages, but never did, he was too much of a soft touch to do that. Danny thought that Poppy might like to share one of their 'chats' that evening, after the restaurant closed. He cancelled a late-night meeting with a couple of his friends, but Poppy seemed content just to go back to her flat. She didn't seem to want to discuss the earlier incident with anybody, although she did thank Danny for his kind consideration of her feelings.

The day was about to get worse for Poppy. When she arrived back at Stonely Parade, her head still spinning like reels on a broken fruit machine, she saw a sight that swiftly took her mind away from her earlier confrontation. As she was parking her car she noticed the tall and imposing figure of Neddy, a well-known dealer from the Marfield estate and an original member of the Keyes brothers crew. What made matters worse was that he was coming out of the back entrance to the flats where she lived. She knew that it was too much of a coincidence to be true. He had to have been visiting Cameron. She hoped that she was mistaken. Her boyfriend knew how she felt about him. He had promised that he would never buy his gear from that source. She ducked down in her car, so that he could not see her as he passed. She peeped up as the footsteps moved further away, spotting his purple dreadlocks hanging down his neck and realising that she had not been mistaken at all. Poppy was clearly not happy, in fact by the time she arrived at her flat she was seething about his visit. She was in the right mood for confrontation this night and an argument ensued within minutes of her entering the flat. Their voices grew louder. The pair of them hurled insults and profanities at each other for ages. Finally, Cameron did what he did best. Slamming shut the bedroom door behind him, he retreated to his cave.

In the street below, lurking in the shadows, a pair of eyes had been watching, studying the reflections of the sparring shapes on their curtains in the front room. Their argument must have seemed like a modern-day Punch and Judy show to any voyeurs below. The small figure had been watching closely and listening intently to every word that had been said during their row. The stalker hiding in the shadows seemed to be fascinated by the couple's turbulent encounter, staring up at the window for almost an hour before leaving.

# CHAPTER NINETEEN

Something was bothering Kayleigh, it had been playing on her mind for some time. She had spent the best part of an hour on the telephone with Krista the previous night, a conversation that had given her even more cause to worry about Bree's erratic behaviour. Some of her concerns were beginning to look as though they were more than just crazy notions rolling around in her head. She was becoming genuinely worried about her best friend's state of mind.

Earlier that morning, an overexcited Bree had called her to invite herself around to her flat. She seemed desperate to fill her in on how her first meeting with 'her sister' had gone and needed Kayleigh's full and undivided attention. Although the girls had been the best of friends for most of their lives, Kayleigh still found it difficult to ask Bree any sensitive questions. They would have 'girlie chats' but there were subjects that could never be placed on the table for fear of upsetting the girl she thought she knew so well.

They had first met when they both attended Oaklands junior school after Krista and Per had bought the beautiful four-bedroom semi-detached house on the upmarket side of Oxley. Kayleigh's parents had just separated, her father moving in with a fellow teacher from the college where he worked, leaving her and her mother sharing a modest abode on the outskirts of the village. The girls seemed to hit it off almost immediately, both sharing their love of the same boy bands and their hatred for certain teachers. They had been 'besties' ever since.

When they started secondary school, the two girls and Jamie became something of a mini-clique. Nobody was allowed into their 'inner circle', especially those that dared to call Bree by her full Christian name, she really hated that. Bree would constantly be trying to keep Jamie out of trouble and stop him from mixing with the small gangs of boys that tried to lead him astray. She had taken an elderly sister role, even back then, despite the fact that she was only a dozen minutes older than her twin. Her and Kayleigh had become so close by the time they were fifteen that many pupils began to think they might be in some sort of relationship. Bree always denied it emphatically, but a mischievous Kayleigh chose to tease her fellow students by suggesting that she might be bi-curious. This of course was nonsense. Kayleigh Hardy was the first girl in her year to lose her virginity and by the end of year eleven she had slept with three different boys, all much older than her, two of them from the same local football team. Bree found her friend's behaviour somewhat embarrassing but chose not to disown her. By the time they had finished their GCSEs, Kayleigh had earned herself a somewhat tarnished reputation. After all, at their small village school in Oxley, secrets like hers did not stay secret for long.

Bree had always had her fair share of attention in those years. Much prettier than Kayleigh, some would say 'a bit of a stunner', she was by far the best-dressed girl outside the school gates. A wardrobe full of designer-labelled clothes and always immaculately presented, she attracted the attention of many admirers. Her mother thought nothing of spending several hundred pounds on a new coat or shoes for Bree, to make her daughter stand out in the crowd. On her sixteenth birthday, Bree received a pair of Jimmy Choo shoes costing over £1200. Kayleigh told her best friend at the time that she thought the purchase was a waste of money and had a better idea for the expensive footwear. She advised her 'bestie' to 'sell those bad boys on eBay and we can go wild in Ibiza for a week'. The excursion to the exotic party island never happened, but Kayleigh was right about the overpriced shoes. Bree only wore them two or three times before they stayed hidden at the back of her wardrobe.

The girls went to different colleges. Bree was far more academically advanced than her friend, as a result of private tuition lessons paid for by her parents. She attended a renowned college in South London, thanks mainly to her superlative exam results and Krista's friendship with one of their board of governors. Kayleigh stayed on for two years at Oxley sixth form, dropping out in the final term and only completing half of her exams. By that time Jamie was at the opposite end of the country at Holme Vale boarding school. The one-time inseparable clique had been well and truly broken.

Despite the fact that Bree and Kayleigh were mixing in different circles, Bree would insist that Kayleigh come to her house, almost every night, so they could chat about the events of the day. It was at this time that Kayleigh noticed big changes in her best friend. She had started dressing in weird dark clothes, she had grown a complex about her mother and every other word out of her mouth was a swearword. She no longer 'didn't like the new toothpaste', instead she 'hated the new fucking toothpaste'. So much for the theory that a well-heeled London college makes you a better person than anyone else, Kayleigh thought, but never shared with Bree, in fear of retribution from her childhood friend. They fell out for a while when Kayleigh started dating a lad working at the

Green Dragon Bar and Grill, the only place that college students ever got served without ID. The relationship did not last long, however, so their fall-out was short-lived.

It was during the time that Bree attended her college that Kayleigh noticed major changes in her attitude. Kayleigh found it strange that Bree would often swear about her mother and the hatred she had for her, but never to her mother's face. Maybe she still remembered the time, several years earlier, when the girls where having a sleepover at Bree's house and Krista had dragged her screaming ten-year-old brother into the bathroom and washed his mouth out with soap for using foul language. Kayleigh herself rarely swore anywhere outside of her comfort zone, which was usually in a horizontal position, with somebody lying on top of her.

As they reached their twenties, Kayleigh had become something of a 'party girl'. She became sexually active, extremely sexually active. There were many drunken one-night stands and holiday flings, none of which ended up leading to relationships. Bree used to tease her that she must be riddled with STDs, having slept with over one hundred men. Kayleigh knew that this figure was not accurate, but in truth, by now she had lost count of the actual number of sexual partners she had really had.

During those years Bree seemed to shun the attention of male company. Kayleigh had set her up with at least three or four possible suitors, but her 'bestie' would always find something she did not like about them. Kayleigh remembered that the longest her friend was seeing anyone for was around six weeks. The man was a young squaddie from Aldershot barracks. He was good looking, athletic and very witty. Jamie really enjoyed his banter when he met him and told Bree that he hoped that his sister would stay with him. Surprisingly, Krista seemed over the moon that her daughter had found a possible soulmate, often leaving the two of them alone in the house, as though she might be encouraging them to have sex. But, as with the other men in Bree's life, it all ended without any explanation being given. It was just Bree, being, well, Bree!

Kayleigh had begun to believe that her friend might be 'asexual'. She never asked her, maybe Bree didn't know herself. It just never seemed right to her that Bree did not seem to have any sexual urges at all. Kayleigh had once met with, and although she would probably deny it to Bree, slept with, one of the few men that had dated her friend. The two of them spent the following morning together, during which time the very forward 'Jack the Lad' gave his own opinion on her sexual preferences. He had taken Bree out several times over a period of around a month, but in his words 'had never even got to first base'. He thought at the time that she was either frigid or, again in his words, 'a closet lesbian, screaming to get out of the cupboard'.

But the question of her sexuality was not the thing that had been on Kayleigh's mind. Of course, she was curious about her friend's lack of interest in relationships, but in truth that was none of her business. No, this was something more concerning – a throwaway line that Krista had used in their phone call and the certainty that her friend had called out a name during at least two of her nightmares. The name was Jess. She knew that it could only be Jess Chambers. Nobody ever mentioned that name to either of the twins after what had happened at the Husavik Straits of Iceland.

Jamie had met Jess during his first week at Bristol University. The two had become an item very quickly and soon became inseparable. Bree really took to his brother's new girlfriend. She liked her outgoing approach on life and her zany dress sense. For a while, Kayleigh seemed to be cast to one side, as Jess, Jamie and Bree became 'the new clique'. Bree would travel to Bristol most weekends and the three of them would go to wild parties together or to music venues to watch indie rock bands. Bree would return, with hundreds of pictures of their escapades on her mobile phone, and if truth be told, Kayleigh was rather jealous.

Around five months after Jamie had first met Jess, the three of them travelled to Iceland on a four-day excursion. They took in the usual tourist sites in the first couple of days, but Jamie had his heart set on seeing the fjords, something Per had often told him was one of the most beautiful places in the world. The small fishing boats could be hired out with a captain, who would get you 'up close and personal' with the whales in the sea, so close you could touch them.

And that is when tragedy struck. The small vessel taking them on the two-hour excursion hit bad weather. Jess, being the crazy carefree girl that she was, stayed on the deck of the boat taking selfies, while the others were sheltered in the cabin. Before anyone knew what was happening, the boat hit a large wave which caused Jess to lose her footing and slip over the side. But it was what happened afterwards that shocked everyone. Jamie, who was a school champion swimmer and a qualified lifeguard, made no attempt to save her, no attempt at all. He simply froze like a statue fixed to the deck of the boat, he couldn't move. He watched on as his girlfriend's body was swept away by the undercurrents. By the time the captain had alerted the coastguard, the poor girl had drowned, her lifeless body pulled from the sea in front of both the twins.

The siblings were left traumatised by the incident. Both attended private counselling and neither of them were seen in public for months. Per took time off work to stay at home with them and eventually Jamie went back to university. But his mind was not right. He would walk out of lectures in floods of tears and began drinking very heavily. He spent every waking hour blaming himself for what had happened. Bree buried herself in her work. She had recently started a new job at the fashion promoters and her boss was very supportive of her situation. She too felt responsible. It had been her idea to go on that excursion. She told Kayleigh at the time that she would never forgive herself for that. As time moved on Jamie seemed to be coming to terms with the tragic event. He said that he no longer felt as if he was to blame, but there was always a look of sadness in his eyes. The usually happy-go-lucky character was a shadow of his former self. The twins made a pact never to mention her name again, asking all their family and friends to follow their lead.

The question was, and Kayleigh was far from alone in thinking it, did Jamie ever really come to terms with the death of his girlfriend? Is it possible that the incident at the Maple crossing may have been suicide? A close friend of Jamie had confided in Kayleigh, shortly after his death, that he had been severely depressed for months. He had not wanted to go to Australia but was doing so because his life was such a mess. He had told him that he hated himself and had dark thoughts most of the time. He was drinking himself into oblivion most days rather than face the reality of his existence. A rumour had circulated amongst his small crowd of friends that Jamie had left a suicide note, but that Bree had found it and destroyed it. She would never want anyone to think that her brother had taken his own life. She would protect his memory with her dying breath.

Could the rumours be true, could this have been a spur-of-the-moment thing? The toxicology report had shown that there were no traces of any drugs, including anti-depressants, inside his body, There was, however, an overwhelming amount of alcohol, over five times the legal drink-drive limit.

And so now the dilemma for Kayleigh was how to ask that awkward question, was there a suicide note? She would need to tread very carefully, her friend was still very fragile, she could tell, but maybe if she opened up and talked about that night, it might help. She knew that Bree would never go to counselling again, she had told her that, after her last series of sessions following the death of Jess. But if her 'bestie' wanted to confide in her, Kayleigh could keep her secret and maybe help her to finally come to terms with Jamie's death. It might also be the answer to stopping her having those awful nightmares, which seemed to be draining all the life out of her troubled friend.

* * *

Bree arrived around midday with an air of unbridled excitement about her. Her words seemed to be firing out of her mouth at one hundred miles per hour as she gave Kayleigh the details of her encounter with Poppy. The overexcited girl used the word 'sister' at least twenty times in the first ten minutes of the conversation, something that Kayleigh found most strange, considering it had only been a few days since she had discovered she existed at all. It was almost as if her newfound half-sibling had been on a very long vacation and that the two of them had finally been reunited. Kayleigh's internet research, however, had told her that Poppy Jarvis had indeed been on an extended holiday, but not on sun-kissed beaches on a faraway exotic island. No, she had recently spent just under four years at HMP Bronzefield. Kayleigh chose not to dampen her best friend's joyous mood, at least not for that moment.

Somewhere around Bree's thirtieth mention of her 'sister' and their first meeting, Kayleigh attempted to change the direction of the conversation and lead on to those awkward questions that were still buzzing around in her head. 'I spoke with your mother last night,' she said. 'She called me from Tampere, she was worried about you.'

Bree looked angry. 'What did that bitch want?' she asked.

'She told me about your conversation. She told me that you were going to meet with this Poppy girl.'

'My sister, you mean, Kayleigh, my sister.'

*There is that word again*, Kayleigh thought, but tried not to be distracted. 'She said that you have stopped answering your phone.'

'She can't handle me knowing the truth. She didn't like the fact that I have found Poppy.'

'She really is worried about you, babe, she wanted the chance to explain.'

'Explain why she has kept my sister hidden from me for more than twenty years? To explain why she never told me that Per was not my real father? I still love him, of course I still love him, but I hate her, I hate her for everything.'

'I told her that you need time, time to let it all sink in. Please don't hate her, babe, she says she only did it to protect you and Jamie. She knows she was wrong.'

'No, Kayleigh, this is the final straw. I really don't want anything to do with that bitch again.'

Not knowing where to lead the conversation next, Kayleigh moved to her kitchen and started to make some coffee. Her friend followed her. Bree still had more to tell her about the previous day. 'I saw where she lives yesterday, it is a real shithole, Kayleigh. She lives in one of those slum estates in South London, you know where all the places look the same. God, her flat is fucking awful!'

'She invited you to her home?' Kayleigh asked, slightly concerned that things were moving a bit too fast. After all, Kayleigh knew now what type of girl Poppy Jarvis was.

'Well, she didn't exactly invite me,' Bree said. 'I sort of, well, I sort of followed her home from work. It is disgusting, there were kids throwing lighted matches into a post box and the smell of cannabis everywhere.'

Her friend shook her head in disbelief. 'You don't know this girl, babe, you can't just rock up on her doorstep.'

'For fuck's sake, Kayleigh! You are starting to sound like my mother.'

'Did you go inside?'

'No, I just watched her from the road, she was having a massive argument with someone in her flat.'

'You shouldn't have gone to her home, babe, not until you get to know more about her, you shouldn't have gone there.'

'I know that she is my sister, that is all that matters.'

The girls took their coffees back into the lounge. The time had come for Kayleigh to open that 'can of worms' she had been holding back on, but first she wanted to give her the lowdown on her newfound sibling.

'Sit down, babe,' she said. 'Let me show you what I found.'

Kayleigh opened her laptop and retyped the search she had made the previous day – '*Poppy Jarvis Prison*'. Over two hundred pages came up on the Google counter. Almost immediately several blurred photographs of the girl Bree had met the previous day appeared. Kayleigh clicked on the top line, an old article for a national newspaper with the headline, '*Getting away with murder*'. She gave time for Bree to read the subtext before moving on to the next newspaper's take on what had happened, its headline much more damning – '*No justice for Billy Keyes as jury says it's manslaughter*'. Bree's eyes raced down the page, barely batting an eyelid as she reached the part of the story revealing that Poppy had been high on a cocktail of drugs at the time she stabbed a youth to death in a fit of rage. Kayleigh clicked on another. 'This is the *Gazette*'s one, you know where we...'

Bree snapped sharply at her friend. 'I know what the fucking *Gazette* is!' she said.

This article had been one of several by the *Southern Gazette* on the Poppy Jarvis case. The last two called for petitions to be started in a bid to have the trial reheard. They wanted real justice to be executed and were seeking a life sentence for the clearly disturbed murderess. The text in these articles was highly emotive, citing the words 'psychopath' and 'deranged' almost as many times as Bree had used the word 'sister' that day. Kayleigh drank her coffee, pondering on how to open the awkward conversation with her best friend, when Bree's comment took her completely by surprise. 'She doesn't look very nice in those photos, does she?' Kayleigh was speechless. Her friend had just read three articles on how her sibling had stabbed an innocent youth to death with a hunting knife with an eight-inch blade and her only concern was that her hair might look out of place in her police mugshot. She was more than worried now, she was alarmed. The girl in the photographs had been jailed for seven years, with a recommendation for psychiatric help, and Bree was talking about her sister as if she had simply received one too many parking tickets.

Before Kayleigh could get around to starting her planned conversation, her best friend started to turn on her. 'So you want to piss on my parade, do you? I have found something in my life that means something to me and you want to knock me back down. What is it, Kayleigh, are you jealous or something?'

Kayleigh was puzzled by her comment. 'Jealous? No, of course not. I am worried about you, babe.' Bree stood up as if she was about to leave. Her friend rose swiftly from the sofa and stood in front of her. 'Don't go, babe, I really need to speak with you today.' Kayleigh had been rehearsing her speech in her head but realised now that her friend was still very vulnerable. Showing her those newspaper articles about her sister would not have helped matters much. She took a deep breath and started. 'It is about Jamie, about what happened.'

Bree stood and faced her friend. She was curious to know where this was going. 'Jamie?' she asked. 'What has me finding my sister got to do with Jamie's accident?'

Kayleigh finally plucked up the courage to say what was on her mind. 'That night,' she asked, 'I don't want to ask you, babe, but I need to know. That night, did he mean to do it? Did Jamie mean to stop the car on the tracks? I know he was depressed, babe, I know what everyone has been saying and I would never have believed it, but…'

Bree interrupted her friend with a look of disgust and hurt on her face. 'Shame on you, Kayleigh Hardy!' she said, gritting her teeth together. 'How could you ever think that my Jamie could do that? Fucking shame on you!'

'Babe, he was still cut up, he never really got over, you know, he never really got over Jess and what happened. He wasn't, you know, he wasn't the bravest person in the world, I didn't even know he could drive. Why would he just crash into that car, and not, and not move?'

'How can you say he wasn't brave, Kayleigh? You are talking out of your fucking arse.'

'But, he didn't, you know, with Jess, he never tried to help her.'

'She drowned, Kayleigh, he didn't have time to help her for fuck's sake!'

'But you know, he loved her, and he didn't even try.'

'You were not there, Kayleigh, you don't fucking know what happened!'

'He told everyone afterwards, he told everyone how guilty he felt. He said he just froze, he couldn't move.'

'But that doesn't mean he wasn't brave. He saved Caroline and Maisie that night at the crossing. If Jamie hadn't used the car to push them off the tracks they would have died.'

'Your mum says he was not himself, that he was really depressed after losing Jess and all the stuff about his real dad was messing with his head. That's why she booked his trip to Australia. She wanted him to have a fresh start. She knew some people out there, distant cousins or something.'

'You never listen, do you, Kayleigh? I have told you before, my fucking whore of a mother booked him that trip to keep him away from me. She would do anything to separate the two of us, she hates me that much.'

'But she thinks,' Kayleigh had to pause a second, this was her real question, 'your mother thinks that he wrote a suicide note. She thinks that you knew about it, she thinks you have hidden it or destroyed it.'

A sudden burst of anger ripped through Bree and she turned on her friend. 'I fucking told you, Kayleigh, he would never have done that, he wasn't depressed, he was pissed off. He was pissed off with our fucking mother trying to control our lives!'

'But he was, babe. I could see he was still hurting over Jess. He wasn't the same after that, he really loved her.'

'He didn't love her, Kayleigh, he only knew her for a few months. Yes, of course he was upset when it happened, we both were, but trust me, he didn't love her like everyone thinks he did. She was my friend too, I was upset about her drowning, but no one ever gave a shit about the way I was feeling, they just fucked me off to counselling and thought that I would be OK. Well I wasn't, Kayleigh! I wasn't fucking OK! But no one gave a shit, it was all about Jamie, it was always all about Jamie.'

'But your mother said that Jess…'

Bree snapped again. 'Stop bringing her into this, my mother doesn't know anything! Why are we talking about a girl that died years and years ago? Trust me, Jamie was not cut up about her, he did not kill himself over Jess. There was no suicide note, Kayleigh, it was an accident, it was a fucking accident!'

'OK, I believe you,' Kayleigh said, trying to calm her friend down. 'I believe you.'

'I don't care if you do or you don't. You are just like the rest of them fucking idiots out there, you are just like my mother. If Jamie was here now he would be so disappointed in you, Kayleigh. Shame on you, you have shown your true colours today, you are not a real friend.'

'No, babe, don't say that. I am your friend, Bree, I will always be there for you.'

'Not always. Sometimes you can be selfish, Kayleigh.'

'Selfish?'

'Yes, you can be very selfish.'

'How can you say that?'

Bree shrugged her shoulders. 'It's true. You are selfish sometimes.'

'No, babe, I have been there for you, I have always been there for you.'

'Like when you tried to bed Jamie, is that what a best friend does?'

'No, that's not true.'

'He told me, Kayleigh, he told me you tried to bed him when he got kicked out of university, when his head was a complete mess.'

'No, babe, I swear, I was just trying to be a friend, to be there for him, after what happened with Jess. He just wanted to talk.'

'But of course he only wanted to talk, Kayleigh, he wouldn't have looked twice at a cheap tramp like you!'

'That hurts, babe, don't say that.'

'Well it's true, let's face it, Kayleigh, you have turned into a real slag over the years.'

'Bree, stop it, you don't mean that.'

'Oh, I do, you are a cheap fucking slag, the standing joke in every bar in Surrey. No, Kayleigh, my brother would not have gone anywhere near you. He told me once that he thought you were ugly, he said you had froggy eyes and you always smelled of piss.'

Kayleigh became tearful. 'Why are you saying that, babe? I never tried to bed Jamie, he was like a brother to me, like you are a sister.'

Bree shrugged her shoulders. 'You are not my sister, Kayleigh. I have a sister, a real sister.'

Kayleigh became more upset and fought hard to hold back her tears. 'I wish I had never found her for you, I wish I had thrown that picture away. What is happening to you, Bree? What is happening to my friend?'

Seeing what her cruel comments had done to Kayleigh made Bree become emotional herself. Suddenly a feeling of overwhelming guilt came over her and she broke down in tears. 'I am sorry, really, I am so sorry,' she said, pulling Kayleigh closer to her and hugging her tightly. 'I just miss him so much, Kayleigh, I miss him every day, I miss him every day.' Large tears escaped from Bree's eyes and rolled down her cheeks, landing gently on her best friend's shoulder. She sobbed loudly as she embraced Kayleigh in a heartfelt grip. She knew she didn't really mean those terrible things she had just said to her only true friend, her emotions were bouncing all over the place at that time. Bree's voice became a little croaky. 'I still dream about him, all of the time. It is like he is still with me. Sometimes I don't want to wake up, I just want to sleep, in the hope that I can see more of him.'

Holding her friend close, Kayleigh tried her best to offer some words of comfort. 'One day,' she said, 'one day things will be OK, babe. I promise that one day all this hurt and pain will go away and you will get your life back.'

Bree broke their embrace and pushed her friend away. 'You don't understand, Kayleigh, you really don't understand. I don't want this pain to go away. If the pain leaves me, it means he is gone, it means Jamie is gone, forever!'

Kayleigh wrapped her arms around her friend again and squeezed her tightly. 'I do understand, babe, I do understand.'

When the crying had come to an end, the girls sat with some fresh coffee and Bree continued to tell her friend more about her encounter with Poppy and how much she wanted to see her again. She promised Kayleigh that she would take her with her next time, so that she could see for herself that this girl was not the deranged monster that the newspapers had made her out to be. Kayleigh smiled and laughed throughout their conversation but deep inside she had the feeling that this newfound relationship would somehow backfire on her best friend and send her reeling back to those dark days she had endured earlier in the year. In her head she really wished that she had destroyed that photograph in Krista's little box of treasured memories.

The girls shared a small box of cakes that Kayleigh had brought the previous day and by mid-afternoon their heated argument seemed to have been forgotten. Bree had said that she needed to leave earlier than planned to pick some things up from a clothes store before it closed. She had begun to say her goodbyes, thanking Kayleigh for always being there for her and assuring her that she would call her before she returned to meet her sister again.

Their earlier differences seemed to have been buried, but just before Bree left the flat, Kayleigh saw a glimpse of the venom that she had witnessed earlier that day. Her friend's face was stern and there was a glint of anger in her eyes. 'And Kayleigh,' she said, grabbing her friend's wrist so tightly that her long nails cut into her skin, 'don't ever talk to my mother again without speaking to me first! Do you understand?' With that parting comment, Bree stomped out of the flat and headed for her car.

Kayleigh looked down at her wrist. The scratch had drawn blood, but it hurt her more inside than out. She hated arguing with the girl she had known for most of her life. Alone in her flat, she realised that she never did get a straight answer to her question. She did not believe Bree now when she said there had been no suicide note.

The *Gazette*'s article on Poppy Jarvis was still staring back at Kayleigh from her laptop. She deleted the pages that she had shown her friend that day and poured herself a large glass of Prosecco. It was early in the day for her to start drinking, but she felt as if she needed some alcohol to calm her nerves. Kayleigh was in deep thought. There was a strange idea rolling around in her head and a sick feeling in her stomach. She wanted to put her twisted theories to the back of her mind, but they were screaming at her so loudly, she couldn't. Before shutting down the screen on her computer she typed in three simple words on the search bar. They were words she never thought in a million years she would place together on her keyboard. Surely these things only happen in strange novels by unknown authors and stories of debauchery in Roman times, she thought. She took a deep breath and typed in the words '*incest between twins*'.

\* \* \*

Bree had lied to her best friend that afternoon. There was no store to visit. She had left Kayleigh's flat in time to visit Jamie's graveside. There were some things that she needed to share with him, important things. When she arrived, she was cheered by the sight of an array of summer flowers blossoming all around the cemetery. The place seemed so much brighter these days.

As she reached her brother's final resting place, she noticed some freshly laid ivory lilies, neatly displayed in the two silver pots. She smiled to herself, knowing that Caroline and Maisie had visited him recently. She sat down beside his gravestone and placed her hands on the top, as if to let him know that she was beside him. 'I have found her, Jay,' she said, crouching closer to his stone. 'I have found our sister.' Bree waited for a couple to pass by before continuing her revelation. 'She is a bit confused, but I understand that. I think that I would be if someone came and told me that they were my sister.'

Bree ran her fingers over her brother's name on the front of the stone. It gave her a small sense of his presence. 'Mum is still being a bitch,' she said, shaking her head. 'She has got Kayleigh on her side now. I don't trust Kayleigh anymore, Jay, but don't worry I will never tell them, I will never say anything.' Bree took out one of the flowers that Maisie had left in the pot and held it to her nose to breathe in its fresh aroma. 'I know that you want to find out more about him, Jay, about our real dad. I am so sorry that I never believed you, maybe I was just scared, maybe I was just scared to know the truth. But I do want to meet him now. I want to know what he is like. I am sure that Poppy will let me meet him, now that she knows that I am his daughter too.'

Stretching out her legs, Bree lay down on top of where her brother was buried. She smiled, as if she felt that she might be lying next to him. Looking up at the clear blue sky she found her mind working overtime. 'I wonder if we look like him, Jay, I wonder if we look just like him. Everyone keeps telling me that I look like her, telling me that I look like our bitch of a mother. You don't think that, do you, Jamie? You always said I was much prettier than her, you always said that I was the prettiest girl in the world.'

Bree smiled, a small, knowing sort of smile and continued her speech. 'When I find him, Jay, when I find our real father, I will tell him what a fine son he had, a handsome, strong and very brave son.' Bree's smile grew larger as an image of her lost brother appeared in her head. 'Oh, and I will tell him that you were funny, Jay, you were always funny. I will tell him how you always made everyone around you laugh.' Bree suddenly became tearful and her voice became a little shaky. 'I miss your laugh,' she said shaking her head, her eyes clouding over with tears. 'Oh, Jamie, I miss your laugh so much!'

# CHAPTER TWENTY

This was not an ordinary Friday in the life of Poppy Jarvis, it was far from it. Despite the appearance of her unwelcome visitor at Chez Blanc earlier that week, she was in a buoyant mood, an extremely buoyant mood. The £400 Matt had loaned her to help with her rent arrears was safely tucked away in a sock beneath her bedroom wardrobe, safely out of Cameron's reach. So with the wages she received from Danny at lunchtime, including £40 of tips for the week, she had more than the £550 she needed to give to her landlord Mr Rahwaz to avoid the eviction. Poppy had arranged to drop the money into his house the following morning on her way to work and he had agreed to cancel the eviction proceedings. She realised that it would be the first time that her rent would be up to date since they moved into their filthy little hovel in Stonely Parade. Poppy felt quite proud of that.

But this was not the only reason she was in high spirits. Following Wednesday's session with Joe Manning she had finally reached the last week of her probation period. She felt so bullish about the upcoming release of her shackles, that she had even spoken with the 'dreaded Mrs Bishop' and agreed to attend a local anger management group for the following six weeks. The woman she had been avoiding for so long had turned out to be much more understanding of her reluctance to prolonged bouts of therapy than she could have hoped for. After a lengthy conversation, Mrs Bishop took it upon herself to change the requirement, reducing the length of the course on the provision that Poppy did not miss a session and the group's counsellor was happy with her involvement. So now she was free of her landlord's nagging phone calls and would soon be free of all the sermons, all the bullshit, and most of all, free of having to face those 'awkward' questions each week in Manning's 'holy' office.

They say that good things come in threes. Maybe the most surprising element of Poppy's new spring in her step was closer to home, much closer in fact. The previous evening, just when she thought that her week could not get any better, she found that an alien life force had taken over the body of her heavy-fisted boyfriend, at least that is what she assumed had happened. He was not high when she arrived home from work, not on his way up or down, he was just, well, just like you would expect a proper boyfriend to be, normal. She was greeted on her return from her shift at Chez Blanc with a cup of steaming hot tea, a plate of buttered toast and an invitation to sit down for a 'chat'. The windows in the lounge were all open and the flat smelled unusually clean. Cameron had even made some sort of effort, not a great one, but an effort nevertheless, to tidy the living room. He told her that he had been sitting in the dark for hours, reflecting on his existence. He said that it depressed him to think how he had spent so much time just wasting his life away. He told her that he now realised that she would leave him if he did not change his behaviour and confessed that he was afraid that he would lose her. After Poppy had searched her flat trying to find 'the real Cameron' they sat and talked, something they hardly ever found time for over the past few months. This was not the first time that Poppy had heard the 'changed man' routine from him, but this time he wasn't on the gear, this time he really seemed to mean it. There was no gain for him, he didn't want anything from her, it was not a ruse to get her to find a wad of cash to feed his habit. Heaven knows he had already had the lion's share of her wages for the past year. No, this time he seemed totally genuine. She did, however, check the 'money sock' beneath her wardrobe when he went to the toilet. She found, to her relief, that it had not been touched.

When she woke that Friday morning, she fully expected to find that the 'old Cameron' had re-entered the shell of her boyfriend. But she was wrong, when Poppy looked into the living room, she was shocked to find her boyfriend studying the situations vacant pages of the local paper. He had already circled a couple of jobs that he thought might suit him, one at a warehouse and the other in a furniture factory. Poppy sat down with him, letting him use the remaining available minutes on her mobile to make interviews with them both. Cameron had also told Poppy that he had picked up a card at the job centre for an organisation that helped people break free from their addictions. He assured her that he would be registering with them and that he was more determined than ever to kick his decade-long drug habit.

Poppy began to wonder, if it wasn't an alien life force from another galaxy who had welcomed her home with that tea and toast supper the previous night, then it might be someone who had been influenced by one of the Reverend Joe's friends. Maybe Cameron had found God, or maybe he met that bloody bloke from that road to Damascus or Dulwich or wherever it was, on his way to the shops, the one who saw the bright lights and turned from sinner to saint. That must be it, she thought, bloody Joe was right all along. People can change, some people do change.

He would need her help though, a lot of help. She remembered what it was like when she went through the process in Bronzefield prison, when she went from having 'drugs on tap' to nothing at all. It very nearly pushed her over the edge. The first two weeks that she was 'on the cold-turkey run' she would wake up screaming in her cell in the middle of the night. Her whole body ached constantly, as if she was living inside a punchbag and the whole world was taking their turn to hit her. She had a recurring dream that she was at the bottom of a dry well, dying of thirst. She would have killed, literally killed, for a glass of water. Poppy never knew why they referred to it as cold turkey. If she had seen a real wild turkey during that time, playfully running across the prison yard, she would have chased it, caught it and kicked the living daylights out of it, simply for being the creature that it was. So Cameron would need her help, but she would be there for him, no questions asked, after all, he had been there for her when Nathan Keyes came calling for revenge for his brother.

Poppy never knew whether or not she really loved Cameron. Love seemed to be such a strange word in her vocabulary, a word that other people used far too frequently. She remembered her friend Nikita's definition of love, telling her that she thought its true meaning was often lost somewhere between people's needs and their desires. 'You want to love someone,' she would say, 'because you want to feel loved yourself.' Poppy and Cameron had got intimate the previous night. It had been something of a fumbled sex session. It was the first time they had shared body fluids in months. Their sexual encounter would hardly be described as memorable. Poppy spent most of the three and half minutes that her boyfriend was bouncing up and down on top of her looking at the spider web that had formed in the corner of their bedroom ceiling. She made a mental note to brush it down the next time she was cleaning the flat. She did not climax, in truth she had hardly got moist at all during those two hundred-plus seconds of animated passion. Poppy had learned so much from Matt over the past few months during their secret sex trysts that her expectation levels were set at high numbers – nines and tens. Cameron may have scraped a three for effort at best, but only if the judge had been in a kindly mood. The Geordie chef could make the whole of her body feel like it was on fire when he was inside her and that little something he could do with his tongue would make her feel as if her whole body were about to explode. Maybe next time her and Cameron had sex she would have to fantasise that it was the ever-willing northerner on top of her, that might just help things along a bit.

Was this a new start? The pair had shared so many good times when they first met, back in the Marfield days. Poppy wondered if they could ever capture that romance again. They were two juvenile cast-offs, kicking back at the world that shunned them in those days, putting a middle finger up to society in unison and telling the world to 'fuck off', much like a budget shop version of Bonnie and Clyde. They were several years older now, but in truth, not much wiser. Maybe that's what happens when you get to your mid-twenties, Poppy thought, maybe some lovers do settle for a tea and toast welcome home and a cosy cuddle-up in bed each night.

So, on this warm and sunny Friday afternoon in early August, Poppy was feeling good, she was buzzing, she was on a real high, without the need of any toxic substances running through her bloodstream. With her wages tucked away in her jacket pocket she decided to treat herself to a few bits from the charity shops at the far end of the high street. She had already picked up some ciggies and topped up her mobile phone and decided to do something that she rarely, if ever, got the chance to do these days: treat herself. She felt like a queen, like a lottery winner, £50 to herself, all to herself. No subsidising Cameron's habit anymore, no more running from the landlord. She had a small, and rare, smile on her face as she strolled along past the shops.

Poppy had one charity shop she visited all the time. It seemed to have more modern clothing in there than the other shops. She often spent a few pounds on a cheap top or two when she had earned some extra tips at Chez Blanc. She browsed through the clothing section. She had already picked out a brightly coloured top when something caught her eye. In the corner of the store, beneath the coat rack, she saw some leather boots. She was immediately drawn to them. They were smart black ankle-length boots with solid heels and small silver studs running down both sides, they were size five. *Perfect*, she thought. She tried them on and studied her reflection in the mirror. *Look at me*, she said to herself, *out in the shops like a normal person, buying normal clothes.* It was the first time in a long time she felt good about herself. She winked at her reflection, as if to say, 'Looking very cool in those, missy.' The boots were £15 and the T-shirt of her choice was £5. A nice crisp £20 note changed hands between her and the shop assistant and she walked out with a smug look of self-satisfaction on her face.

Her walk had become more of a strut as she continued her shopping trip along the high street. She still had an hour or so to kill before she had to start her evening shift and she still had money to spend. The images of the girl who had come to Chez Blanc to talk about her father had gone, so had all the other thoughts in her head. Today, Poppy Jarvis was relaxed. Suddenly something in a shop window brought her walk to a halt. It was a poster in the travel agents. She wasn't sure why it had drawn her attention. Maybe her temporary position of wealth had gone to her head. The poster was of a couple, a young couple, walking along a sandy beach. It wasn't like the beach at Bournemouth, it was massive, miles and miles of golden sand. The water was crystal clear and so very blue. Anyone would want to swim in that sea, she thought. The couple looked as if they were in love, their hands clasped tightly together, savouring the beautiful experience they were sharing. Maybe that would be her and Cameron one day, perhaps the pair of them had finally grown up, become real adults. They would get married, get old together. Maybe Cameron had seen the error of his ways, he was going to be a better person, to treat her like his real girlfriend, to love her. That's all she really wanted, to feel truly loved. The sex would have to improve though. Maybe he could ask Matt for tips. They could become friends, drinking buddies. Maybe if Cameron was too tired to perform Matt could step in, a substitute, waiting patiently for his chance to shine.

Her mind began to run away with her. What was she thinking? She never had daydreams like this, she never thought that her life would ever be anything but a mere existence – live, struggle, die. Poppy began to feel like she was living someone else's life now, a normal life. She was finally beginning to believe that, somewhere, amongst all that bitterness and anger she held inside her head, there was a good person waiting to escape.

When she entered Chez Blanc, Matt could sense a change in her. He didn't know what it was, she just looked different to him. Maybe, he thought, helping her to clear her rent arrears had been a good thing. She seemed to be much more relaxed, almost happy. The happy-go-lucky chef caught her looking in on the dining area. He knew the reason why. 'Don't worry,' he said, 'that posh tart hasn't been back. Danny told me to get rid of her if she does.' Poppy laughed. Again, the chef sensed that it was a different sort of laugh, it was almost a believable laugh. Something good seemed to be happening inside Poppy's head. Surely that could only be good news.

Danny joined the two of them to sample a seafood dish that Matt had been working on for the evening menu. The restaurant owner drank mineral water, but let his staff finish a half bottle of Moobuzz Pinot Noir with their meal. Poppy was still in high spirits, joining in with most of the conversation and amusing both her boss and the chef with a throwaway line about stealing a couple of bottles of the luxury red wine for herself for the weekend. It was never truly known if the large number of bottles of this fine wine that found their way into Matt's wine rack at home were ever truly part of an arrangement, but Poppy enjoyed teasing Matt with their shared 'secret' at every opportunity.

Chantelle joined them at the meal table before the evening service started. She had a long face and whiney tone to her voice, nothing unusual there. The scraggy teenager spent most of the time complaining that her parents had gone away that day, leaving her to fend for herself for the coming weekend. Poppy ignored the young waitress's rant. She was rapidly becoming tired of the girl's constant moaning and 'spoilt brat' attitude. Danny was in the same camp, finding an excuse to leave the table. Matt, however, stayed to offer Chantelle a sympathetic ear, but that was Matt, too much of a 'nice guy' for his own good.

Friday nights were always busy in the restaurant. More than thirty diners had pre-booked and with walk-ins Chez Blanc was expected to be extremely busy to say the least. The tables filled up quickly and Matt and Anton were tested to the full. Chantelle's continuing bleating about her parents' excursion did not help matters. She was only one wrong step away now from being on the receiving end of Poppy's sharp tongue. Danny spent a fair amount of time at one table where a couple of his business contacts were enjoying a night out with their wives. The owner of Chez Blanc was keen to impress this group of diners as they had a substantial influence with the local golf club. The wily old restaurant owner was always looking for new ways to bring in a better class of clientele to his establishment. He hoped that the free bottle of expensive wine he gave these visitors would be well received. He was right. Before the end of the evening he had taken a booking for twenty 'business heads' for the end of the month.

Anyone who had been served by Poppy during a prior visit to the restaurant must have been wondering who the new waitress was. She looked identical to the sour-faced cow who never cracked a smile and had only ever been mildly polite with her serving manner. This new girl was bouncing around the dining area, laughing at customers' jokes, even complimenting several guests on their appearance. Poppy also went out of her way to find some crayons and a colouring book from the back storeroom in a bid to pacify a hyperactive young child, much to the delight of his exhausted parents. She received the biggest cheer of the night when she called out loudly to her fellow waitress, 'Not to worry, she can have her crayons back at the end of the night.' There were roars of laughter from many of the diners. Chantelle was far from amused and sulked for the rest of the evening. Danny was extremely pleased to see this side to his loyal staff member, confiding in one of his business friends that if he had ever had a daughter, he wished she would have turned out just like her.

By eleven thirty the last of the diners had departed and Danny had left the staff to sort out the clean-up between themselves. It had been a good night for tips, with Matt, Anton and Chantelle each receiving £20. Poppy pocketed almost double that, with a big hug from her boss thrown in for good measure. So now she was set, she had more than enough money to cover the rest of the rent arrears owed to Rahwaz and around £60 of cash to do with as she pleased. It had been a long time since she could afford a trip to the hairdressers, but that extra money should cover it. After all, she wanted to look nice for her 'new' boyfriend from now on. If he was going to make as much effort as he had promised, then so would she. There was still one small problem, however, a problem in the shape of a stocky Geordie with a foolish grin. On the one hand she wanted to tell him that their secret sex sorties would have to come to an end, but something in her head told her that she still needed to feel his manhood between her legs. Unfortunately, tact and diplomacy were never going to be Poppy's strong points, something that was evident when she decided to express her feelings to him that night.

Matt had seen Poppy put her jacket on and make her way out to her car. She had left without even saying goodbye, something that was unusual, even for her, unless of course she was in one of her foul moods. He chased her to the end of the car park and intercepted her just in time. 'Hey!' he shouted. 'Don't go. I thought we could have a catch-up when 'Little Miss Stroppy' goes home. I think she was just about to order a taxi.'

Poppy shook her head. 'No, Matt, I need an early night. It's been a really long day and I just want to get home.'

The Geordie was not going to be brushed aside that easily. 'Come on,' he said, with a glint in his eye, 'I will make it worth your while, you know I will. We can go back to the flat and try out the new sheets I bought online. They are pure silk, black silk.'

Poppy laughed. 'Fuck, Matt, you are so corny. But I said no! And I meant no!'

Matt tried one last time. 'You know you can't resist me, you know you're aching for it down there. Come on, make a lonely northerner happy tonight.'

It was obvious to Poppy that he was not going to take no for an answer. Maybe a small part of her wanted him to grab her, roughly, as he had done that first time they had sex, and just fuck her senseless, there and then on the back seat of her car. But the 'new' Poppy simply played with his erotic affections. 'It's easy, Matt, just listen carefully,' she said. 'When I click my fingers, like this, that will tell you when I want your dick inside me. That will be your cue to come running. So until you hear this,' Poppy belittled the amorous chef by clicking her fingers in front of his face, 'I suggest that you just fuck off home and play with yourself. Oh, and try not to make too much mess on your new silk sheets!'

As her car pulled away Matt looked slightly confused, a dejected figure in the dark and empty car park. He stood in deep thought for a few moments before he decided that he didn't like this new waitress. The old Poppy was a stoney-faced, moody cow, ignorant, arrogant and churlish, with nothing good to say about anyone. She could be a real bitch at times. But he liked her, he wanted the 'old Poppy' back!

\* \* \*

When she arrived back at her flat in Eltham, she was still in high spirits, but Poppy's good mood was soon dampened when she exited her car. He was there again, she could see that towering figure coming down the stairway. She knew it was Neddy, she could recognise him a mile away, six-foot four with those long mauve dreadlocks. But nobody ever laughed at the lanky white man for pretending that he had Rastafarian roots, in fact no one ever laughed at Neddy at all. When she got closer she could see his bulging eyeballs, surrounded by dark circles. Years of substance abuse had not been kind to this giant freak and at thirty-something he already passed for being middle-aged. They did not speak when they passed each other, a mutual hatred that derived from the Marfield days. She was still sure he had been present when her friend Nikita had been subject to that terrible ordeal at the back of the estate. She would never forgive him, nor any of the others, for that night.

Poppy had always had one over on this drug-dealing thug though, the fact that she knew his real name. Poppy had been present at Southwark Crown Court on the day he had been called in for sentencing for stealing cars and assault. She almost fell off her chair laughing when she first heard those words, 'Neville Edwards'. The name 'Neddy' might strike fear into the average nobody on the Marfield, but if it was known on the estate that his real name was in fact Neville, he would struggle to hold his own with the year nines in the local school playground.

He had been friends with Cameron since their teens. The pair had spent some time together in prison for a racial attack. For some strange reason they were both proud of the fact that they had removed foot-long fluorescent light bulbs on a train journey and slashed the face of a young Asian boy. They did this for no other reason than he was Asian. Poppy was surprised when she had heard about the level of violence that had been used, simply because the boy was 'different'. She was not a fan of Asians herself, not after Nikita had told her that she had fallen prey to a small group of Pakistani men who used her for sex when she was only fourteen years old. But despite the fact that she had no time for the Asian community, she would never have carved her initials into someone's face with a broken light fixture, simply because of the colour of their skin. She would always need a valid reason to hurt someone, whatever their race or religion.

As they passed one another, Neddy gave her a knowing stare and sucked his teeth loudly. This was another aggravating trait he claimed he had originated from his Jamaican heritage. She could see his face clearly now. With his bloodshot eyes and haggard features he resembled an extra in a zombie film. It was obvious that they were not going to stop and chat, there was still that bad blood between the two of them. Poppy simply walked on for a few paces and used the only word that she knew that accurately described this lowlife from her past. 'Cunt!' she muttered under her breath.

Poppy was still determined not to let his visit dampen her mood. If Cameron had been truthful and was going to give up, or at least cut down on his drug taking, then scum like Neville Edwards would soon be a thing of the past. But as she neared the front door to her flat she sensed that something was not right. *Why would Neddy visit Cameron if it wasn't something to do with drugs?* she thought. The overwhelming stench of freshly smoked skunk hit her hard as she walked up the stairs. She bit the corner of her lip, very hard, but chose to to use a different approach when she entered her home. Maybe giving Cameron the benefit of the doubt would be the best thing to do, after all, there would be no point telling her boyfriend who he can and can't have in his life. Maybe it would be a good thing if he was offered some 'gear' by Neddy. It would test his resolve, show her if he was serious or not about giving up his habit.

'I brought some chicken fillets back from the restaurant, I thought we could heat them up for our supper,' Poppy said, in a gentle tone, as she entered the flat. There was no response. She tried again. 'We could watch a film later if you like, but I am going to need to have a bath first, I stink.' Still nothing. She made her way into the living room where the television was blaring out loudly, with nobody watching, as it was most nights. He was asleep, he was sound asleep on the sofa again. Poppy hung up her jacket and threw the bag with her shiny new boots and top into the corner of the room. *No tea and toast waiting for me tonight!* she thought. She was still in a passive mood and determined not to let the presence of Neddy spoil things for her, but when she turned back she saw something that was bound to change that. The table was littered with small bags, some with pills in them, some with white powder. Her brain told her instantly that this was all down to Neddy. 'Cam,' she said nudging him in his ribs. 'Cam, get up.' He ignored her.

Suddenly, something hit her, it struck her very hard. It was the most daunting feeling of reality, a feeling that made her feel sick to her stomach. She raced into the bedroom and searched frantically beneath her wardrobe. It was gone, the money had been taken. Their only chance of having that normal life she had yearned for had vanished in a split second. She flew back into the living room, the veins on her neck began throbbing, the bitter anger in her eyes apparent. Cameron was awake now and sitting up. He started to rub his eyes. 'What the fuck!' he said. 'What the fuck are you shouting about?'

Poppy showed him the empty sock. 'The money, Cam, where has the fucking money gone? Please don't tell me you have given in to the no-good fuck-wit Neddy!'

Cameron raised his hands as though he wanted the chance to explain. 'We are gonna double that cash with this stuff, girl, everything is gonna be good.'

Poppy shook her head vigorously. 'No, Cam, I want the money back, I want it back now!' She ran to the window to see if Neddy was still in view, he wasn't. She returned to the sofa where Cameron sat. He did not seem too concerned. Poppy raised her voice, but still in a calm and controlled manner. 'You need to call him, you need to call him right now and tell him you want that money back. Do it now, Cam, do it now or I swear…'

'Swear what?' he asked. 'Swear what? I have done a deal for this food and I ain't going back on it. Neddy would think I was a right cunt if I did. I have already got three or four people in the line to buy the stuff, so stop stressing, just give me a couple of days and you will get your fucking money back!'

'Give me Neddy's number, Cam!' Poppy yelled. 'Give it to me now!'

'I said no! Don't you ever fucking listen to me? Anyway, where did you get all that cash from? You didn't get that in tips at that shithole where you work.'

'I was saving it, Cam, it was for Rahwaz, you know he wants to kick us out. You might want to live on the fucking streets, but I don't. Now give me that number.'

Poppy began to feel that rush of blood rising in her body. She screwed her hands tightly. There were whispers in her head. She didn't need them to tell her, she already knew what she was going to do. To hell with those calming colours, she thought, if he didn't give her that number now, right now, he was dead, she would kill him. But as she turned around to square up to him she suddenly felt the back of Cameron's hand. It hit her across her cheek with an almighty force, sending her flying over the coffee table and onto the floor. She was not down more than three seconds before she was back on her feet, her legs carrying her forward at a searing pace towards her boyfriend. Lowering her head as she neared him, she caught Cameron full on in the centre of his chest, winding him slightly and knocking him down onto the sofa. She raised her fist high into the air, but he caught it on its way down, twisting her arm and throwing her sideways onto the carpet. In a split second she was back up again, hurtling towards him, screaming like a deranged Indian war chief, but this time her charge had no impact, he stood his ground. She wasn't giving up, she changed tack now, pulling back her leg and swinging her foot hard in the direction of his genitals. Unfortunately for Poppy, the kick completely missed its target as he turned her body sideways, doing minimal damage to his thigh. She suddenly found herself out of breath. She struggled to muster another kick. Now it was his turn. She had spent most of her energy, he hadn't, he was ready for this encounter. He reached down and grabbed her by the hair. Yanking it hard he swung her over onto her back, kicking her twice in the side as he dragged her across the carpet. 'I fucking warned you not to come for me again, you bitch!' he yelled. 'You aren't ever gonna beat me, when are you gonna fucking learn that?' Poppy swung an arm upwards in an attempt to catch his face, but there was no power there, he simply parried the blow. He dragged her as far as the bathroom, giving her a kick or two en route, before lifting her onto her knees. Pulling back her dangling mane, he continued his tirade of abuse as he systematically pushed her head against the bathroom door. 'Don't ever come for me again or I will finish you,' he said, aiming one final kick into her shoulder as he released his grip on her hair.

As he walked away Poppy heard the voices in her head. They were telling her to get up, to find a blade, a knife, anything sharp, to stab him, to kill the bastard. But her brain told her that he was too strong for her, he always was, this was not a battle that she could win. In truth this was a conflict she should never have started. Cameron scooped up the bags of pills from the coffee table and cradled them in his arms before carrying them into the bedroom, his actions mirroring those of a big kid not wanting to share his sweets with his little sister.

And then, it was as if he had heard those thoughts in his girlfriend's head. His next task was to clear the kitchen drawers of the tray of knives, forks and all other sharp objects. They too ended up somewhere in his lair, tucked under the pillow where Poppy would usually lay her head. Cameron felt a little safer now that those weapons had been secured, safe enough to give Poppy one last piece of his warped mind. She offered little resistance this time as he grabbed her by the neck and turned her head towards his face. He had that usual vacant look in his soulless eyes as he told her what he really thought of her. 'Listen to me, filthy skank, I helped you when you needed it and all you have ever given me is grief. Well, them fuckers from the estate are welcome to you now, I ain't putting my neck on the line for you ever again. Stay or go, I don't give a fuck what you do now.' Cameron could not resist cracking her head one last time against the bathroom door, adding a token kick into the small of her back, before walking away.

Poppy closed her eyes as she heard the bedroom door slam hard against its frame. Gone were the crazy ideas that had spun around in her head that day. Her daydreams had been replaced with reality, a stark reality that had literally picked her up and kicked the living daylights out of her that night. She was beaten now, she had nothing left to give. She crawled into the bathroom, using the side of the sink to pull herself up. As she lifted her arm to reach the flannel, a sharp pain ricocheted through her body. She screwed up her face in agony as it carried on upwards to the side of her head. She swallowed her pain and ran some cold water, gently dowsing her face and neck. It didn't help. She turned off the tap. Poppy found her reflection in the mirror. It wasn't the image of the girl that had put on her makeup that morning, the one with all those half-baked notions of a happy future in her head. No, this girl was just the shell of that person, a shattered replica of the girl with all those crazy dreams. As she sat holding the damp flannel against the back of her aching head, Poppy promised herself that, whatever happened in her life now, she would not forgive him for what he did tonight. She would never ever let Cameron get the chance to hurt her again.

# CHAPTER
# TWENTY-ONE

The sinking man continued to stare aimlessly out of the hospital window, his tired and ghostly reflection peering back at him from the rain-covered glass. In the streets below, the pavements were deserted, the reflections from the neon signs glistening in the puddles below. The undercurrents of the gloomy waters around him were still dragging him down, further and further into the depths of his own despair. He hoped that his journey through the smokescreens of his past would bring him some answers, some reasoning behind it all. It may save him from his fate. But the lights on the shores were far away now, those waters were too deep. He could feel them pulling him down, he was beginning to realise that they had him now.

'I would never have known,' Dean said, hoping that the figure in the bed would finally acknowledge his presence. 'I would never have known if I hadn't bumped into that Millie woman outside that gym, the one where the boy, where Jamie works.' He explained his comment to the statue-like figure wrapped up in those warm bedsheets. 'She never liked me, Millie, her friend, she never liked me. She was always telling Krista to finish things with me. Always poisoning her mind against me.' Dean pulled the lapels of his long coat together. There was a colder chill in that room now, an icy chill. It was strange because the window was shut tight and the radiators were still warm. 'She told me about the boy, she thought I must have known. She never gave me a straight answer of course, but I could tell by her face. I bet she raced home to call Krista. Maybe it was her, maybe his mother warned him off me.' Suddenly, Dean looked across at the bed. He thought he heard some movement behind him, but he was mistaken. 'They have a girl, Krista and her bloke, they have a daughter, her picture was on the lad's Facebook page. God, she looks so much like her mother. So my lad has a sister, he has a little sister. No, I can't really call him that, my lad, my son, I can't really call him that. He wouldn't know me from Adam, would he?'

The self-pity kicked in again as Dean searched for some consolation, not that any was likely to be forthcoming. 'I just wish he would have called me. I just wanted to meet him, maybe just once, you know to talk, just to see him. He is handsome. Did I tell you I saw his photo on that Facebook thing? Such a good-looking lad with a big smile on his face.'

Dean turned to look around the room that had stolen his life away. He desperately wanted to get out of that place, it was draining every bit of energy left in him. Nothing ever changed in that hospital room – the broken clock on the wall, the untouched glass of water on the bedside cabinet, even the newspaper seemed as if it had the same picture on the front page each day. Tapping the face of his watch, he scratched beneath the strap. It was becoming more irritating by the minute. 'And now my bloody watch has stopped working,' he said. 'Cheap foreign shit!'

The streets below remained empty. One or two cars passed by. It seemed as if the whole world had now taken refuge from the downpour. 'I thought that was going to be the last time that I saw her, that day at the clinic, where she…' He stopped mid-sentence and shook his head. 'I thought that she had done it on purpose, getting pregnant I mean, she was like that. I thought that she was trying to trap me, just like Hannah had done. When Krista told me she was pregnant, it was like a reality check. I knew then that it couldn't carry on.' Dean frowned as he faced the reality of what had really happened that day. 'I should have worked it out sooner. The things she said, the way she was. I should have known. I know now why she came to see me that night. Oh, my beautiful Persephone you certainly got one over on me there, didn't you? God, I must have been such a fool, such a bloody fool!'

Krista may have used a much stronger word than 'fool' for him if she was here now. It may have been one of the rare occasions that she needed to find a harsh profanity to describe the man she had once loved. But on that night, all those years ago, she still held onto a small hope, a hope that her dreams had not yet been shattered. She had thought it through. Somehow, she still hoped that the two of them could get through the crazy mess they had created. She had worked it all out. He would not have to leave his sick wife and precious daughter, she would accept that. It was a fact that Krista had never planned, nor wanted, to have children. It would probably happen at some time or another, why not now? Why not now with the man she truly loved? So she would share him, as she had done these past few years. She would continue to share him with his wife and daughter. She would bring up the twins, Millie could help her. Her best friend had brought up her five-year-old son on her own, it can't be that hard. Then Dean could come round to see them, to see her and his beautiful twins. She was convinced that once he saw how it all worked out, he would be back in her life. Their feelings for one another would be as strong as ever. It would be just as it had been before. After all, he had told her that he loved her, the night of the awards dinner. He meant it, when he said he loved her. She had waited all those months to hear those words, he must have meant it. So why give up on the dream, when the dream is not over?

Krista Nylund was a highly intelligent and resourceful woman, but she was a lost soul blinded by her obsession with a man that would never be hers. She was prepared to sacrifice everything, including her pride, in her quest for utopia. That dark and chilly night in February 1998, while excited young lovers were planning how to spend Valentine's evening, it was time for her to carry out her plan, a simple plan, one which would end in her producing the small blurry image of the beautiful creations that would bond her and Dean together forever. But the man she adored would show his true colours that night, a side to the him that would bring Krista crashing back down to earth.

They were meeting at the Castle Moat public house, the very place where it had all started on that crazy spring evening almost three years earlier. Krista stood outside the bustling bar, in a slight daze, just watching the world go by. A young couple crossed the road in front of her, holding hands, laughing, wrapped up in a picture of sheer happiness. Why couldn't her relationship with Dean be like that? she thought. Uncomplicated, carefree, exciting, the way it used to be. Why did everything have to change?

He was late, nothing new there, but he was not as late as he usually was. Fifteen minutes was an acceptable delay. Maybe this was a good sign, maybe it had finally dawned on him what he might be about to lose. She desperately wanted to give him a simple peck on his cheek, but as soon as she felt his breath on her neck, that all changed. She wrapped her arms around him tightly and kissed him fully on the lips for at least a full minute. She did not care that passers-by were staring at them. She wanted that kiss to last for as long as possible. Somewhere deep inside, she feared that this may be their last embrace.

Inside the pub Krista refused his offer of a drink, making a feeble excuse about picking up Millie from work later that night. She realised when she sat down that the smart Yves St Laurent dress she was wearing was getting too tight for her. She kept her coat done up. She did not want to reveal the seven pounds that she had already gained in weight. Dean was certainly in no mood for copying her alcohol abstention, sinking three pints and two whisky chasers before they had started any sort of real conversation. Krista was still smitten with the man beside her, holding his hand tightly each time he returned from the bar. But Dean could see that all was not right. For the first time ever he saw something different in her eyes. Those mesmerising whirlpools of enchantment would still drive men to insanity, but there was something unfamiliar about them, a look of sadness, the sort of look a child would give you if they had lost their way home.

'Hard day at the chateau, Nylund?' Dean asked. 'You look a little tired.'

Hardly the best way to start a conversation, Krista thought, but she responded with a knowing smile. 'Yeah, something like that.'

'God, it seems so long since I saw you. I know it wasn't the best of places to go, but we did the right thing, you do know that, don't you?' Krista waited for him to say more, but he didn't. His conversation drifted away and he started to tell her about a new job he had applied for in Birmingham.

She wanted to scream out loudly at him, 'Is that it? Is that really it? All forgotten, we just pretend it never happened? Is that really what you expect me to do?' But she said nothing, she listened to him as he droned on about new products and sales targets, losing a tiny bit more respect for him each time he opened his mouth. Suddenly out of nowhere she found some words to change the direction of his pointless conversation. 'How are things at home? How is Hannah?' she asked.

It had worked, he was caught. He took a large mouthful of lager before answering. 'Still much the same,' he said. 'She has good days and bad ones. But I do my best for her.'

Krista wasn't finished there. 'And your daughter, how is she?'

Dean wasn't quite sure where this conversation was leading, she had never asked about his home life as directly as that before.

'Poppy,' Dean responded. 'You know that her name is Poppy. She is OK, causing havoc, you know like most two-year-olds do. I think they call it 'terrible twos' or something like that.'

Krista smiled and nodded. 'But she is three soon right? It is her birthday in the summer, the eighteenth of July, isn't it?' Krista only remembered that date because of their amazing experience at the boating lake, the date she discovered some time later was the day that Poppy had been born.

Dean took another drink. 'Yes, she is three in July, but that's five months away. How did you remember that?'

Krista shrugged her shoulders. 'Oh, you know me, I am just good with dates and stuff like that.' She wanted to hit him with that glass he was holding now. Why had that night at the lake always meant so much to her and not to him?

Dean made his way to the bar to fetch some more drinks. As he waited to be served he looked back at Krista. He sensed that there was something different about her. It wasn't just the fact that the sparkle had gone from her eyes, he wasn't sure what it was, but he didn't feel comfortable. He began to wonder if there was something she might be hiding from him. Maybe she had found someone else, maybe she had come to tell him that they were over. The friendly barmaid gave him a big smile when she served his drinks. 'Cheer up,' she said, 'it may never happen.'

Dean returned the smile and laughed at her comment. 'Let's hope so,' he replied.

When he arrived back at the table, Dean delivered a large glass of white wine to Krista. 'I told you I couldn't drink tonight, I am picking Millie up.' He apologised and returned to his conversation about his new job prospects, but Krista wasn't listening, she had more to say. 'She is new, that girl who served you, the one with the spiky hair. Do you know her?'

Dean shook his head. 'Of course not, she was just being friendly.'

Krista stared at the bar and looked her rival over for a second or two. 'A bit overfriendly if you ask me,' she said.

They sat in stony silence for a few minutes. Dean was in no mood to have another conversation about her uncontrollable jealousy. They had visited that subject more times than he cared to remember over the past twelve months. Krista was still formulating her plan, trying to think of the best way to drop her bombshell, the one which was going to determine how this evening and indeed the rest of her life would play out. Dean, being Dean, had simply assumed that the two of them could resume where they had left off before the trip to the clinic. But he knew now that all was not right with Krista. An alarm bell in his head told him that he was sitting next to a different person this evening. He wasn't sure if he wanted to be there anymore that night.

Krista now decided that she would follow her original plan, the one that would mean Dean could have the best of both worlds. Where better to start, than to see how he really felt about having children. 'So, Poppy, are you going to do anything special for her birthday?'

Dean grinned. 'No, I don't think so, I think we might give her a party. She can invite her friends from playschool.'

He was on the end of her hook now, so she continued. 'What about presents? What is she into, you know, what cartoons or stuff does she like?'

Dean was slightly confused but still answered the question. 'Eh, I don't know really, I suppose anything with bears in it. Hannah has not been well recently, so we have not really had a chance to talk about it, besides it's months away from now.'

Krista became agitated that he had brought his wife into the conversation, she had only wanted to talk about Poppy, about other children, about little brothers or sisters for his daughter. He was obviously not going to play her game, so out of nowhere she simply lashed out. 'She looked OK to me, Dean, your sick wife looked OK when you were at Croydon shopping centre last week. Hannah didn't look like a recovering alcoholic crazy woman to me.' Dean was totally stunned but Krista hadn't finished yet. 'Is that holding hands thing part of her new therapy? It seemed to be working, she seemed happy enough to me. That is definitely helping her depression.'

'You were at the shopping centre?'

'Yeah, I go there sometimes. Don't worry I wasn't going to make a scene.'

'Why would you go there? You don't live anywhere near Croydon.'

'I just fancied a change of scenery.'

Dean's facial expression had now changed. Krista had seen she had touched a raw nerve. 'You were spying on me! You must have followed us from the house.'

Krista did not want to admit that he was right. Her stalking expedition had started right outside his front door, so she lied. 'Relax, Dean. It was a coincidence. I did follow the two of you around for a while though.' Krista was really enjoying watching him squirm. 'God, she does like some terribly drab clothes shops, doesn't she?' Adding sarcastically, 'Maybe that is part of her illness.'

She had angered Dean with that comment, but she didn't care, she was feeling as if she had nothing to lose now. Maybe it was her unbalanced hormones or the fact that he had been flirting with the new barmaid. Whatever it was, she was in the mood for straight-talking. She was devastated to think that Dean had lied to her for three years about the true mental state of his wife. She wanted to just come out and say it, to reveal the truth – 'You are going to be a father of twins, you need to get used to it' – but she also wanted to retain her dignity, the small shreds of self-worth that she had left inside her fragile body. Krista was waiting for Dean to explain, but his eyes would not meet hers, they were staring at his drink, as if he would find the answers to her questions somewhere at the bottom of the pint glass he was holding.

Finally, but not before he had finished half of the contents of that glass, he found his voice. 'You have made a big mistake, Krista, coming to my house, spying on my wife. I thought you understood, I thought you got it.'

Krista's retaliation was instant. 'It was all bullshit, Dean,' she said. She was in no mood to be patronised. 'Everything you have told me about her is just bullshit. Helping each other through rehab, keeping each other dry, it is all crap, Dean. Jesus, ever since I have known you, all you have ever done is drink. I have often wondered what it would be like to spend a full day with you sober.'

Dean shook his head but something deep inside told him that she was right. The truth was staring back at him from those empty glasses on the table. Krista was still waiting. She knew Dean well enough now to know that he would invent some line or another to convince her that he was the 'good guy' in all of this, after all. In her heart she was hoping that she would hear those lies, that he would fight to save their relationship. *God*, she thought, *is it even a relationship anymore?* Krista knew that she didn't want to lose him, she loved him, they could still make it work, but her original plan was falling apart at the seams. *Why isn't he speaking?* she thought. *Why isn't he at least trying to salvage the situation?* But his excuses were not forthcoming. Dean sat beside her in deep contemplation, as though he knew that things had finally come to an end between the two of them. Krista suddenly realised that her badly timed admission to following him and Hannah at the shopping centre had backfired, it had changed everything. He confirmed her fears with a few simple words which tore at her soul and ripped a massive hole in her heart. 'I am still in love with her, with Hannah, I still care for her, I still love her,' he said.

Krista felt herself slump back in her chair. Those words echoed around in her head for several seconds before she found a voice, a tiny shaky voice. 'What?' she asked, desperately hoping that she had misheard him. But Dean's next sentence told her that there was nothing wrong with her hearing.

'I came here tonight to tell you that I think it best that we call it a day. We need to end it.'

Dean could see her bottom lip start to tremble and her facial expression change to one of despair. He moved his hand across hers in a bid to comfort her, but she pushed it away. He looked around the bar and then down at those glasses on the table. He couldn't look her in the face anymore, but he needed to say more. 'I want to give it another try with Hannah,' he said. 'We both owe it to Poppy to be together, as a proper family.'

Krista wiped a tear or two away from the corner of her eye. Everything around her seemed to grind to a halt, as if the world had suddenly stopped turning and she was about to fall off. It was only not that long ago that he said that he loved her, that he told her he could not be without her. Something inside her wanted to scream out very loudly and not stop, not until he told her that he was lying, that he had made up wanting to be with Hannah, that she was the one he wanted to be with.

She felt so foolish now. Her plan had been ripped to shreds before she had even had a chance to show him the scan picture of his twins, yes, his twins, resting in her womb. She was so sure that those shadowy little figures on that dark background would have sent him into a state of uncontrollable euphoria. She had got carried away with her fantasy, even researching several books and finding some suitable names from his crazy world of mythology. She was going to tell him that she wanted to call their twins Apollo and Artemis, their own little god and goddess. They could have both laughed about that. But she didn't feel like laughing now, she just felt numb. Her whole world felt like it had just ended.

When he tried again, to put his hand on hers, she rose swiftly from the table and headed for the door. Krista knew that she was going to break down and cry, she knew that there was a flood of tears sitting behind her eyeballs. She didn't want him to see them, that would only make things worse. As the fresh air hit her, so did a sharp intake of reality, that terrible feeling of emptiness in the pit of her stomach. She was so torn up inside with both grief and anger, that she did not notice the cars flashing backwards and forwards around her as she crossed the busy road. Dean had left half of his drink, something most uncommon for him, and made his way out of the bar to find her. He received a few nasty glares from the patrons of the Castle Moat, who had clearly seen the look of distress on his companion's face. He followed Krista across the road to the tube station. Catching up with her he tried to grab her arm, but she pushed his hand away. Although he felt he had made things clear to her, Dean seemed to be concerned, but it was not about her welfare or how she might be feeling. All that was worrying him was whether or not she would revisit his house to reveal the truth to Hannah. He knew that would break his wife and send her reeling straight back to the bottles of cheap vodka from the supermarket. Krista may not have believed him, but his wife's condition had not been exaggerated. She was only ever one stressful moment away from returning to her former life in the gutter of alcoholism.

He tried speaking to Krista, but she wasn't really listening, she was still trying desperately to hold herself together. Pushing past an elderly couple, he caught up with her again on the escalator, standing in her path as it reached the bottom. Dean didn't know it at that moment, but it would be the last time he would ever see her face. They stood in silence for a few seconds, as commuters brushed past them on their way home. He could see that her eyes were red, they were no longer shining. Those dancing flames had been replaced with fading embers. 'Please, Nylund, just stop, just stop and talk to me,' he said.

Through her tear-filled eyes Krista answered him. Even her voice sounded different, like that of a helpless child. 'I gave up everything for you, Dean, I gave up everything. But I know now, I know that it is time for me to grow up, to stop kidding myself that this is anything more than a crazy fantasy. You and I will never be together, I have to accept that now.'

Dean moved forward in an attempt to put his arms around her, but she pushed him away. A passer-by on his way to the platform seemed to be concerned. He asked her if she was OK. She nodded, but she knew that inside her shredded heart she was far from OK. Krista looked up at the man that had captured her heart and broken it. 'So let's just leave it now, you have taken everything that I have, Dean. I don't want to do this anymore, it is killing me inside.' Dean went to speak but she cut him short, raising her fingers and pressing them against his open lips. Shaking her head, she smiled her beautiful smile at him for one last time. 'Sometimes it is better just to say nothing,' she said and turned away.

Dean stood and watched as his beautiful goddess walked towards the platform. He felt somewhat confused but also strangely relieved at that moment. His brain was finding it hard to separate his emotions. Deep down inside he knew that this was the right thing to do, never realising for one moment that the pain that would follow would stay with him for a lifetime.

Krista didn't turn back, she knew if she did that the fountain of tears she was holding on to would explode from her eyes. Her head told her to keep walking, she had to ignore what her heart might be saying. Dean watched her disappear from his view and turned back towards the escalator, dragging his feet slowly as if he had been wounded in battle. As soon as he stepped onto the escalator he noticed the first advertisement board to his left. He saw her face on the shoulders of a model advertising skin cream. He felt a sense of guilt, and then on the next one, her smile was beaming back at him from the face of a woman promoting a temping agency. His guilt turned to shame. By the time he had neared the top, she had appeared in almost every frame. His head began to spin, he panicked, he suddenly felt as if he was in a dark alleyway with no side doors, his mind was in turmoil. He gritted his teeth together as he heard the screeching of the brakes of the tube train as it arrived at the platform beneath him, the train that would be taking her away, taking his Persephone away, for good. The sound sent an ache ripping all the way through his body. Suddenly, Dean spun around and began to make his way back down the escalator, fighting the forces of nature and pushing past several irate passengers in his path. He jumped as soon as he neared the bottom and sprinted as fast as his legs could carry him. 'Krista!' he screamed. 'Krista, wait, please wait.' But it was too late, he arrived on the platform just as the train began to pull away. He suddenly felt sick, not from the running, not from drinking on an empty stomach, no this was a real sickness that he could never remember feeling before. He could feel it swelling up in the pit of his stomach. He looked dejected as his feet shuffled back towards the escalator, swinging out a leg and taking a hefty kick at a litter bin en route in a bid to vent some of his frustration. When he stood back on the escalator he covered his eyes. It might have been that he didn't want to see those pictures on the wall again or maybe he was trying to hide the tears that were desperately trying to escape from beneath his eyelids.

But if Dean Jarvis had looked back down at that precise second, a life-changing moment may have occurred. A moment that could have altered his destiny and that of all those around him. A split-second decision which may have saved him from the torturous turmoil that would rule his life from that day forward. Krista had appeared from the place she had been hiding, behind one of the side tunnels of the station. She watched him through her misty eyes as the escalator carried him slowly away, leaving her behind, leaving her life for good. Her heart told her to scream out his name at the top of her voice, but the sanity inside her head persuaded her not to. This was it, the fantasy was finally over. Looking down at the small bump beneath her coat, she made a promise to herself as she dragged her feet back to the platform. She promised that she would sacrifice everything in the world, even the man she truly loved, to protect those two beautiful babies that were growing inside her.

* * *

Back at the window of the hospital room Dean began to reflect on that night, the night he lost her. He suddenly felt alone, more alone than he had ever felt before. 'She blocked my number you know,' he said, to an audience that clearly had no sympathy for his plight. 'Changed her job and moved out of her flat before I ever got the chance to tell her how I really felt.' He never realised that without his 'chosen goddess', everything that he lived for would be lost. Dean would tread the waters of regret for most of his life, totally unaware that resentment can be such a heavy load to carry.

The drowning man felt isolated now. He realised that the figure in the bed behind him would offer no words of comfort. He was a castaway, stranded somewhere in his sea of bitterness. He knew that the time was approaching. The currents in those dark and murky waters of his past were finally dragging him down to a place of no return.

# CHAPTER
# TWENTY-TWO

S taring at her bathroom mirror Poppy flicked several strands of greasy hair away from her face. She was relieved to see that no noticeable marks had been left by Cameron's brutal backhander. She applied a thick layer of concealer and some makeup to her drab features, feeling a sharp pain in her side each time she bent her arm. Holding her hair back behind her ears, she swivelled her head to see if there might be any signs of the beating she had received the previous night. In truth it was hard to tell if the red swelling on her neck was from the day before or the remains of the scalding she had received previously. Whichever it was, it still ached. She felt slightly sick inside to think that she had let him do that to her again.

She was no longer worried about the missing money or indeed the fact that Rahwaz would now carry out his threat and have her and Cameron evicted from the flat. It didn't feel like a real home to her this morning, it didn't feel like a safe place to be anymore.

But this time it wasn't so much the big bad wolf that might come knocking at the door that concerned her, it was the one that she had been sharing a bed with. Poppy had lost count now of the times that Cameron had hit her over the past twelve months, but she knew in her heart that last night's violent assault on her would be the last.

She had managed to leave her flat without disturbing her brute of a boyfriend. The last thing that she needed this morning was him getting physical with her again. She had not managed to pack many clothes. Most of them were in the wardrobe in the bedroom where Cameron was sleeping. She did pack some underwear which had been drying on the bathroom radiator, as well as her new T-shirt and some toiletries. She pulled on her new boots, maybe wishing she had been wearing them when she aimed those kicks at her boyfriend the previous night.

There were more than two hours before her and Matt were due to start their shift, two full hours for her to show Matt what he could enjoy on a more regular basis now, providing of course he was willing to put a roof over her head and if he agreed to stop grinning like a Cheshire cat. She planned to visit him before the start of her shift and give him what he was hungry for, what he was always hungry for. And if she could drag herself away from the hot and steamy sex session during those couple of hours, she could wash her mangy hair with his expensive shampoo. It would be a 'win-win' situation for each of them. *God*, she thought, *I am even using some of his expressions now.* Maybe she really did like Matt, more than she realised.

After parking her car in the Chez Blanc car park, Poppy applied some further makeup to her pale features. A planned seduction rarely works without a bit of effort. She made the best job she could with her tatty hair and left her vehicle to make the short walk to Matt's flat. She called in at the coffee shop in the high street, ordering a black coffee for herself and a cappuccino with four sugars for Matt. As she waited for the drinks to be served she thought of one or two clever one-liners to open the conversation. Maybe when he opened his door she should simply click her fingers and say to him, 'OK, big boy, I want you now.' He would find that funny, mind you Matt usually found most things funny. Almost as soon as she had started the walk to Matt's home her mobile rang. It was Rahwaz. She ignored the call. She certainly wouldn't be thinking about him and his overdue rent for the next two hours. By the time she arrived at his flat she had changed her mind about her opening line and decide to settle for something less direct. He may have not been impressed with her put-down the previous day, he was, after all, a sensitive sort of guy.

She managed to slip in through the security door at the front of the flats as one of the other occupants was making their way out of the building. Poppy practised a smile as she approached his door, a 'Yes, I am bitch but you can still like me' sort of smile. She rang his doorbell, no response. She had to ring again and then a third time before she achieved a reaction. 'Alright! I am coming,' she heard, as Matt made his way to answer his door.

'You took your time,' Poppy said as the door opened, completely forgetting the funny one-liner that she had intended. 'You wasn't sleeping, was you?' Matt stood in front of her, bare-chested. Nothing but a pair of dark green Calvin Klein briefs stood between him and her sexual desire. His face was bright red, as if he had been working out or running. Poppy offered him the drink she had just purchased. 'Cappuccino, with four sugars. Trust me, Matt, you are gonna need all the energy you can get today!'

But as Poppy went to push past him and make her way inside, something stopped her in her tracks. It was a small voice from inside the flat, a squeaky irritating voice, one that she recognised instantly, one that she did not care much for. 'If that's the taxi,' the scratchy voice declared, 'I am not ready yet, Matt, I can't find my knickers.' Poppy took a step back. Her reaction was partly in disbelief, partly in anger. Her face told its own story.

'It's not what it looks like,' Matt said, his shaky voice telling Poppy that it clearly was exactly what it looked like.

At that precise second Chantelle's adolescent frame appeared from Matt's living room door, wearing nothing more than a look of shame and one of his smart T-shirts. Chantelle was completely unaware who was standing on the other side of the door until she caught Poppy's stare full on. 'Oh shit!' the small girl shouted. Now recognising the visitor, she rapidly retreated to the safety of the lounge.

Matt was looking more nervous now and repeated his statement. 'It really isn't what it looks like.'

'So what is it then, Matt?' Poppy asked. 'Are you helping her with her homework or something?' Matt was lost for words, but Poppy wasn't. 'She is fifteen, Matt, you do know that, she is just fifteen. They have words for people like you.' Poppy took a step back, still clinging onto the drinks in her hand, an expression of calmness hiding her feelings of complete disgust. Her thumbs slowly loosened the tops of the plastic cups as Matt looked back into his flat to make sure Chantelle was in safe hiding. He knew what Poppy was capable of now. He wanted to get back inside himself and lock the door, but his feet seemed to be glued to the spot. Finally, Matt struggled to find the right words to explain his predicament, but Poppy wasn't really listening. 'It just happened,' he said. 'It was a mistake, it just happened.' But before he could explain further, he noticed the lids of the cups fall to the floor and both vessels launched in his direction. His bare chest took the full force of one of the hot drinks, while his designer underwear offered little protection from the other. Matt let out a small shriek and doubled over in agony as the boiling hot coffee made direct contact with his genitals. Poppy stared at the wounded Geordie for a few seconds and shook her head.

As she turned and walked away, back towards the direction of the high street, she left Matt with her own take on his choice of sexual conquest. 'Paedophile!' she declared loudly, as her feet gathered pace. 'That's the word they use for people like you, Matt, fucking paedophile!'

Matt watched her walk away, making sure that she was out of view before slipping back into his flat. He grabbed some towels and covered the area that his crazed colleague had just targeted. Chantelle was still in the lounge, sitting on his sofa. She was in tears. But she was not crying because of the assault on Matt, she did not seem too concerned by the large red marks glowing on his chest and thighs. No, she had other things she needed to worry about. 'I hope she doesn't tell Danny,' she said. 'I will lose my job if she does.'

Poppy did not know where she was going as she walked through the bustling high street. Her head was scrambled. The hissing sounds had returned, the voices seemed to have woken from their slumber. Everyone she passed seemed to be speaking loudly, she was sure that they were talking about her. She almost knocked over a couple of women as she lost concentration for a few seconds. Her feet were moving, but she didn't seem to be going anywhere. Her mind was working overtime. Why had she been so stupid, why should she be upset? It was just sex with Matt and the sex was rubbish, she told herself. But another voice told her that it wasn't, the sex was amazing, the sex was always fucking amazing, the best she could ever remember. He made her feel so alive when they were having sex, he made her feel so wanted. She felt something she had never felt before. *But now he is fucking Chantelle, a child. He is sick.* She felt ashamed of herself now. She had been having sex with someone who was sick in the head. Maybe, she thought, Matt was actually more sick in the head than she was. It is him that needs help, not her.

\* \* \*

314

Halfway down the high street, Poppy picked out a brick from a skip parked at the side of the road and launched it with great force. It found its target, leaving the sounds of shattering glass in her wake.

The sun had started to go down before Poppy realised where she was. She didn't know how long she had been sitting on that concrete floor in front of the lock-up garages. The scratches on the front of her new boots and the newly created dents in some of those shutter doors told their own story. She still felt the dull pains of her recent beating in the small of her back. Her head was hurting too, from the million and one thoughts that had been running through her brain. It seemed the whole day had just gone. The time on her phone told her that she had missed the lunchtime session and was already late for the start of her evening shift at the restaurant. She studied the missed calls and messages on her mobile. Danny and Rahwaz both featured heavily in her list. Part of her told her not to give a damn, but the other part told her that she needed to pull herself together, she needed her job, she needed Danny, she was homeless now, she had nowhere to live.

\* \* \*

The warm August weather meant that many of the early diners seated in Chez Blanc had not bothered with coats and jackets. Sitting chatting on one of the tables of the restaurant were Bree and Kayleigh. They had both enjoyed a mini chicken kiev starter, washed down with some expensive Merlot, and were waiting for their main course to arrive. The pair had begun to think that it may have been a wasted journey. There was no sign of Poppy, and the young waitress serving them had simply pulled a face when asked where she might be. Bree had bought a new cream-coloured top from Escada that morning. She wanted to look her best for her reunion with her newfound sibling. She had also endured a mini-makeover at the local beauty parlour. It was the first time that Kayligh had seen her best friend make any real effort with her appearance for years. Her friend didn't want to tell her, but she found her uncanny resemblance to her mother almost frightening now. Suddenly Kayleigh received a sharp kick in her ankle beneath the table as her best friend declared, 'She is here! She just came in through the back way, that's my sister!'

It was early evening, almost eight o'clock. Chez Blanc was not too busy at that time. A table of four sour-faced women, two pairs of elderly pensioners and a couple with an infant child were seated. The main topic of conversation in the dining area was the unexplained damage caused to the travel agent's window in the high street. Patrons were concerned that the random act of vandalism may have been down to some travelling football fans on their way to a game. If only they knew!'

Danny had stopped calling Poppy at around seven o'clock and cancelled his night out to cover for his missing waitress. He feared that she may have had another altercation with Cameron. He hoped that was not the case.

There was nothing wrong with Bree's eyesight. Poppy had walked in through the back entrance of the restaurant and could clearly be seen hanging up her green bomber jacket. As she made her way into the kitchen she brushed past a terrified-looking Chantelle who was carrying some bread rolls through to the dining area. Poppy didn't need words, the stare she gave the shaking young waitress was enough to cause her to tilt her plate, leaving a trail of breadcrumbs across the restaurant carpet. Poppy made her way to the large refrigerator and helped herself to some ham and a piece of cheese. She was hungry, she hadn't eaten a thing that day. If nothing else, she knew that she always had free food at her place of work. Reaching into the cutlery drawer she grabbed a bread knife and reached for the French stick on the side of prep table. Matt had been busy at the stoves and had not realised that she had arrived. He caught a first glimpse of her as he turned for some seasoning. 'Shit!' he said. 'I didn't see you come in, you made me jump.' Poppy looked him square in the face as she cut two slices of bread. That knife in her hand was certainly doing nothing for the Geordie chef's nerves.

'I didn't think you were coming in,' Matt said, watching Poppy add some pickle to her ham and cheese roll. Her eyes never left him once as she sampled her food. The usually confident northerner was lost for words. As he watched Poppy use the sharp instrument in her hand to cut another slice of bread, he felt the need to try to explain his actions. 'We need to talk, Poppy, about this morning, we need to talk.' Poppy remained silent. She was enjoying this moment. She placed the knife which had been giving the Geordie chef so much concern onto the side of the draining board and chewed hard on the crusty corner of her roll, teasing him, as if to say to him, 'What do you think I will do now?' Her silence made him nervous, very nervous.

Danny suddenly appeared and made his way past the pair of them, heading for the storeroom. 'Hello, love,' he said as he passed by. 'I didn't know if you were coming in tonight.' Poppy still said nothing. Her eyes seemed to be fixed on Matt's twitching features. Danny returned with a high chair that had clearly seen better days and began wiping it over with a dish cloth before making his way back to the dining area. 'I wish these bloody people would tell me when they are bringing bloody babies in here,' he said. 'They will have to make do with this now.' As he walked away, the restaurant owner's parting comment gave Matt even more reason to be anxious. 'Have you told her that the bloody girl is here, that she has come back?'

Playtime was over for Poppy. The expression on her face changed quickly as his comment sank in. Gone was the smirk of someone taunting the chef about his encounter with the waitress. It was replaced with a look of anger, real anger. Matt reacted quickly, brushing the bread knife along the work surface, out of reach of Poppy's hand.

'I told her,' Poppy said, her voice raw, her tone angry. 'I told her not to come back here.' Matt stood in front of her, feeling slightly braver now that there was less chance of him being on the receiving end of that sharp blade. 'I fucking told that bitch!' Poppy screamed, her eyes now full of venom. Matt grabbed both of her wrists and looked down at her. He had seen her when she was angry, very angry, but had never seen that look of rage in her eyes before, not with the loudmouth large woman that had threatened her, not with him when they had shared that first encounter. This was something completely different. Poppy's face began to twist and turn. She bit hard on the corner of her lip. 'I fucking told her!' she said again, through gritted teeth. 'I fucking warned that bitch!'

Matt tried to reason with her, reaching out and holding her arms. 'Let's go outside,' he said. Poppy tried to free herself from his grasp, but the chef asked her again, 'Let's go outside for a walk.'

But in Poppy's brain that mellow hissing sound had already started. A few laughing voices began to echo around inside her head. She tried to look past Matt and focus on some colours, some warm colours, any colours, but they were not there. All she could see was the face of that girl, that terrible girl that had twisted her mind around the previous week. Matt could see that she was beginning to hyperventilate, she was no longer in control. 'Poppy,' he said with genuine concern in his voice, 'talk to me!'

Again, she searched her brain, trying to find something – the sun, a stream, a river. *Where are the colours?* she thought. *Where are the colours?* Matt tightened his grip slightly on her arms and spoke in a calm and measured voice. 'You don't want to do anything stupid, Poppy,' he said. 'Remember, you don't want to go back there, you don't want to end up in prison.'

Poppy began to breathe more deeply, still searching for some peaceful thoughts to enter her scrambled mind. 'You can do this, Poppy,' Matt said. 'You can do this, keep taking deep breaths. Remember the colours, the blue sky, the bright sun, everything will be OK.' As she breathed out longer breaths she slowly began to see those colours back in her head. They were faded but they were good colours – blues and greens and even yellows. She saw the stream, she saw the lake. It was alright, everything was going to be alright.

'I am OK now, Matt,' she said. 'You can let me go.'

Matt shook his head. 'Just wait one more minute, Poppy. Just hold onto me for one more minute.' She took several more long breaths and slowly her head began to clear. The hissing sounds were still there but they were fading, the echoes of laughter had all but gone. The moment was over. Poppy took one more deep breath and released herself from Matt's grip.

'I need a drink,' Poppy said and turned to enter the dining area. Matt went to speak but she got there first. 'I am OK, really, Matt, I am OK. I just need a drink now.'

When Poppy entered the seating area she did not look left or right in fear of seeing the reason for her anger. Moving directly to the bar, she poured herself a double vodka and downed the drink in one go. She felt slightly more at ease and repeated the exercise. Again the drink barely touched the sides of her mouth before it had been fully devoured. Matt stood in the doorway for a few seconds and was joined by his latest conquest who had been hiding in the staff toilets. Danny was busy trying to assemble the table on the front of the high chair. He was completely oblivious to what had just happened in the kitchen. Chantelle's squeaky voice suddenly piped up. 'She is a fucking nutter!' she said. 'She should be locked up!' Matt shook his head at the dizzy-headed teenager as though to warn her not to say anything more.

Poppy stared down at the stainless steel sink behind the bar. Things were still not right in her head, she knew that. She hoped that the alcohol would have helped calm her nerves, but she was wrong. That hissing sound had been replaced by a fuzzy whirring noise. Strange images began to appear in the unwashed wine glasses in front of her. She closed her eyes tightly. She knew she didn't want to look, she knew she shouldn't look, but a laughing voice called out somewhere deep inside her brain. It was not a random voice, like all the others, it was that girl's voice, it was Bree's voice. It was calling out to her, it was mocking her. Lifting her head slowly, Poppy looked directly to the middle table and saw both Bree and Kayleigh staring at her. One whispered something to the other, they both laughed. That image was enough, it was all Poppy needed. Suddenly that sound inside her head increased tenfold and was accompanied by an orchestra of gaggling laughter. Her face twisted, she bit the corner of her lip harder than ever before, her fists tightened, her head was spinning. She closed her eyes and muttered under her breath, as her headspace searched desperately for the calming colours to return. *Why didn't she stay away?* she thought. *Why didn't she just leave me alone?* Poppy could feel the rage now. It began to climb inside her, like molten lava rising in a dormant volcano. One last time, her inner conscience screamed out for some shades of soothing colours to appear, but they wouldn't, they had deserted her now.

In a split second Poppy's arm swung violently to the right and sent the CD player flying into the wall. Her other arm swiftly followed, hurling four wine glasses crashing over the side of the bar. 'I told you!' she screamed at the top of her voice as she moved forwards at a rapid pace from behind the bar and headed into the dining area. 'I fucking told you not to come back here! I fucking warned you!' Danny turned away from his task with the high chair and took a step forwards, into Poppy's path, but her momentum could not be stopped. She shoved him to one side and sent him flying head first over the high chair, his shoulder crashing against the side of the dining table, causing the startled mother to clutch her baby close to her chest.

The whole restaurant fell silent as Poppy marched over to the table where Bree and Poppy sat. The girls looked up in total shock. There was a brief pause. Most of the diners in the restaurant froze, as if they were playing a game of statues. The mother holding the small child watched on as her husband lifted his arms halfway in the air, as if he thought that this was a hold-up. Before she realised what was happening, Bree felt Poppy's hand on her throat and found her sister's face less than six inches away from her own. Kayleigh began to lift herself from her chair. 'Let her go!' she yelled. 'Let her go!'

Poppy's other hand pushed Kayleigh firmly back into her seat. 'Shut up!' Poppy snapped. 'This is fuck all to do with you!' Bree's hand reached across her newfound sibling's wrist as she tried to free herself from her grip, but Poppy had no intention of letting her go. 'I told you not to come back here!' she barked. 'Why couldn't you just leave me alone!' Bree was dumbstruck. She wanted to say something, but it was difficult to speak with Poppy's hand wrapped around her throat.

Kayleigh tried again to reason with Poppy. 'Just let her go, we can sort this out, just let her go!'

The rage in Poppy's eyes now fixed firmly on Kayleigh. 'I told you to keep your fucking mouth shut!'

Bree's 'bestie' reached forward and tried to free her friend from Poppy's grip. 'She is your sister! She is your sister!' she screamed.

Poppy shook her head and made her feelings clear. 'She is no fucking sister of mine!'

Across the room Danny was struggling to get to his feet. Chantelle cowered behind Matt. The chef did not seem to have an appetite for this conflict. Everyone else was still playing statues. The elderly couple had their forks raised halfway to their mouths, small bits of meat dangling from them. The small child's father had now lowered his hands and began searching in his jacket pocket for his mobile phone.

Poppy's attention had switched back to her unwelcome visitor. 'I told you he was not my dad. Why couldn't you just listen, why did you have to come back?' Poppy tightened her hold on Bree's neck, causing her to gag slightly. Kayleigh instinctively rose to her feet and reached out in a bid to protect her friend, but Poppy was ready, Poppy was always ready! Her head swung back and jolted forwards with alarming pace and accuracy, butting Kayleigh fully on the side of her cheek and sending her crashing to the ground. With her other arm, she pushed her hand with great force into Bree's throat, sending her reeling backwards over her chair and slamming her body into the adjoining table. Without any hesitation Poppy grabbed the neck of the bottle of red wine the girls had been drinking and raised it high into the air. A second later it was brought down onto their table, shattering tiny fragments of glass everywhere.

Poppy held the half-broken bottle at arm's length, as if to warn off any of the restaurant's patrons that might want to get involved in this argument. But in truth no one in that restaurant was even thinking about taking the crazed waitress on, least of all Matt, who seemed to be rooted to the spot. The Geordie lad may well be a bad boy in the bedroom, but he was clearly out of his depth here. Poppy looked around her. She had an audience now, no one was saying anything, no one was doing anything. Holding the jagged edge of the bottle at arm's length, Poppy made a statement. Her voice was a little shaken, but her words were clear. 'That's it!' she said. 'You can all stare. You can all stare at the crazy girl. You got what you wanted, this is what you all fucking wanted!'

Danny was sitting upright now, rubbing his battered head. He tried to reason with his waitress. 'No, Poppy, put it down, please put the bottle down, we can sort this out.'

Poppy shook her head. 'No, Danny, we can't, not anymore, we can't sort this out, not now!'

Bree was still sprawled out on the restaurant floor. She moved slightly and put her hands up at her sides and appealed to her sister. 'I came here to talk, Poppy, I only wanted to...' She didn't get to finish her sentence. 'Shut up!' Poppy barked. 'Shut up, all of you. You have done it now, all of you. You push me and prod me and keep fucking pushing me, until, until this!' She looked over at the anxious-looking chef who hadn't moved an inch. 'You wanted to see me at the limit, Matt, you wanted to see me go over the edge. Well, I haven't even started yet!'

Kayleigh started crawling on her hands and knees, doubled over in pain, sobbing as she clutched the side of her badly swollen face. The woman with the small child was in tears too, holding the frightened baby so close to her she was in danger of smothering him. Her husband was looking away from the scene of Poppy's floorshow, his hands fumbling around under the table. The old couple had now dropped their cutlery and were clasping hands across the table, as if judgement day had arrived.

Breathing heavily Poppy looked down at the culprit for all this mayhem, her sister. Bree was still perched on the floor, her beautiful designer blouse sporting the dark red patterns of the spilled Merlot. Suddenly, Bree started to shuffle herself forward, across the wine-stained carpet. She was still in a state of shock as she reached out for the support of a table. Her hand slipped at the first attempt to grip the top of the edge, but it found its mark on the second. Slowly she began to pull herself up, looking over at her wounded best friend who was curled up in a ball just a few feet away. Poppy had not moved an inch, tiny streams of red wine trickling down her sleeve from the weapon in her hand, her face still filled with twisted anger. Her breathing became more rapid as she turned from one way to the other, the jagged edges of the broken bottle pointing a clear warning to all those around her. The restaurant was silent, deadly silent.

And then, almost in slow motion, right in front of her sibling's eyes, Bree stood tall. It is said in times of great danger that your brain gives you two options, fight or flight. Bree was certainly not going to run away. She was just a few feet away from her angry sister now, and despite the fact that her first instinct had been to move backwards, her feet did not listen to her brain. Taking small steps, she was clearly shaken, but her face had a look of determination about it, as though something was drawing her closer to the danger. Nobody made a sound. Poppy's eyes moved from side to side as her heart pounded harder in her chest. Her nostrils flared as her sister took another step forward. Bree was now just inches from the serrated edge of the bottle. She could almost taste the trickle of expensive vino sliding down its brim. The atmosphere was palpable.

Poppy's trembling hand held the outstretched bottle firmly as she looked at the brave but foolish girl in front of her. She had told her not to come back, she had warned her. Is this what she wanted, is this what she really wanted, for her pretty face to be cut to pieces? Poppy's eyes looked straight ahead, directly into her sibling's gaze. She expected to see a look of fear, total terror, but she was wrong, her sister was calm, she didn't look frightened at all. Stretching her head forward a few inches, Bree found her neck nestled against the jagged edge of the broken bottle. She stared deep into her sister's eyes and spoke calmly. 'I know that you won't hurt me, Poppy, I am your sister.'

Suddenly, Poppy felt something strange inside her head. She knew that she should be searching her mind for those colours, but a small voice in her head told her that she didn't need to, that this girl was right, she couldn't hurt her, it was a voice of reason. The two girls never lost eye contact for those few seconds, as their standoff reached its crescendo.

Kayleigh began to wriggle around on the floor. She was conscious of the impending danger to her friend. Her arm began to slide across the restaurant carpet to reach for her bag. She knew that this was going to end badly. She needed to grab her phone to call the police. She had all but reached her target when she found the sharp heel of Poppy's new boot crushing down on her fingers. Kayleigh let out a scream of agony and rolled away from the feet of the monster that towered above her. Bree wanted to do something to help her friend, but could not move with the edge of the bottle still nestling beneath her chin. Poppy smiled as a tiny ripple of blood seeped out of Bree's neck, trickling slowly down her visitor's throat and onto her designer top. Bree tried again to reassure her sibling that her intentions were good ones. 'I just want to talk, Poppy. I can't walk away from you, we are sisters.'

Poppy's eyes began to twitch as mixed signals raced through her head. 'No!' she screamed. 'We are not sisters, I am not your fucking sister!'

Suddenly, everyone's attention was drawn to the side, to the place where the couple sat with their baby. There was a muffled sound coming from beneath their table. 'Emergency services, emergency services, which one do you require?' The man stared, first at his wife, still clutching their small child tightly to her bosom and then at Poppy. He did not know what to do for the best. He froze, he did nothing.

Poppy's gaze returned swiftly back to the front. The girl was still there, she hadn't moved. The edge of the bottle had drawn more blood on Bree's neck, not a deep cut, but enough to send another stream of bright red fluid racing down her neck. The voice beneath the table could be heard again. 'Emergency services, can I help you?'

As she stared down the neck of the bottle at the small traces of blood sliding down her sister's throat, Poppy heard the voice of reason once more, but this time it was not in her head, this time it was to the side of her. 'Just go,' Danny said. 'Don't do it, Poppy love, just go, it will be alright, I promise you everything will be OK.'

Everyone was staring at her, waiting for Poppy to make her next move. They didn't have to wait long. She gave Bree a telling stare, as if to let her know that this was all her fault, but also to serve as a warning that she meant what she had said, she wanted nothing to do with her. Lowering her arm, she placed the broken wine bottle on an empty table behind Kayleigh's outstretched body and made her way towards the back entrance. Both Matt and Chantelle took several steps to their left to give her a wide berth, the large Geordie lad clearly still stunned by her actions. Before she left, she looked over at Danny, still rubbing the back of his head and offered him a half-smile. The restaurant owner nodded gently as if to let her know that he thought she was doing the right thing. Nobody moved a muscle as she grabbed her jacket and bag. Her audience looked on, hoping that this performance did not merit an encore.

When she had tightened her jacket, Poppy stepped behind the bar and grabbed a large bottle of vodka, Grey Goose, the expensive brand. If this was going to be her Armageddon, she thought, then she was going to go out in style.

She exited the restaurant through the same door she had come in, saying nothing at all. As soon as the frozen spectators at her floorshow heard her vehicle leaving the car park, the restaurant came back to life. Matt and a the two elderly patrons rushed over to help Kayleigh while Danny put a reassuring arm around Bree to comfort her. The diner at the table called for the police as his wife comforted their child. This was the first and last time they would ever visit Chez Blanc.

# CHAPTER
# TWENTY-THREE

P oppy sat ashen-faced behind the steering wheel of the Omega. Her hands were still shaking. The car had travelled for less than twenty minutes to find this familiar location, but she did not know why. She began to rock backwards and forwards. A weird kind of fuzziness was unwinding inside her head again. Small voices, some she recognised, others she didn't, were telling her that they were angry with her, that she should have finished that girl off. Her face screwed up tightly as the noises in her brain grew louder. She suddenly found herself mimicking the words of her unwanted visitor at the restaurant. 'I am your sister, Poppy, I only want to talk, Poppy. You will not hurt me, Poppy, you are my sister, Poppy.' The angry voices grew louder in her head as she thought about Matt's betrayal. She imitated the northerner's apology. 'It is not what it looks like, Poppy, it is not what it looks like.' She closed her eyes for a few seconds and then a few more, but the tormenting sounds would not go away. Some familiar voices were back now too – her school friends from her birthday party, the American woman from the prison, Mrs Houghton. They were laughing, they were all laughing at her. She looked to her side, slowly raising her head to see the window of her flat. Those shapes were dancing all over the closed curtains, like a puppet show of silhouettes. He was in there, that bastard was up there in her flat. The voices told her that he was laughing too, laughing louder than anyone.

Poppy opened the bottle of vodka perched on her passenger seat and took a large swig, followed by another. She could not remember driving back to the flat. It was as if her car had used some sort of spiritual guidance to get there by itself. She looked back up at the lights in her living room. She didn't want to go in there, she wanted to drive away, far away, but the noisy demons in her head were calling out to her. They were telling her she had not finished, not yet. They were demanding blood, they wanted vengeance for her.

The turbulence grew inside Poppy's head as she took another large mouthful of alcohol. Maybe, she thought, if she just got drunk, really drunk, she could wake up and none of this was happening, it was all just a dream, a terrible nightmare. Poppy's head sank into her hands as she tried one final time to rid herself of the torturous voices in her brain, but they were going nowhere. If anything there were more of them and they were getting louder now. Joe Manning was in her head now, sitting in his big chair with a bible in his hand. 'You are a sinner, Poppy Jarvis, an evil sinner!' he said, as he began laughing, laughing very loudly. 'You will burn in hell.' Neddy was standing behind Joe's chair. He was pointing at her and sneering, so was Meghan Masters and Mr Donovan, they were all mocking her. *Where are the colours?* Poppy thought. *There are no colours.* Poppy screamed out loudly at the ghosts that surrounded her. 'Go away! Go away!' But the gathering crowd of monstrous characters from her past simply found her shouts amusing and laughed louder.

Poppy reached for the bottle and took another gulp of the stolen Grey Goose. Her attention was drawn back to her flat. He was up there, she knew he was up there, laughing. She closed her eyes one final time but could find no safe sanctuary from those dark thoughts inside her head. Screwing the top firmly on the stolen bottle of alcohol Poppy threw it in the footrest of the Omega and left her car. Opening the boot of her vehicle she looked down and saw the tyre iron. She heard another voice, it was shouting at her. The tyre iron, it was screaming up at her, 'Take me, I will do the job, I will fuck that bastard up for you!' She didn't need telling twice, she reached inside and grabbed the rusty tool from beneath the punctured tyre. It was heavy, she thought, heavy enough to crack his skull open. Her head began to spin and the blood in her veins pumped faster as she made her way to the stairs at the back of her flat. A couple of drunken revellers called out to her as she passed the takeaway beneath her home, but she was in no mood for conversation.

Poppy climbed the stairway to her flat. There was no plan in her head, just a stealthy determination in her walk, as if her feet were being guided to her target. As she reached her front door she was met with the terrible stench of rotting food and stale cannabis. She turned her key gently to open the door and crept into the living room. She stood in complete silence for a minute or two, stalking her prey. He was fast asleep on the sofa. Half a dozen empty lager cans and a half-smoked joint littered the carpet in front of him. The television was blaring out in the corner of the room. It was showing a documentary on untamed wildlife, maybe a fitting background for the scene that was about to unfold. There were silver wrappers on the table sitting alongside some Rizlas and a small bag of weed. A half-eaten sandwich kept this assortment company.

Her boyfriend was in a deep slumber. Barely nine o'clock and he was dead to the world. A small grunting sound, like that of a snoring boar, escaped from the head of the large-framed body sprawled out below her. The voices in her head began to guide Poppy. She could hear them echoing around inside her brain. She needed to punish Cameron, she needed to hurt him, to hurt him badly. One tiny voice was still trying to reason with her, trying to get her to abandon this act of revenge, but that voice stood alone and was soon drowned out by the others. Poppy closed her eyes for a few seconds. Maybe she could still find the sun, it would shine again. Maybe the calm lake would return to comfort her, to make these evil thoughts disappear. But there was nothing there now, just darkness, a void. All she could feel at that moment was the scalding water he had poured on her neck and the aches and pains that had been left from his size ten feet.

As the voices became louder, the lava in her volcanic temper slowly began to rise again. In an instant Poppy lifted the tyre iron high above her head and brought it crashing down with an almighty force onto Cameron's cheek, the blow cutting deep into his skin. His head moved sharply, but before he knew what was happening the weapon had been raised and lowered again, this time catching the side of his temple. He was dazed, he was disorientated, he felt the pain, but he was still half asleep. Suddenly he let out an ear-piercing howl, like that of a wounded animal as the third blow cracked against the side of his face. Cameron rolled off the sofa onto the floor, desperate to escape the onslaught. Poppy moved swiftly. Standing directly over him, she yanked back the rusty metal tool and unleashed it again, this time catching the back of his skull. Cameron screamed again, his hands moving frantically from side to side and then upwards to protect his face. But it would be in vain. A further blow landed fully onto the side of his cheek, carving a deep gash just below his eye. The six-foot brute was now fighting for his life. His survival instincts kicked in and he rolled up into a ball, his blood-spattered hands now desperate to protect his head. But Poppy wasn't finished. The voices in her head were screaming at her now, egging her on. That burning venom inside her would not let her stop. Once again the hefty iron bar was hoisted high above her head, this time catching the lampshade and sending it spinning around above Cameron's body. Poppy brought her weapon crashing down, but this one missed, the metal bar bouncing back off the floor. Blood began to seep out through the wounds in Cameron's face as Poppy lifted the weapon high again. Her next blow seemed to be twice as hard as the previous one, maybe trying to make up for the fact she had just missed her target, the crushing blow landing across her boyfriend's unprotected ribs, the impact causing him to let out a wild scream and a cry for mercy. 'Stop, you bitch!' he said, his voice both weak and muffled. 'Fucking stop now!'

Poppy's eyes were still full of rage. The screams of little Callum Baxter and the last breaths of Billy Keyes joined the orchestra of voices echoing through her brain. She raised the weapon for one final time and looked down at her pathetic boyfriend, cowering like a small child. His sorrowful eyes were open, they seemed to be begging for mercy. Trickles of blood were dripping from his forehead. Some of the voices in her head were telling her that he was beaten. He pleaded with her again. 'Stop!' his voice much fainter than before but his words still audible. 'Stop, you fucking bitch!' But this was not over for Poppy, not yet. She raised her other hand to grip the weapon tightly and stood over her prey, like an executioner wielding an axe at a medieval beheading. Poppy let out an almighty scream as her final blow came crunching down onto Cameron's skull. He barely mustered enough energy to cry out, choosing instead to swallow the excruciating pain he felt.

Poppy surveyed the damage caused by her savagery for a few seconds, before throwing the bloodstained weapon against the wall of her flat. Looking down at this giant of a man she had maimed so badly, sneering at him as he groaned in agony, she felt nothing, no pity, no guilt, nothing at all. Why should she? When she looked at the blood-soaked sleeve of her jacket, she noticed her hand. It wasn't shaking now. She felt neither good nor bad, she simply felt nothing at all. Poppy reached into her pocket and pulled out a wad of notes, the balance of the money she had strived so hard to gather to clear her rent arrears. It meant nothing to her now, this was no home for her anymore. One by one she ripped each £20 note into tiny pieces and showered it over Cameron's body, like confetti, bloodstained confetti. When the last of the notes had been shredded, she looked down at the messy bone-chilling bloody work of art she had just created. She nodded and laughed to herself. It was a masterpiece, she thought, she was proud of her creation!

Poppy turned slowly and headed for the door. Her task was complete, there was no need for her to stay. But as Cameron's groaning faded, he managed to muster a few words aimed at his former partner, thoughts he may have wished he had kept to himself. 'Fucking bitch!' he muttered, his faint voice barely recognisable. 'I will find you and I will fucking kill you!' Without any hesitation Poppy turned around and launched herself back into the fray, swinging back her right leg and bringing it forward at great pace into the head of her boyfriend, almost like a footballer dispatching an accurate penalty kick. Her shiny new boot caught Cameron full on the side of his head with a sickening thud, spreading his nose, like mashed pulp, across his face, and silencing that foul mouth of his once and for all.

As she left the flat, pulling the tatty brown door closed for the last time, Poppy could make out the cast of familiar voices in her head. They were cheering loudly, she could hear their applause, she had done well.

When she climbed back into her Omega, she could sense that the voices in her head were fading. Small glimpses of several bright colours began to appear in front of her. She picked up the bottle that was rolling around in the footrest of her car and swallowed a large mouthful of vodka. There was a sense of tranquillity, a sense of newfound freedom. She realised that whatever happened now, she was free from him, free from his violent tempers and his heavy-fisted abuse. She did not know whether Cameron was dead or alive and in truth she did not care. This was not a time for contemplation, this was a time for celebration. Poppy raised the vodka bottle and looked up at the window of her flat, as if she wanted to toast her new-found freedom. Those shadowy images were still dancing on those tatty curtains. 'Good riddance!' she said with a wry smile on her face. 'Good riddance to bad rubbish!'

When she started her engine, she had no idea of her destination. Maybe the spiritual sat nav which had led her back to her flat would decide her destiny.

# CHAPTER
# TWENTY-FOUR

The twittering of a few wild birds was all that could be heard at the picturesque setting in the heart of the Surrey countryside. A small but welcoming breeze brushed through the tops of the sycamore trees as the sun began to climb in the sky above. The silence was broken by the shouting of two overexcited youths, as their bikes raced past Poppy's stranded car. Her eyes peeled open, very slowly. They felt as though they had been stuck together with glue. She winced and closed them tightly as the piercing sunlight blinded her vision, pulling her bloodstained jacket over her head to block out their lethal rays. A few seconds later she was awoken by the sounds of the young boys again. They seemed to be riding backwards and forwards past the Omega, as if they were trying to goad her.

The side of Poppy's head began to ache as she tried in vain to return to her slumber. She rolled her tongue around the inside of her cheek. There was an evil taste in her mouth, it made her gag slightly. Looking down onto the floor of her car she saw the empty vodka bottle lying next to some chocolate bar wrappers and an empty cigarette packet. It was small comfort to her, but she knew now why she was feeling as if she had been on the losing end of an argument with a baseball bat. She tried to close her eyes again but the noisy duo on their bikes had returned, their high-pitched laughter a clear sign that they thought their tormenting behaviour was somehow amusing. Luckily for them, Poppy was not in any fit state for confrontation.

Poppy finally gave up any hope of peace and quiet. She sat upright in the back seat of her car and put her hand across her face to block out the powerful sunbeams. Her eyes were weary, she could feel a throbbing inside her head, a slow thud, banging away like a huge bass drum. It seemed to be getting louder, echoing around inside her brain. She knew that all this pain she felt had been self-inflicted. The excessive alcohol she had consumed and the headbutt she had delivered to the girl in the restaurant were the cause of her torment. She reached down for the cigarette packet. It was empty. 'Shit!' she said in a muffled voice that was struggling to leave her mouth. Her head slid down onto the back seat of her car as the images of the previous night's events slowly returned to haunt her. She wanted to put those thoughts out of her mind. She really didn't want to face up to the reality of her actions, not yet, not while she was feeling so fragile.

Looking through the windscreen of her car, Poppy watched on as the two mischievous young cyclists finally rode off into the distance. She thought about lying back down, but something inside her aching head told her that she needed to get into the fresh air. She looked out of her side window, across a small section of grass leading to a stretch of water that was no more than fifteen feet from her. Despite the fact that she was barely able to focus, she recognised it instantly. It was the lake, she was back at the lake. In the background she could see the familiar shape of the pavilion with its long white fence. The sun was bouncing off its large shiny windows. To the right of her, just across the water, was the small jetty. She could make out a few small rowing boats swaying gently on the lake, patiently waiting for their passengers.

The thumping sounds inside her head continued, they were unrelenting. Poppy tried to work out how the hell she had got here. The last thing she remembered was driving down a darkly lit country lane that seemed to go on forever. She couldn't remember stopping. Maybe that spiritual sat nav, the one that had taken her back to the flat, had guided her car to this place. Slowly the events of the previous day began to filter through to her brain. She looked down at her feet and noticed the thick brown stain on her right boot. She knew what it was, it was blood, it was Cameron's blood. Her tired eyes moved slowly upwards and she studied the cuts on her hands and the spatter of bloodstains on the sleeve of her beloved jacket. She knew now that it was bad. Was he dead? Did she kill him? Had she killed Cameron?

The thoughts of her actions were enough to start Poppy moving. Something told her she had to make some big decisions and make them fast, but her aching head was still telling her to lie down and to sleep it off. Reaching over to the front seat of the Omega, Poppy grabbed her handbag and looked inside for her purse. She had just two £5 notes and several coins. She searched her bag in the hope she had some cigarettes in there. Just one would do, just one would ease the pain, but there were none. Taking out her mobile, she switched it on, hoping that the battery would not be dead. She was in luck, the phone came back to life. She knew that things were bad. Maybe in a few seconds she would find out just how bad they really were. Her mobile revealed that there were twelve missed calls, five from Danny, two from Rahwaz, two from the restaurant number and three from a withheld caller. She knew that those ones would be from the police. There were several voice messages, but she couldn't face those, not without a cigarette or two. There were also half a dozen text messages waiting to be opened, but they would also need to wait.

Her body ached all over and the bass drum continued to beat loudly inside her head, playing its own punishing tune, one she did not care too much for. Suddenly Poppy began to feel a watery sensation starting to build up at the back of her throat, as if there was a noxious substance that was screaming to be released. Zipping up her jacket, she pushed open the car door and swiftly made an exit into the fresh air. The blazing rays from the sun hit her like a sledgehammer, making her giddy and completely distorting her vision. She choked loudly, as if she knew that she was about to vomit. She didn't try to hold it back. Bending forwards she spewed up at least half the alcohol she had consumed the night before, together with an assortment of foul-smelling bits of food. Her eyes watered as she released a second load. This time it was more liquid than anything else. A passer-by, walking his dog, watched on in disgust as she gagged loudly, before clearing the remaining contents of her stomach with one final stomach-wrenching effort. The man with the dog did not stop, why would he?

As she stood upright and spat out the tiny fragments of vomit left in her mouth, Poppy had a much clearer view of her surroundings. This was the lake she had visited as a child. She was confused as to how she could have found this place after all this time. Maybe it was a dream, maybe everything was a dream, she had not gone crazy last night, maybe everyone was OK. But looking down at the stains on the sleeve of her jacket and the cuts on her knuckles, she knew that this was far from a dream.

As Poppy wiped over her face with her sleeve, she noticed that the pavilion was open. The screams and shouts of children's unbridled excitement ripping through the morning air, as families began queuing for the rowing boats. Through her bleary eyes, Poppy could make out the shapes of the small army of toddlers, dressed in colourful T-shirts and shorts, dragging their parents' hands toward the small vessels moored at the edge of the lake. For a few seconds her mind took her back there, to when she was one of the small excited children, when she was the little girl who always sailed in the best boat and had the best captain on the lake. She began to wonder if Captain Stripey and Captain Hooknose still visited this place. Maybe they came here with their grandchildren now. Maybe she would see them again, maybe she would remember how good it used to feel to be here, long ago, before she ever knew the bitterness of rejection.

Poppy's Omega was not in a good state, its bodywork was covered in scratches and dents and the passenger side wing mirror was hanging by a thread. The vehicle looked as if it had been abandoned by joyriders. The car's bonnet was pointing directly at the lake, as though its purpose had been to carry its driver into the water. Poppy asked herself that question. Was a watery grave meant to be her final ending? In truth she did not know the answer, she had been so drunk the previous night she was capable of anything. Maybe that was it, perhaps she had decided that she had finally had enough. Maybe she wanted to finish things, to put an end to her miserable existence. After all, who would really miss her if she died? Danny could find a new waitress, Cameron could find a new punchbag, Matt already had a new fuck-buddy and her so-called sister, well, in Poppy's mind, she could just 'fuck off and die!' Maybe the Reverend Joe would hold a service for her, in memory of that 'screwed-up sour-faced sinner' who never listened to his advice and refused to follow the path to righteousness.

Dragging her feet across the increasingly familiar fields, Poppy made her way towards the pavilion. She could feel the fresh breeze from the water on her neck and smell the algae blooms resting at the edge of the lake. As she neared the jetty and heard the laughter of children echo around her, the ghosts of her past life began to appear in her head. 'Row faster, Daddy, row faster, they are catching us,' she would bark at him. Those big strong arms and bulging muscles would never let her down. She could see his body now, moving backwards and forwards at the head of the boat, his firm hands gripping tightly onto the oars. 'Faster, Daddy, faster.' He would pull those silly faces at her, making all sorts of weird grunting noises as their boat glided across the lake. She would be yelling her instructions at him and he would be laughing loudly at the 'slowcoaches' in the other vessels. A sudden chill ran down her spine as she strolled past the empty boats that were swaying in the water, waiting for their new captains to board. Maybe it was a sign of a sudden change in the warm air or could it be one of those ghosts from her past, reminding her that this place had not been so bad after all.

As she passed the long white fence and entered the pavilion, Poppy attracted several stares from the families seated at the tables. Who could blame them? She looked a complete mess. She noticed immediately that the interior of the cafeteria had not changed. The main seating area was painted in bland cream and brown shades, the same as she remembered it. Old black and white photographs of the lake, taken during the 1940s, still hung proudly on the walls. They may have been moved around, but they were the same pictures. The refreshment counter with the ice cream freezer was still in the far corner. Even the display of sweets had not changed its position. Time had stood still in this pavilion for more than two decades. Even the women behind the counter had a familiar look about them. In her throbbing head, Poppy began to wish that time had stood still for her too.

She thought that it might be best to have a small makeover before venturing to the counter. Her somewhat bedraggled appearance and pale features were already a talking point of most of the customers. She made her way to the toilets. They too were still located in the same corner of the tea room. In truth that was probably the only place they could be. Poppy sat down in one of the cubicles and relieved herself of the remainder of the large bottle of vodka that was still floating around in her system. She rested her head against the side panel for a few seconds, still feeling somewhat weary, her eyelids feeling heavy. She was desperate to return to her slumber. Her rest was cut short by the sounds of a woman calling out to her daughter who had strayed into the toilets. They say that there is no rest for the wicked, that would certainly be true on this day.

Poppy left the temporary sanctuary of the cubicle and made her way to the washbasins. A small smile cracked on her troubled face as she remembered on her last visit here how she could barely see the top of her head in the large mirror that was now facing her. As she searched in her bag, hoping to find a hairbrush, a small but very familiar tone sounded out in her head. It was unmistakable, it made her skin crawl, it made her jump. 'What have you done now, Popsy?' the tiny voice asked. 'What have you done now?' As she looked up, she heard it again. 'Why did you do it, Popsy girl, why did you do it?' Poppy began to shake. Her senses could not take in what was happening, and then, before she had the chance to find some sanity, an image of the girl appeared in the mirror. She was standing behind her, Nikita was here with her.

Poppy stared at her reflection and then beyond it, she could see the small figure of her friend standing behind her. She was as clear as anything. The mirror was telling her that it was her, those messy double buns sitting proudly on her jet-black hair told her that it was her, but her brain refused to be fooled by the image. The waif-like figure asked her again, 'Why, Popsy girl, why did you do it? You have spoiled everything now.' Poppy began to tremble, as the face of the figure in the mirror became much clearer to her. The little pixie shook her head and continued. 'Nothing to say for yourself?'

Poppy responded. Her voice bore something of a tremble. 'You can't be here, I know you can't be here, Nix, I know this isn't you.'

'And you can be here. You can be at this place, can you? What gives you the right to be here?'

'It was my memory, Nix, not yours, the lake was always my one place, I told you that.'

The tiny figure in the background laughed, that beautiful high-pitched laugh that always made Poppy smile. 'Well, maybe it is my place now,' she said. 'Maybe I have taken this away from you, like you took everything away from me.'

'No, Nix, no!' Poppy shouted. 'I told you what happened, I told you everything. It wasn't my fault that they took him away, I swear.'

'But it was, Popsy girl, we both know that it was your fault.'

Poppy was still shaking, still trying to come to terms with the vision in her head. She closed her eyes tightly for a few seconds. But when she opened them, she was still there, Nikita was still behind her, she was still smiling. 'Why did you stop, Popsy, why did you stop at the edge of the lake?' she asked.

'What do you mean?'

'Didn't you want to join me? We could have so much fun again, you and me. It could be just like old times.'

'No, Nix, you are not real! You are not real!'

'Poor Popsy girl has messed up again, this time it's her boyfriend that she cuts up into pieces. And poor Popsy girl has no one else to blame but herself. Poor, poor Popsy girl!'

'No, you are not real, Nix! You can't be real!'

The figure behind her laughed, that impish little laugh that told Poppy that she was there, her friend was there with her. 'You see, I was right,' Nikita said. 'I told you that one day we would both be famous.'

'No!' Poppy yelled at the mirror. 'I don't want to be famous, I never did!'

'Poor Popsy, now she doesn't want to be famous.'

'You are wrong, Nix, I heard the voices again, they told me to do it, they always make me do it.'

'Still blaming those voices, Popsy girl. Come on, that's old news now, I know that, you know that, all those bloody shrinks knew that!'

Poppy became very agitated, she wanted to lash out, but she couldn't, she would never have hurt Nikita. She closed her eyes again and screamed loudly at the mirror. 'It's the voices, Nix, you know it's the voices. You need to leave me alone! You need to go away!'

Suddenly the door swung open and Poppy's attention was drawn to her side, to the entrance for the toilets. A startled woman stood there. She was holding the hand of a small child, she was just a few feet away. She gave Poppy a strange look before walking back out into the tea room. Poppy looked back at the mirror but saw only her own reflection. She was gone, her pixie friend was gone. She turned on the taps of the basin in front of her and dowsed her face with cold water. She was still shaking slightly. Her friend's grinning features were now fixed in her brain, she couldn't get Nikita out of her head. She splashed more water across her head to flatten her hair. Her reflection in that mirror told her she resembled a scarecrow, no wonder everyone had been looking at her. Before she left the toilets, Poppy looked into each of the cubicles to see if her friend was hiding in there. She knew that it was not possible, she knew that she wouldn't find her little pixie, but your brain can tell you to do strange things when you know that your time is coming to an end.

Pushing past the woman and the young girl who had been waiting outside the toilets, Poppy returned to the cafeteria area inside the pavilion. It was busier now, most of the tables were full and the queue for the refreshments had doubled in size. Poppy desperately needed a cigarette, a shot of alcohol, a fix, anything, anything at all to make this numb feeling in her body go away. Joining the refreshment queue, she gazed down at the families seated around her. They all looked so happy, so full of life, not a care in the world.

As she neared the front of the queue, Poppy felt the throbbing pain return. She touched her forehead and rubbed the bump above her right eye. An image of the girl she had butted the previous day came into her mind. She didn't want to deal with those thoughts, not now. Her eyes began to squint as the bright fluorescent lights behind the counter drew nearer. She was still a little unsteady on her feet, something that a few of the people in the queue felt worthy of conversation. Poppy stared back at the toilets and closed her eyes. Maybe when she opened them she would see her friend appear, she would be sporting those crazy buns in her hair and that mischievous smile would be beaming all over her face.. She would know what to do now, Nikita would have the answers. She would help Poppy get through this nightmare. But she didn't, Nikita never would appear again.

'Can I help you?' the calm and welcoming voice said. 'Can I help you, young lady?'

Poppy opened her eyes and found herself at the front of the queue. The kindly-looking woman in a bright green apron smiled at her from behind the counter and asked again, 'Can I help you?'

'Tea,' Poppy replied. 'A mug of tea and do you sell cigarettes?'

The woman shook her head. 'No, love, afraid not, the nearest shop for tobacco is on the Crawley road, about two miles away.'

Poppy scrambled some coins together to pay for her drink and carried her cup over to a table by the window. She could sense now that she was the topic of conversation of many of the friendly faces sitting at the tables. She found herself sitting opposite a table with two small children – a pale-skinned girl in a yellow dress and a slightly older boy who had his head buried in a comic. The woman sitting with them was busy on her phone, complaining about the roadworks that had held up their journey that morning. Poppy sipped her tea at first and then took some larger mouthfuls in the hope that the taste would soothe the terrible furry feeling in her throat. She looked down at the sleeve on her coat. The blood-stains were much clearer now and seemed much darker beneath these brighter lights. She peered out of the window, across the lake. Several boats had now entered the water and were already halfway round the island in the middle. She remembered how her father would tell her that there was treasure on that island, real treasure. He told her that one day they would land at the island and dig up all the treasure and they would be rich. He said that they could buy their own boat with all the money, a much bigger boat, too big for the lake, one that was made for the sea. They could go on a real adventure then, across the ocean, where they would find people that only spoke in a different language. They would catch fresh fish and cook it, adding fried chips with lots of salt and vinegar. They would eat their meal on their boat and then play games with all the other children on the sandy beaches. It always made Poppy happy when he told her that story. She wanted to believe him. But they never did land on the island, they never did find that treasure.

As Poppy looked over at the table opposite, the small girl in a yellow checked dress was staring in her direction, looking at her in a strange way, as though she could see some food on her face. The child wasn't smiling, she just sat there, observing Poppy's every move. Poppy felt conscious that her appearance may be scaring the little girl. She brushed the straggling strands of unkempt hair behind her ear and continued to drink her tea. The young girl was still staring though, watching Poppy as if she was some sort of circus act. Her observer began to chew on the end of a straw, biting off the end of it as if it was edible. Poppy recognised something in the girl that she had seen many years before, a tiny child full of big dreams, her head full of mischievous thoughts and made-up games. Poppy wanted to be that little girl, she wanted to be that normal child, sitting there with her normal family, living a life that normal people live. If only she could get the chance to be that little girl again and have a different life. She would not be here now, sat in a room full of strangers, no one to care for her or love her, an empty shell of a person who had nothing but bad memories for company and nothing in her life that was worth living for.

Poppy's mobile rang twice while she was unknowingly entertaining the bemused child. The first call had been from Danny, the second a withheld number. She answered neither. She was desperately searching her mind to consider her options, but in truth she knew that her fate was inevitable. The money in her pocket might buy her a few days, maybe a week, if she slept in her car. But she knew that she would be kidding herself if she thought that she would be able to run forever. A strange sense of guilt hung over her aching head at that moment, not for what she had done to Cameron or that girl in the restaurant, not even for scalding Matt with the hot drinks. No, the only person she felt any sense of remorse for was Danny. She had let him down, after all that he had done for her, all the faith that he had shown in her. She had thrown it all back in his face. She hung her head in shame.

The small girl with the front row seat at the circus was still watching the star attraction as she finished her tea and zipped up her bomber jacket. Poppy thought she might try something approaching an act of comic humanity in a bid to get a reaction from the child. She poked out her tongue and pulled back the sides of her eyes, making something of a scary face. But the girl was not amused. Her facial expression remained unchanged, she simply chewed on her straw. Maybe she was disappointed with this act, maybe she would be asking for her money back. After all, the real Poppy Jarvis was meant to be a lot more entertaining, much more brutal, a psychopath. The real Poppy Jarvis screamed at people and held broken bottles and knives in her hand. The small girl in the pretty yellow dress would surely not be recommending this tame version of the show to any of her friends.

The fresh air hit Poppy hard in the face as she made her way out of the pavilion. She still felt a little nauseous and was conscious that she may bring up the mug of tea that was making its way through her system. She still felt slightly unsteady on her feet, so sat on one of the large wooden benches overlooking the lake. It had something of a familiar feel about it. She felt as if she had sat in this place before. She watched on as the small boats moved gently through the water, small cries of laughter echoing out from the other side of the island. A couple with a very small child, no older than two years old, were breaking bread and feeding the ever-growing number of ducks down in front of her. She smiled to herself. She never did like those bloody ducks at the lake, they always seemed to get in the way of her father's boat. To her right, Poppy could see a man walking his dog. She perked up for a second. It wasn't the sight of his four-legged friend that brought her to her feet, he was smoking, he had cigarettes. Poppy did her best to tidy her hair as she approached him. She didn't want to give him the impression that she was just some homeless scrounger. The man was getting on in years, somewhere in his early seventies, maybe older. He was small in stature and had a tiny grey moustache which looked in need of a serious trim. He wore a quarter-checked flat cap and large boots as if he was going hunting rather than for a simple walk around the fields. His dog was a Golden Labrador. He was lying down, taking in the view and the gentle breeze from the lake. Poppy stood beside the pair for a moment or two. She watched them closely. The man spoke to his dog as if it were his child, patting his head and praising him each time he sat or lay down at his request. But Poppy wasn't interested in the good behaviour of his animal friend, she desperately needed a cigarette. She approached the man from the side, so she would not alarm him. Sorting through her bag, she found a couple of pound coins amongst the mess of tissues and held them outwards in the palm of her hands. 'Can I buy a couple of those ciggies off you?' she asked. 'They don't sell them in the canteen.' The man looked her up and down, his wise old eyes studying her weary face and scruffy appearance for a few seconds. Poppy thought that maybe he had not understood her. She offered him the money again.

The man reached into his pocket and pulled out a packet of Marlboro cigarettes. He checked inside and saw that there were half a dozen left. 'Here, have these,' he said. 'You look like you need them.'

Poppy offered him the money, but he shook his head. 'Don't worry about that,' he said. 'Do you need a light?' Poppy nodded and he lit up her cigarette. She breathed in deeply. That first intake of tobacco felt heavenly as it raced around her lungs. 'If you don't mind me saying so, you look a bit lost,' the elderly gentleman observed. 'Do you need any help?'

Poppy took another long drag on her cigarette before replying. 'No, I know this place, I used to come here when I was young.'

'It hasn't changed much,' the man said, looking out across the lake. 'Apart from the fact that the bloody tea has gone up to two quid for a tiny mug and they don't let Toby in the pavilion anymore.'

'Toby?' she asked and then quickly realised that he had meant his four-legged companion. 'Oh, Toby, yes I see.'

'It is none of my business, but you look like, well, like you might have been in a fight or something.'

Poppy wasn't sure what to say, so she said nothing. She appreciated the fact that he had given her the cigarettes, but she wasn't going to share her thoughts with this stranger.

The three of them stood there in silence for a moment or two, Poppy, the elderly man and Toby, all looking out across the water, all with different thoughts on how the coming hours were going to play out. Despite his ageing years, the man seemed astute. He had already identified the bloodstains on the sleeve of her jacket and was becoming more inquisitive. 'Are you in some sort of trouble?' he asked. 'I know it is nothing to do with me, but, well, it might help to talk to someone about it.'

Poppy shook her head. 'No, I am fine, I just had a bad night, that's all.' The man did not believe her, but said nothing more. He knew deep down that the girl with his cigarettes in her jacket pocket was troubled, deeply troubled. It did not take a genius to work that out. They stood in silence as Poppy finished the remainder of her life-saving shot of nicotine.

The lake was alive now. Around twenty boats had been launched onto the still waters. The family of ducks had been fed now and moved backwards and forwards across the water, much to the annoyance of some of the revellers in the boats. The elderly man took in a deep breath of the country air and ushered his four-legged companion to his feet with a simple call. 'Come on, fella!' he said. 'You and I can get some exercise now.' Poppy decided to stay a little longer, after all, it was becoming easier for her to deal with the reality of her past than that of her future.

Despite the fact that the stranger had been a little too interested in her personal problems for her liking, she felt somewhat obligated to show her gratitude. 'Thanks,' she said. 'For the ciggies.'

The man pulled out a disposable lighter from his pocket and passed it to her. 'No problem,' he said with a small look of concern on his ageing face. 'You will probably need this too.' But before he turned to leave, he gave Poppy a simple piece of advice. 'Take it from someone who has probably made more mistakes than most in their life, you can't hide from them. If you don't own your mistakes, they will follow you around, until they wear you down.' With that he gave Poppy a friendly smile and walked away with his faithful companion in tow. 'Be lucky, girl!' he said. 'Be lucky!'

Poppy lit up another cigarette and stared into the tranquillity of her surroundings, the place where everything was peaceful, no shouting or screaming, no plates being thrown across the kitchen, no fighting, nothing, just a pure and simple place where she once felt at peace with the world. She was still trying to work out how she had arrived here, to the ghosts of her past, back to this place. There was nothing spectacular about it, it was a couple of dozen wooden boats floating their way around a small island in the middle of an ordinary stretch of water. But as those images of her childhood swayed through her consciousness, one dark thought came back to haunt her. It was always lurking there, somewhere at the back of her mind. Is this where her father hid her? Is her mother's body lying somewhere at the bottom of that lake?

Poppy was in something of a daze as she walked back to her car. The sight of Nikita in the toilet mirror was still with her. She was finding it impossible to get the girl's image out of her head. As she sat in her Omega, she looked over the missed calls and text messages in her mobile. The calls from the withheld number seemed to have doubled since she last looked. She knew that it would be the police, they would be giving her chapter and verse on the benefits of a voluntary surrender. She did not want to hand herself in, but it was rapidly looking like her only option.

Her head was still throbbing. It didn't make things any easier for her. She was trying to remember exactly what happened the day before, some of it was still a blur. Was he dead, had she killed Cameron? She knew that she had hit him with that bar, hard, hard enough to hurt him, but had she killed him? The voice of reason told her that he couldn't be dead, he was invincible, Cameron was invincible. What about the time he took a pasting from the motorcycle gang? They beat him black and blue and just a few days later he was kicking a football around on the green. Her mind was working overtime now. *No, he must be dead*, she thought, *he wasn't moving, when I left him, he wasn't moving.* She changed her mind again. Was he moving? Maybe a bit, maybe she heard him groan when she was leaving. Yes! That's it, their neighbour would have heard the noise, they would have called an ambulance, he would be alright, it was Cameron, he would be alright. Maybe he didn't even tell the police what really happened, he wouldn't have grassed her up, not Cameron, he was no grass, he hated the police. Maybe he did, maybe he did grass her up. He hated her now, maybe the big hard man told the police everything. But she could tell the police that she hit him in self-defence, tell the police he started it, it was just a row that got out of hand. Poppy could not decide what the best outcome for her would be. Maybe it was better if he was dead, maybe that would be better for her after all.

The gentle breeze wafted across the beautiful greens surrounding the lake, reaching Poppy in her moments of reflection. It was all coming back to her now. All her brutal actions of the previous day were being replayed on a big-screen television in her troubled mind. *I hurt Danny*, she thought, *I didn't mean to, it was her fault, Danny, it was that bitch who says she is my sister, it was her and her trouble-making friend. That smarmy cow deserved everything she got, but not you, Danny, not you. You saw her, Danny, she is crazy, she wanted me to cut her with that bottle, that broken bottle. My god, she walked right up to me, she wanted me to slice her up, you saw her, Danny, you saw her, she is a mad bitch, she was asking to be hurt. Why did she have to come back? I told her not to. She did this, her and her big-mouthed bitch of a friend. They caused all these problems, them and Matt. Yes, Matt, he started it all.* Poppy was struggling now, she began to realise the amount of people that she had hurt the previous day, but she still tried to find some reasons to justify her actions. *He was fucking her, Danny, Matt, he was fucking Chantelle, that squeaky-voiced little slut, he was fucking her. God, she is only about fourteen or fifteen years old, I don't know, maybe older but not old enough. He is a pervert, Danny, I hope you have sacked him, he started all of this, he made me angry, he made me so fucking angry, he started the voices off inside my head.*

Poppy reached into her jacket pocket to light up another cigarette but just as she did her phone rang, causing her to jerk backwards and drop the lighter. She knew the time had come. This was the withheld number. She knew deep down inside that she could not run away from this. *Let's talk to the police*, she thought, *let's just get this shit over and done with.* She answered the call. 'Hello.'

'Oh hello, is that Poppy, Poppy Jarvis?'

'Yes.'

'Thank goodness, I have been trying to reach you for the past couple of days.'

'OK.'

Poppy had spoken to many women police officers and court officials in her time. She sensed that this woman on the phone was not one of them. She was right.

'You are related to Dean Jarvis, is that correct?' the woman asked.

'Yes, I am…' She didn't want to use the words, but she felt that she had to. 'I am his daughter, who am I speaking to?'

'My name is Angela Napier, I am the hospital administrator from St Andrew's Hospital in Southwark.'

'Is it about my father?'

'Yes, it is is, Miss Jarvis. I am afraid I have some bad news for you.'

350

# CHAPTER TWENTY-FIVE

Maybe, when you can't accept that reality is the only truth and that everything else means nothing, nothing at all, maybe then you must begin to accept the fate that lies ahead of you.

But Dean Jarvis still believed that if you simply don't tell someone something, then it is not a lie. He had lived by this rule for most of his life, but if ever there was a time to find some peace in this world and the one that lies beyond, the time was now. This might be his final chance.

The currents surrounding the sinking man were growing ever stronger, pulling him deeper into the abyss. His hopes of survival were fading fast as the tides of his self-despair carried him further away from the shores of redemption. Any help he received at this late stage would be the equivalent of a small rubber ring fighting the rage of a tidal wave.

The drowning man was still looking for solace, not that anyone was likely to believe his tales of woe, least of all his companion in that hospital room. He tried again, however, to justify himself to that lonely figure beneath the bedsheets. He began with a lie, one he had told himself many times over. It was not a convincing lie. 'I tried my best for Poppy, I did everything I could, but she was better off with them, better off in care. They had professional people, you know, ones that could help her with her problems. I know she was better off with them.' The flashing monitor beside the man in the bed registered a few small bleeping sounds. Maybe it was a way of acknowledging the fact that he was listening, maybe it wasn't.

The blinds at the hospital window were closed now. The rain had stopped falling and the sirens of the ambulances were idle. The clock on the wall was still showing twenty minutes past the hour, but it was clear that the second hand was fighting to move forwards. Time was no longer on Dean's side, it would be now or never. He decided to follow a different path. 'Poppy thinks I did it, you know that, don't you? Poppy thinks that I killed her mother. She asked me once, she asked me if she should stop hoping that her mother was safe and that she would come back home. I think that might have been the last time I saw her. She was in that shitty kids' home, the one in Bluebridge, she hated it there. How could she think that I would have murdered her mother? I loved Hannah, maybe I never showed it enough, but I loved her, I just hated what she had become. All that booze and those pills she used to take, but deep down I still loved her. I stopped seeing her after that – Poppy – I didn't want to see her anymore. It broke me in two, every time I held her tiny hand and had to let it go again. I don't know why the police never found Hannah. I wanted them to, I wanted them to find her.'

In his mind Dean was still convinced that he could reach the shoreline. The sinking man was fighting harder than ever to escape his destiny. But the small morsels he had offered in his final bid for forgiveness had fallen on deaf ears. By now, the tiny lights in those small houses were getting further and further away. The angry currents began to pull harder on Dean's torso. His resistance would be futile. He realised now that he was getting weaker, much weaker. The colours on the small screen beside the man in the bed flashed rapidly for a few seconds and the machine made an unusual sound which distracted his attention. Dean reached into his pocket and took out his mobile phone, a relic from the 1990s, the Nokia C16 handpiece that he had owned for more than a quarter of a century. 'I still think that it will ring, you know,' Dean said. 'I know it sounds crazy, but I still think that one day it will ring, and it will be her. They all laughed at me, all those fools with their shiny new iPhones. I suppose I just hoped, maybe one day, that she would find my number and call, just once, that's all, she would only need to speak, to talk to me. I just wanted to hear her voice one more time.'

Those that might choose to forgive him might assume that elusive call he had been hoping for was a call from his daughter or his missing spouse. It might have bought him some time, stopped him from plunging further downwards, to the bed of his ocean of regrets. But as usual his selfish thoughts had turned to Krista, they always turned to Krista, but Dean knew in his heart that call would never ever come.

\* \* \*

If only the drowning man knew that it would not be so long that he would be joining his son, the one he never met, the one he didn't want, another offspring that he had abandoned. Fortunately for his boy, the world had been a kind place during his short life. Although he never got to fulfil his dreams and ambitions, he was loved. For the twenty-two years that his beautiful soul was amongst the living, he was truly loved. Maybe, if by some miracle Dean's final calling took him to the house of the righteous, he might meet him there. Maybe his son would reveal that he also had another child, one who could not be with them, not just yet, but maybe soon. He might tell him that his second daughter, the one he never even knew existed, was herself in turmoil. That his father had left behind two deeply troubled souls, who, for different reasons, were both crying out for their own salvation. Perhaps this would be his punishment, an eternity of never knowing the truths that had surrounded him all these years. If only he had looked sooner, if only he had looked harder, this union may well have been a happy one.

The drowning man had almost sunk to the bottom of his sea of despair. Those distant lights were becoming dimmer by the minute. There were no life jackets being thrown in his direction, no outstretched arms beckoning him to safety. He was alone now, he was completely alone. It began to get darker, much darker. He had one final chance to reflect on his life. Maybe if he hadn't been sleepwalking through his existence for the past twenty-odd years and could join the dots together, he might realise why he was here now, alone in this desolate hospital room. He might blame his drink problem for why he regularly beat his wife, or the two-year-long police investigation into her disappearance which caused the first of his two nervous breakdowns. He could say that there was someone else to blame for the sixteen jobs he gained and lost over the past two decades. Maybe it was the stress from that situation that caused him to be locked up in prison for nine months, for the accident he caused whilst under the influence of his beloved alcohol. And if he searched deep enough, maybe, just maybe, Dean could blame someone, anyone, else for what happened to Poppy. He could try to convince anyone who might listen that it was the fault of genes that his mentally unbalanced mother had passed down to him, the frenzied cocktail of out-of-control chromosomes that now raged like a wildfire inside the framework of his troubled daughter's body. There would always be a scapegoat, always someone else to curse for his sorrows. He could always pass the blame onto someone or other.

But who could he blame for the cancer that had started in his liver and had now eaten away most of his vital organs? The cancer that had weakened his resistance day by day and left him helpless in his ocean of self-pity. Maybe God. If no one will listen and all else fails, blame God!

As his weary eyes fought hard to stay open he began to hear sounds of small voices echoing around his head. The lights were becoming much brighter now. His vision was somewhat distorted but be began to make out the shapes of familiar faces. His stepfather, Peter, he was there, he was polishing his shoes, he must be going to work soon. His mother was there, in the corner of a long white room. She was sitting in her big chair, she was brushing her hair, she was looking straight at him, but she didn't seem to know who he was. He wanted to cry out to her, 'It's me, Momma, it's your Dean!' She was fading away now, disappearing from those bright white walls surrounding her. He could see her shadow moving away from him. And now to the left of him he could see his old school teacher, Mr Matthews. He was at the front of the classroom. 'Reach for the stars, Jarvis,' he said. 'And if you get over the trees you will have done bloody well for yourself.' Roger Morris was there too, his best friend Roger. They were both laughing at the teacher's funny comment. The images continued to appear at a frantic pace. He could see a young couple, they were strolling in the countryside, they were smiling, they were happy, they walked straight past him, he didn't know why!

Dean's body began to move around. He couldn't feel his arms, it was as if they were tied down. The light became brighter, much brighter and was hurting his eyes. The images of days gone past continued to drift across his line of vision. Mrs Barnes, his next-door neighbour, was there now. She was with her dog. She waved at him, but he couldn't wave back, his arms were too tired. The church bells, he could hear the ringing of the church bells. Hannah, he could hear her voice. She began to walk towards him, but then she stopped. She was wearing her wedding dress. She looked just as she had done all those years ago. He wanted to call out to her, but his mouth wouldn't open, it seemed as if his lips were sealed together. She began to walk away. He wanted to shout out loudly, 'Don't go, Hannah! Don't go! I am here,' but the words would not leave his mouth. He was too late, she was out of view. Suddenly, he could feel something in his arms. He looked down. It was Poppy, it was Poppy, she was so small, just a tiny baby. He could smell her freshness and feel her soft skin. He touched her tiny fingers, touched her smooth face. He wanted to tell her, to tell her that he was sorry, that he was sorry for everything, but in a split second, she was gone, taken away from his grasp.

A helplessness began to overwhelm Dean now. The visions were becoming blurry as if his eyesight was deserting him. Where was Poppy? Where was Hannah? He wanted to call out to them, but his lips were so dry, his mouth would not open. And now he could hear her voice calling him, he could hear her clearly, she was there with him, Krista was back with him. A brief recollection of their first meeting, her welcoming smile, he could see the fires burning brightly in those dangerous eyes. She was calling to him, enticing him to come to her. He could see her arms stretched out towards him, luring him in, calling him closer to the shore. She was there, Krista was there, she was offering him a final chance of salvation. The jumbled thoughts in Dean's head were mixed with cries of laughter and pain. They slowly began to fade. He suddenly felt a bright ray of light searing through his eyelids. Through a small crack in the bottom of one eye he could make out the shape of the clock on the wall. The second hand was working now and had moved onwards to twenty-five past the hour. All of a sudden, everything became very loud inside his head. The sounds were deafening. Through a tiny slit at the bottom of his eyelid, somewhere through the burning light, he could make out the kindly face of a woman. She was dressed in a nurse's uniform. He could feel the warmth of her fingers as they wrapped around his hand. He didn't know who she was, but he felt comforted by her touch.

In the darkening corner of his mind he could still hear her. Krista was calling out to him, the tones of her voice running through his head like the most beautiful song he had ever heard. His body was moving closer and closer to the rocks. He could see them now, the sirens, their faces were so clear, she was there, she was with them, Krista, she was beckoning him towards her. His breath shortened as he gazed at the incredible beauty before him. He was going to be safe, Krista was holding out her hand. It was so close, so close, he moved forward, he tried to raise his arm, but he could not reach her.

Suddenly, without any warning, the bright lights became dim and the image of Krista disappeared. Inside his head everything became dark and then darker, his vision began to fade from grey to black. The sea was totally still, he could no longer hear the waves, there was complete silence.

The drowning man was no longer sinking, his struggle was over. He had finally drowned.

# CHAPTER TWENTY-SIX

P oppy sat in the car park of St Andrew's Hospital and smoked the last of the cigarettes she had been given by the kindly gentleman at the lake. She didn't know what to feel. There was a kind of elation, almost as though she should celebrate the fact that her father had died. But a large part of her felt cheated that he was no longer there. The bitterness that had shrouded her mind had gone. She realised now that she had no one left to blame for any of her past actions. In truth Poppy Jarvis could well have been holding back a river of tears in those ice-cold veins of hers. Whether self-inflicted or not, her scars, both physical and mental, would have broken people much stronger than her. But Poppy did not feel like crying, there was a hollowness in her body, almost as if she felt no emotion whatsoever.

At the reception area Poppy was invited to take a seat and wait for Mrs Napier, who kept her waiting for almost an hour before introducing herself. Not that Poppy had anything else to do that day. It would give her time to make some decisions about her final port of call.

Mrs Napier, a neatly kept middle-aged woman in a smart black trouser suit, greeted Poppy with a solemn face, probably a feature she practised regularly in her mirror at home. She invited Poppy to join her in a small office at the end of a long corridor. No further words were spoken until the two women sat down opposite each other. Mrs Napier started the conversation. 'We didn't really know who to call,' she said. 'He never had any visitors in all of the time that he has been here.' Poppy simply nodded and let her continue. 'He had an old phone, a very old phone, it was a Nokia, I believe. We couldn't find a charger for it, but one of the other patients got their father to bring one in.' Poppy wasn't really interested in her story, but nevertheless did her best to give her the impression that she was. 'So when we went through the text messages on his phone, we realised that you must be his daughter. I have tried to reach you for the last couple of days but...'

Suddenly, Poppy decided to speak up. 'I have been very busy, so I couldn't get back to you,' she said.

A sympathetic smile appeared on the face of Mrs Napier. 'Of course, of course, I understand. I am just pleased that we managed to contact you.'

Poppy decided at that point to make her position perfectly clear. 'We were not close, my dad and me, we were not close. I haven't seen him for over fifteen years.'

The kindly lady nodded. 'We sort of got that impression from the text messages. We realised that things were far from perfect between you, but you are his next of kin.'

Poppy shrugged her shoulders. 'So, there was no one else at all?' she asked.

'He has been with us for several months. As I said, he never had any visitors. We did find a number for his landlord at his bedsit, but he told us that he didn't think that he had any family.'

'Bedsit?' Poppy said, her first realisation that her father's life had not exactly been a bed of roses without her.

'Yes, I think his landlord sold off his belongings to pay for his overdue rent.'

'What did he die from?' Poppy asked, in an almost nonchalant manner, as though her recently deceased father had been a small family pet.

'Liver cancer,' Mrs Napier replied. 'He had been in our intensive care unit since early this year. He wasn't conscious for most of that time. He wouldn't have really been in any pain, the morphine would have helped with that.'

Poppy felt anxious. She really wanted to get this ordeal over and done with. 'So what happens next? I don't have any money or anything if you are expecting me to pay for his funeral.'

'I have no doubt that the state will have to take care of that, Poppy,' the woman said in a reassuring manner. 'But there are one or two things you need to do.'

'Like what?' Poppy asked.

'Well,' Mrs Napier said, reaching into a filing cabinet drawer, 'these are his belongings. There is not much here, but we are dutybound to hand them over to his next of kin.' The woman handed Poppy a large padded envelope and asked her to sign a preprinted document. The hospital administrator was somewhat surprised at Poppy's lack of emotion, but it was not her place to discuss the cause of their rift. It was, however, her role to ask her the next question. 'Would you like to say your final goodbyes?' Poppy seemed quite stunned by her comment, but let the caring woman continue. 'He is in our chapel of rest.'

'I don't think so,' Poppy said, shaking her head. 'As I said we were not close or anything. I don't even really know why I came here today.'

'It can help, closure can sometimes help,' Mrs Napier said, a solemn look appearing on her face. 'Whatever you felt about him, Miss Jarvis, he was still your father.'

'I am not sure,' Poppy replied. 'It is sort of like, he is gone now, so it might just be best to remember him as he was.' Poppy was tempted to add the words 'selfish, unreliable, drunken and bastard' but kept those thoughts to herself. There was a small silence with the two women staring at one another, both waiting for the other to speak. Finally Poppy nodded her head at the woman. 'I think you are right, I should see him, I should say goodbye to him.'

Mrs Napier nodded back and stood to leave the room. 'Give me a few minutes,' she said, leaving Poppy clutching the remains of her father's existence in her lap. 'I will let them know you are coming down.'

Why did she say she wanted to see him? Poppy thought. She didn't, she really didn't want to be reminded of him ever again, he could rot in hell for all she cared. She thumbed over the outside of the padded envelope. His whole life was resting in her hands now. Not much to show for all those years, Poppy thought. She wanted to feel some emotion inside, but the bitter memories of her past years pushed up her barriers to prevent her.

Mrs Napier returned around fifteen minutes later and asked Poppy to follow her down a side corridor. The lady with the smart trouser suit and the kindly facial expressions started a meaningless conversation in a bid to make Poppy feel more at ease. 'Did you have to come far?' she asked.

Poppy shook her head. 'Not really, I live in Eltham.'

Mrs Napier tried a little harder. 'We never got to know him very well, your father, as I said, he was in and out of consciousness most of the time he was with us.' Poppy said nothing, she would have preferred this woman to keep quiet. She didn't feel that she needed any more information than she had already been given. Something kept telling Poppy that she should feel something inside her at this moment, an emotion, anything, love, hate, bitterness, anger, but she still felt nothing at all. Everything seemed so surreal. She was sure that she would wake up any minute and realise that none of this was happening. She felt as if she was hallucinating.

It was certainly a stranger experience than the side effects of any of the substances she could remember taking in her past. Maybe, she thought, it wasn't just this that was a dream, maybe nothing had really happened the previous day after all, maybe Cameron was OK, maybe Danny would be calling her any moment asking her why she was late for work. But as the large brown door of the chapel of rest came into view, the cold chills of reality washed over her body. Poppy suddenly felt a little unsteady on her feet, almost dropping the package containing her late father's effects.

'This is it,' Mrs Napier confirmed. 'He is in here, they have prepared him for your visit.'

Poppy nodded. She started to wonder if she would be able to recognise him. 'Does he, does he look...' Her question was intercepted by the kindly woman who seemed to know all the right things to say. She had probably stood in front of this door a hundred times before. 'He looks at peace,' she said. 'He looks totally at peace.' Mrs Napier could clearly see that the visitor was a little apprehensive about entering the room. 'Take a moment or two if you are not ready,' she said. 'I can come in with you if you want me to.'

Poppy shook her head. 'No. I would rather see him alone.' She braced herself and took a deep breath. 'I just want to get this over and done with.'

The door was opened for her and Poppy slowly made her way into the room. She noticed the smell when she first entered. It was a musky smell, like decaying flowers. She made her way to the table at the end of the narrow room where a teak coffin rested on top of a cloth-covered table. It was open. She prepared herself, first looking up at the dimmed lights and then, after a huge intake of breath, down at her father.

Her eyes moved along the inside of the casket at the still figure, a light linen cloth shrouding his stiffened body. The first thing that she noticed was his hair, it was almost completely grey. There were strong lines on his forehead and his face was a pasty shade of white, as though some makeup had been applied to his features. He seemed so thin. His cheeks had sunken inwards and his mouth seemed to be so much smaller than she had remembered. But this was him, this was her father. He seemed so weak now. Those bulging shoulders and strong arms had gone and been replaced by the fragile shell of a man. It had only been seventeen years or so since Poppy had last seen him, but it suddenly felt like a lot longer. He had become an old man before he had died, a frail, weak old man, and she hadn't been with him to witness any of those changes.

As Poppy looked down at him, she was still trying hard to find something inside her, anything at all, but there was just nothing there. She tried telling herself that she should cry or at least pretend to cry, that's what people do, they cry. But Poppy didn't feel like shedding any tears, she still felt cheated. She never had the chance to tell him how much hurt and pain she had been through since he abandoned her. She never got the opportunity to see if he was truly remorseful about what he had done, whether he had spent his life regretting his decisions, whether he would have done things differently if he had the chance over again. But probably, most importantly, she never got the chance to look him in the eye and ask him what had really happened to her mother. She knew that she would never know now.

Poppy took one last long look at her father and turned to walk away, bringing an end to all that built-up anger and pain that had been churning around inside her for countless years. Yes, he had cheated her alright, she would have no one to blame now for the way her life had panned out. She could no longer feel that sour bitterness towards him, he was dead.

Around halfway back to those large brown doors, Poppy suddenly stopped. She was curious, she wanted to know what was in the envelope. Maybe there was a confession. Is it possible he would have felt a dying urge to reveal the true fate of his wife, her mother? After all, they can't lock you up in prison when you

363

are dead. Maybe that was it. She would respect him for that. If there was something that let her know what really happened, she might just feel the tiniest molecule of respect for him. She reached inside the envelope and pulled out the contents: a tatty wristwatch with an alligator strap, some spectacles, an old and battered Nokia mobile phone and a wallet engraved with his initials. Mrs Napier had been right, he did not have much to show for his sixty-plus years in this world.

Poppy opened the wallet, still hoping to find something relating to her mother. Inside there were three £10 notes, some paperwork regarding an overdue electricity bill, a couple of torn tickets for a football match, and a flyer from a fitness centre in Oxley village. Poppy looked inside the side compartments to find three or four business cards and an out-of-date bank debit card, but no letter, no confession. Even now he was going to keep the truth from her. She suddenly noticed that behind the bank notes there was a photograph. It was folded in half. She opened the picture. It immediately brought a small smile to her face. It was a picture of a man sitting down at a wooden table, a table identical to the one she had sat at the previous day. He was holding a young girl, a pretty girl, wearing a bright blue T-shirt. She instantly recognised the man, he was lying down behind her now, resting. But he looked different in the picture, he had those big strong arms and his face was tanned, he didn't look pale and pasty at all. His arms were wrapped around the small child. He was holding her tightly, so tightly, as if he would never let her go. She studied the picture of the young girl closely. She remembered the bright blue T-shirt, she remembered those black jeans, she even remembered the flowery trainers that the child had on her feet. But she didn't recognise that little girl. She could see that she was smiling, a huge smile, she looked happy, so happy, she looked so innocent, so very innocent. Poppy ran her fingers over the photograph, as if she was trying to bring the people in that picture to life. She wished for a few seconds that the man lying behind her was not dead, that she could speak to him. But those thoughts did not last longer than those few seconds.

As Poppy began to replace the remnants of her father's life back into his wallet, she noticed a tiny compartment at the back. There was something inside, it was hard, it felt like coins. When she unzipped the small pocket, it dropped out. It was an object that made the hairs stand up sharply on the back of her neck. She held it in the palm of her hand and began to shake. It was broken now, both the letter 'T' and 'D' were chipped in half, the lion had lost its tail, but she remembered that keyring as if she had only bought it the day before. Why had he kept it all this time? Why had he done this to her? It wasn't fair, she didn't want this, she needed to despise him, she didn't want to remember him in good ways. Why had he kept this token of her affection for all these years?

Suddenly, something happened, something very strange, an overwhelming feeling of vulnerability hit Poppy. She felt very weak, as if her knees were about to collapse beneath her. Just then, her lip began to tremble and then a tear, a large tear, escaped from the corner of her eye and ran down her cheek. She wiped the tear away as if to dismiss it. There was no way that she would give this man, dead or alive, the satisfaction of seeing her cry. But she could not stop the second or the third tear as they slithered down her face. Before she knew what was happening both of her eyes had clouded over and that mountain of ice in her veins had begun to melt. She felt a pain, as if someone had kicked her in the stomach. It hurt, it hurt so differently to any pain she could ever remember. She clutched the tiny souvenir and held it close to her chest. Her mouth was dry, but she felt the need to speak. Her voice was weak and croaky, but her words were distinct. 'They broke me, Daddy, they all broke me, and you let them do that!'

The tiny trickles of tears had suddenly become a stream, an unstoppable stream. 'You just left me there, you just left me there, alone. I never knew why you didn't come back for me, Daddy, you promised you would come back for me. I waited there, at the big window, every Saturday, I waited there, looking out for you. I thought we would go out, away from that place, I thought you would take me somewhere, anywhere. We could have had ice cream, the mint one, with the chocolate sauce and the hundred and thousands. You knew that was my favourite, you always knew that, Daddy, didn't you?'

Poppy wanted to stop speaking, but she couldn't, her heart would not let her. 'They laughed at me, all of those other kids, they just laughed at me. They told me that you were never coming back, but I still waited, every week, I still waited at the window. I just wanted to see you again, Daddy, I needed to know that you still cared about me.' As Poppy dried some of the tears from her face with the bloodstained sleeve of her jacket, she looked at the photograph of her and her father again. She had a different feeling inside now, she didn't know what it was. 'What did I do that was so bad that you would just leave me with all those evil people? I tried my best to be a good girl, to make you and Mummy happy. And now this is what you have made me, this, this terrible person, this monster, you did this to me, Daddy, you made me like this.'

Just when Poppy thought that she had said enough, that she should stop, there was more, she couldn't hold back now, she had to tell him everything that had been burning inside her for all these years. 'I wish I knew, I wish you was here to tell me, to tell me what I did that was so wrong that you would just give up on me. I just need to understand.'

Poppy turned around slowly to look back down at the silent figure, lying peacefully beneath her. 'I never said I hated you, Daddy.' She took a moment's silence, perhaps remembering some better days, maybe at the boating lake, maybe somewhere else. Moving her arm forward she reached down and touched his face gently. 'I never said I hated you, I never said that, even after what you did to me. I can't ever forgive you, Daddy, but I will never ever hate you.' With those words, Poppy kissed her fingers and pressed them down onto her father's cold lips. Something very real began to evolve inside her troubled mind, as if she had suddenly realised that this would be the last time she would ever see him.

'Goodnight, Daddy!' she said, just as the innocent little girl in that photograph had done all those years before.

* * *

Shortly after leaving the hospital Poppy made a journey to some local shops. She knew that she needed petrol for her car but felt sure that her trusty Omega would get her to her last destination. She spent most of the £30 that she had just inherited from her father on some essentials: a toothbrush and some toothpaste, two £5 pay-as-you-go SIM cards, some sanitary towels and some tobacco and Rizla papers. Making a small slit in the wrapper of the towels she pushed the SIM cards inside to conceal them inside the box. She knew that these would provide a small bargaining tool in the place where she would end up that day. She had originally toyed with the idea of spending the money with a dealer she knew, close to the Marfield. She was still in a state of bewilderment. She thought it might be a good idea to take something, maybe take the edge off the terrible moment that she was living in. But something told her that she would be better off having a clear head for the trials that lay ahead.

Arriving at Chez Blanc, she was a little surprised to see that most of the lights were turned off inside the restaurant. The car park was empty, apart from Danny's vehicle parked in the corner. Riffling through her glove compartment Poppy found an envelope. It was a bit creased and grubby, but it would have to suffice. She searched her bag hoping to find a pen but had to settle for an eyebrow pencil from her makeup bag. Poppy pondered on her thoughts for a few seconds before scribbling some words down on the envelope. '*Danny, please sell car to help pay for damages. I am giving myself up.*' Placing her car keys inside the envelope, she sealed it and sat in deep thought for a few minutes. This place had been good to her. The restaurant and Danny had always felt like another safe place in her life. She looked over at the dimly lit windows of Chez Blanc and remembered how good it had felt when he had called her that day to tell her that she had got the job. There were some good moments from here that she could take with her, despite everything that had happened in the past few days. They would always be good memories that might help her get through her next ordeal. Turning the envelope over Poppy added a few simple words with her pencil, in the hope that Danny would not judge her crazy actions too harshly. He had truly been one of the only people she had ever met who cared about her as a person. Someone who was prepared to forget her past and accept her for what she really was. Someone she had felt that she had been truly able to call a friend. Poppy scribbled her final message for him. '*I am sorry. Please don't hate me. P x*'

As Poppy left her car, she noticed some movement inside the restaurant and walked slowly to the back window, peering through the glass at a slight angle so she would not be seen. Most of the lights were turned off but she could make out the shape of someone sitting at a table in the dining area. It was Danny, he was alone. A very big part of her wanted to enter the back door and give him a hug, a very tight and very long hug, to tell him that she was sorry. Maybe she would never let him go. A crazy thought entered her head as she rubbed the glass to see him more clearly. Maybe there was another way out of this mess. If she asked him, she felt sure he would help. Maybe he could hide her in his wine cellar, she could live there, at least until the police stopped looking for her. She wouldn't want anything, maybe some of the leftover food each day to keep her alive and she could clean the restaurant for him in return. In a few weeks the police would stop looking for her. She could change her hairstyle, maybe cut it all off, she could pretend to be someone else. 'Nikita', she could say that her name was 'Nikita'. It seemed mad but just for the tiniest moment in

Poppy's mixed-up brain it all made sense. If anyone in this world was going to give her another chance, it would be Danny.

But as the image of the restaurant owner became clearer, she could see that Danny was not totally alone. There on the table in front of him was a bottle of brandy, a large bottle of brandy. It was half empty. Her sudden rush of blood to the head was replaced with an overwhelming feeling of guilt. For the second time that day, Poppy had a feeling that was totally alien to her, it was a feeling of shame. This was her fault, this was all her fault. Her face slowly changed to one of despair and she dragged her feet across the car park to where Danny's car was situated. She slid the envelope underneath his windscreen wiper and began the short walk down the high street in the direction of the police station. This was it, there was no way out for her now.

\* \* \*

It wasn't very busy inside the police station. There was a young couple being seen to by the duty officer, and a black woman with a teenage boy were sitting on the chairs in deep conversation. Poppy gave her name to the woman at the desk and stated the reason for her being there. The woman raised her eyebrows and looked Poppy up and down, as though she was already sizing her up for her new prison uniform. While she was waiting, Poppy checked over the items she had bought earlier and packed them in a small carrier bag. It was so very quiet and peaceful in the reception area, she could hear most of the discussion between the woman and her teenage son. They appeared to be rowing over whether they should tell the police who they thought had stolen his pushbike. The boy seemed to be arguing the point that he was better off without his transport than facing the wrath of the group of lads who he had seen take it. Poppy reached into her jacket pocket, remembering that she still had the souvenir tucked away in there. As she looked again at the chipped keyring, the symbol of a day she was unlikely to forget in a hurry, her eyes lit up as she suddenly remembered the morning she had given it to him, how her father had hugged her tightly when he unwrapped it and told her that it was the best present he had ever received.

She was still deep in thought and had not noticed the main door opening behind her, nor had she seen the three burly police officers and the WPC rushing towards her. Suddenly Poppy's legs were taken from beneath her and her forehead hit the floor, the weight of two of the big brutes in uniform forcing her downwards, while the others grabbed her arms. They were all shouting at her, telling her not to resist. An officer's knee pushed down hard on the back of her neck, despite the fact that she was making no attempt at all to struggle. Both of her arms were twisted up behind her back and she suddenly felt the sharp squeezing on her wrists, as the handcuffs were forced into place.

As she lay there on the floor of the police station, she could see it, somewhere between the shiny shoes of one of the police officers. The keyring. It was only a few inches from her face. She wasn't sure why, but it gave her a reason to smile. And that is when it hit her, that is when Poppy knew that she was back, she was back where she belonged, the world would not miss her, it would be a safer place now that she was in custody.

Something in her head told her that it would be a very long time before she would see freedom again.

# CHAPTER
# TWENTY-SEVEN

A dark gloom had settled over the walls of Downview prison, the blackening skies above giving a clear sign that the unusually mild November weather was coming to an end. Bree was out of her comfort zone, a million miles out of her comfort zone. Her pink cashmere coat stood out like a giant colouful lollipop amongst the scruffy jeans and tacky tracksuits of the other visitors. She felt nervous, yet excited. She was still finding it hard to take in the fact that her sibling had agreed to her visit. She did her best to avoid eye contact with any of the people around her as she shuffled her feet along to join the small queue leading into the prison.

As the small crowd of visitors moved through the entrance gate, Bree clutched her precious Louis Vuitton bag close to her chest, not realising that this would be the last place on earth that anyone would try to steal it. She listened closely to the conversations around her. *They seem like normal people*, she thought, *just like me, just visiting their loved ones in this daunting arena.* Her heart raced faster as she entered the main prison building. It had been five weeks since she had last seen her sibling in court and nearly three months since the incident at the bistro. Bree was trying hard to think of things to say, but for that moment her mind was totally blank.

The guards went through their usual search procedures and one by one the visitors were ushered into a small hall. Everything seemed so surreal to Bree. Never in her wildest dreams would she have thought that she would be in a place like this. She studied her surroundings as she sat in a seat in the middle of the visiting room. The walls were bare, they were a dirty shade of vanilla, the tables were old and wobbly and looked as if they had not been cleaned for weeks. Her fellow visitors were laughing and joking amongst themselves as they waited for the captives to arrive. They all seemed to be taking this in their stride, as if it was a day out to the funfair or the zoo.

A large cheer went up amongst the visiting crew as the first of the inmates appeared from behind a door in the corner of the room, followed closely by several more. Bree was expecting to see stripy prison suits or bright orange all-in-ones, like those she had seen in American crime movies. But she was wrong, the inmates were all dressed in standard clothing. The only thing that made them stand out were the bright red bibs covering their tops. Two uniformed guards, one male, one female, led the prisoners into the arena and watched on as the exhibits were met by their loved ones. Bree was fascinated by the array of women adorned in bibs. Most of them looked so rough. Bright and menacing tattoos stood out on some of their necks and arms, some were missing teeth, one or two, however, looked, well, just like normal people. The last inmate to appear was Poppy. She bowled into the hall as if she owned the place. Bree overheard the girl at the table to her side whisper to her visitor, 'That's her, that's the mad bitch I told you about.'

As soon as Poppy had entered the fray Bree raised her arm, but her sibling had already seen her and was making her way towards her. As she neared the table Bree sensed that her sister looked smaller than she had remembered. As her washed-out features and disheveled appearance slowly became more apparent to her visitor, she could see scratch marks on her knuckles and she was wearing a bandage on her right wrist. As Poppy sat down Bree could not help but notice that she also had cuts and bruises on the side of her face and her left ear seemed to be twice the size it should be. When she was opposite, the bright fluorescent light above her head revealed the two old scars on her neck. They were long and deep, as if someone had once attacked her with a knife. Bree breathed in deeply, the moment had finally arrived.

Poppy looked around the room, handing out a harsh stare to the mixed-race girl sitting at the adjacent table, before opening the conversation. 'Fuck! Are you wearing perfume, missy?'

Bree nodded. 'Creed Aventus,' she said, her mouth feeling dry as the words left her lips.

'You did know where you were coming today?' Poppy asked.

'Yes,' Bree muttered, realising that the generous spray of her fragrance was now lingering around their table.

'I don't know why you wanted to come, missy,' Poppy said. 'I said all I had to say in the restaurant.'

Bree's mouth was still dry, but she found a small voice again. 'I wanted to come here to see you, err… I wanted to err… Thank you for letting me come.'

Poppy shrugged her shoulders. 'I can't really stop you anymore, can I?'

Bree's heart was racing, she was here, she was sitting opposite her sister. She had been waiting for this day for weeks, but now she was lost for words. She sat up straight in her chair and tried again. 'I bought you these,' she said, handing Poppy two fashion magazines. 'I was going to get you a book, but I didn't know what…' Poppy interrupted her. 'A book! A fucking book?!'

Bree quickly realised her mistake. What in God's name ever made her buy those magazines? she thought. She quickly changed the subject. 'They searched me when I came in, they had dogs sniff inside my bag.'

'They search everyone,' Poppy replied. 'Even the posh fuckers with snooty labels hanging around their necks.'

'Oh, what for drugs and stuff?'

'Drugs, blades, SIM cards. You didn't manage to sneak any of those in, did you?'

Bree shook her head and laughed. 'No, of course not.'

'Shame!' Poppy said, her attention once again distracted by the girl on the table to her side.

'What's it like, prison?' Bree asked. 'What's it really like in here?'

'Oh, it's just one big fucking hen party from start to finish,' Poppy replied, hoping that her visitor would see that she was being sarcastic.

Bree was still staring at the bruises on her sibling's face. 'Did you do that in here?'

'It comes with the territory.'

'And your hand?'

'Why did you want to come here? It's not to talk about my welfare in prison?'

'You are my sister.'

'Let's get this straight. If your mother really did fuck my old man, we are half-sisters, not full sisters, we are just half-sisters, have you got that?'

Bree nodded. 'But we are still related.'

'Oh, so you want to come here every week now and tell me how my new family are doing? Which uncle bought a Mercedes and what you thought of the fucking play you went to see at the theatre?'

'No, of course not. I came here to see how you were, to see if we could, maybe, I was hoping that we might be able to clear the air.'

'What, and you bring me fucking magazines! Jesus Christ!'

'I am sorry, I got that wrong, OK. I just thought that maybe, if we got the chance to talk again, we could, I mean, that I could understand. I didn't expect all these people, I thought it would be a private room.'

'A private room! Do you live on another planet or something? You know you are not so out of place in here, missy, this prison is full of weirdos. Just look around you, these women are murderers, druggies, thieves.' Poppy moved closer and raised her voice. 'Stalkers!'

'What do you mean?'

'I saw you there, at the sentencing hearing. That was you wasn't it, sitting next to Danny?'

'I went there to support you.'

Poppy laughed. 'God give me fucking strength, support me! You really don't have a clue, do you?'

'I tried to persuade Kayleigh to drop the charges before we knew how you were going to plead.'

'That's your friend, the mouthy one, from the restaurant?'

'Yes.'

'Stupid bitch, she was asking for it. I warned her, I told her to keep her fucking beak out of it.'

''You fractured her cheekbone, Poppy, she is scarred for life. Don't you feel any remorse at all?'

'Oh, boo-hoo-hoo, poor fucking Kayleigh. Tell you what, I will make her a 'get well soon' card in my workshop and send it her if it makes you feel better.'

Bree was slightly angered by her sibling's heartless comment but persevered. 'You pleaded guilty, to everything!'

'As if I had any choice.'

'It was GBH wasn't it, grievous bodily harm?'

'You were there, you heard everything.'

'But he was OK, that Cameron guy, apart from some broken bones and scars, he wasn't damaged permanently?'

'If he has brain damage it is down to all that poisonous shit he puts in his body, not down to me.'

'The newspapers said he was in some residential rehab centre in Portsmouth or Southampton or somewhere down there. They said he was recovering well.'

'Another fucking waste of tax payers' money. Cameron is a lost cause, he will never get off the gear.'

'Five and a half years, they sentenced you to five and a half years, so you will be out in half?'

Poppy laughed. 'Don't kid yourself, missy, these bastards are never going to let me out of this place now.'

'What do you mean?'

'They have got me now, they will find a reason to keep me in here this time, trust me.'

'Because of what happened before, to that young kid?'

'Young kid?'

'Billy Keyes, the young boy that you, well, you know, what you did, I read about what happened.'

Poppy sat back in her chair and looked around the room. She was angry, she didn't want to show it, but she was seething inside. 'Don't believe everything you read in the papers, missy.'

'You killed him! You stabbed him more than twenty times. He was only a kid, barely seventeen, I read it, the whole story, it was all over the internet.'

'Yeah, yeah, poor innocent Billy fucking Keyes, what an angel!'

'Well, what's the truth then?'

Poppy laughed and looked her visitor straight in the eye. 'You couldn't handle the truth, missy.'

'Try me.'

Poppy pondered for a few seconds. Maybe, she thought, maybe this was her chance to get rid of this nuisance in front of her. She decided to give the girl opposite the full uncensored version of events. She leaned forward, she wanted her newfound stalker to hear every word clearly. 'Billy Keyes was a grade A cunt,' she said, gritting her teeth. 'His brothers ran the Marfield estate with an iron fist and Billy was their recruiter.'

'Recruiter?'

'He gave schoolkids free booze and fags to start with, and then introduced them to free weed, sometimes ecstasy. Before long he had them hooked, got them onto harder stuff – coke, spice, crack – fuck, some of them poor kids were on brown before they were fourteen years old.'

'Brown, that's heroin, right?'

'Wow! I am impressed, missy is learning fast.'

'For free?'

'Get real, missy, nothing is for free in this life. Once those kids were hooked on the gear, the Keyes brothers could charge what they liked. Kids were giving away their Nintendos, selling their designer trainers, stealing cash from their parents. They would do anything for their next high.'

'Did you buy drugs, I mean did you buy from him, from Billy?'

'Sometimes, the brothers ran the Marfield, you had to travel miles to get your fix elsewhere.'

'Is that why you killed him? Was it an argument over drugs?'

Poppy took a deep breath and clenched her fists tightly. 'I had a friend. Don't look so surprised. She was a good friend, she gave me a place to stay, looked after me and all that.' Poppy paused for a few seconds, she never found it easy talking about Nikita. 'She had her baby taken away by Social Services, so she was on a massive downer, that little kid was her whole world. So she needed something, something to help her, something to make her pain go away. She didn't have any money, the Social had sanctioned her benefits, she had been on the rattle for four days. She told me that Billy was going to fix her up, he would give her something. I begged her not to go, I pleaded with her, I knew what he was like. She had no money, she would do anything to score that day, I knew it would be favours.'

'Favours?' Bree asked.

'Blow jobs, sex, blow jobs. Fuck, what it must be like to live in your little world!'

'So what happened, did she go there?'

Bree could see the rage building in Poppy's face as she continued her story. 'So the 'angel' Billy Keyes gets her to blow half a dozen of his mates on the Marfield for a bag of brown.' Poppy paused again as the memory of that day came back to haunt her. She bit her lip hard and continued. 'They filmed it, on their mobiles, his fucking mates, they all filmed it. Her fucking blowbang show was up on the internet before she had wiped the last drops of spunk from her face.'

'Is that why you...?'

Poppy suddenly snapped. 'She died, you fucking idiot! He gave her a bag of bad gear and she fucking died. After his mates had finished with her Billy threw her a bag of bad shit and she used it all, she died.' Bree could see how much her sister had cared for the girl she was talking about. 'They found her the next morning in an alleyway. She was lying there amongst the dog shit and chip wrappers. My friend, my only fucking friend in the world and he killed her. He humiliated her and then he killed her.'

Bree was shocked. 'Jesus! I didn't know.'

'That's why I sliced that no-good cunt up. I did the Marfield a favour, good riddance to bad rubbish. Fuck Billy Keyes! I hope he rots in hell!'

Poppy could see that her visitor was too shocked to respond. Maybe she would finally leave her in peace now and drop all of this 'long-lost sisters' nonsense. 'They don't print shit like that in the *Guardian* or *Times* or whatever newspaper you read, do they?' she asked.

Bree still had questions, she wanted to know everything. 'Why did the media crucify you? Why did they all want you to go to prison for life if that's what really happened?'

'I had a good brief.'

'What!'

'My brief said that if I told the court that I was high on drugs and pleaded guilty to manslaughter, it would be a seven-to-ten stretch, diminished responsibility or some shit like that.' Poppy mimicked her submission to the court at her murder trial. 'Oh, look at me, judge, another poor victim of drug addiction. I would never have done it if I was clean. Please help me, I am just a victim of society.' Poppy laughed. 'And it worked for me. The jury never got all the facts, they never got to hear the real reason I did it. So the public all hated me, they wanted me to be shoved in a loony bin for the rest of my life. But the jury said, 'Poor little cow! She didn't know what she was doing.''

'And were you, were you high, when you stabbed him?'

Poppy's eyes narrowed and a sinister smile cracked on her face. 'I knew exactly what I was doing when I carved up that fucking weasel, trust me. The only high that I was on was revenge.'

Bree could not believe how brazen her sister was, telling her the reason she had stabbed Billy Keyes to death, as if she had been describing a trip to a shopping centre. It was strange, Bree should be in total shock, but rather than feel scared she was somewhat in awe of her sibling. She wanted to know more, she wanted to know much more about this side of Poppy's life. 'So, the guy at your flat, this Cameron fella, he was your boyfriend?' she asked. Poppy didn't answer, her attention was once again drawn to the girl and her visitor at the table to the side of them. She could hear them talking about her. Poppy stared full on at her fellow inmate before blowing her an imaginary kiss. The girl swiftly turned her head away, but not before Bree had caught a look at the other side of her face. It was covered in bruises and her right eye was half closed. She looked as if she had been in a boxing match. Bree said nothing to her sister, it didn't take Einstein to work out that this girl was not exactly Poppy's best friend inside the prison.

'Your boyfriend!' Bree asked again. 'You were going to tell me what happened, that night, after you left the restaurant.'

Poppy stretched her arms. She was becoming tired of her sibling's questions. She did, however, have one of her own. 'That night, in the restaurant, when you were there with your friend, the gobby one, was you being brave or are you really that dumb?'

Bree knew what she meant, but in truth did not know the answer herself. 'I knew you couldn't hurt me, Poppy, I knew that you wouldn't hurt me, not once you knew that I was really your sister.'

Poppy stared at her opposite number for a few seconds before letting out a small laugh. 'You have balls, missy, I will give you that, you have balls, but don't kid yourself, you really don't know anything about me at all!' Despite the fact she had acknowledged her sister's bravery, Poppy still felt the need to correct her sibling. 'And I have told you before, missy, we are not sisters, we are only half-sisters.'

Bree was aware that the time was passing fast. One hour visiting time was never going to be long enough to ask all the questions she had in her head. She changed the direction of the conversation. She was eager to learn more about the man who was responsible for bringing the unlikely duo together. 'What was he like?' she asked. 'Your father, my real father, what was he like?' Poppy pondered on the question for a moment before declaring, 'He was just a waste of space, a selfish waste of space. Trust me, you were better off not knowing him.'

'But when you were younger, did he, I don't know, did he ever take you to ballet lessons or come to watch you in school plays or stuff like that?'

'Why is that important to you?'

'I don't know, I am just curious. I know you say he was a waste of space but there must have been good times, it can't have been all bad?'

Poppy smiled. 'I don't think you want to know what he was really like, missy. Let's just say, he wasn't your average dad.'

'Did he ever hit you?'

'Sometimes, just, you know if I made too much noise or answered him back. It was the drink, once he was on the drink, it was best to just keep out of his way.'

'He was an alcoholic?'

'I only really knew what other people have said about him. He dumped me into care when I was eight. I didn't see him much after that.'

'Is that why you don't like to talk about him?'

'You have got a lot of fucking questions, missy. Let's just leave it there, you were better off not knowing him.'

Bree paused for a few seconds. She could see that Poppy was not going to discuss her childhood. 'You did go though?' she asked. 'To his funeral, you did go, didn't you?'

Poppy leaned forward and sneered at her opposite number. 'I am surprised you were not there, wrapped up in some black Gucci number for the occasion, you seem to love all of this family reunion shit.'

Bree shook her head. 'No, I didn't even know where it was. Was he buried or cremated?'

'Cremated,' Poppy said and suddenly laughed out loud. 'Fuck, he was even late for his own funeral, the car with his box in went to the wrong crematorium. Now that was funny, it was worth the day out just to witness that shit.'

Bree noticed that the two guards were now looking at their watches. Time must nearly be up. She knew that this would be the last time she would see her sibling. She did not want to go without letting her know that her father also had a son. She started a well-rehearsed speech. 'I get it, Poppy, I get what you have been through, but it doesn't mean that we can't...'

Poppy interrupted Bree's patter, she was clearly angered by her sister's comment. 'You get it! You get what?'

Bree quickly realised that her comment had not gone down well. 'I didn't mean to...'

'No, missy! Don't come here with your perfectly painted nails and your designer fucking coat and tell me you get it. You don't get it! You could never get it! You could never walk a fucking day in my shoes or have lived through what I have. Don't stroll in here like 'Lady Shit' and tell me you fucking get it!'

Bree began to backtrack, she tried to explain but only made things worse. 'I want to understand, Poppy, I want to try to understand why you, I mean what you, I am sorry, I didn't mean to, I am just trying to understand.'

'Well don't! My life is my life, it has fuck all to do with you!'

'I am really sorry, Poppy, I say things sometimes without thinking. It has been a really tough year for me.'

'Tough? Yeah, sure it has, what happened? Did your round-the-world cruise get cancelled or something?'

'I lost my brother, my twin brother,' Bree said, looking down at the table. 'My brother, he was our brother, a year ago, a year ago today.'

'Lost?'

'He died, there was a terrible accident.'

Poppy shrugged her shoulders and looked around the room again. She didn't have any words of comfort for her visitor. 'What do you want me to say, 'sorry for your loss'? I never knew him.'

Bree wiped a tear from her eye. 'He would have liked you, Jamie, he would have loved your free spirit and your 'fuck everyone' approach to life.'

Bree sneered at her sibling's revelation. 'Oh right, I get it now, so twin bro has fucked off and left you and you want me to replace him. That's why you were so desperate for me and you to be best buddies, that's what all this sisters bullshit is about!'

'No, I just wanted to know you, to say I had met you, that you knew about me and Jamie.'

'Life don't work like that, missy, shit happens, people die. You can't just replace your brother with some fucking random girl that happens to have come from the same spunk that you did.'

It was Bree's turn to be angry now, Poppy had overstepped the mark. 'You can't replace Jamie!' she snapped. 'No one can. He was my life, he was my whole world. Mock me all you like, Poppy, but don't say anything bad about Jamie.'

Poppy sighed and slumped back into her chair. 'So, I guess that's a card for your mouthy friend and a sympathy card for dead bro. Fuck, I am going to be busy in the workshop this week!'

Bree was fuming. She had finally had enough of her sibling's put-downs. She reached forward and grabbed the bandage on Poppy's arm, squeezing it tightly, watching her sister's face twist with pain. 'I told you, don't ever speak bad of Jamie, do you understand?'

Poppy winced as Bree tightened her grip and she felt a pain shoot upwards through her arm. 'Woah!' she said. 'I have touched a nerve and suddenly missy has grown a backbone. Now let go of my arm before I rip those cute fucking eyes out of their sockets.'

Bree stood her ground, gripping tighter on her sister's injury, watching her stern face twist as the pain intensified. 'Do you know,' Bree said, 'I came here today hoping that I might get the chance to find out more about you, maybe make the peace with you. I thought you would at least listen to what I had to say. But no, something in that sick fucking head of yours wants to shut everyone out, people that may give a shit about you, people that might care!'

Poppy moved in closer to show her sibling that she held no fear, the look of pain on her face swiftly replaced by one of rage. They were now just inches apart, they looked full-on into the opposite's eyes, searching, deeper and deeper in the other's soul. It was a strange experience, it was as if they were both staring into a hollow mirror, each seeing the thoughts of the other, embedded at the end of a long dark tunnel. 'I am not scared of you,' Bree said, finally releasing her grip on her sister's arm. 'I will never be scared of you, Poppy.' Neither of them moved and no further words were spoken. It seemed as if they had found something in that last exchange, something disturbing. Neither of them knew what it was. It sent a chill running through their bones.

Suddenly, the sharp tone of the bell in the corner of the room broke the stony silence. The sound indicated that the visiting hour was over, it was time for Poppy to leave. Within a matter of seconds most of the inmates began heading one way, while their visitors headed off in the other. Some romantic gestures and heartfelt promises were made by the parting couples, a young child burst into a flood of tears as his mother waved him goodbye. Poppy had been the last to arrive in the visiting room and she would be the last to leave, kicking her chair backwards and heading for the queue of fellow inmates without so much as a 'by your leave' for her sibling.

As she joined the huddle of prisoners preparing to exit the side door they had arrived from, Poppy looked back at her visitor. Bree hadn't moved, she was still sitting at the table, her head bowed, a forlorn figure. Her newfound bravado seemed to have disappeared and been replaced with a look of total rejection. Suddenly Poppy called out to her, her voice echoing around the walls of the emptying arena. 'Hey Rhianna, Brianna, whatever your name is, it's time to leave, you can go home now.'

Raising her head slightly, Bree stared at her sister. 'It is Bree,' she muttered under her breath. 'My name is fucking Bree!'

As Poppy neared the exit door to enter the confines of the main prison she called out to her sibling once more. 'Hey, missy, he did come to watch me in a school play, one Christmas, I was about six, he was steaming, off his face on booze. The teachers threw him out halfway through the show, he was sound asleep, snoring like a baby.' Bree's face suddenly lit up. Her sister had finally acknowledged her existence. It was enough for Bree, just hearing that was enough, her journey had not been wasted. She didn't want her to go now, she wanted to know more, anything, anything at all. She needed to know more about her, about them, her and her father. Just as Poppy was about to disappear she left her sibling with a parting remark that brought a broad smile to her sad features. 'And really, girl, get a grip, can you imagine me in a fucking ballet dress?'

A small tear appeared in Bree's eye as her sister disappeared from her view. It was a tear of sadness. She suddenly felt empty inside, empty and lost, because she knew in her heart that this would be the last time that she would ever see her sister. 'Goodbye, Poppy' she said, her smile replaced with a small frown. 'I hope you find some peace in your life.'

En route to her cell Poppy gave the mixed-race girl a long hard look. The altercation the two of them had been involved in the previous day had seemed trivial at the time, but Poppy wanted her fellow inmate to be under no illusion that she was no pushover. The damaged girl with the fierce temper was frightened of no one and she was willing to carry out her own brand of punishment on anyone who messed with her. The girl avoided her stare, giving Poppy an immediate psychological advantage over her new enemy.

Poppy entered her cell with a strange feeling inside her. She felt as if she had met Bree a long time ago, it was as if she had known her her whole life, despite the fact she had only ever seen her a few times. She didn't know what it was, but it felt as if they had a connection, a real connection. It confused her slightly.

As she sat on her bed, she looked over at the crumpled photograph of her and her father. The picture was stuck to the wall courtesy of some Blu Tack supplied by her cellmate. As she studied the photo more closely, she pushed gently against a small object that was swinging from the makeshift shelf beside her. It was a simple object, a slightly battered keyring that was to become her constant companion for the years ahead. Taking a closer look at the fading picture, something brought a smile to her face. Part of her wanted to tear the photograph into a thousand pieces but a bigger part of her wanted to laugh out loud. 'Poor cow!' she said. 'She even has our fucking nose.'

There were three hours to kill before dinner, three long and arduous hours that would be more taxing on the brain than anyone could ever imagine. The constant sound of fellow inmates whinging and whining across the landing, the woman in the adjacent cell who seemed to burst into tears at least once an hour and the hawk-like eyes of the prison guards scrutinising her every move. Poppy pushed the tiny souvenir of her past to keep it swinging, staring at it intently as if she was hoping that she would be hypnotised by its backwards and forwards motions, sending her to sleep, taking her away from this stark reality. It didn't work, but she found its presence to be a comfort to her.

Poppy picked up the items left by her sister and lay back on her hard pillow. She began to flick through the pages of one of the fashion magazines, sneering at most of the bright images of stunning zero-sized models clad in highbrow clothing, before declaring, 'God! What sort of people read this fucking shit?'

# CHAPTER
# TWENTY-EIGHT

T he clouds above the prison walls had fulfilled their earlier promise and the rain had begun to fall as Bree made her way back to her car. She took a few minutes to take in the final image of where her sister was to be housed for the foreseeable future before driving to her intended destination. There was so much more she would have liked to know about Poppy, a thousand questions she would never have answered. But she felt that she had made the peace with her sibling and that would make her final journey that much easier.

Bree arrived at the Maple crossing just as a freight train hurtled by, its noisy engine ripping through the damp air, polluting the peaceful countryside setting. Seconds later the barrier was raised and she drove to the other side. A small shudder ran through her as she sensed the stark reality of this location. This was the first time she had been here since it happened, but she had an inner resolve today, she felt stronger than she had felt in a very long time.

She parked her Mercedes in a nearby side street and made the short walk back to the crossing. It was strange, it seemed to be welcoming her return, as if it was pleased she had come back. She immediately noticed two displays of fresh flowers that had been left by the barriers. She didn't have to guess who the ivory lilies were from. It warmed her inside to know that Maisie and her mother had not forgotten the anniversary of Jamie's death. The other display was a colourful assortment of carnations and germini, with a card showing that Preston and Jamie's friends from the gym had earmarked the date of the event. Bree never did like Preston very much, but for the few seconds it took her to read his personal inscription on the card, he had turned from sinner to saint in her eyes. His words seemed heartfelt as if he genuinely missed the antics of his work colleague.

The grey sky was becoming darker and the rain was falling more steadily as Bree stood at the crossing in sombre silence. She looked down at the dark puddle that was growing beneath her feet and began to remember what a fuss she had made over her new boots on that fateful day. She suddenly felt ashamed of her petulant behaviour. Nothing should have mattered that day, or any other day since Jamie left her. She did not speak in those small moments, she didn't need to. She knew that it would not be long before she could tell her brother everything she had been wanting to say since they parted. She picked off the two small cards that had been left with the flowers. She wanted Jamie to know how much he was truly missed.

Bree's second port of call was one that she did with a heavy heart. She posted a letter in a small post box on the outskirts of Oxley village. It was a simple letter, addressed to foreign shores. She had checked the postage carefully the previous day to make sure it would reach its destination. The letter was not addressed to her mother, although in truth it should have been. Even at this late juncture in her troubled life, Bree was not prepared to give her parent the respect she craved. The letter had been with Bree for some time, locked safely away in a drawer in her bedroom, but she had never felt the desire to relay its contents to her parents before today. It was not a long letter and was self-explanatory. The words written some time before would ensure that her mother would be left in no doubt as to the irreversible damage she had done to her children when she tried to tear apart the unbreakable bond that existed between them. The message in the letter would cause great pain to the woman who divided the love the siblings had shared and explain why Jamie was no longer here. Perhaps, Bree thought in hindsight, she should have addressed the letter to her mother rather than to Per. After all, he would always find a way to make the words of the note sound softer, more comforting. He would be the support that would get her mother through the tragic truth she was about to discover. Bless Per, she thought, he might just be a puppet in her mother's eyes, but he would always be the best father she could ever have wished for.

She posted the letter at 4.12pm and made her way back to her car. A small crack of thunder could be heard in the distance as the light began to fade in the skies above. She was ready now, she was ready to make that short journey that would take her to her final calling. She had made a promise to herself, a promise that she had postponed several times before, it had never been the right time. But today, the time was right, today it was perfect.

Bree made the seven-minute journey to the east of Guildford town centre and entered the multi-storey car park. This was not a random choice of venue, she had chosen this place some months before when she had been on one of her shopping trips. She carefully manoeuvred her Mercedes up through the winding concrete pathway. There was plenty of room for her to park on both the fifth and sixth floors, but she chose to drive her car all the way to the roof area. There were only a few other vehicles here, so she was unlikely to be disturbed. After parking her Mercedes, Bree took a moment before applying some makeup and a thin coat of lipstick. She wanted to look her best today. She plugged her mobile phone into the car speaker and found the treasured video of her beloved brother singing at the wedding reception. She watched the footage two or three times, running her finger gently across his smiling face as he danced across her small screen. She could feel his presence in the car, he was here with her, she could sense it. Bree pressed the replay button on her video setting and turned up the volume on her car system so that the sound of her brother's singing would accompany her on her journey. She felt happy, she felt at peace with the world.

The falling rain had now gathered pace as it dropped from the blackening clouds, but it did not bother Bree when she exited her car. If anything, she welcomed the downpour, it added something special to the occasion. She threw her pink cashmere coat onto the back seat, leaving her car door open as she made her way to the rear of her vehicle. She wasn't bothered about how wet the seat covers might get, she needed to hear his voice, singing out to her from those tiny speakers. She retrieved a garment from the boot of her car. It was something special, something that she had been hiding in her wardrobe drawer, something that she had been hiding for too long. She smiled a warm smile and hurriedly slipped the precious item of clothing over her body, laughing as she pulled the hood back from her head. It was beautiful, a bright shiny yellow sort of beautiful. It was long, very long, and big, far too big for her small frame. Bree's tiny hands could barely be seen at the bottom of the sleeves, but she adored it, it was perfect. It immediately made her feel like she belonged here, on this wet and windy rooftop. She walked through the small streams of rainwater that had formed on the car park roof and began to dance, spinning around like a small child, kicking her way through the puddles and pirouetting like a ballerina in a West End show. Jamie's song could be heard in the background. She tried to copy his dance moves, but she couldn't. In her eyes no one ever danced as good as he did.

Bree glided her way across the rain-drenched rooftop in the direction she had travelled from that day. Despite the falling rain and the fading light, there was a clear view. She could see everything that she needed to from that corner of the roof. She had a bird's eye view of the Maple crossing. Bree lifted herself up onto the side of the fence and onto the top of the solid brick wall. There was no hesitation in her step, no fear, she had rehearsed this day so many times in her head, the time she had been waiting for with such eager anticipation had finally arrived. She slipped slightly as she climbed over the small barrier that separated the rooftop from the wall on the outside of the building, but it did not stop her. Standing up on the narrow stretch of bricks she looked down. There was nothing protecting her now. The drop to the street was more than a hundred feet, but it could have been a thousand, ten thousand, she would not have been deterred. Suddenly everything in her line of vision seemed so small. Cars were coming and going beneath her feet and people were rushing across the busy roads below, hiding under their umbrellas, desperate to escape the atrocious weather. Bree stood there for a few seconds before pulling down the hood of her bright yellow raincoat. What did it matter now if her hair was a mess? She closed her eyes for a second or two as the rain lashed down. There was a tinge of excitement running through her veins at that moment. She held no fear whatsoever, she knew that when she jumped that Jamie would catch her, he would hold her in his arms and they would be together again for all eternity. This was to be her 'perfect moment'.

Bree took another look down at the miniature circus below before raising her head towards the sky. 'Isn't this beautiful, Jay?' she said. 'Isn't this rain so sweet and so beautiful?' Stretching her arms out wide to embrace the showers that were falling from the skies, she continued. 'It takes me back, Jay, back to that night.' Bree closed her eyes and took a deep breath. She wanted to smell the air, to taste the rain, it was going to be so special for her. 'It's my time now, my time, Jay. It's time for me and you to be together again. I am not scared, really, I am not scared!'

Above her, the skies continued to darken as the narrow ledge beneath Bree's feet became damper by the second. 'I went to see our sister today, I went to see Poppy. She is a bit, well, you know, she is a bit fucking crazy, Jay, but I like that about her. And she likes me, Jay, I could tell that she likes me now. She told me some things, about her, about him, about our father. Is he there with you, Jamie? Did you find him? Is he up there with you? I hope so, I hope you have found him now.'

The downpour began to increase in intensity, growing in stature as if it was doing its best to mirror the fateful night from the previous year. Bree's hair was now wet through and trickles of rain had found their way inside her bright raincoat and were running down her neck. In the distance she could make out the sounds of a police siren from the busy town centre. She looked down again, the dimming lights below seemed to be making a pathway for her, as if they were calling out to her, inviting her to jump.

'Do you think I look beautiful in this coat, Jay? Do you think it suits me?' Bree asked, pushing back her soaking wet hair. 'Do you remember, Jamie, do you remember that you said that to her? You said that to Jess, on the boat, you said that she looked beautiful, you said that this coat suited her, do you remember, Jay?'

Suddenly one of her feet seemed to lose its grip on the slippery surface and Bree's feet wobbled beneath her. She reached behind her back and grabbed at the barrier in a bid to steady herself. 'I hope she is not with you, Jamie, I hope Jess is not up there with you. You stopped telling me that I was beautiful when Jess came along, you stopped telling me that I was special. It was her then, Jay, it was always Jess, she was always your special one then.'

Bree's thoughts had suddenly become clouded by the memory of her brother's girlfriend and her mood began to take a different turn. She needed to say something. 'I told you that she was no good for you, Jay, I told you so many times, but you never listened to me. You thought you knew her, you thought you knew everything about Jess, but you didn't.' Bree brushed back her hair from her face again, conscious that her brother might be watching her. *He needs to know*, she thought, *he deserves to know*. 'I knew she couldn't swim, Jamie, that's why she didn't want to go on that boat trip. I knew she couldn't swim, she told me, but she didn't tell you, did she?' Bree could not hide the bitterness she was holding onto for much longer, there was a tinge of anger in her voice now. 'I hated you being with her, Jamie, she was no good for you. I knew that you and Jess were talking about me, you were always talking behind my back. You thought I never heard you, Jay, but I did.' Bree looked down at the busy streets below. They seemed to be screaming up at her now, beckoning her to join them, begging her to jump, to end her torment once and for all. Bree's expression slowly changed to one of anguish. 'I heard you, Jay, I heard everything.' She ran her hands up against the side of her face and pushed them against her ears. 'The noises, those noises when she was in your bed, I hated them, I hated them so much, I could hear everything in my room. I cried every night, but you never heard me, you never cared about me anymore, everything was about her, she was your special one then, Jay, everything was always about Jess.'

The sounds of thunder cracked in the distance. The storm was growing and the worst of it seemed to be heading towards the place that she had chosen for her final act. But Bree was oblivious to the deteriorating weather conditions. 'I never felt guilty, Jamie, I have never ever felt bad about what I did. She was no good for you, I never felt anything when I...' Bree smiled, a twisted knowing smile and cut short her confession. 'You don't want to hear that, Jay, do you? You don't want to hear that. But I don't want her to be there with you now, please tell me Jess is not with you. Tell me that you just want me to be with you again, that's all that matters, isn't it? You just want us to be together again.'

A crack of lightning caught Bree unaware and caused her to lose her footing. She clasped more firmly at the rail behind her as if she still needed more time. She still had more to say. 'I could have helped her, Jamie, when she was in the water, I could have helped her, but I didn't, I just watched. I know I should have called you, I should have shouted for you and the captain, I should have told you. But I just watched, Jay. I just waited. I waited until her arms stopped moving and the waves were over her head. I knew I had you back then, Jamie, I knew we could be together again.'

Bree stood in silence for a few seconds, maybe her guilt was finally going to surface, maybe this would be her moment of remorse. But that was not the case, the twisted anger on her face portrayed the darker inner thoughts she truly felt for her brother's lost love. 'She didn't look very beautiful when they pulled her out of the water, did she, Jamie? She wasn't very fucking special then!'

Bree began to feel a bitter emptiness inside her body, as though something precious had been stolen from her at that moment, a frightening realism that she should not be here. She was starting to rethink her whole plan. 'I know that you are with her now, Jay, I know that Jess is there, I know you are both laughing at me.'

Suddenly Bree's legs began to tremble beneath her. Her heart began to race as she looked down and faced the reality of her situation. She seemed to be higher now, so much higher than before. It was too high, she thought, this is too high. Her body began to shake, she started to feel giddy. In an instant her fearlessness had been replaced with total panic. All her bravery had vanished, she grasped tightly onto the barrier and pulled her legs carefully over the railing to safety. Her heart sank deep into her chest and large tears appeared in her eyes. This is not what she wanted, she needed to be with him today, she wanted to feel his touch and hold him tighter than she ever held him before. She had planned this day for so long, but she couldn't find the strength to go through with it, not now, not knowing that Jess might be there too. She didn't want to share her brother with her, not again.

Bree tried to find an escape route, some comfort in the fact that she might have something to live for now. 'I can't be with you,

Jamie,' she shouted at the blackening sky, as though her brother might be looking down, waiting for her to fulfill the promise she had made to him. 'Not today. I can't be with you now, Poppy needs me now, I need to be here for her. I need to help her, Jay. She will get to like me one day.' Her lip began to tremble and her voice became shaky as she faced the harsh reality of her cowardice. 'She may even love me one day, love me like a real sister. I have to be here for her now, you understand, Jay, don't you?'

The dark skies opened wider, unleashing a further torrent of heavy rain. It fell harder and louder on the rooftop around Bree's feet. She pulled her bright yellow raincoat tightly around her neck but seemed to be fighting a losing battle to stay dry. Her dampened face began to show some signs of real concern. She didn't want her brother to think that she had let him down, she hoped in her heart that he would see why she could not go through with her plan. But now she was lost, she was in no man's land. She couldn't join him, but she didn't want to stay here without him. Her mind was full of confusion, her heart was full of pain.

Bree was now deep in thought. Her head was a minefield of bitterness and bewilderment. The more she thought about the past, the angrier she became. There was something more that she needed to say. It broke her in half to do so, but she knew that she could not leave this rooftop until she had told him everything.

'I know you saw me, Jamie, I know you saw me do it. But I wanted you to hurt, the way that I was hurting inside, I wanted you to know what it felt like. What it felt like like to lose someone, someone special. But she was no good for you, Jess was no good for you.'

Bree pushed her soaking locks of hair back behind her ears and looked back up at the darkening storm clouds above. 'You lied to me, Jay, you lied to me when you told me that you loved me, you lied when you said that we would always be together. Why did you want to go away and leave me again? If you really loved me, you would have been there for me. So you lied, Jay, I knew you were never coming back.' Bree became tearful and her voice trembled. She had to shout now to be heard above the constant downpour. 'God, I hated you so much that night, Jamie. She was there again, Jess was back in your thoughts. Why, Jamie, why? Everything was changing again, you were leaving me on my own. After all I did for you, I sacrificed everything to be with you. I never wanted anyone else but you, Jay. I never knew anyone else but you. How could you have been so cruel to me, if you really loved me, like you said you did?'

Suddenly, amidst the swirling rain and fading light Bree found a smile, a sinister self-satisfying smirk that beamed across her soaking wet face. She looked up and laughed at the sky. 'They still think that you did it, did you know that, Jamie? They all think that you wanted to end it all, because of what happened to her, because of what happened to that stupid bitch Jess.'

The tears left her eyes and grew bigger as they rolled down her cheeks. Bree knew he had to hear everything if he was to understand, after all, she was the only living soul that knew what really happened that tragic night at the Maple crossing. 'You were always the weak one, Jamie, always so weak. I couldn't let you go, not when you were still thinking about her. You would have told someone, you would have told them what I did.' Bree's body began to shake violently as she tried to justify her actions. In her bitter and twisted mind she had convinced herself that he might understand. 'But you know that I wanted us both to go, Jay, I meant for us both to go together.' Bree stopped for a second or two. She had lived with the torment of her actions for so long she was still finding it hard to say the words that might free her. 'I am sorry I never came with you, Jamie, I am so sorry I got out of the car. I never meant for it to be that way, believe me, I wanted to come with you!'

Bree shook her head and began to laugh loudly at the sky. It was the laughter of a soul with no conscience, a bitter and twisted girl that knew that she had wronged her brother but had no sense of true remorse. And now she aimed her vindictive bitterness at the woman who had sacrificed everything to bring her into the world. 'She will soon know the truth, that bitch will soon know what really happened. Our mother will know that it was all her fault, everything was her fault. I hope she feels as much pain as I have felt these past years, I hope it rips her up inside, Jay, I hate her so much.'

Bree moved back towards her car, her feet trudging slowly through the deepening puddles. She did not feel like singing along or dancing to the song playing through her speakers anymore, she felt inside as if her life had already ended. She knew that she no longer needed to make that sacrifice. 'I want to be with you, Jay,' she said, looking back up through the gloomy storm that surrounded her. 'But not now, Jay, not now.' She stretched out her arms and screamed as loud as she could at the howling skies above. 'I can't be with you, Jamie! Not now I have Poppy, do you understand? She needs me, she needs me, my sister needs me, I have to be here for her now!'

As the skies grew darker, Bree bowed her head. Her windswept hair began to take the full force of those punishing rains. The dark clouds loomed to the left of her and to the right. There were dark clouds above her head and dark clouds inside her head. She could see no escape from this torture. Her soul was to be terminally condemned. She prayed for some respite. Maybe the gods would show her some mercy.

But the gods lurking in those dark clouds above were not here to absolve her of her sins for her treacherous acts. These heaven-sent rains could never cleanse the soul of someone so damaged and heartless. No, these rains were here to remind her that they would always be there, watching over her, never ever letting her forget. The angry gods in those black skies above her would never forgive her for her sins.

The End